SO-BNK-639

3 1526 04649020 4

APOCALYPSE BOW WOW

James Proimos III

illustrated by

James Proimos Jr.

BLOOMSBURY

NEW YORK   LONDON   NEW DELHI   SYDNEY

Copyright © 2015 by Welcome Literary LLC
All rights reserved. No part of this book may be reproduced or
transmitted in any form or by any means, electronic or mechanical,
including photocopying, recording, or by any information storage and
retrieval system, without permission in writing from the publisher.

First published in the United States of America in January 2015
by Bloomsbury Children's Books
www.bloomsbury.com

Bloomsbury is a registered trademark of Bloomsbury Publishing Plc

For information about permission to reproduce selections from
this book, write to Permissions, Bloomsbury Children's Books,
1385 Broadway, New York, New York 10018
Bloomsbury books may be purchased for business or promotional use.
For information on bulk purchases please contact Macmillan
Corporate and Premium Sales Department at
specialmarkets@macmillan.com

Library of Congress Cataloging-in-Publication Data
Proimos, James, III.
Apocalypse bow wow / by James Proimos III ; illustrations by James
Proimos Jr.
     pages   cm
Summary: Apollo and Brownie are unaware that the apocalypse is
at hand, but when their owners do not return and they run
out of food and water, the dogs venture into the world, where
they team up with a police dog, a flea that quotes Sun Tzu's
The Art of War, and others in an attempt to survive.
ISBN 978-1-61963-442-8 (hardcover) · ISBN 978-1-61963-443-5 (e-book)
1. Graphic novels. [1. Graphic novels. 2. Dogs—Fiction. 3. Survival—
Fiction. 4. Humorous stories.] I. Proimos, James, illustrator. II. Title.
PZ7.7.P76Apo 2015   741.5973 — dc23   2014016674

Book design by John Candell
Printed and bound in the U.S.A. by Thomson-Shore Inc., Dexter, Michigan
2 4 6 8 10 9 7 5 3 1

All papers used by Bloomsbury Publishing, Inc., are natural,
recyclable products made from wood grown in well-managed forests.
The manufacturing processes conform to the environmental
regulations of the country of origin.

For Apollo and Brownie

The
Prologue

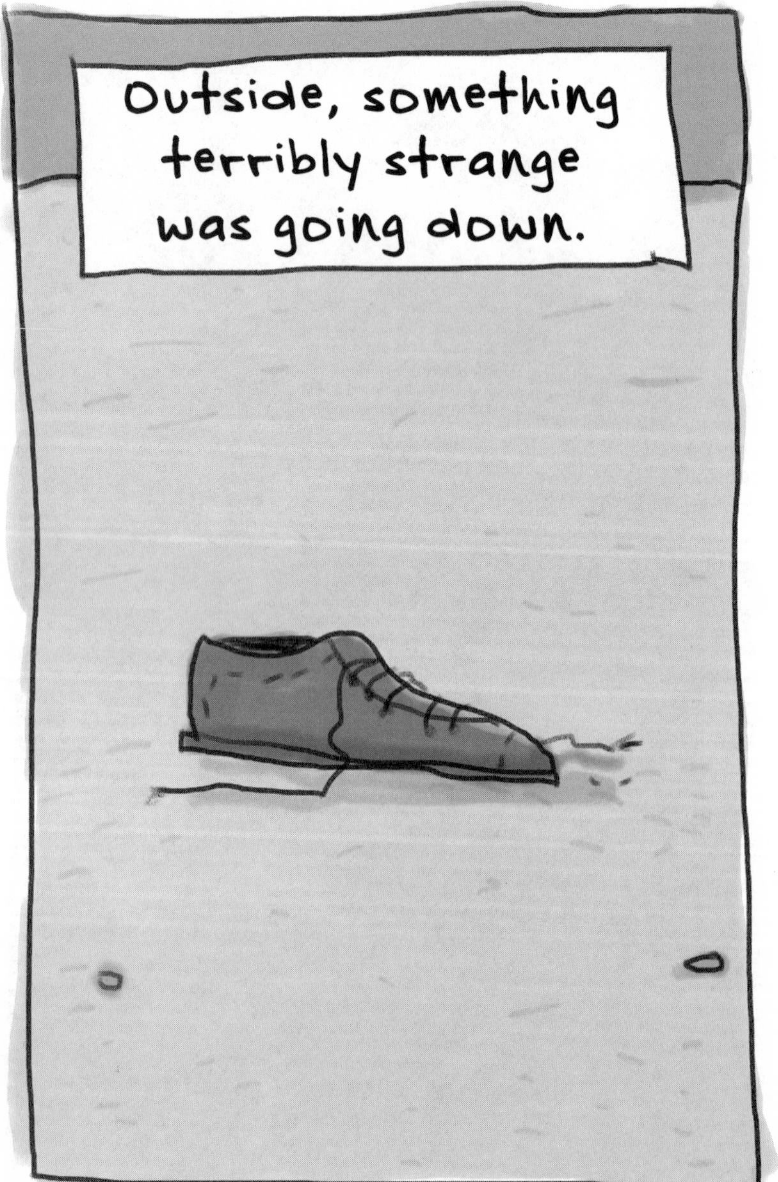
Outside, something terribly strange was going down.

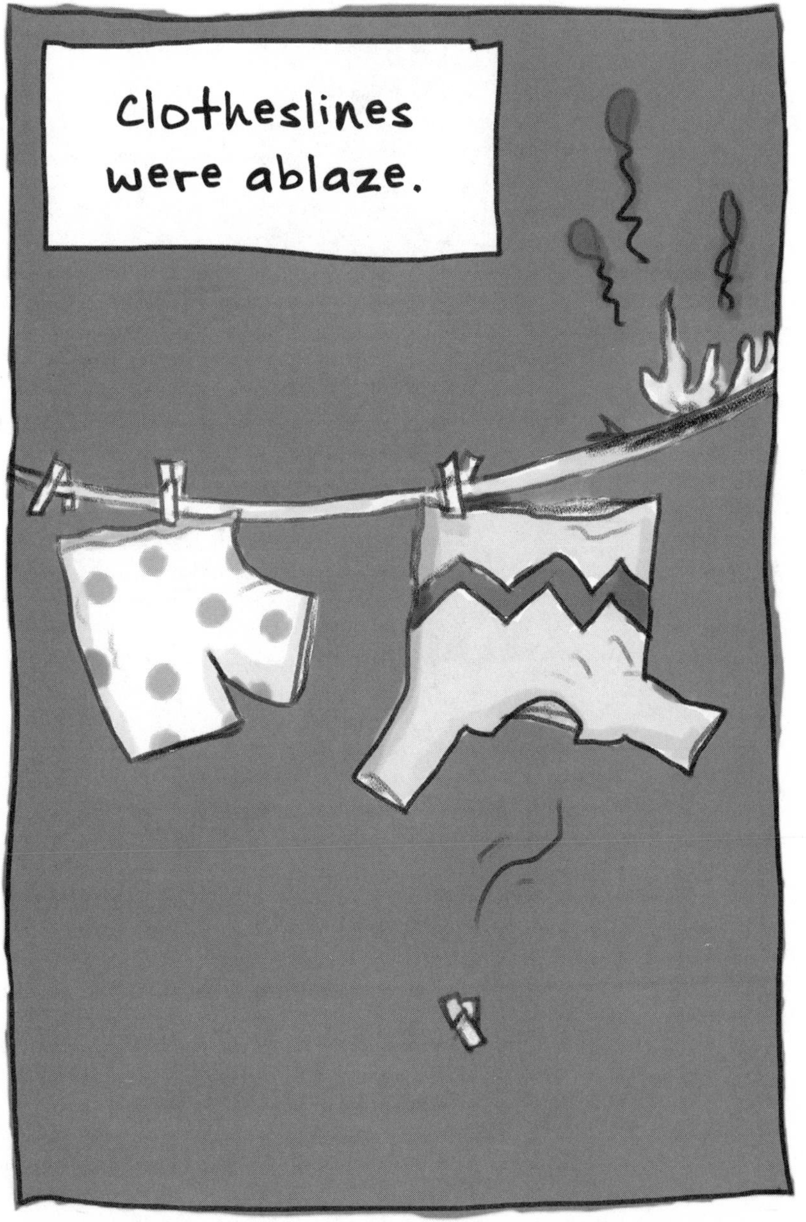
Clotheslines were ablaze.

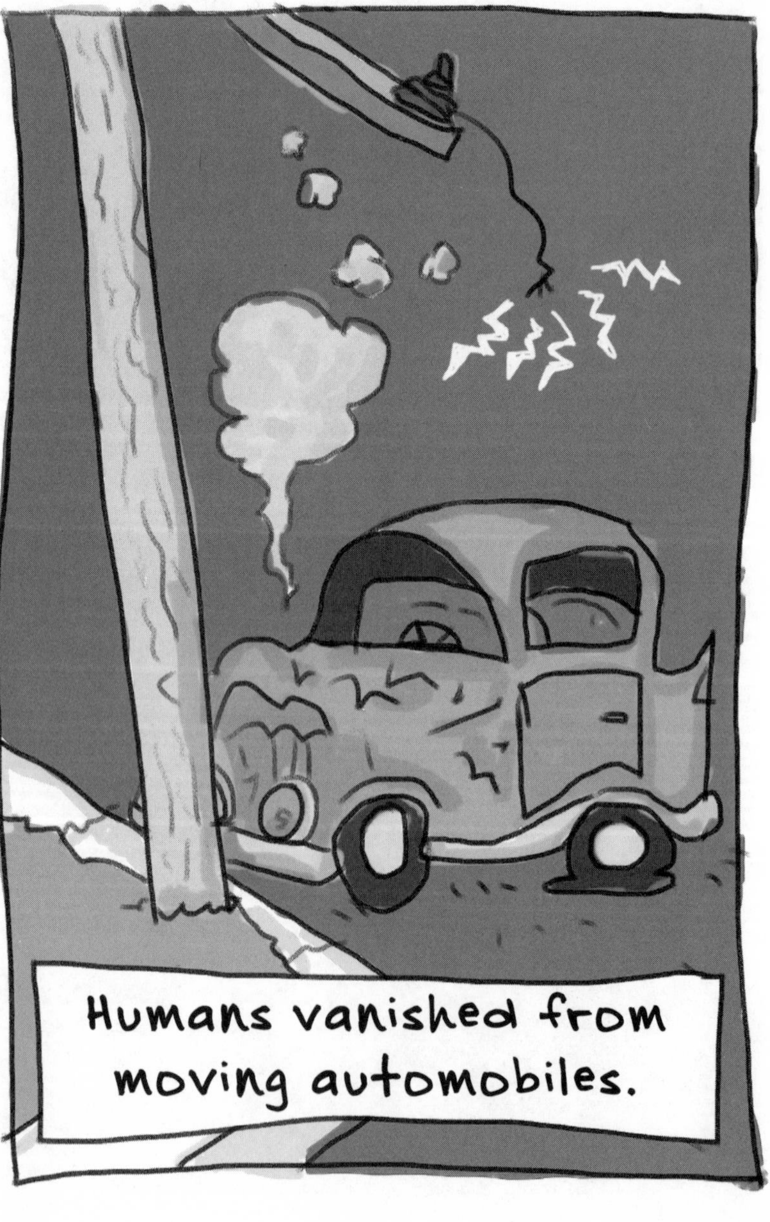
Humans vanished from
moving automobiles.

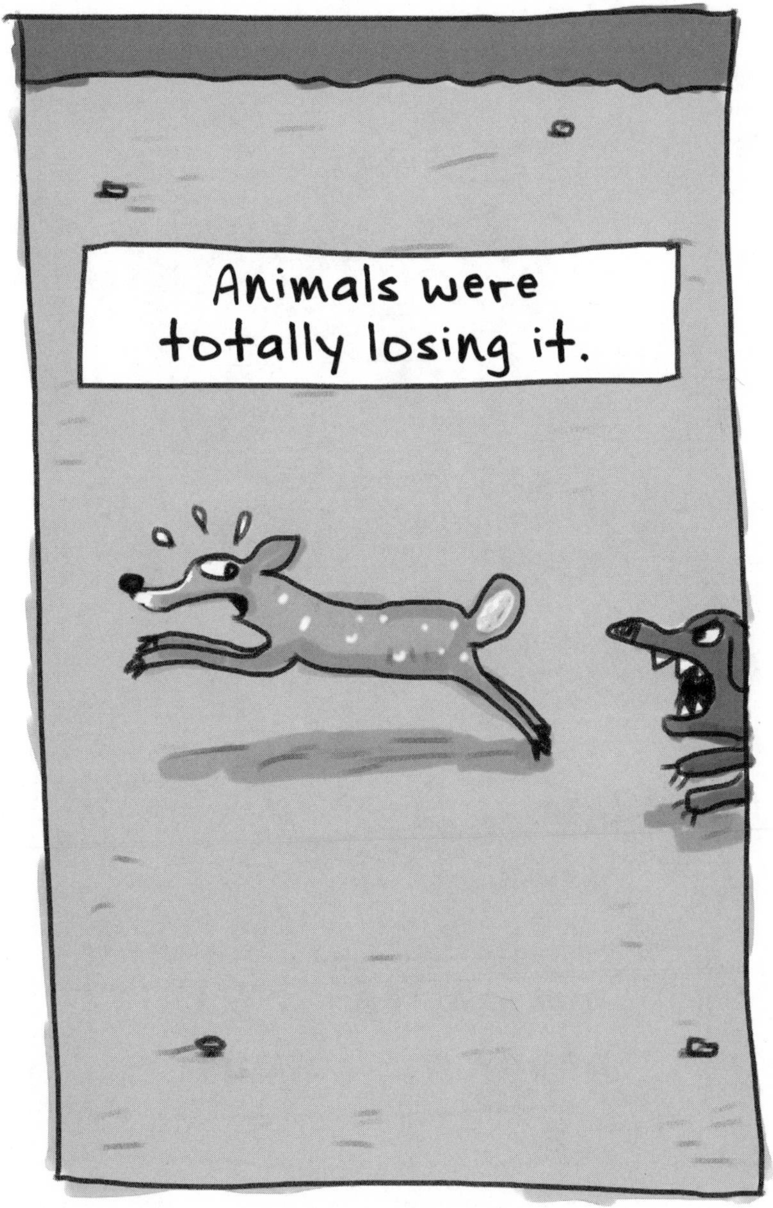
Animals were totally losing it.

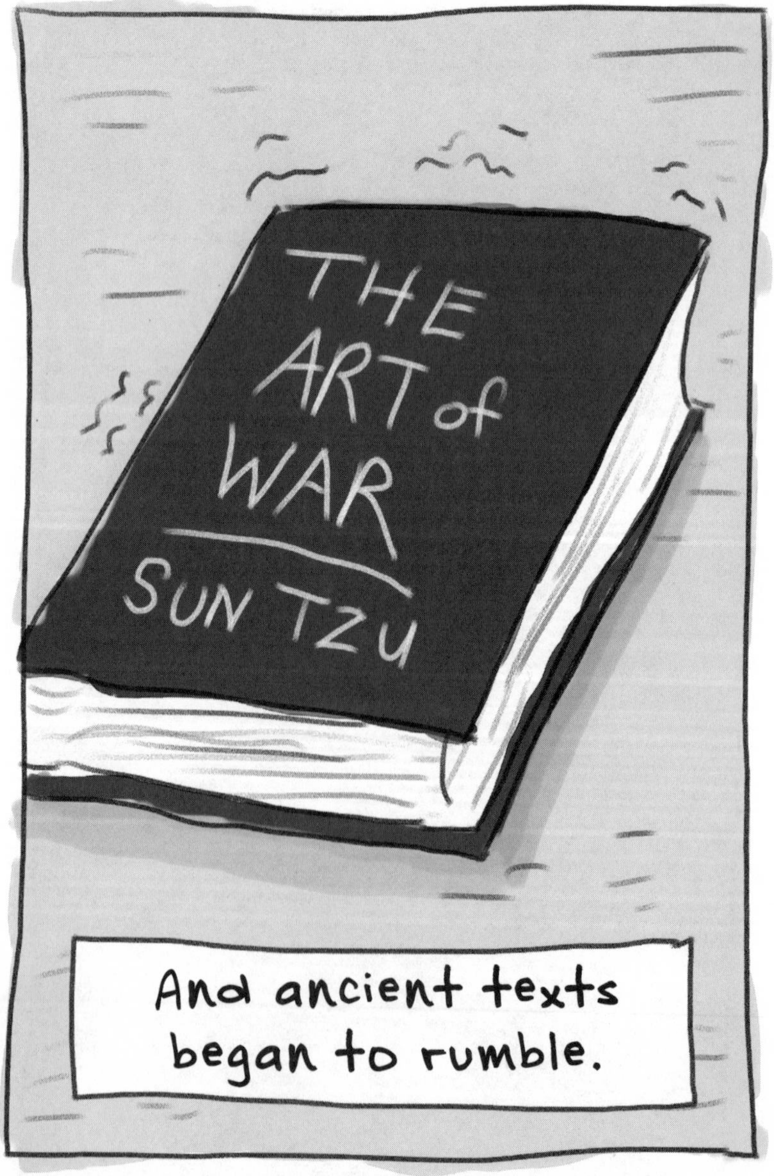
THE ART of WAR
SUN TZU
And ancient texts began to rumble.

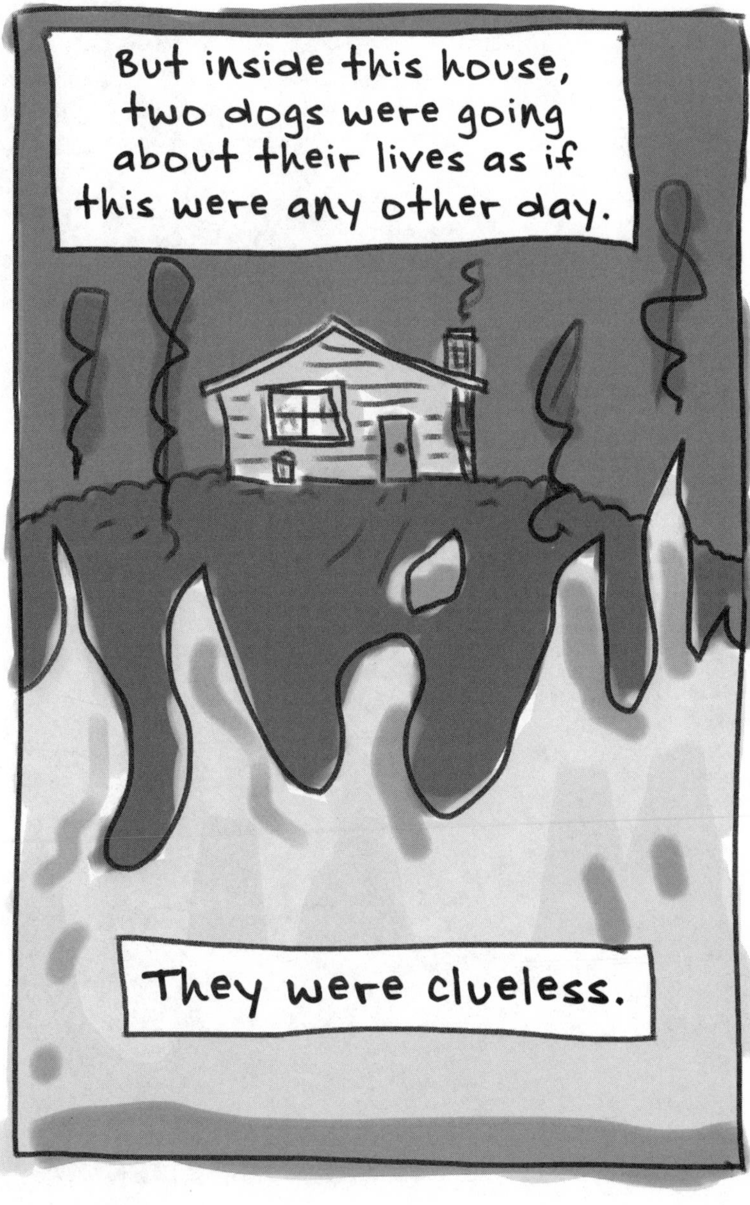
But inside this house, two dogs were going about their lives as if this were any other day.
They were clueless.

Scene
One

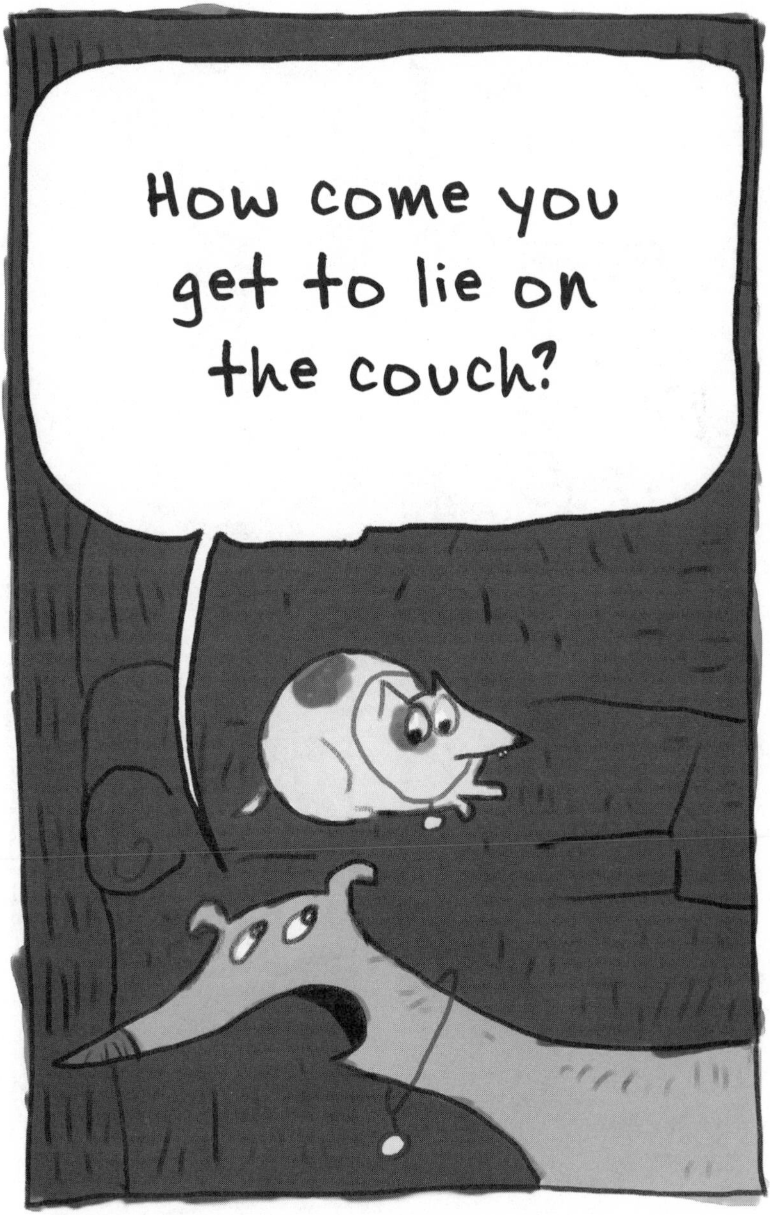
How come you get to lie on the couch?

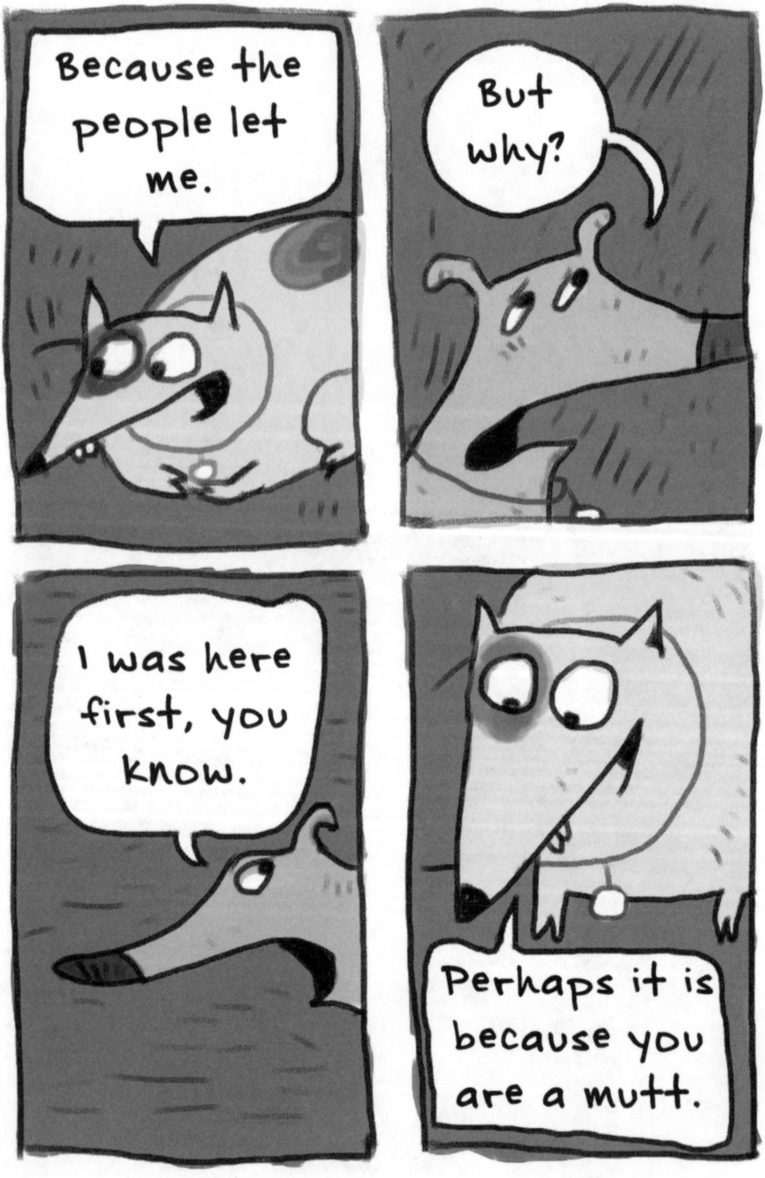
Because the people let me.
But why?
I was here first, you know.
Perhaps it is because you are a mutt.

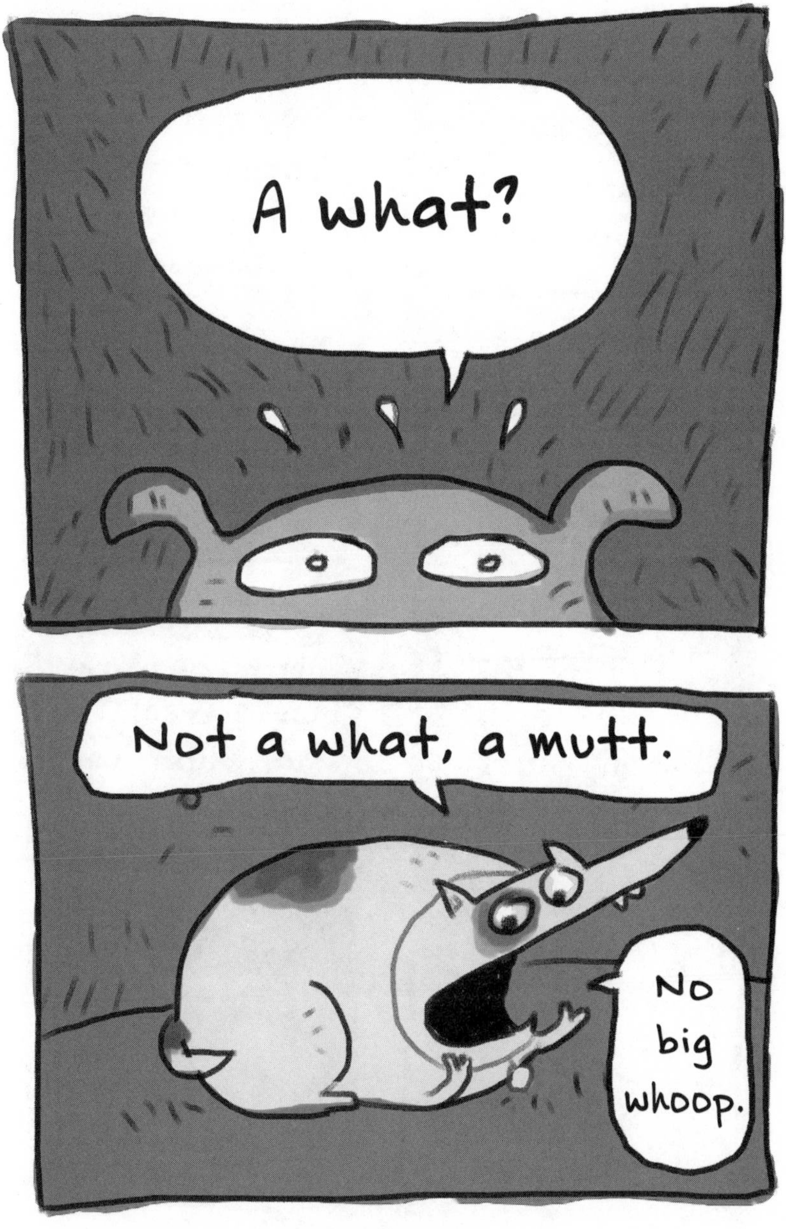
A what?
Not a what, a mutt.
No big whoop.

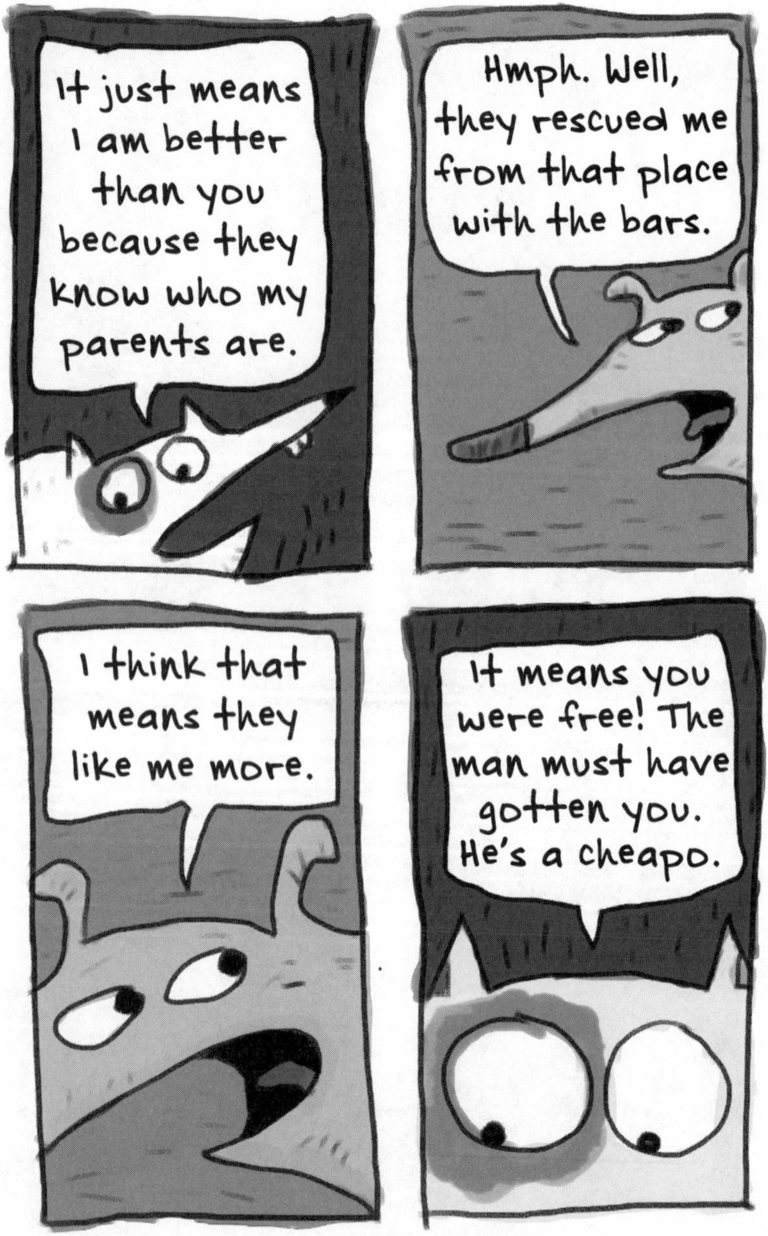
It just means I am better than you because they know who my parents are.
Hmph. Well, they rescued me from that place with the bars.
I think that means they like me more.
It means you were free! The man must have gotten you. He's a cheapo.

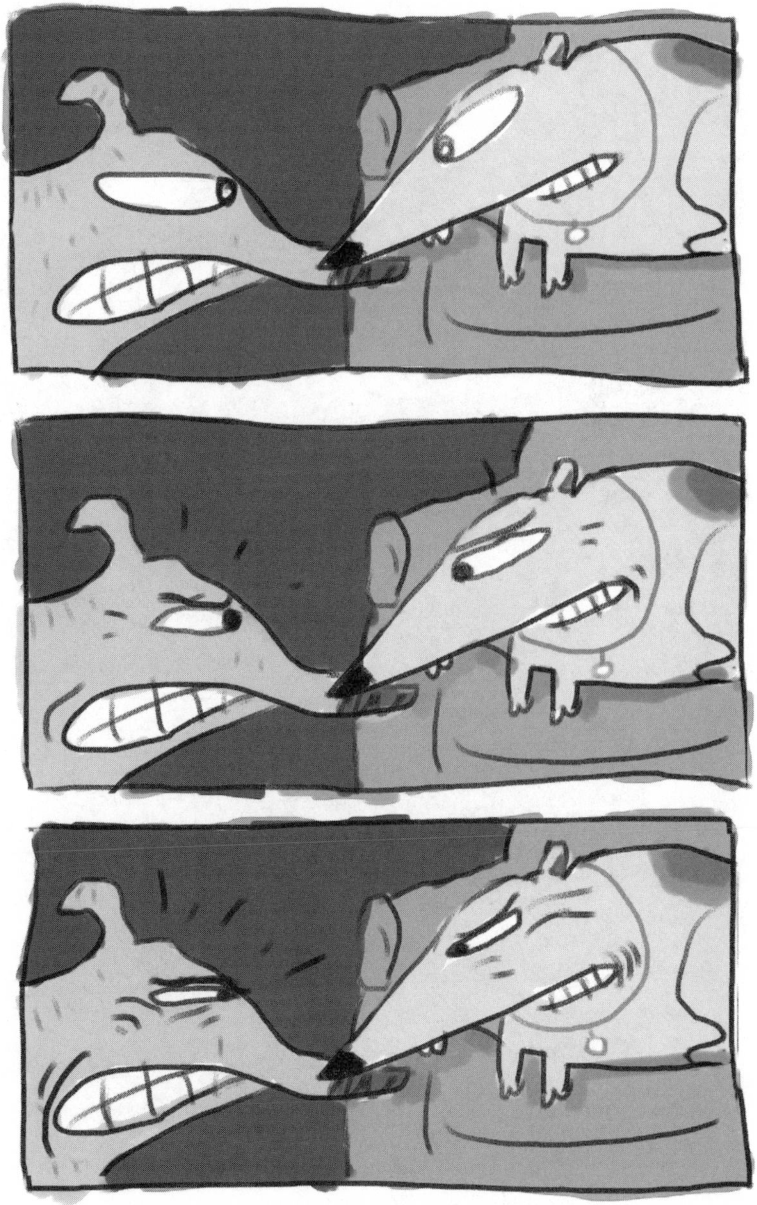

Scene
Two

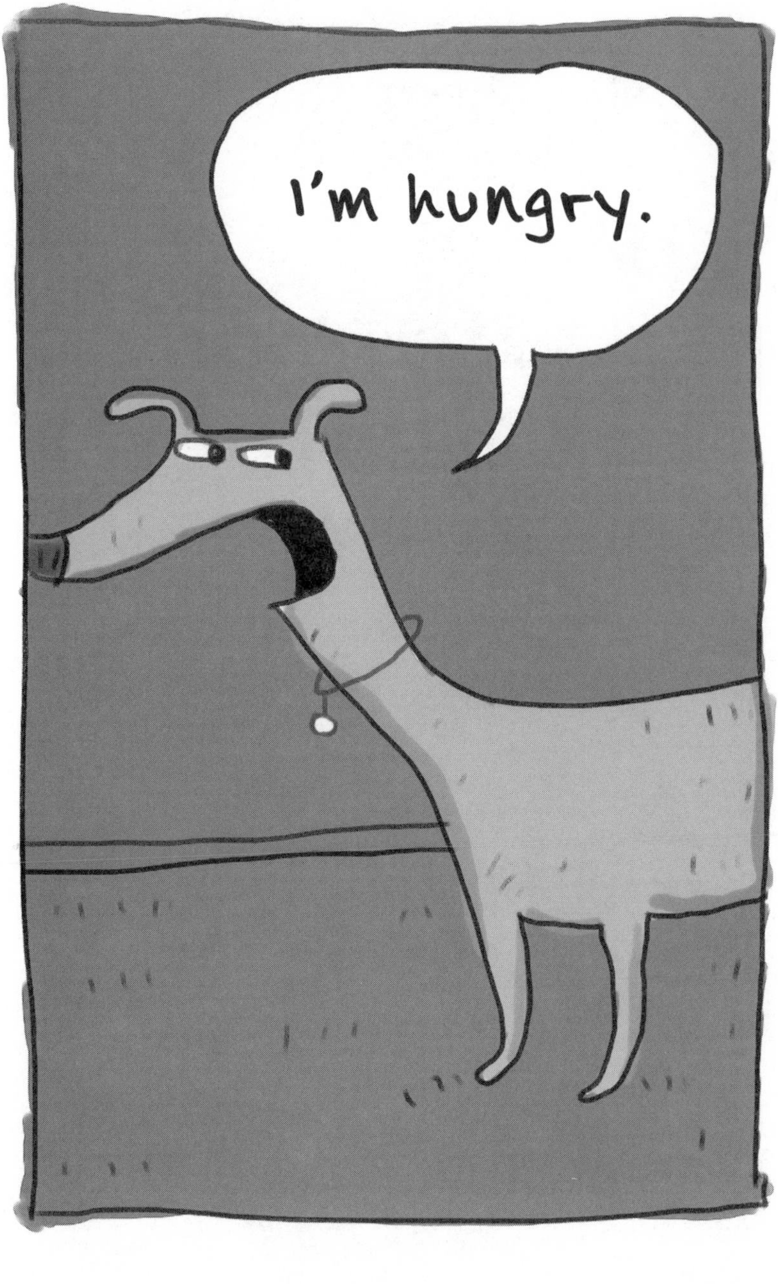
I'm hungry.

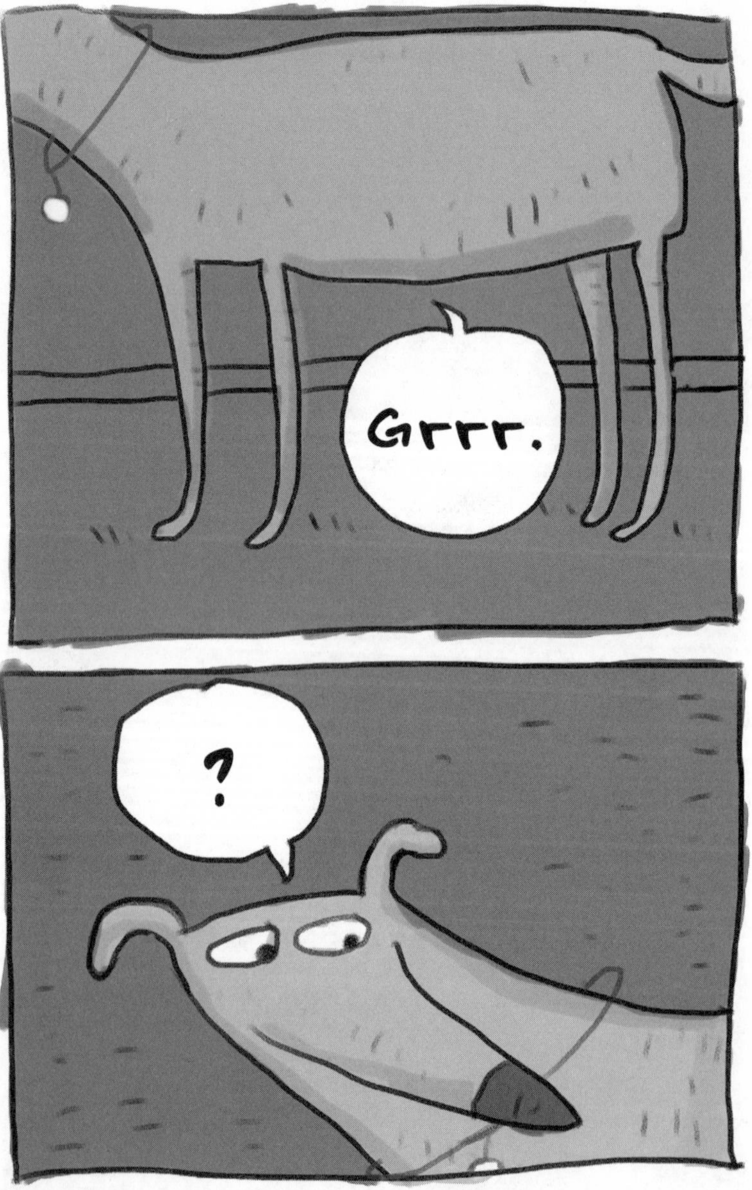
Grrr.
?

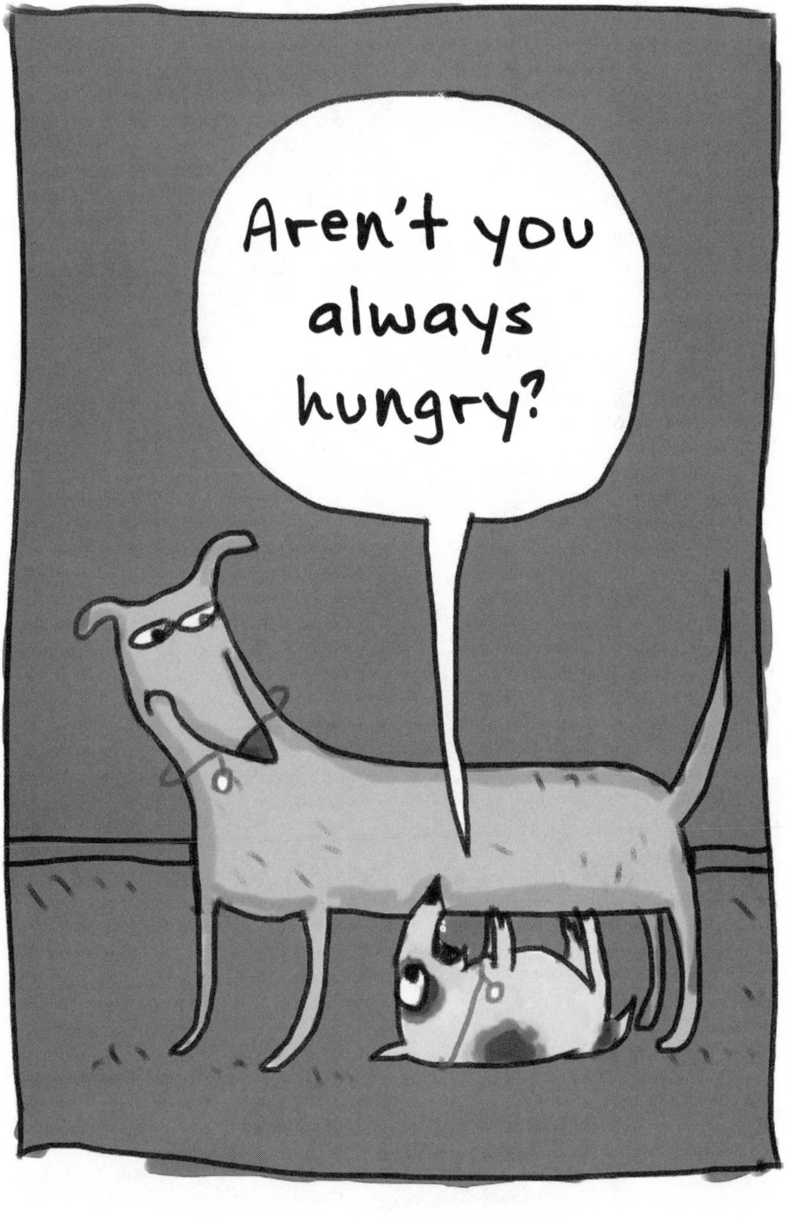
Aren't you always hungry?

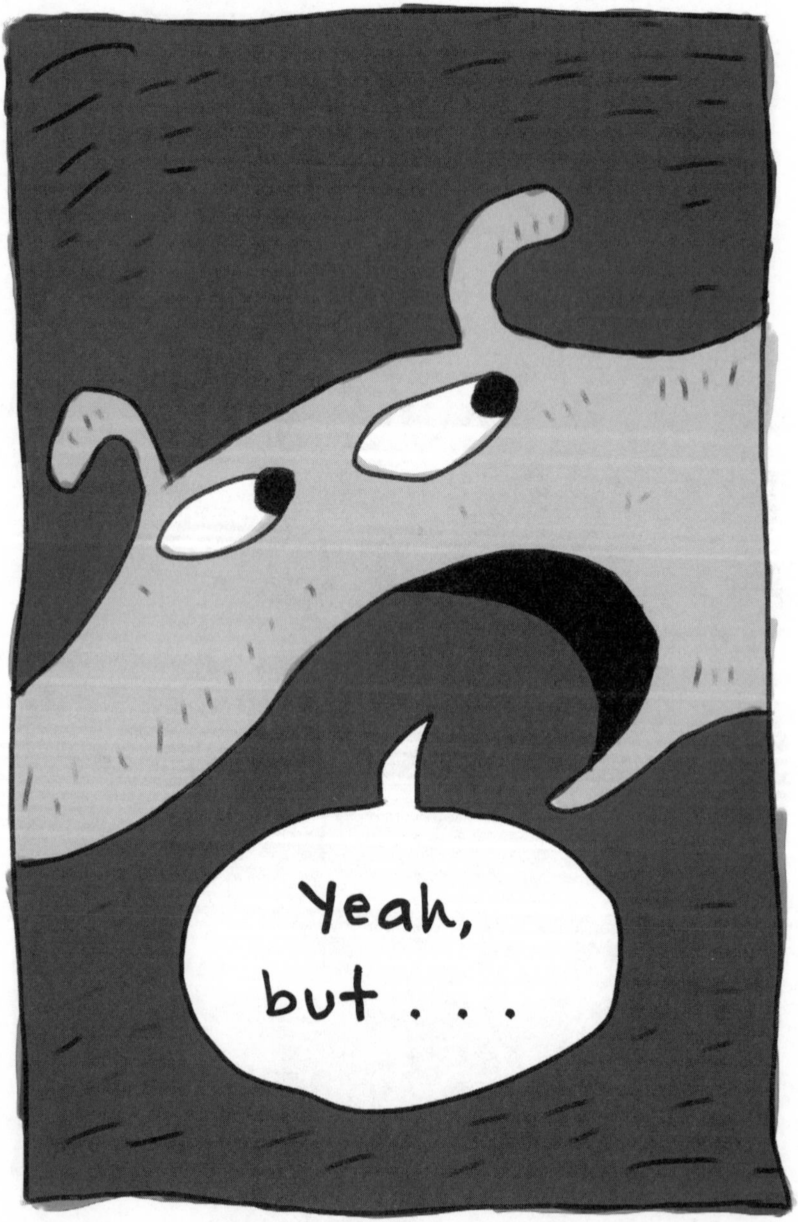
Yeah, but . . .

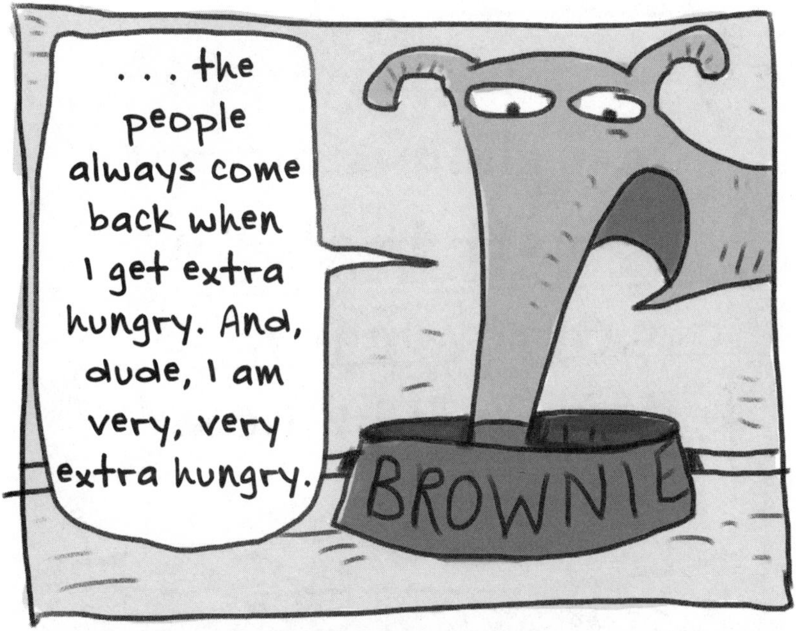
. . . the people always come back when I get extra hungry. And, dude, I am very, very extra hungry.
BROWNIE

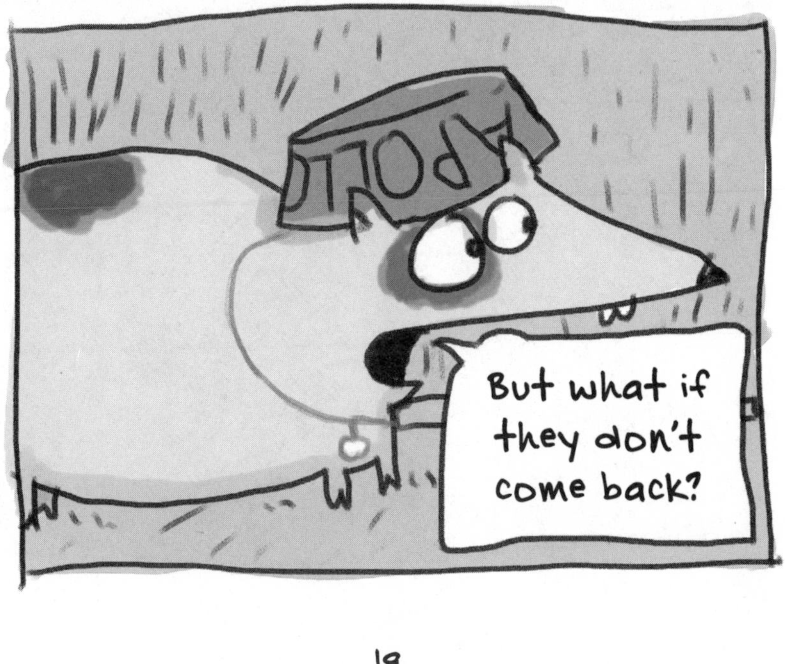
POLO
But what if they don't come back?

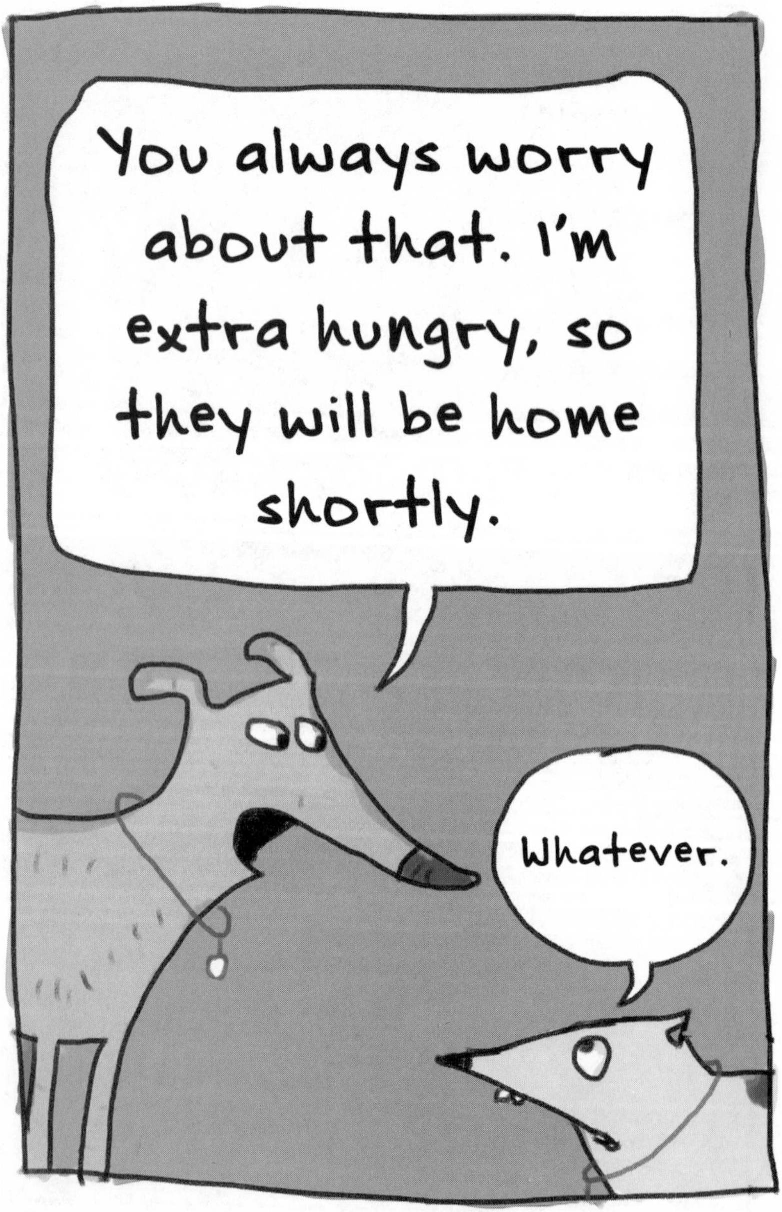
You always worry about that. I'm extra hungry, so they will be home shortly.
Whatever.

Scene
Three

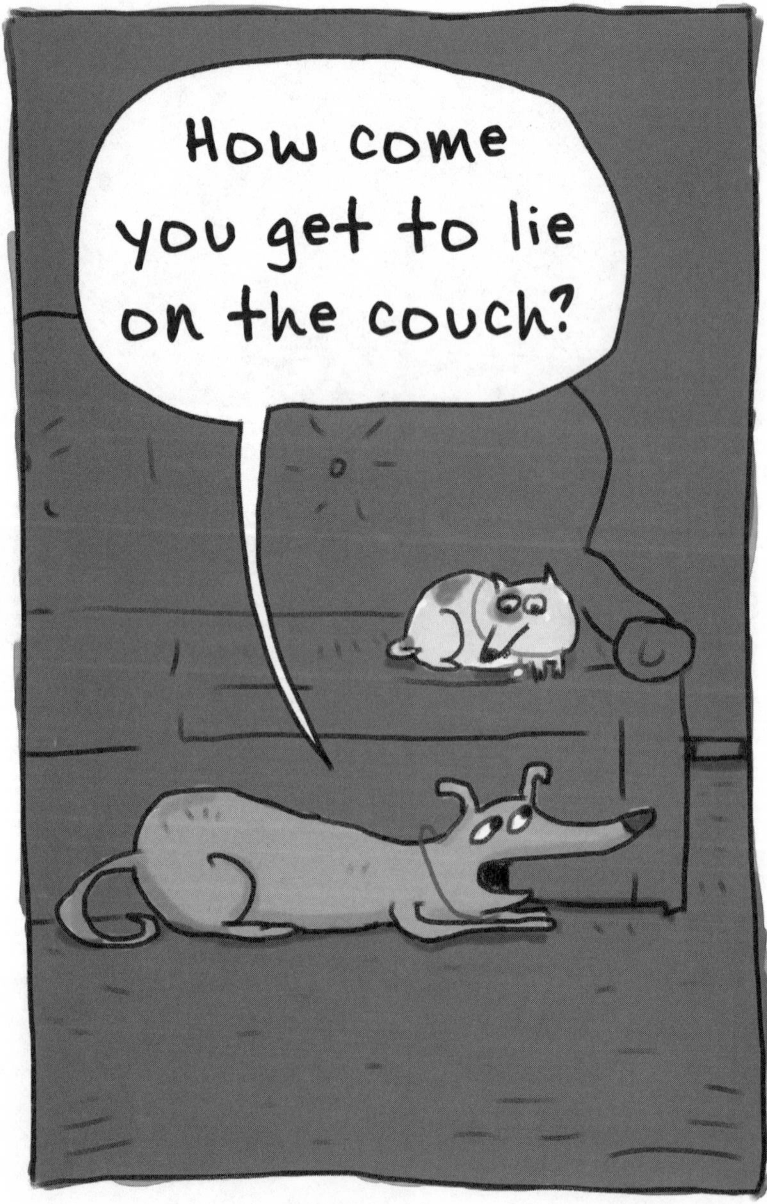
How come you get to lie on the couch?

Scene
Four

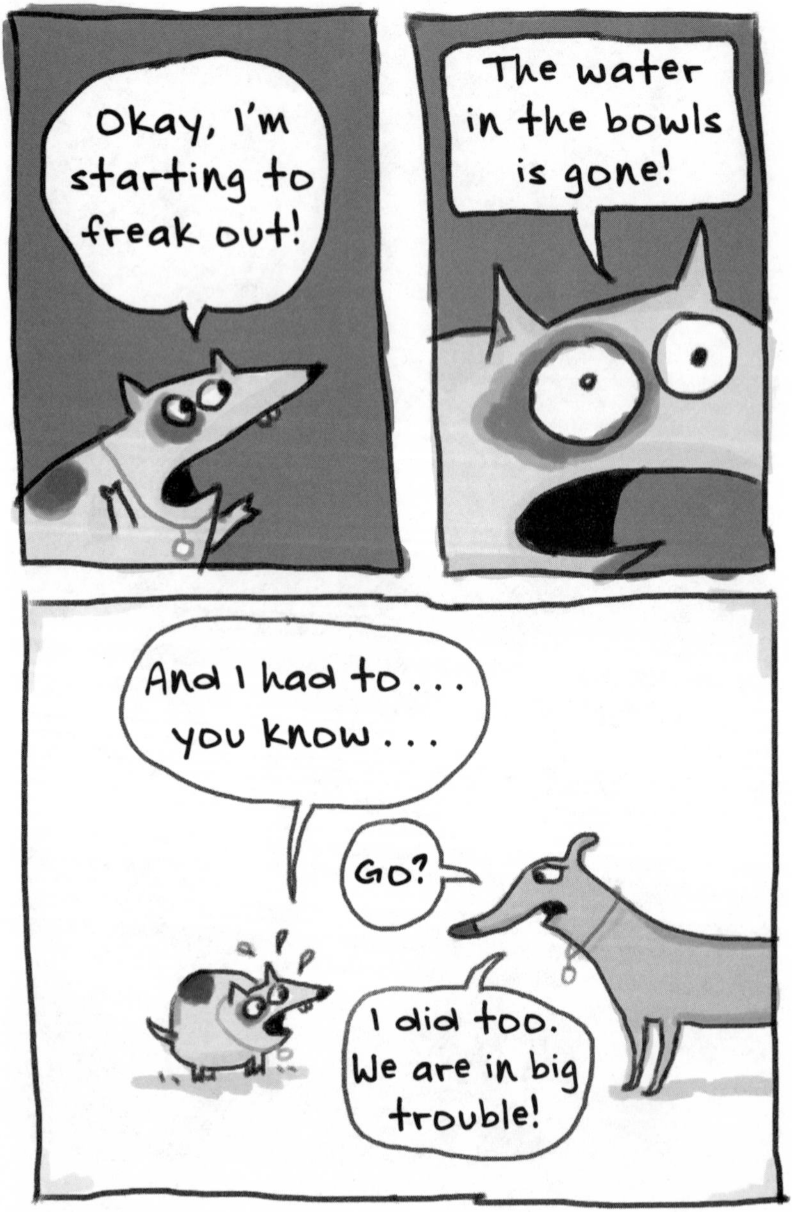
Okay, I'm starting to freak out!
The water in the bowls is gone!
And I had to . . . you know . . .
Go?
I did too. We are in big trouble!

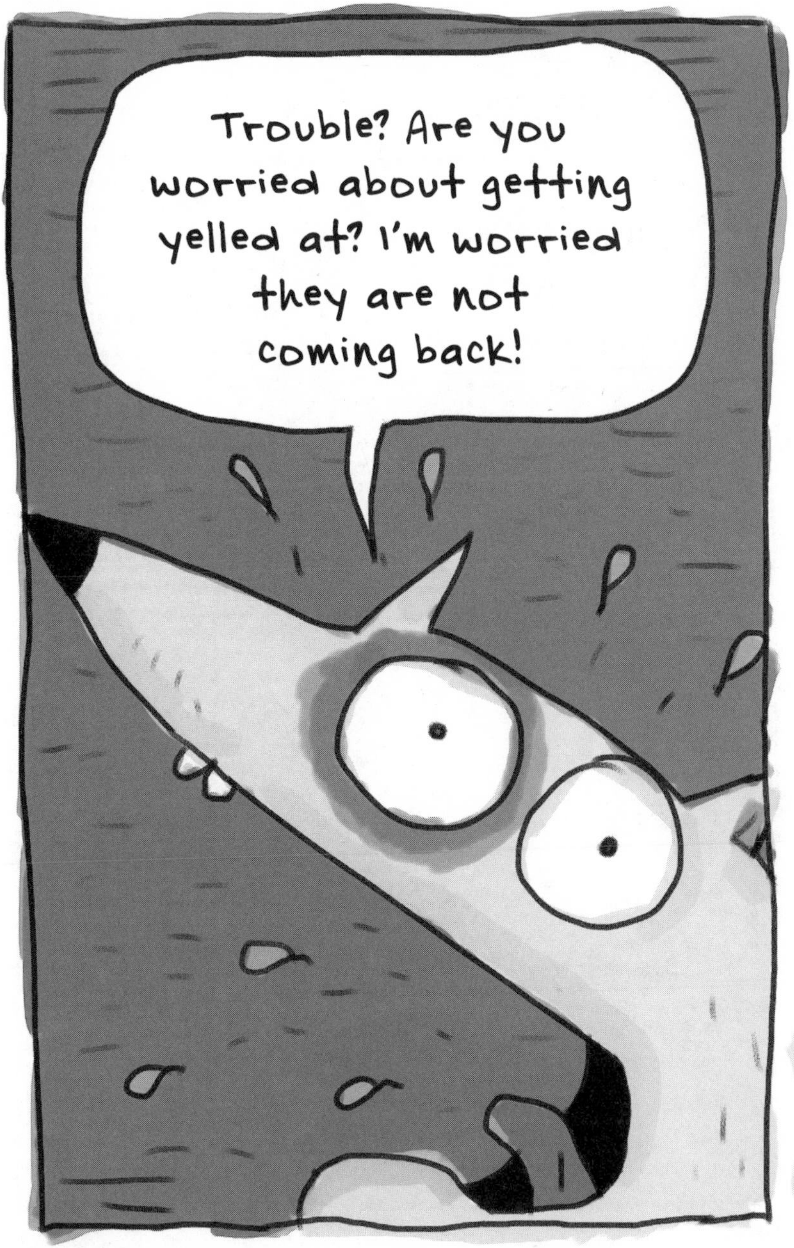
Trouble? Are you worried about getting yelled at? I'm worried they are not coming back!

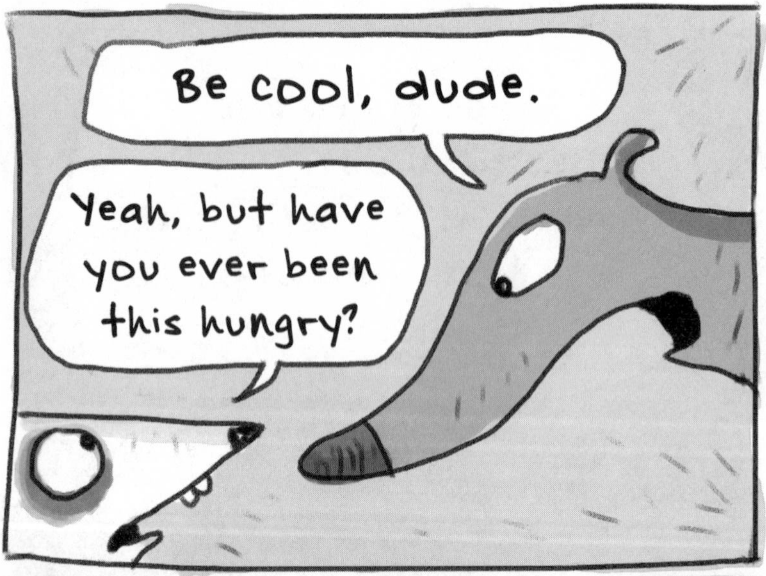
Be cool, dude.
Yeah, but have you ever been this hungry?

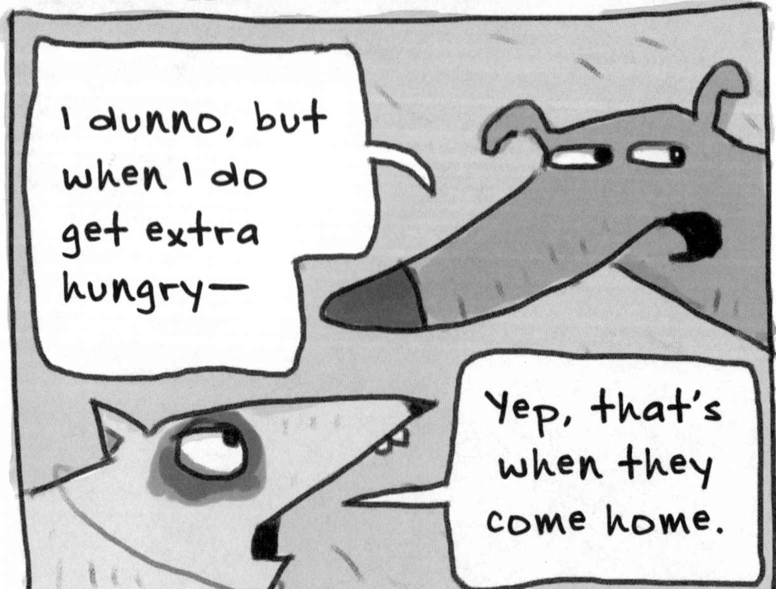
I dunno, but when I do get extra hungry—
Yep, that's when they come home.

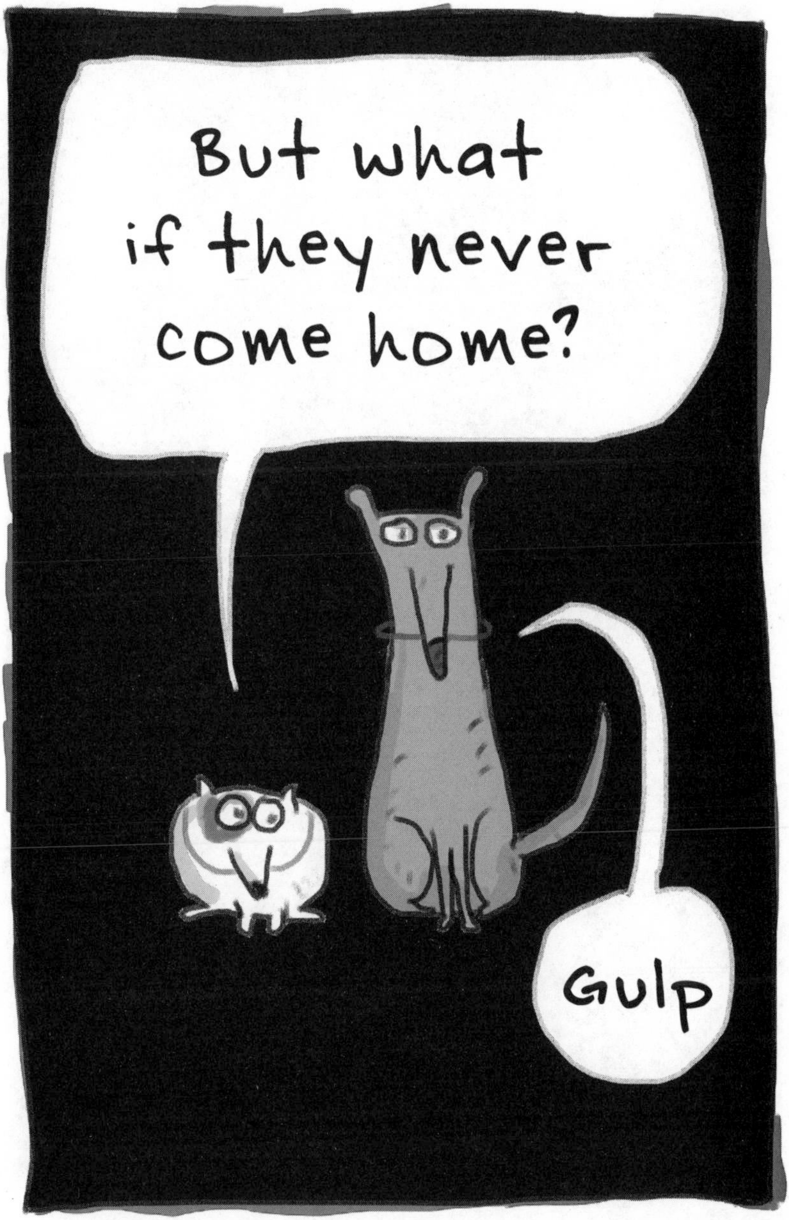
But what if they never come home?
Gulp

Scene
Five

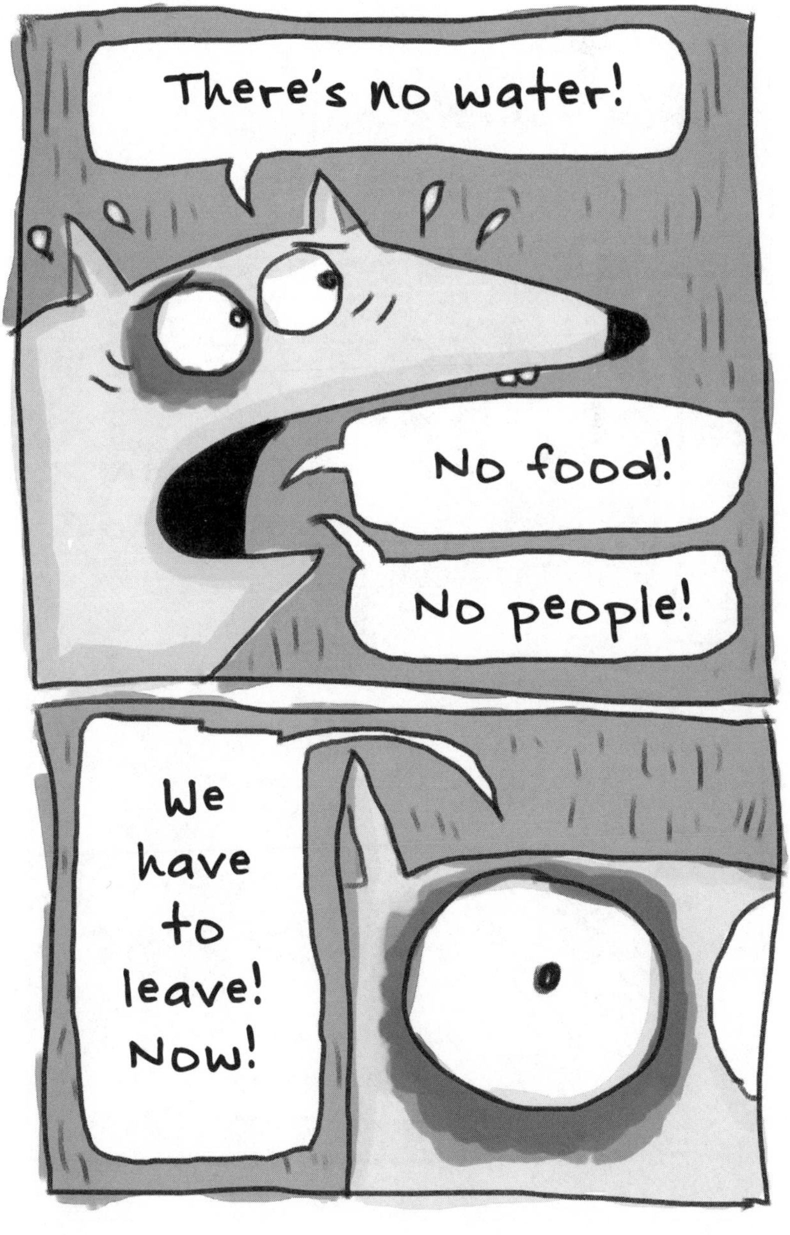
There's no water!
No food!
No people!
We have to leave! Now!

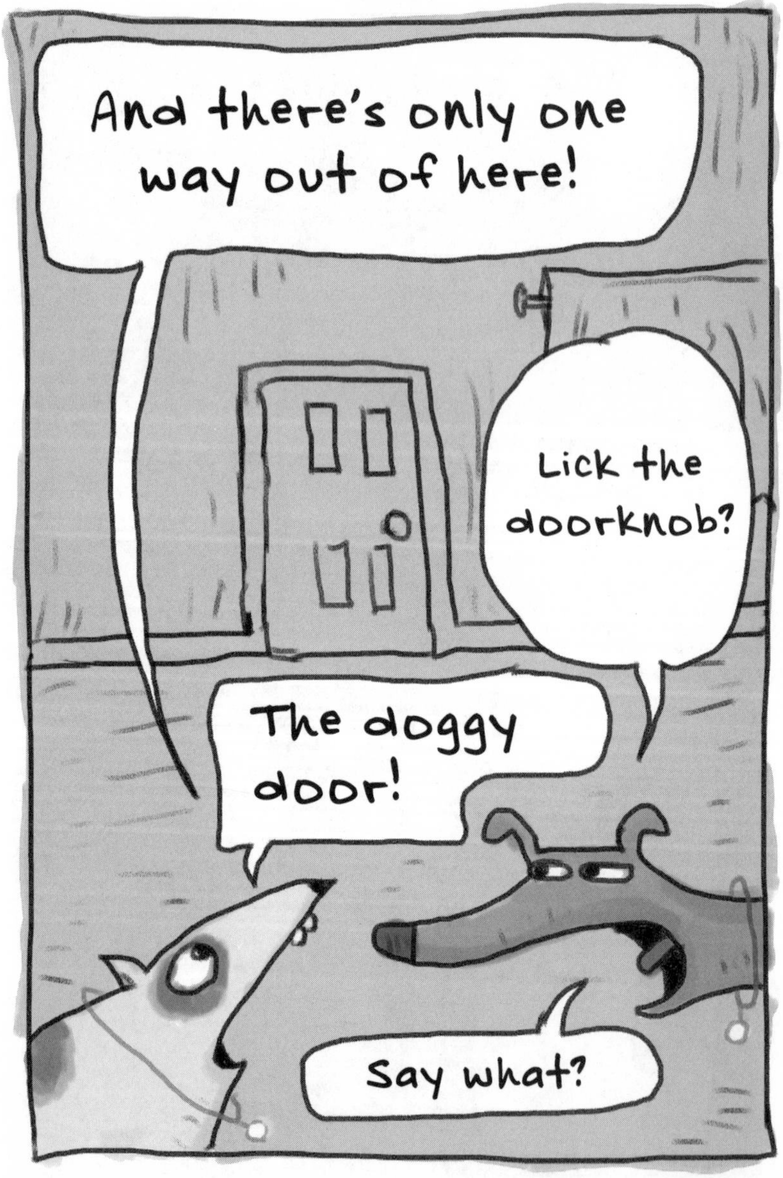
And there's only one way out of here!
Lick the doorknob?
The doggy door!
Say what?

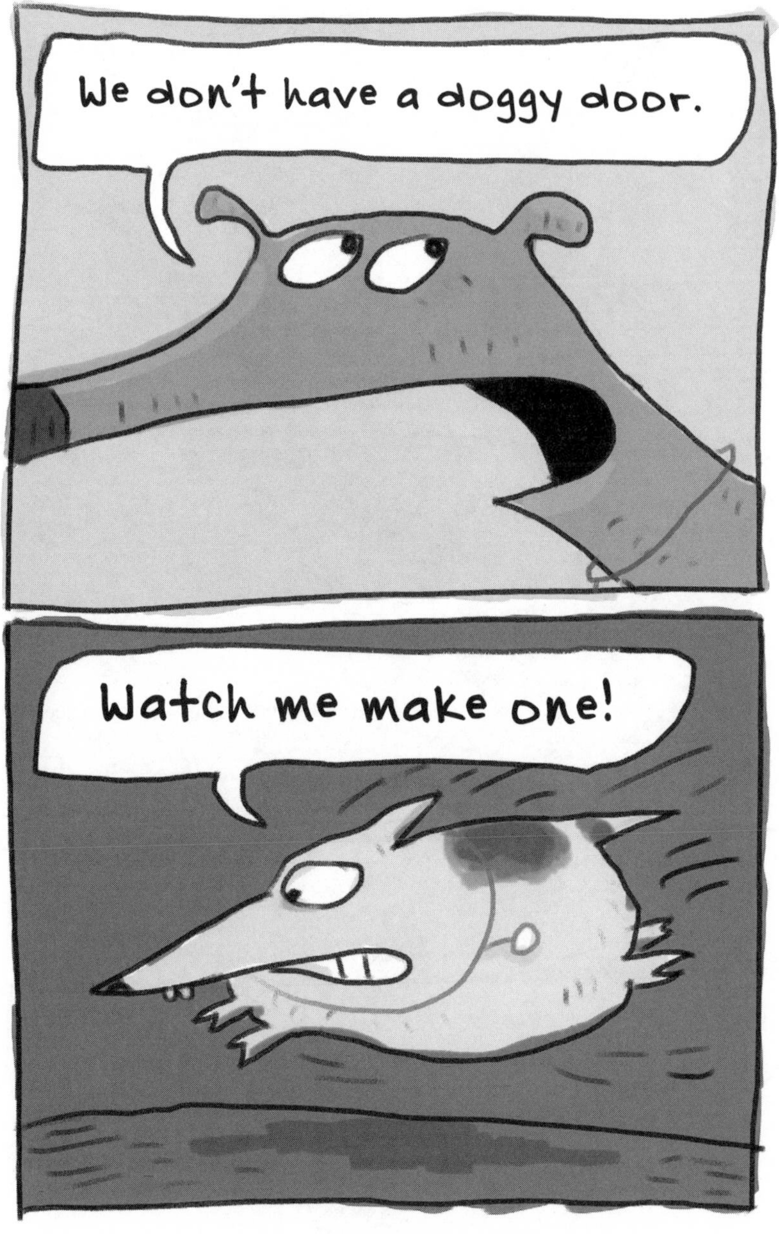
We don't have a doggy door.
Watch me make one!

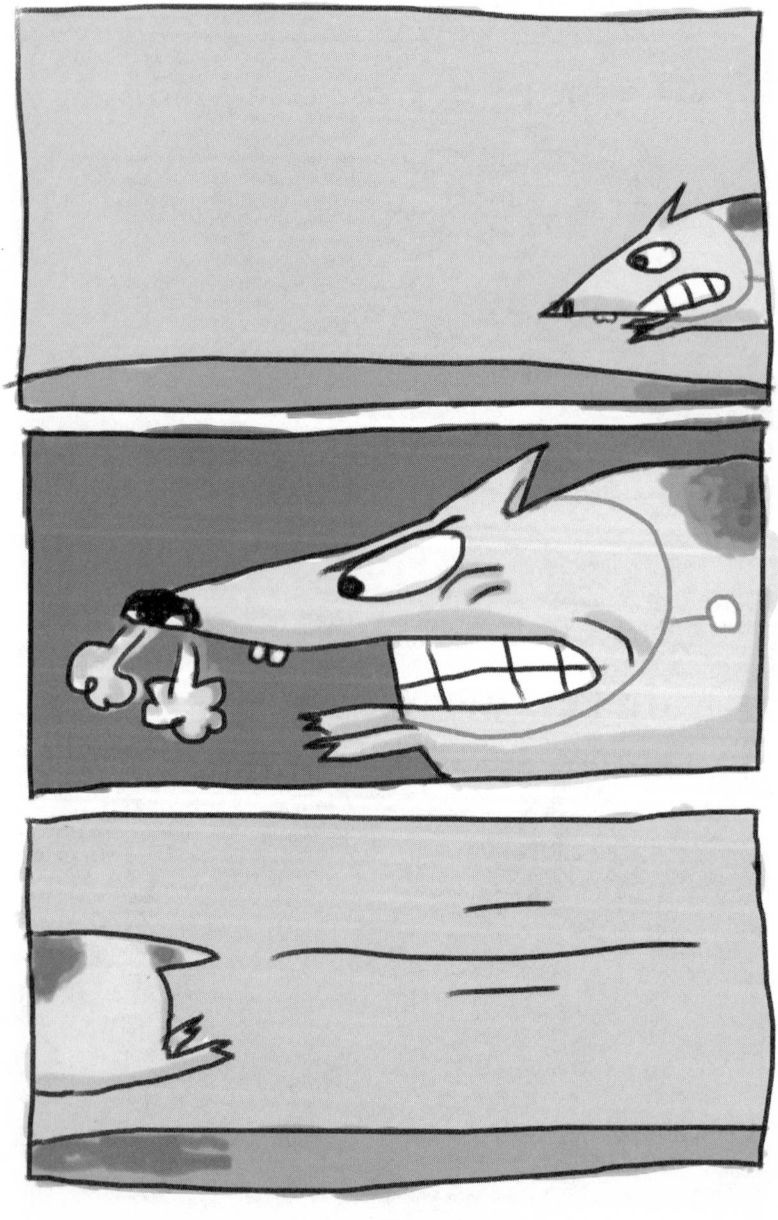

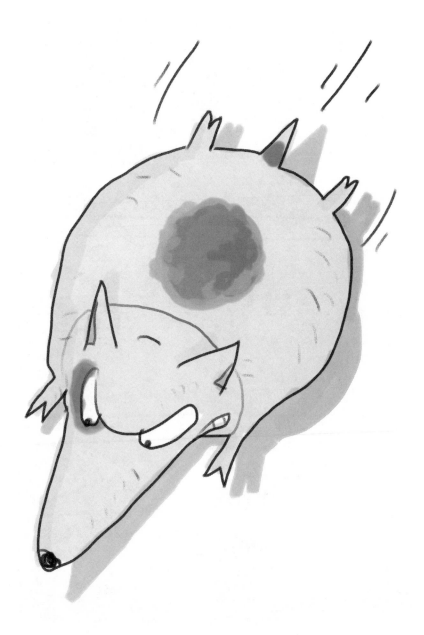

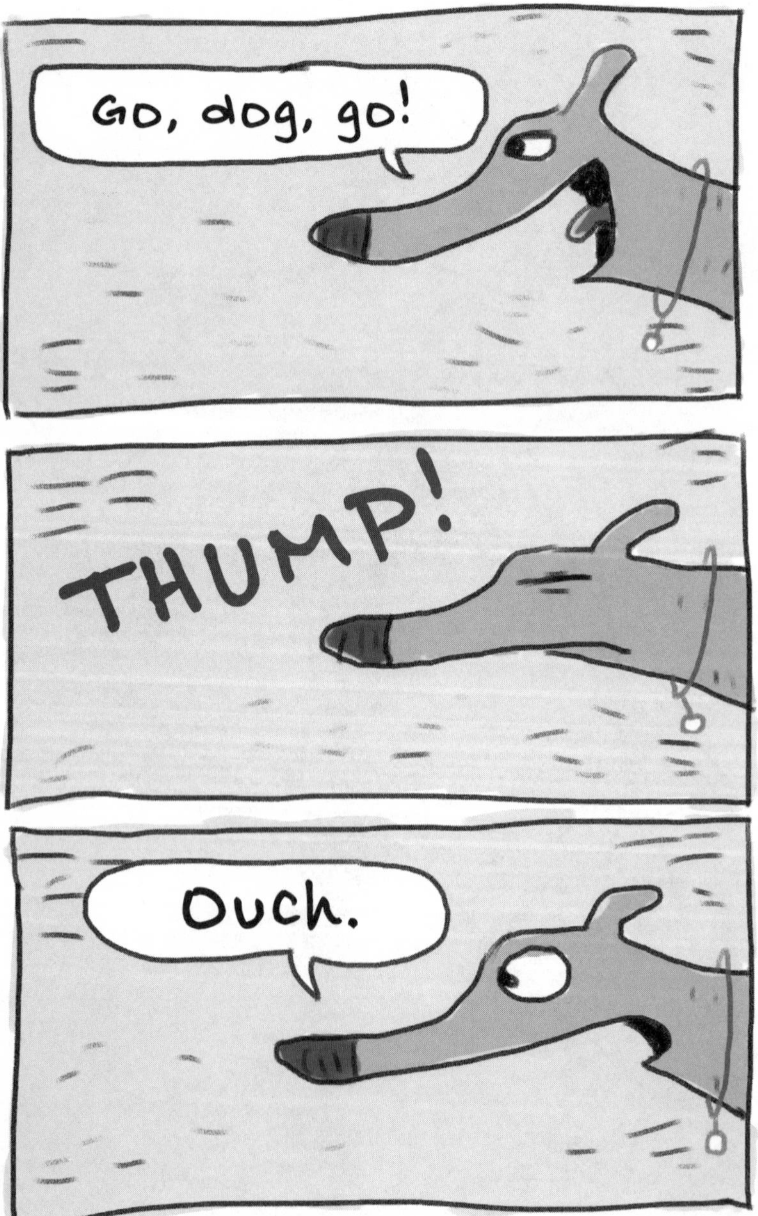
Go, dog, go!
THUMP!
Ouch.

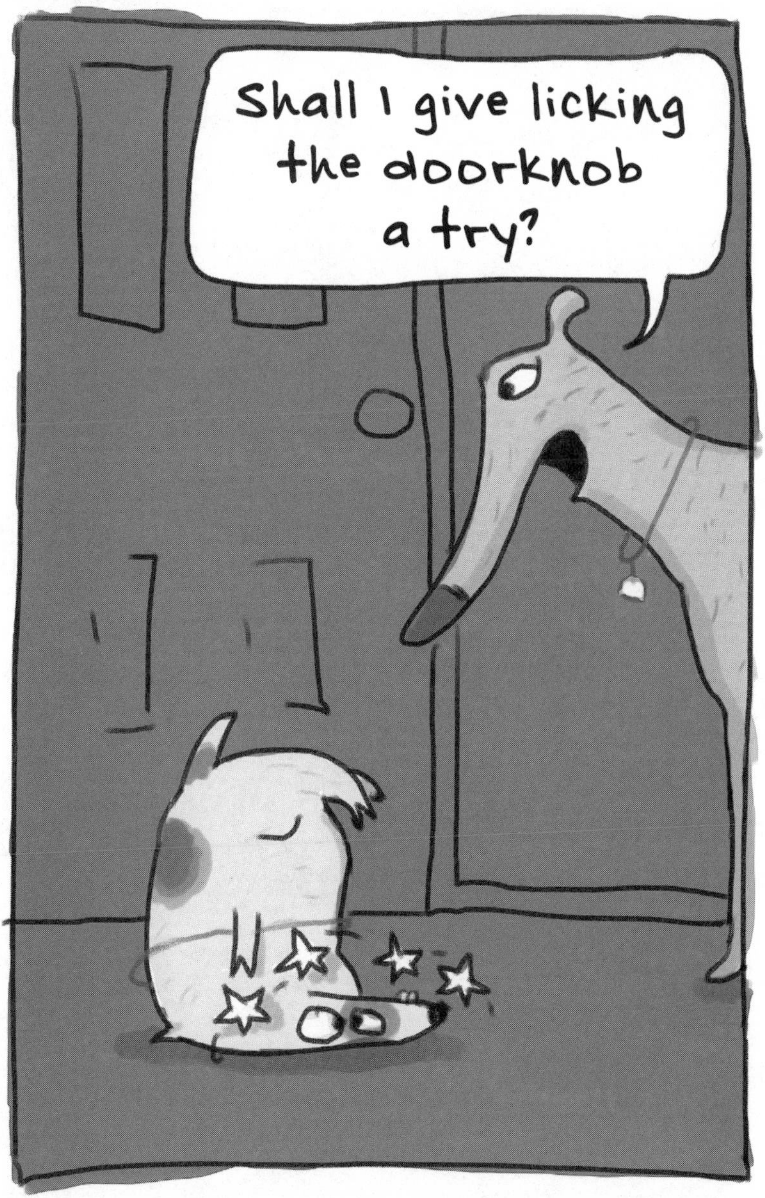
Shall I give licking the doorknob a try?

Scene
Six

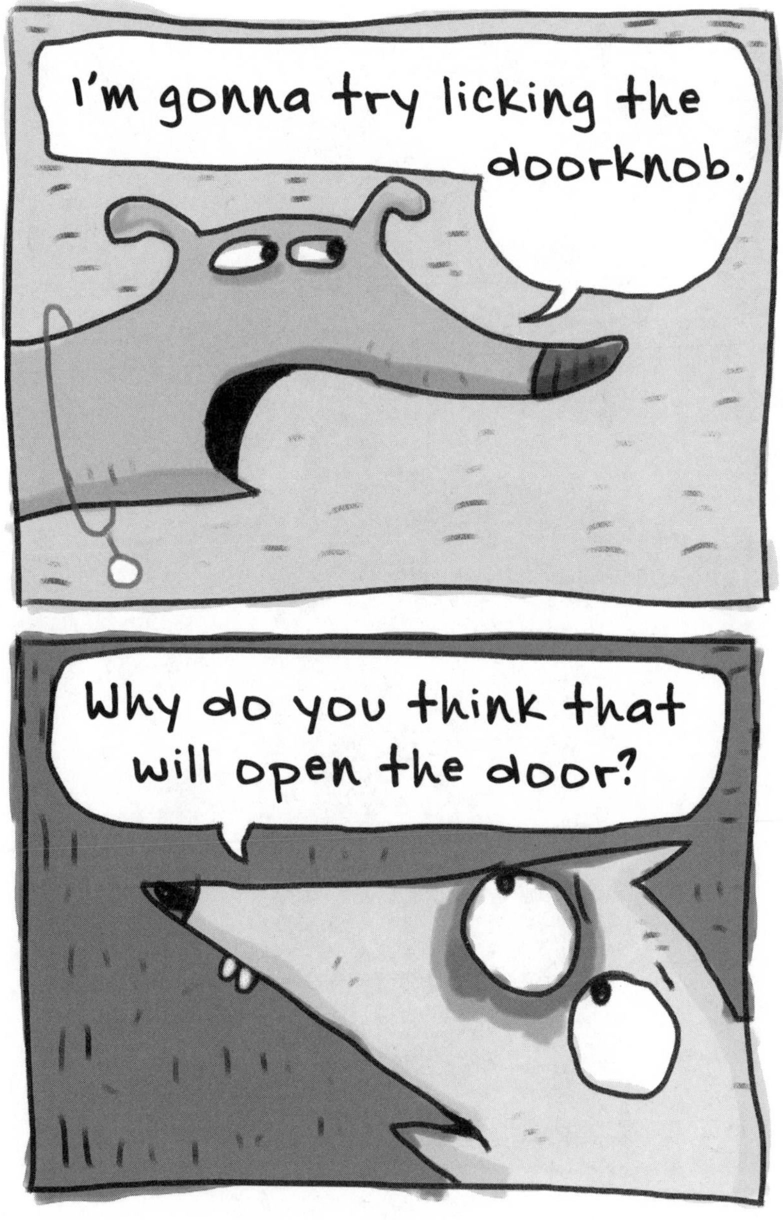
I'm gonna try licking the doorknob.
Why do you think that will open the door?

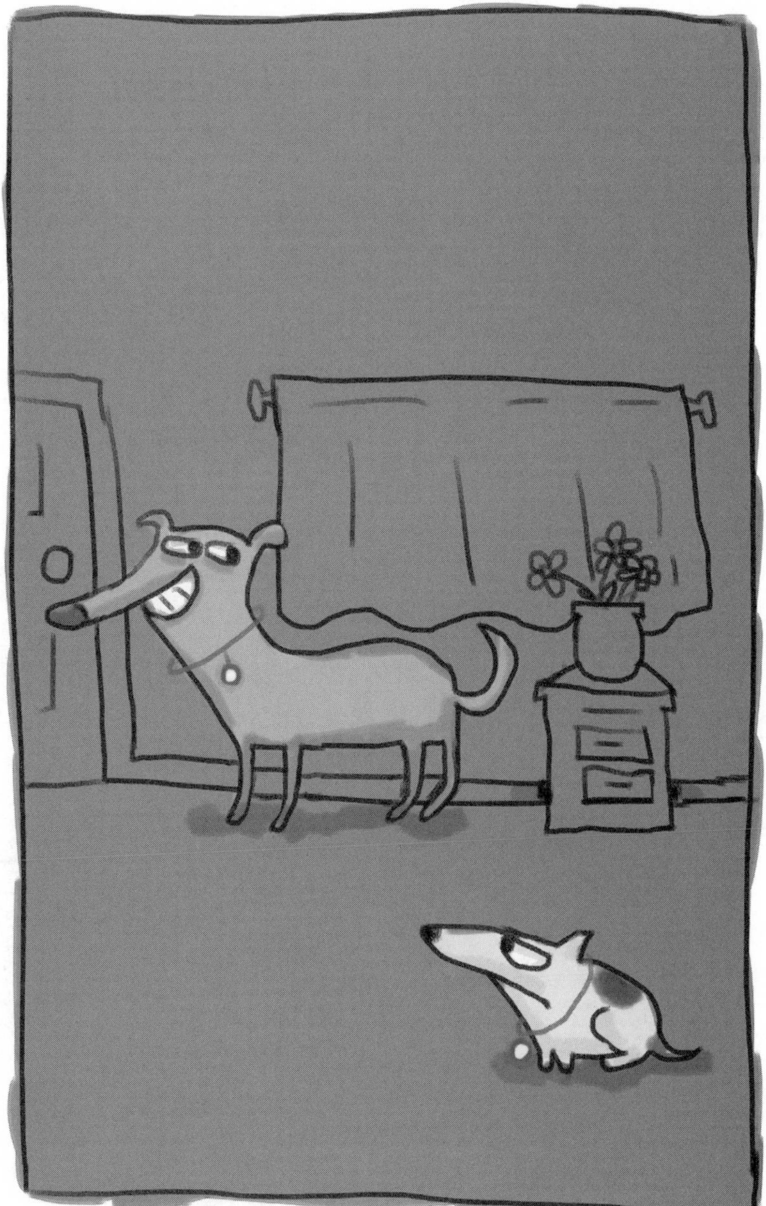

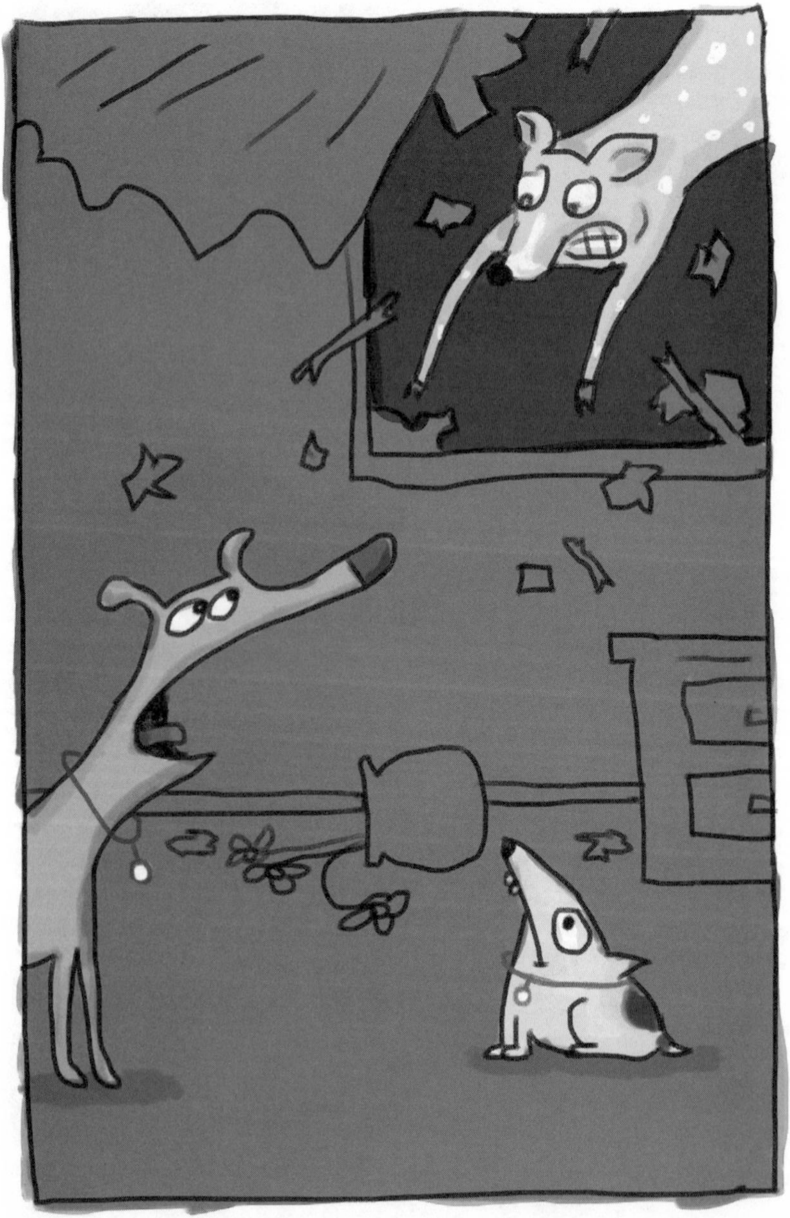

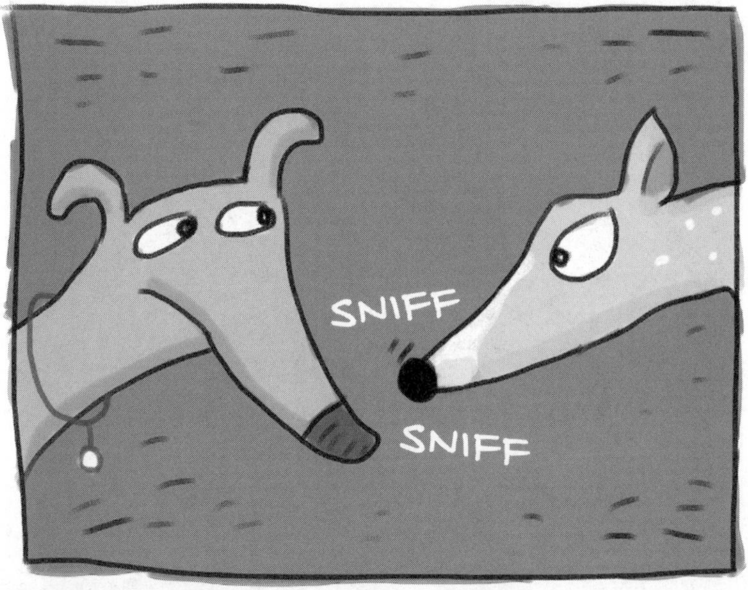
SNIFF
SNIFF

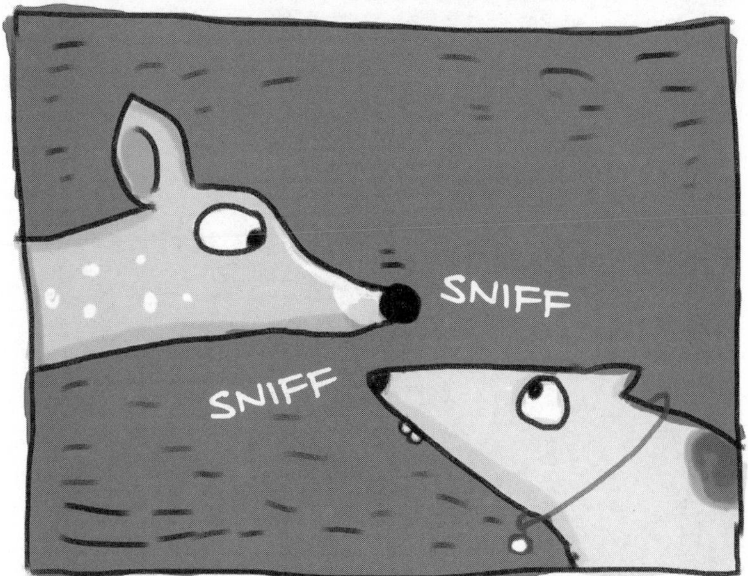
SNIFF
SNIFF

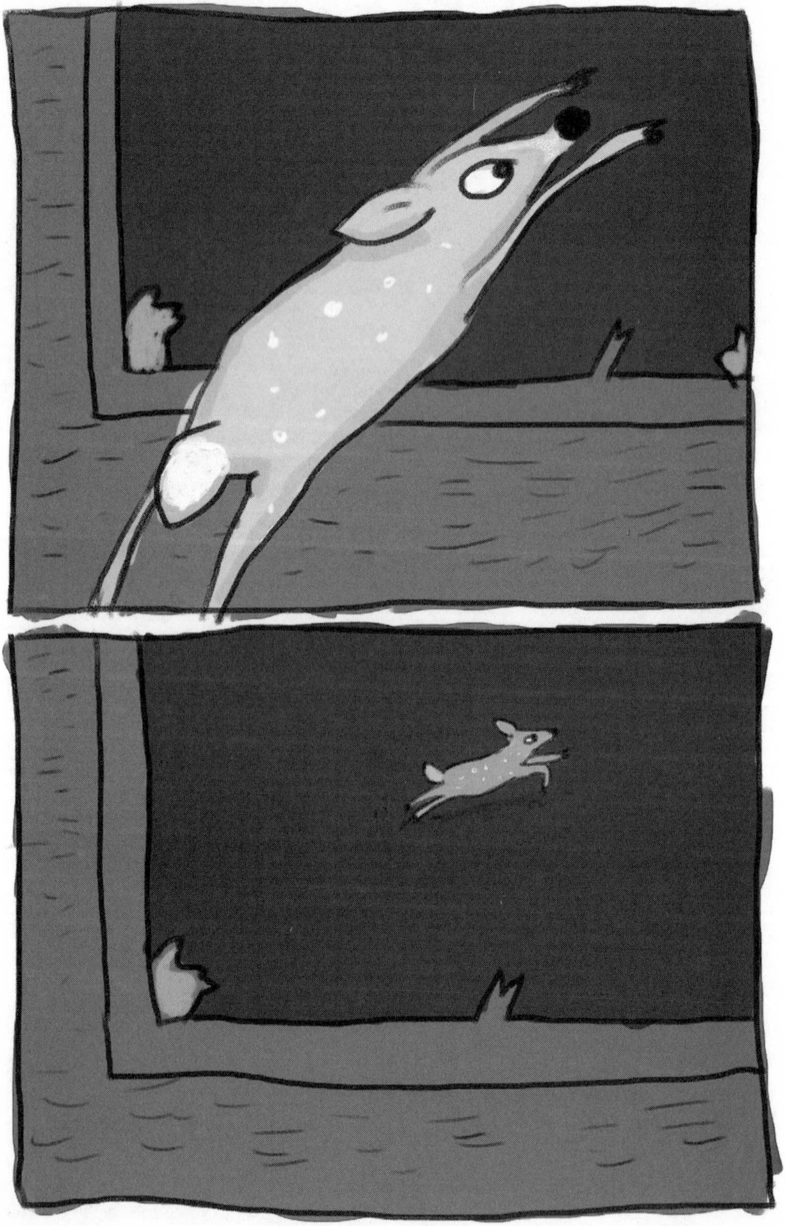

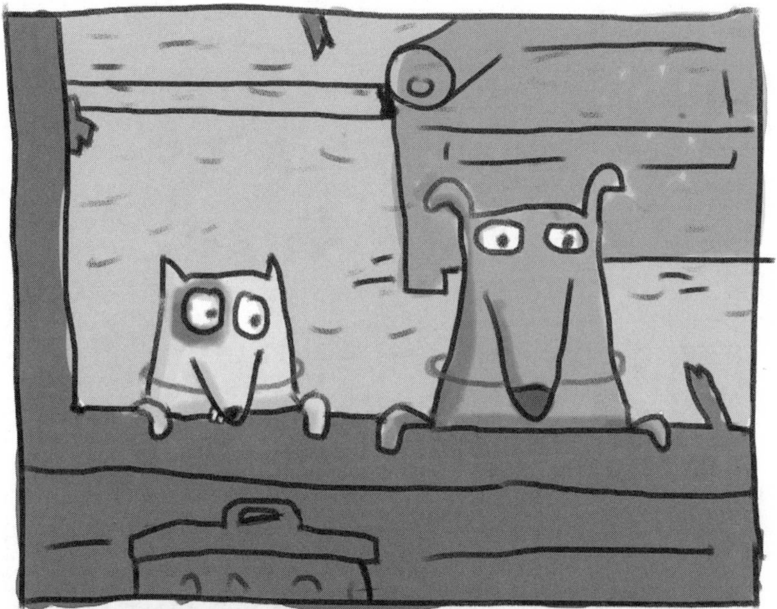

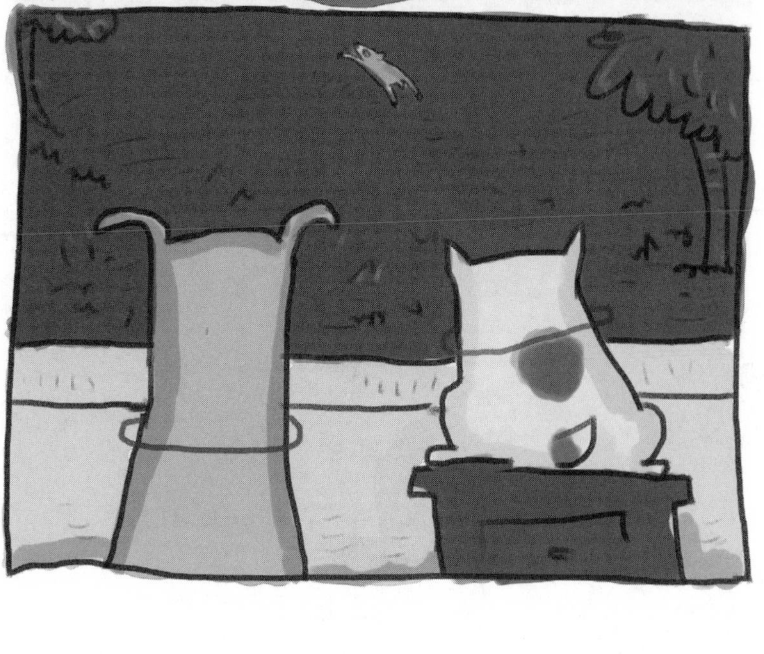

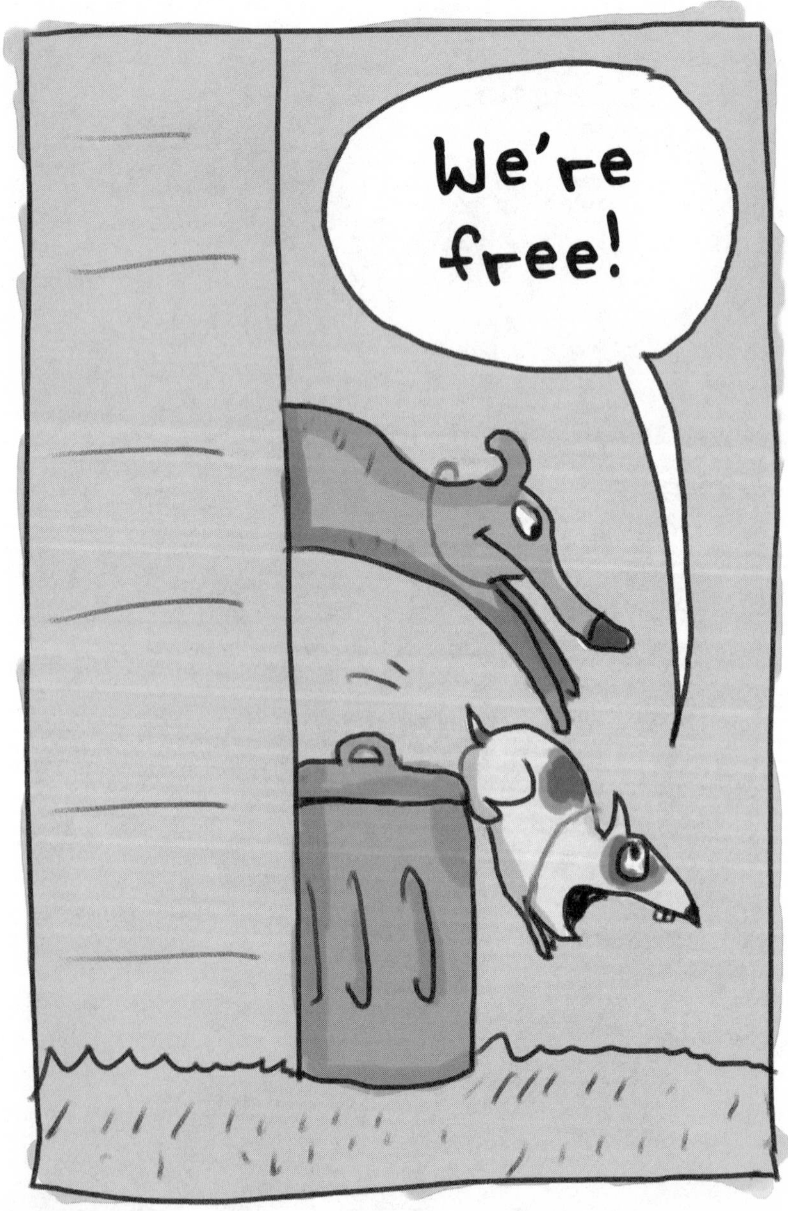
We're free!

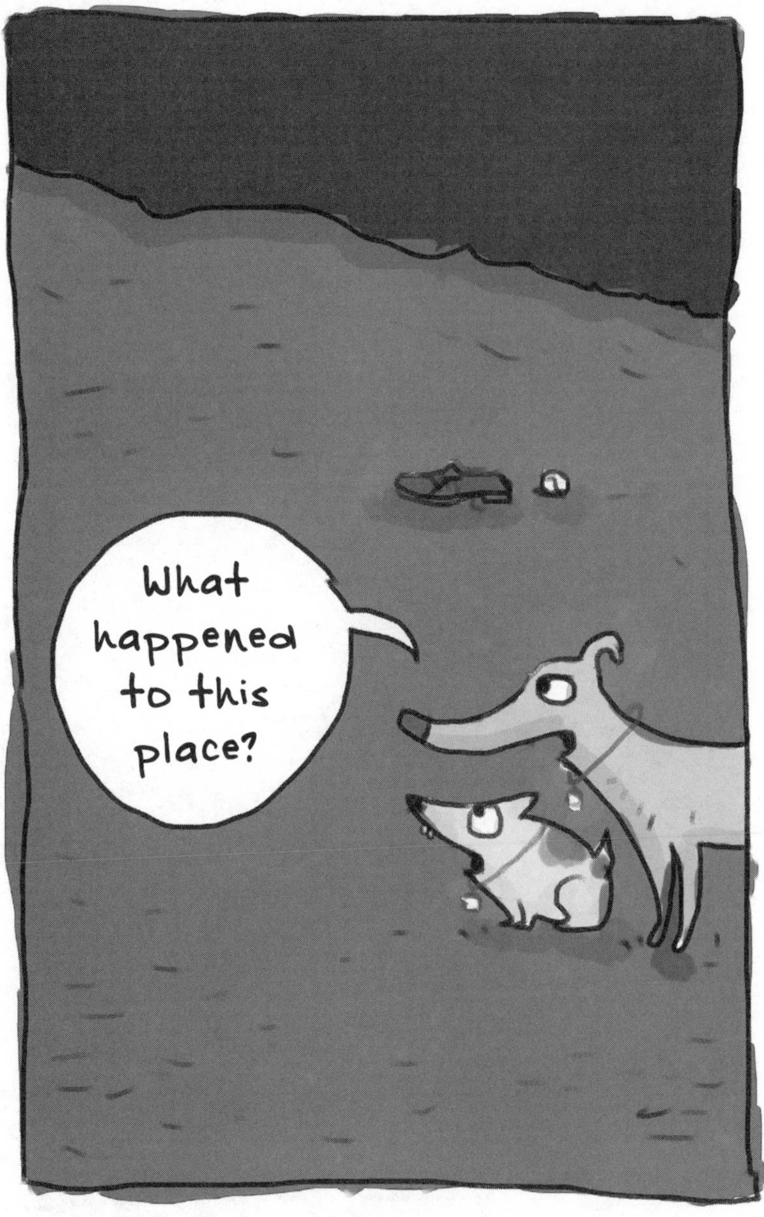
What happened to this place?

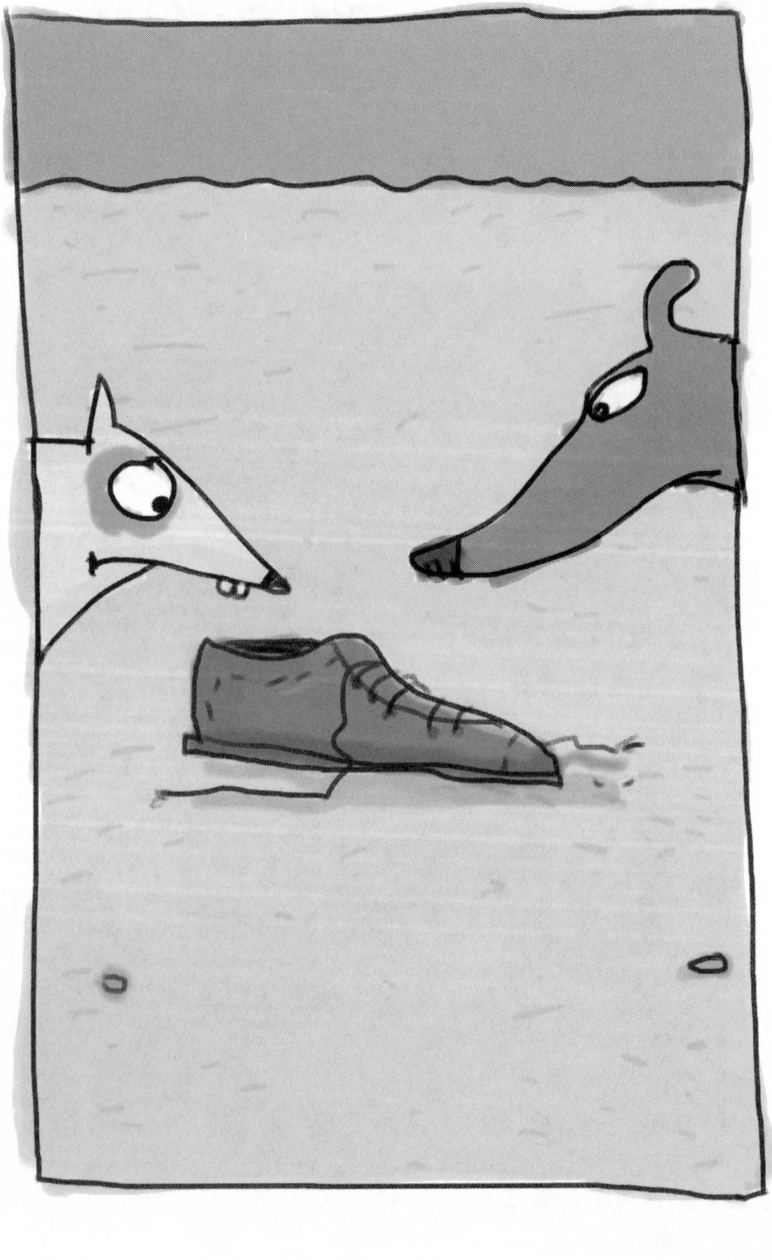

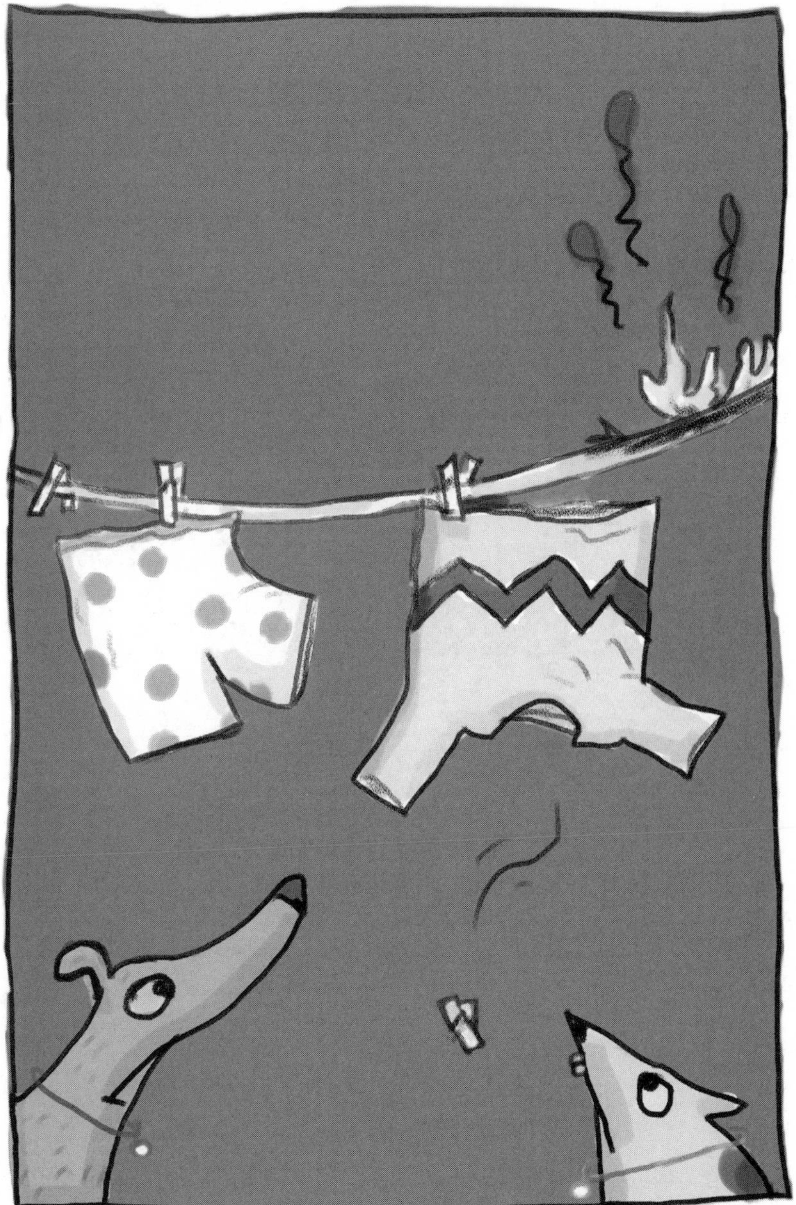

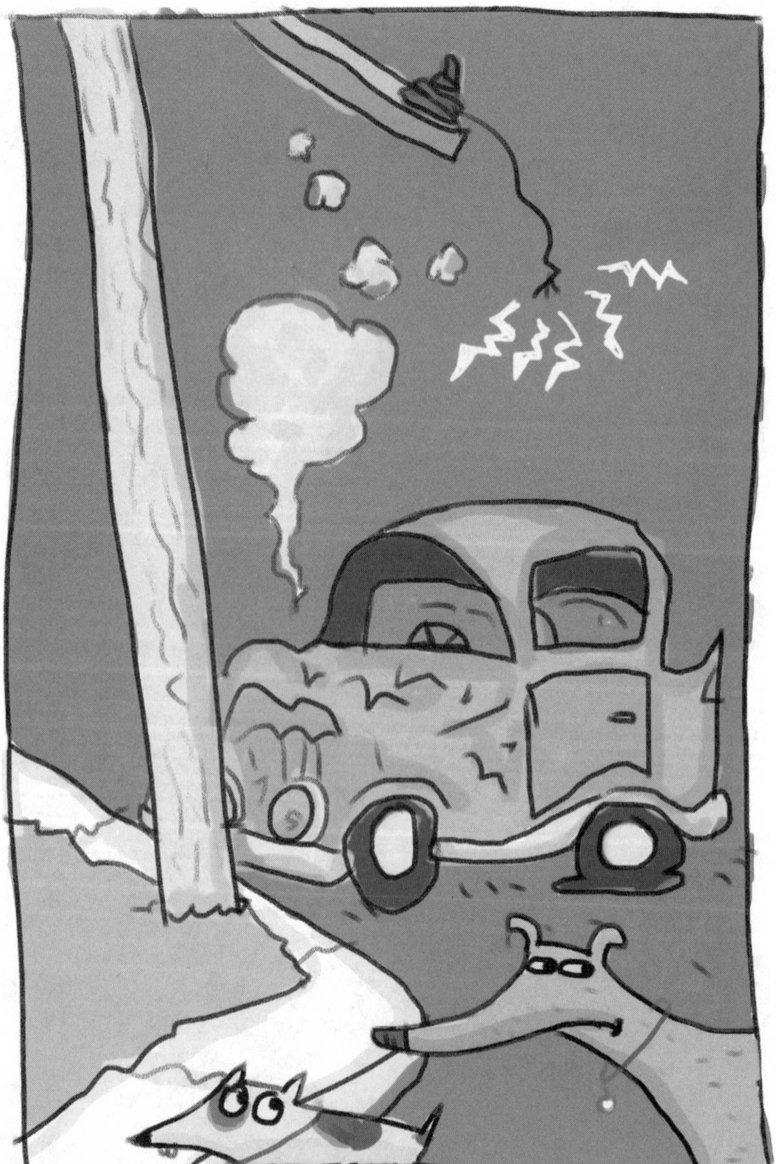

Scene
Seven

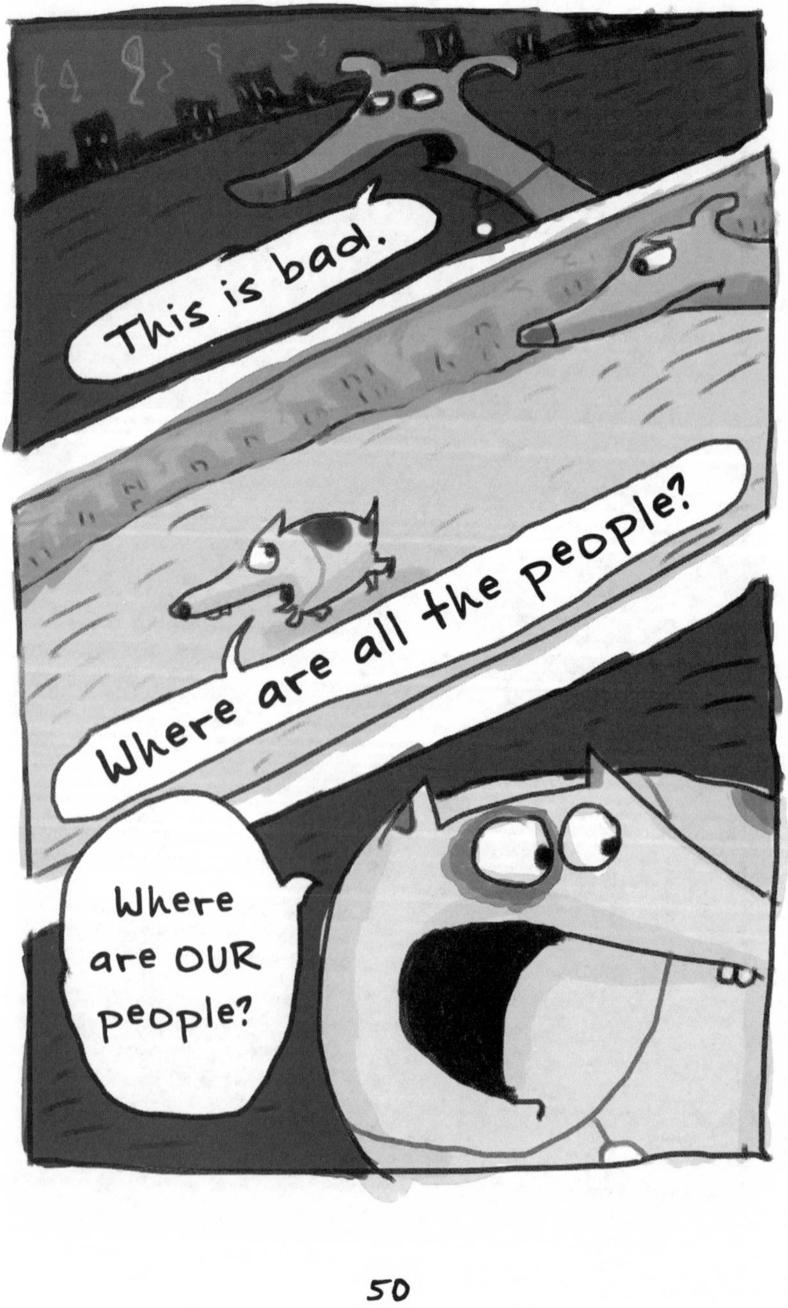
This is bad.
Where are all the people?
Where are OUR people?

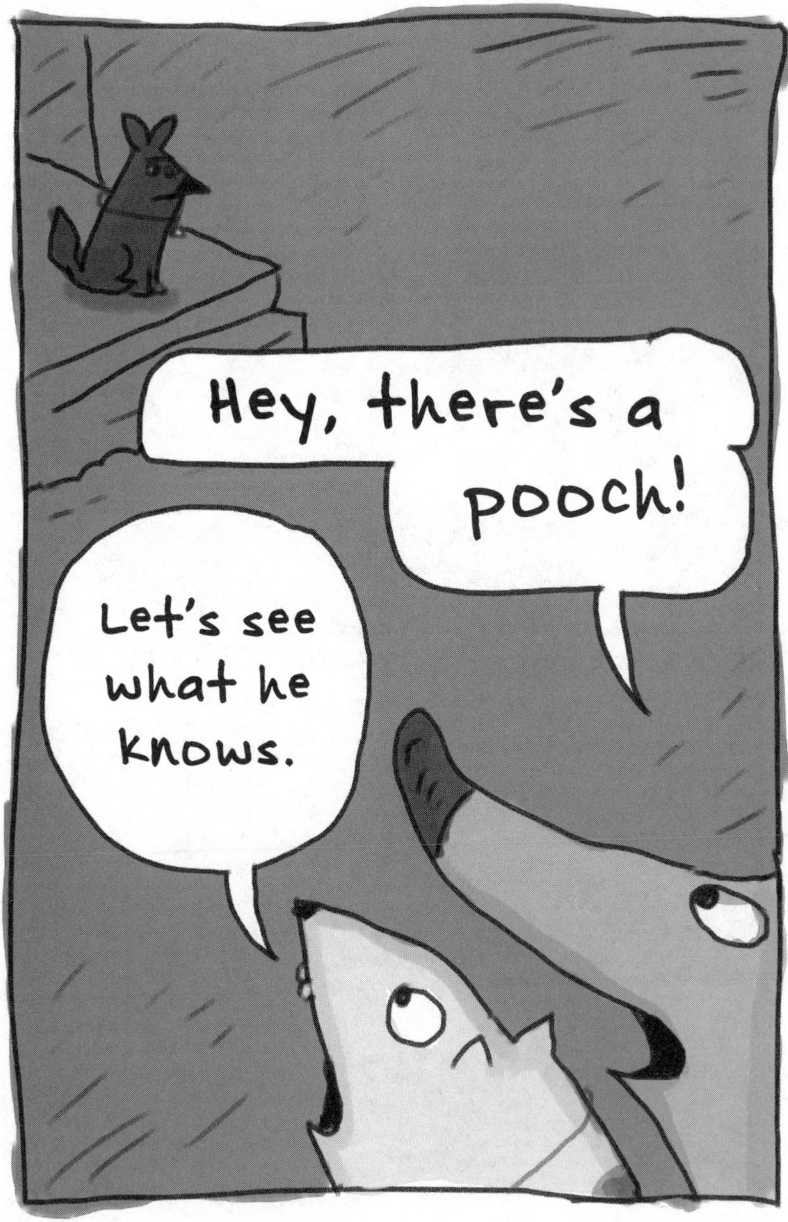
Hey, there's a pooch!
Let's see what he knows.

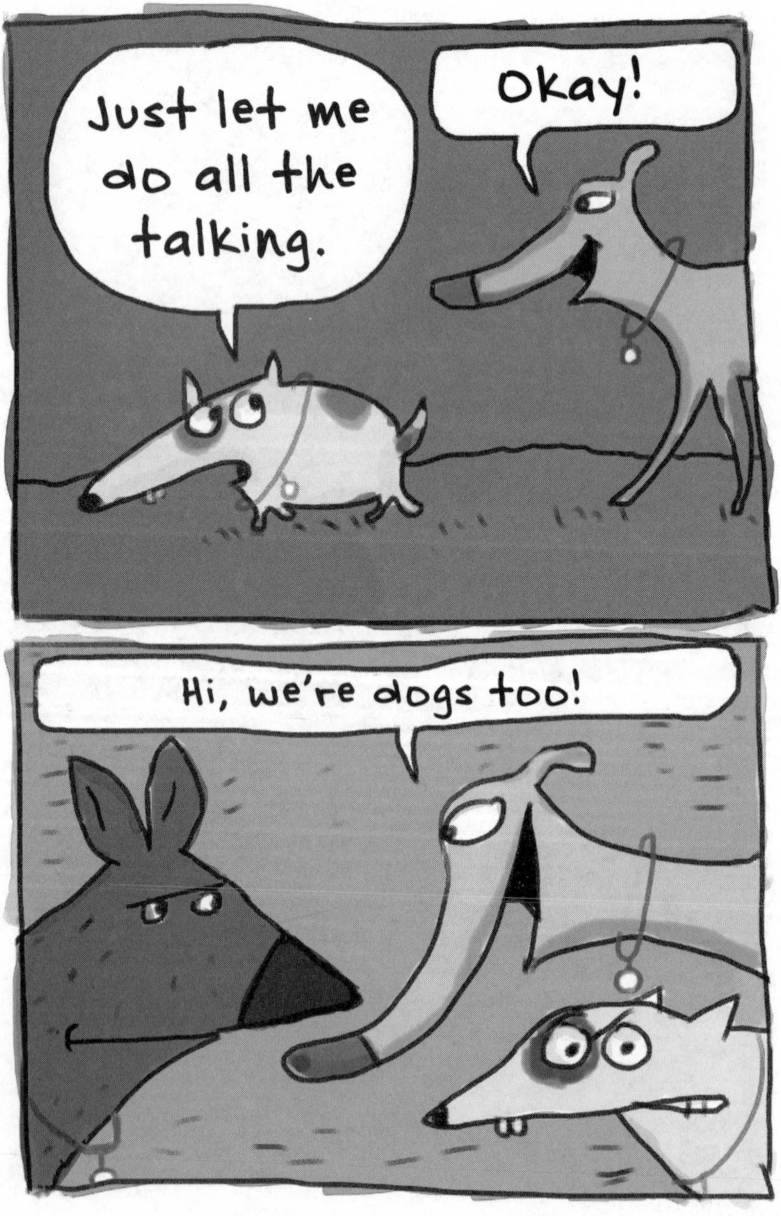
Just let me do all the talking.
Okay!
Hi, we're dogs too!

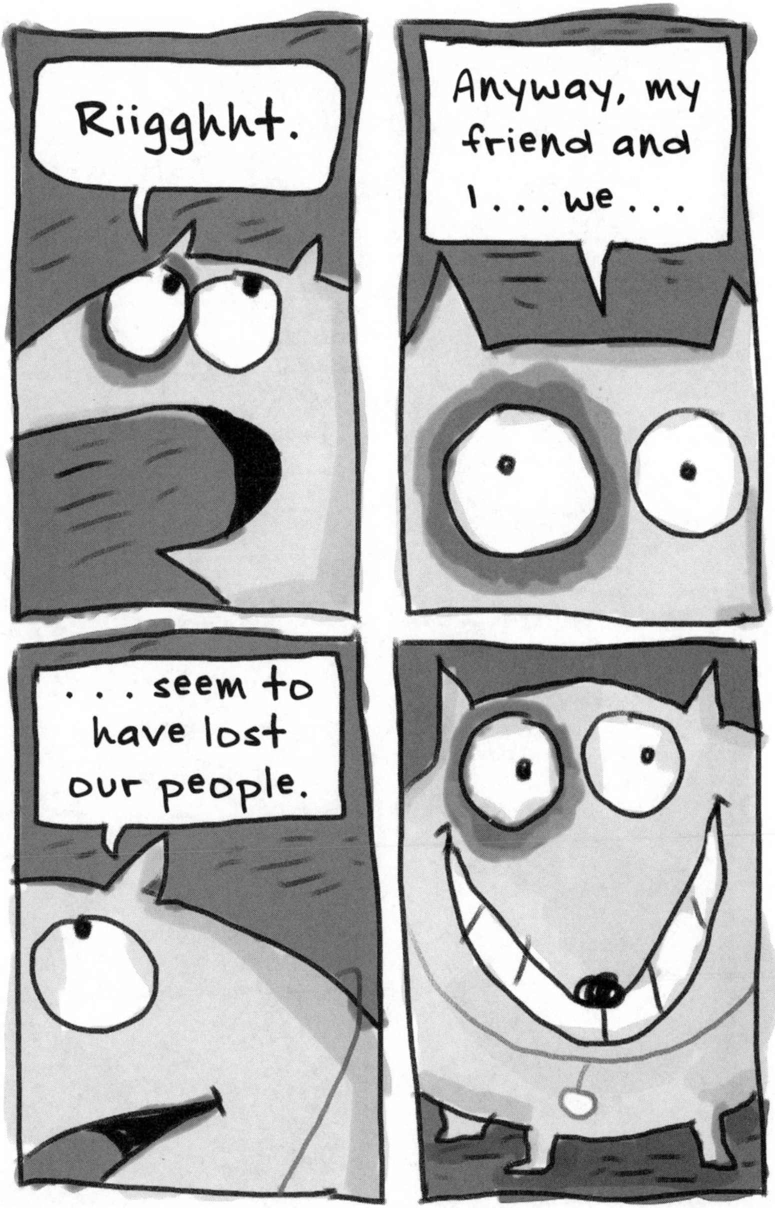
Riigghht.
Anyway, my friend and I . . . we . . .
. . . seem to have lost our people.

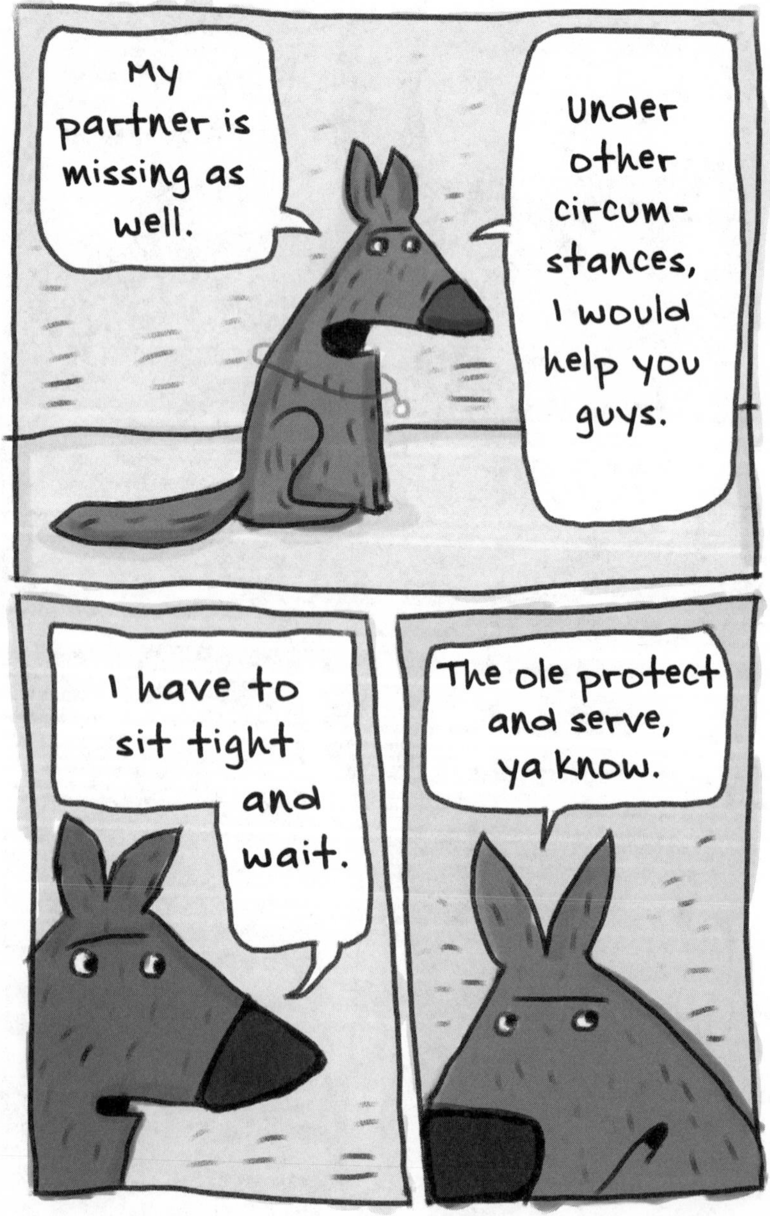
My partner is missing as well.
Under other circum-stances, I would help you guys.
I have to sit tight and wait.
The ole protect and serve, ya know.

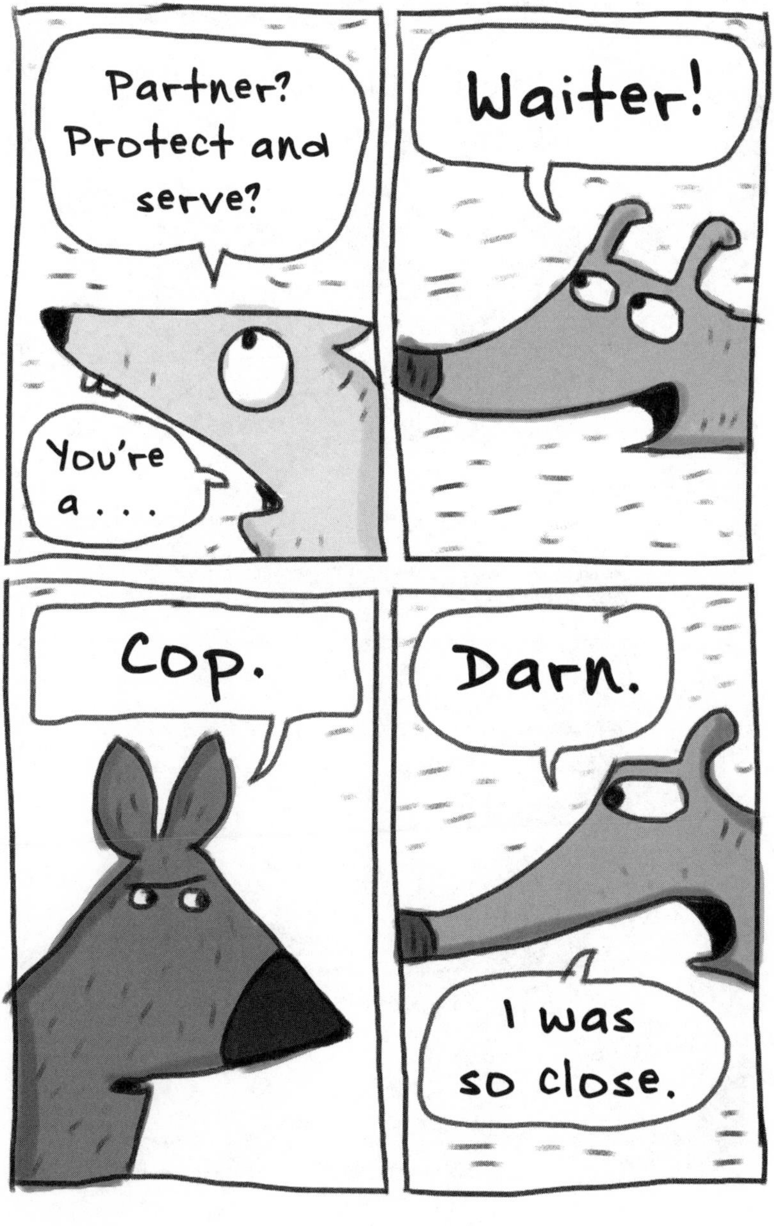
Partner? Protect and serve?
You're a . . .
Waiter!
Cop.
Darn.
I was so close.

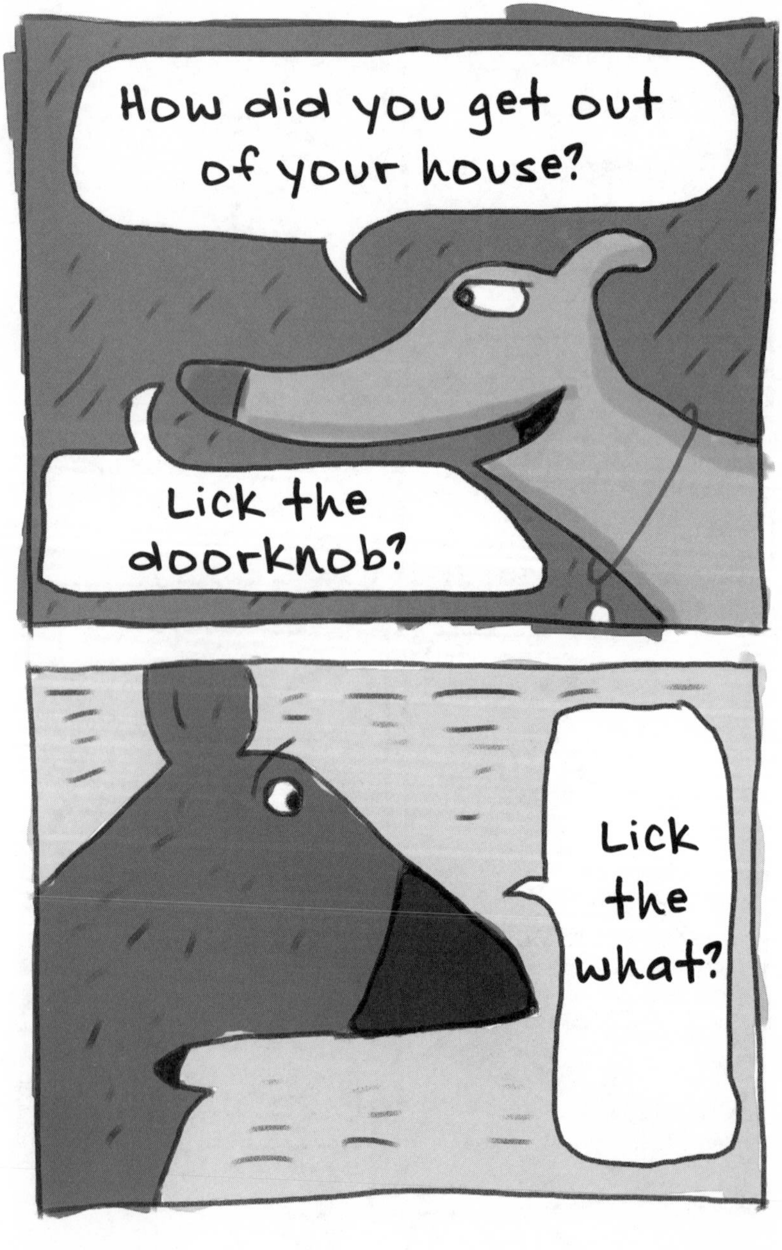
How did you get out of your house?
Lick the doorknob?
Lick the what?

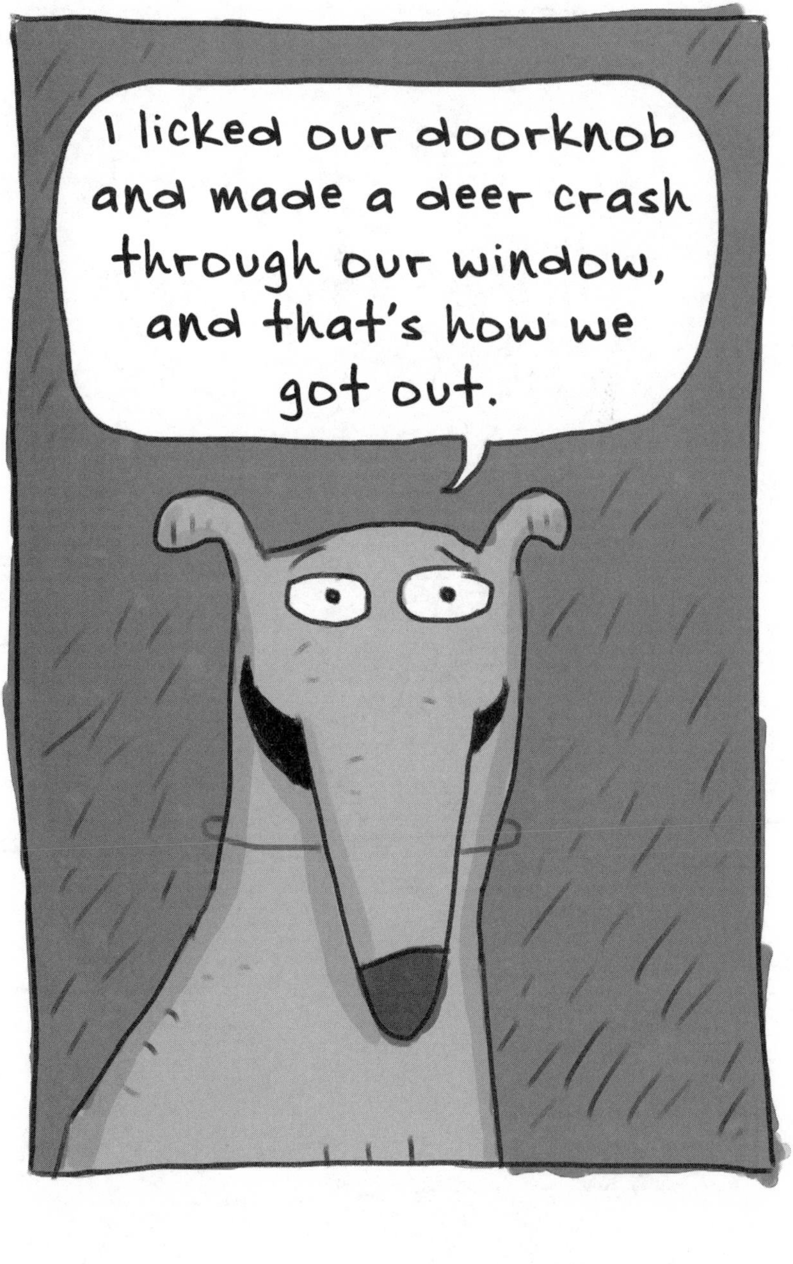
I licked our doorknob and made a deer crash through our window, and that's how we got out.

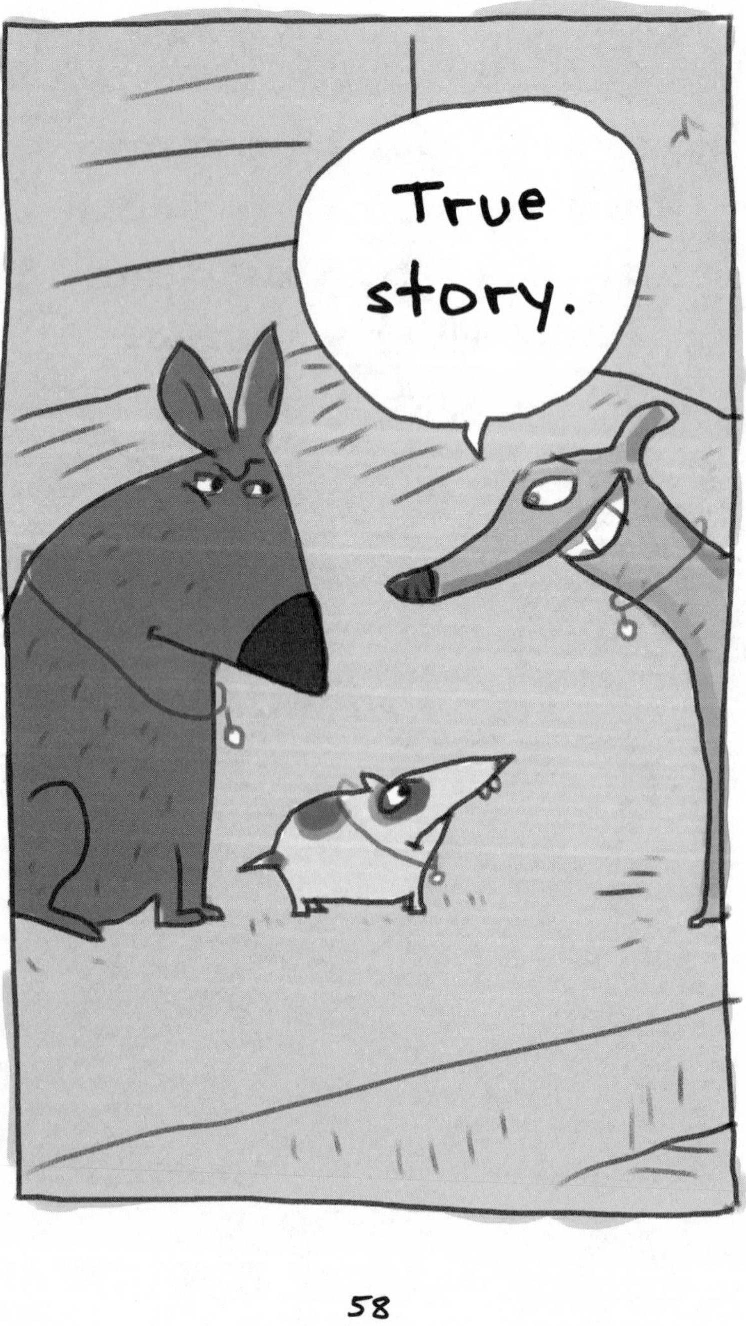
True story.

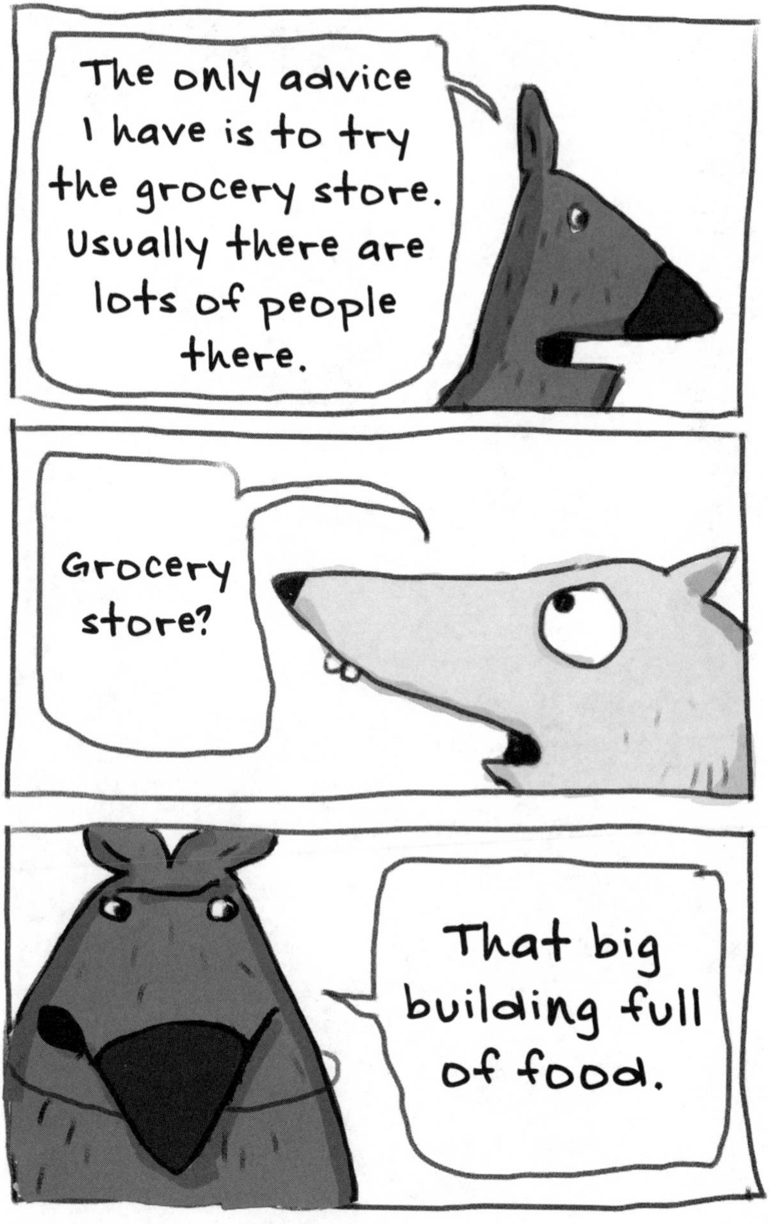
The only advice I have is to try the grocery store. Usually there are lots of people there.
Grocery store?
That big building full of food.

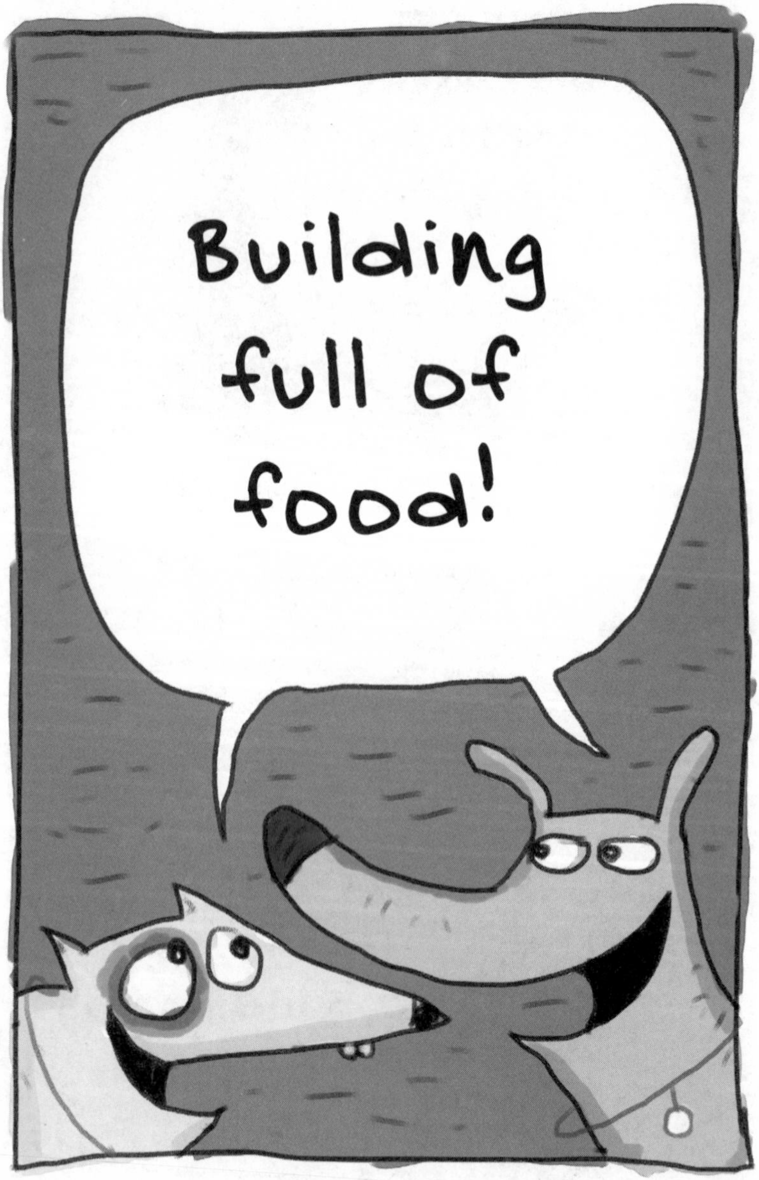
Building full of food!

Scene
Eight

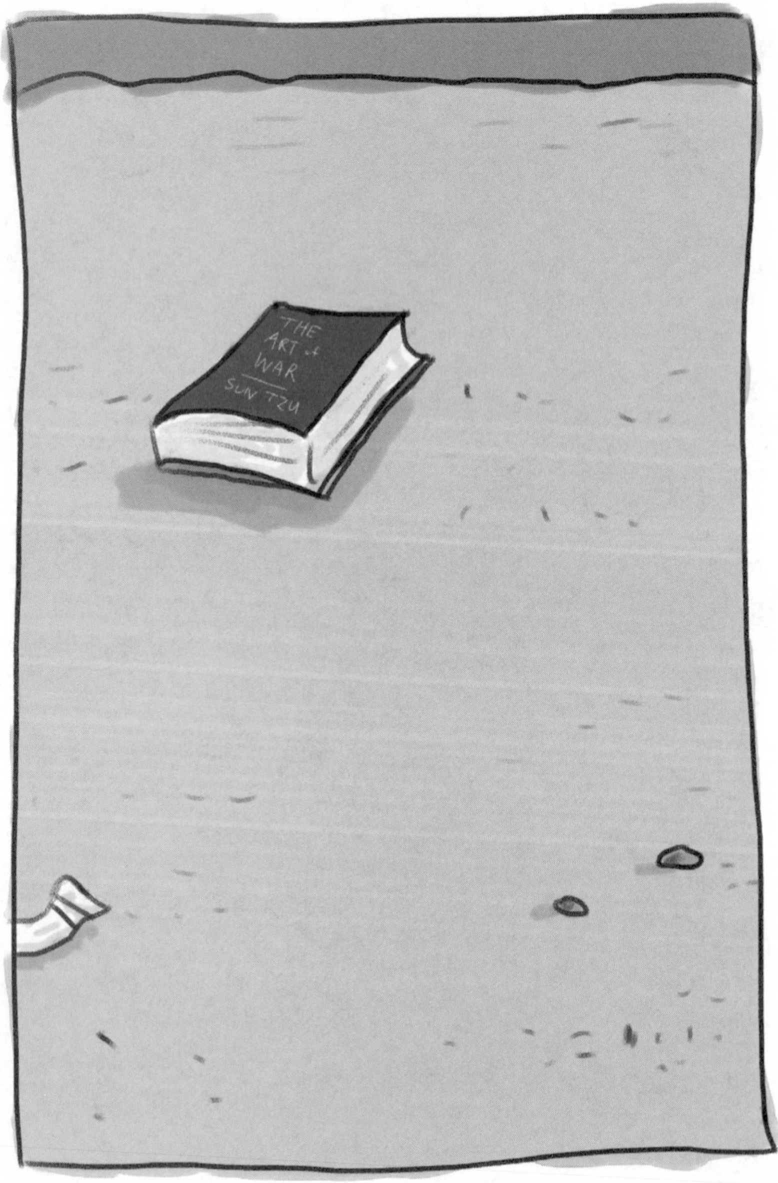
THE
ART of
WAR
SUN TZU

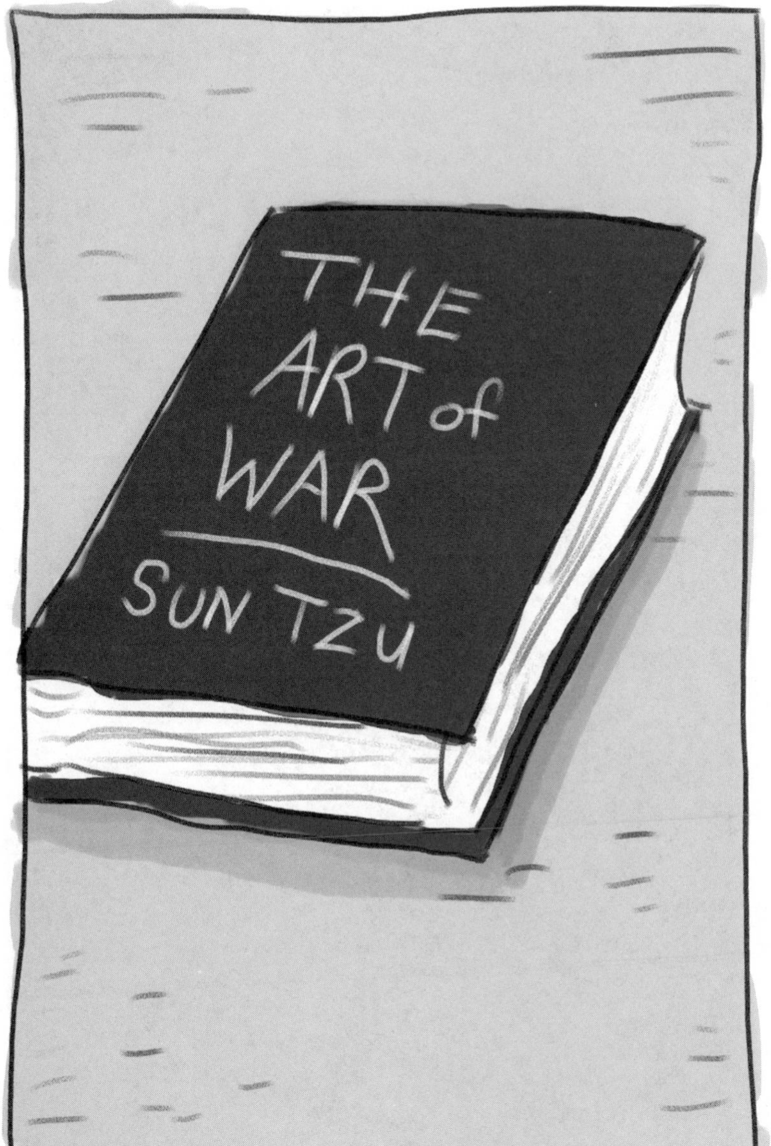
THE
ART of
WAR
SUN TZU

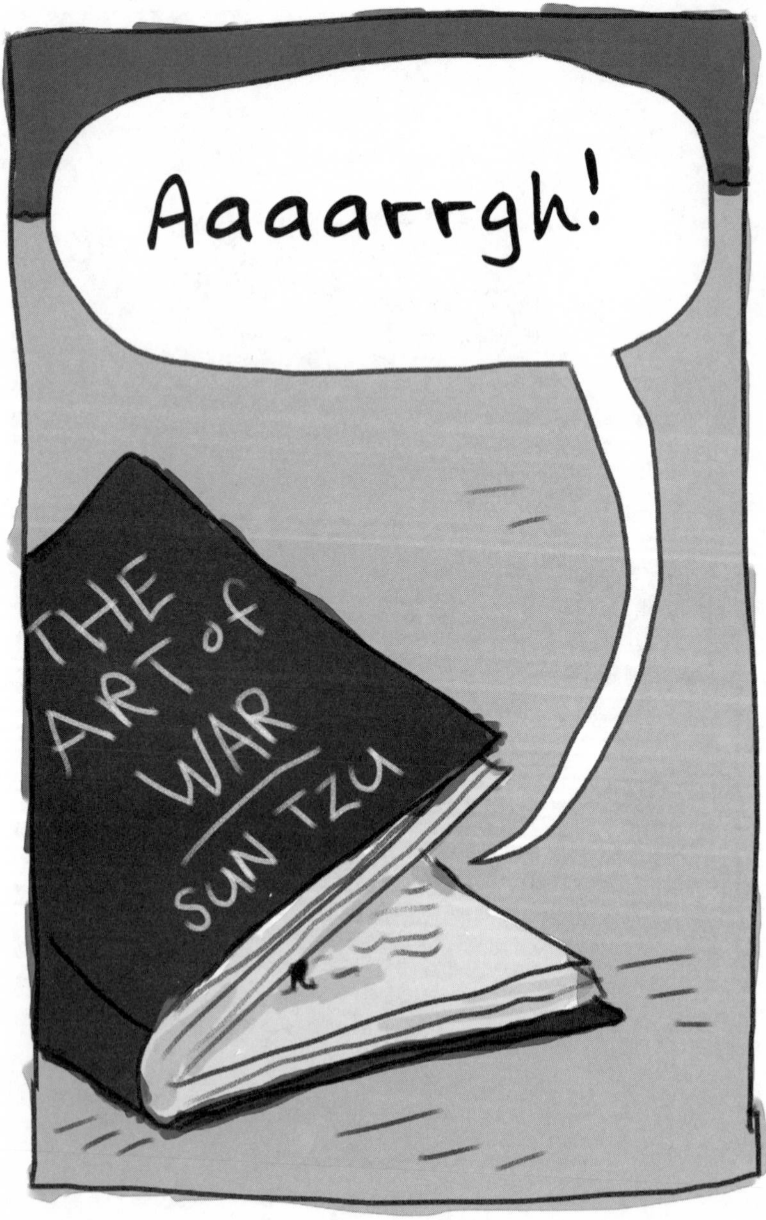
Aaaarrgh!
THE ART of WAR
SUN TZU

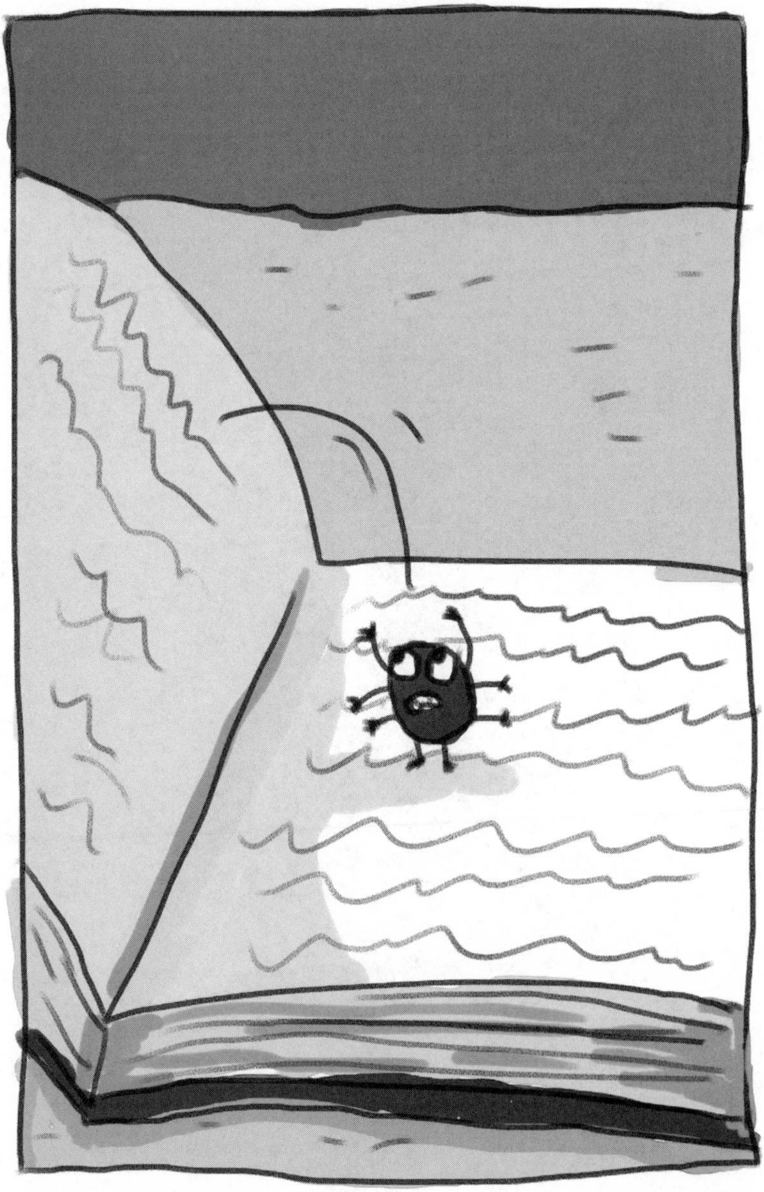

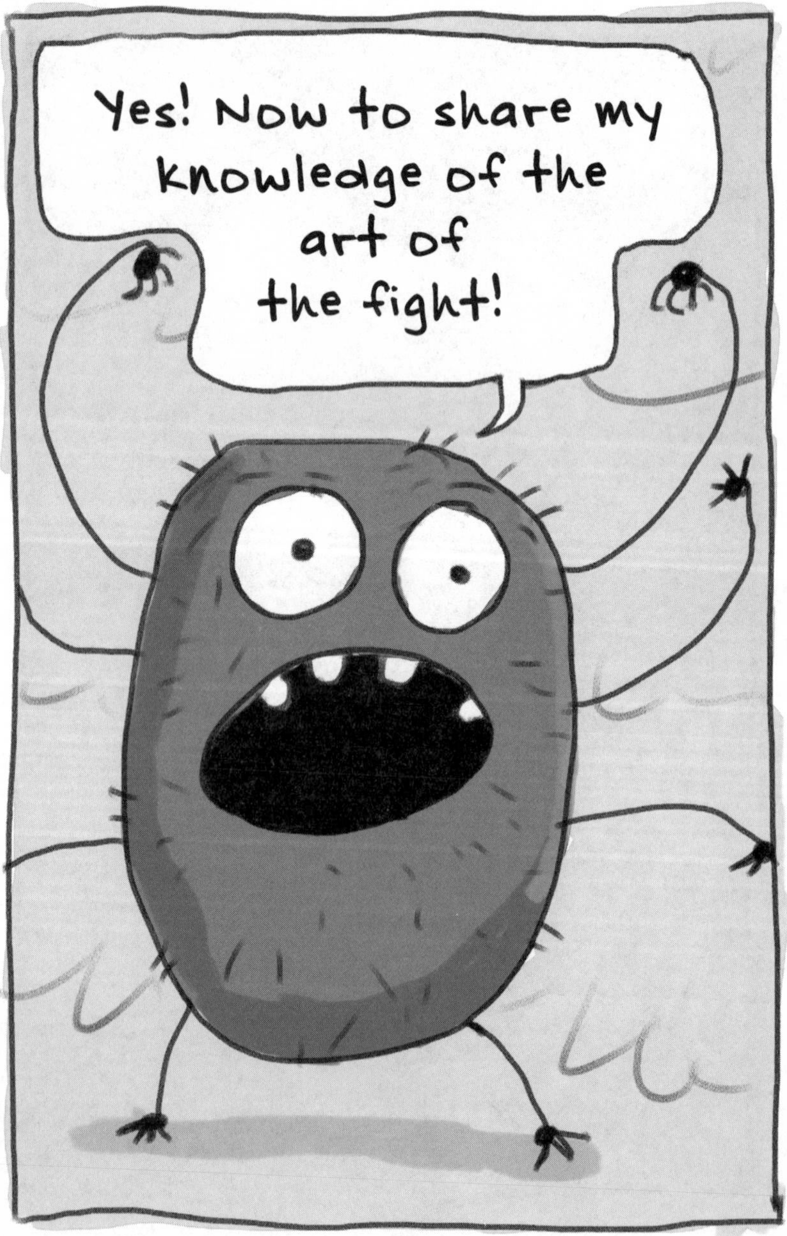
Yes! Now to share my knowledge of the art of the fight!

Scene
Nine

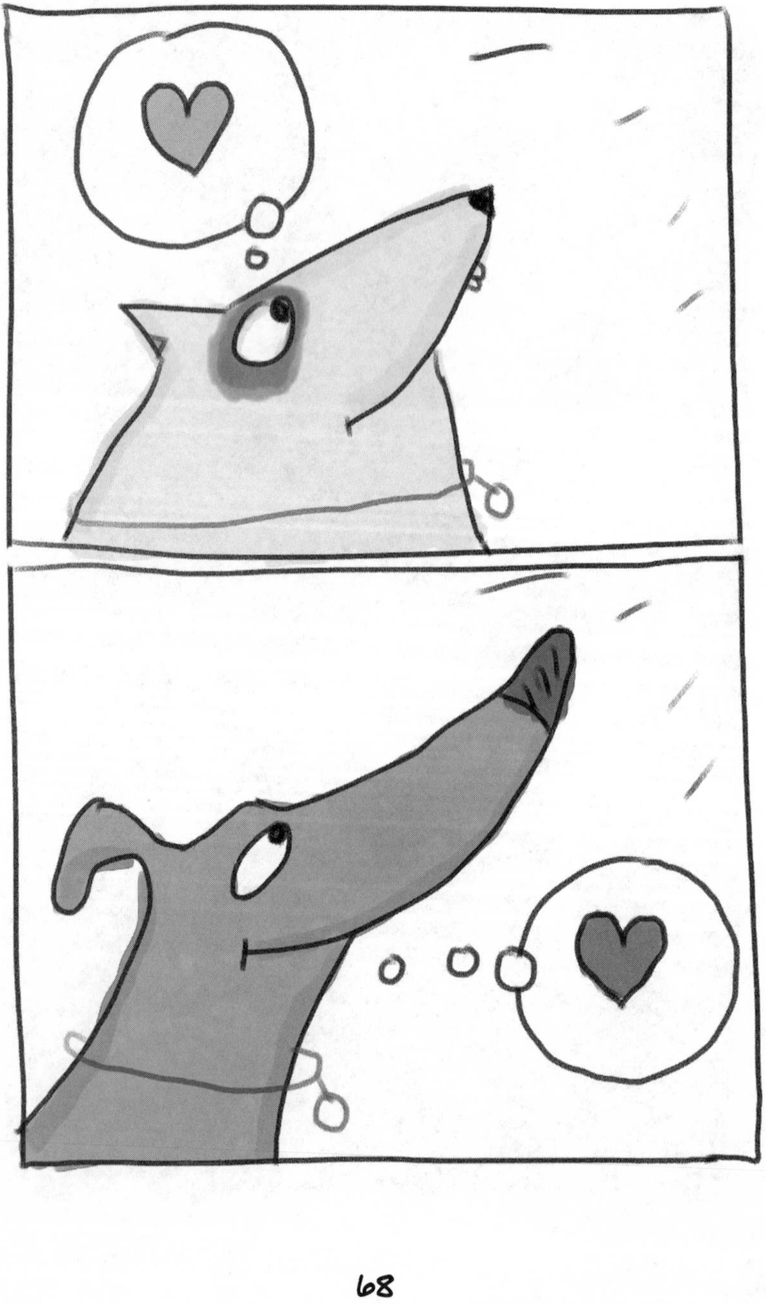

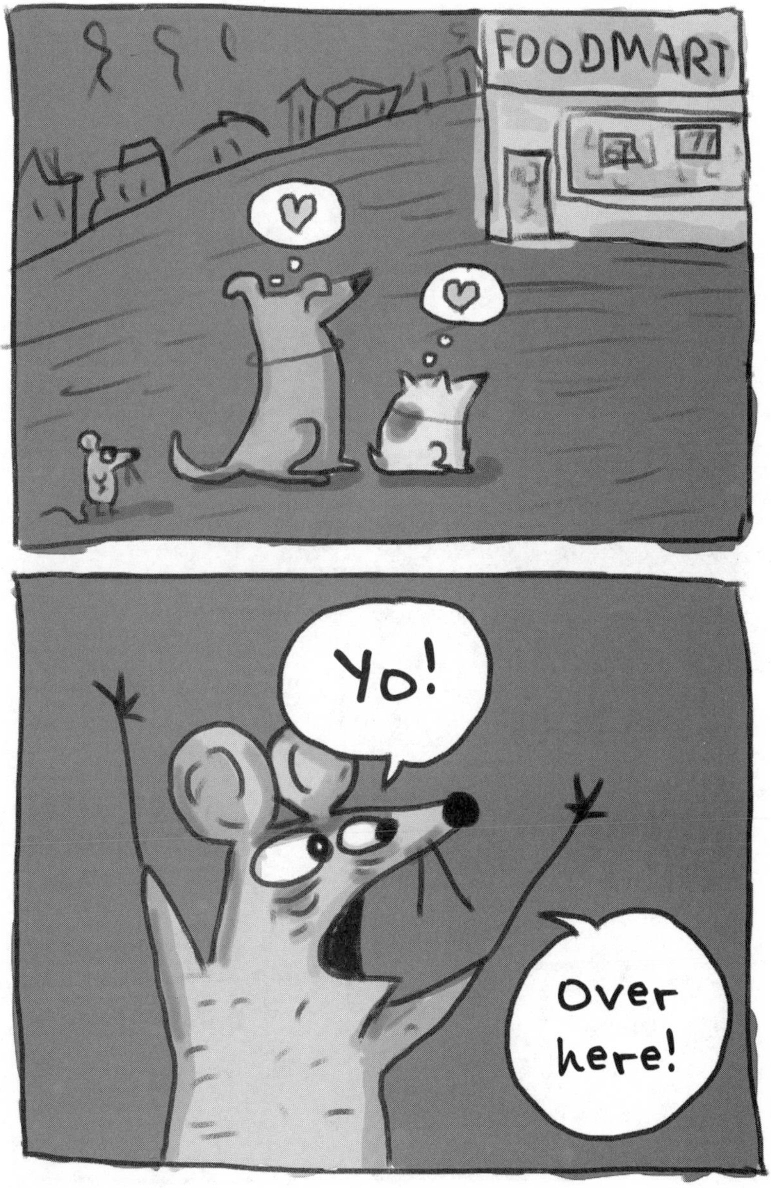
FOODMART
Yo!
Over here!

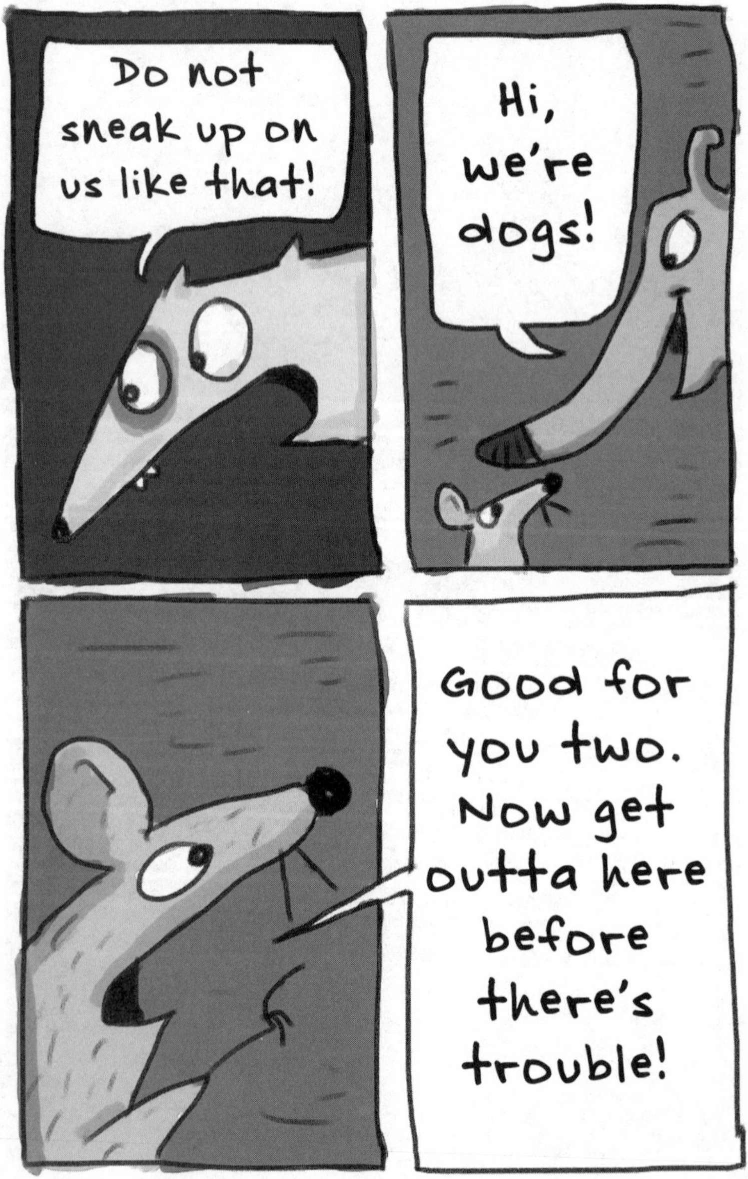
Do not sneak up on us like that!
Hi, we're dogs!
Good for you two. Now get outta here before there's trouble!

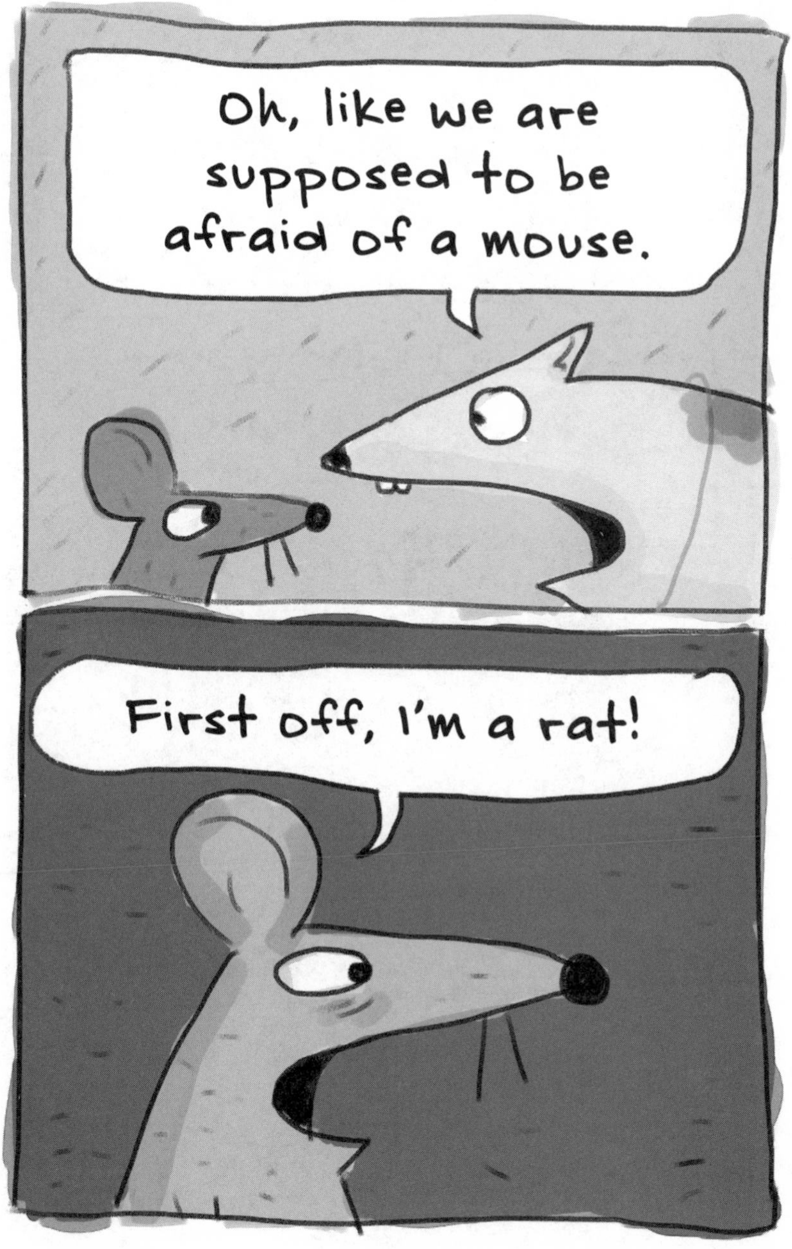
Oh, like we are supposed to be afraid of a mouse.
First off, I'm a rat!

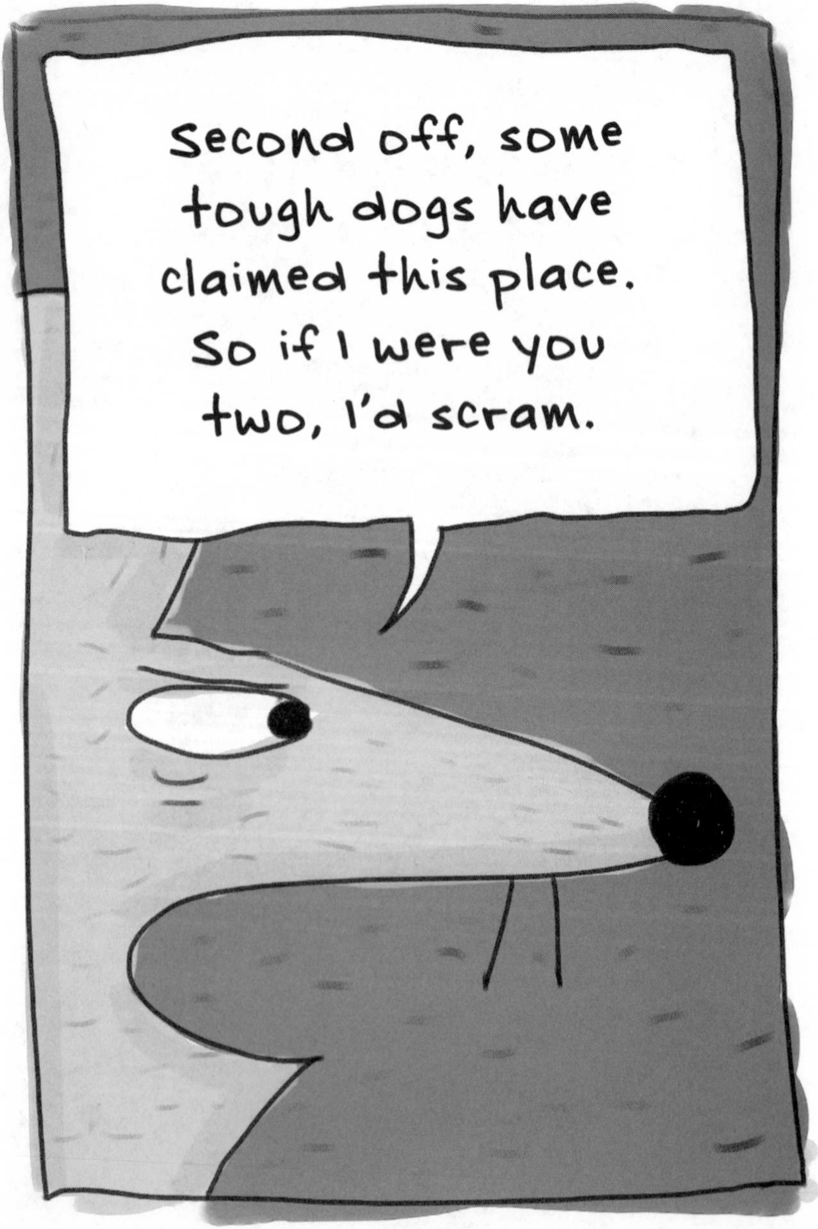
Second off, some tough dogs have claimed this place. So if I were you two, I'd scram.

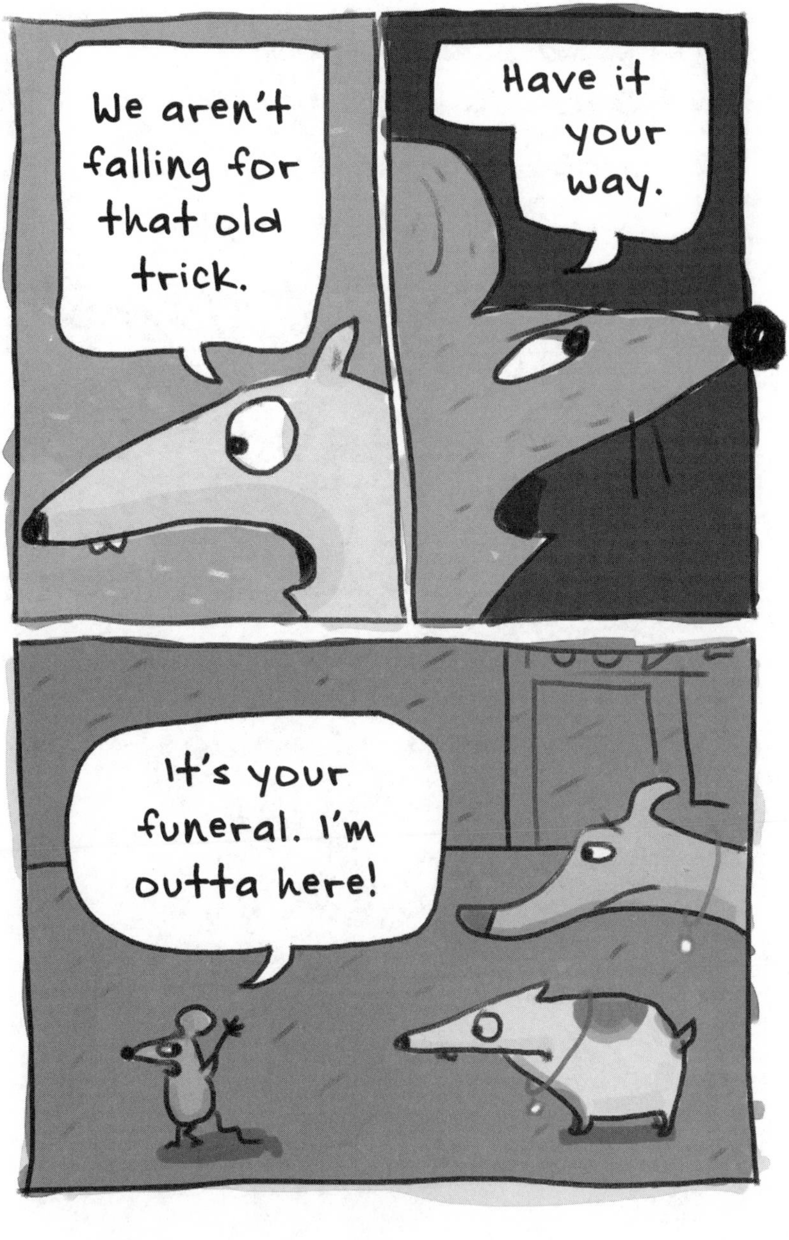
We aren't falling for that old trick.
Have it your way.
It's your funeral. I'm outta here!

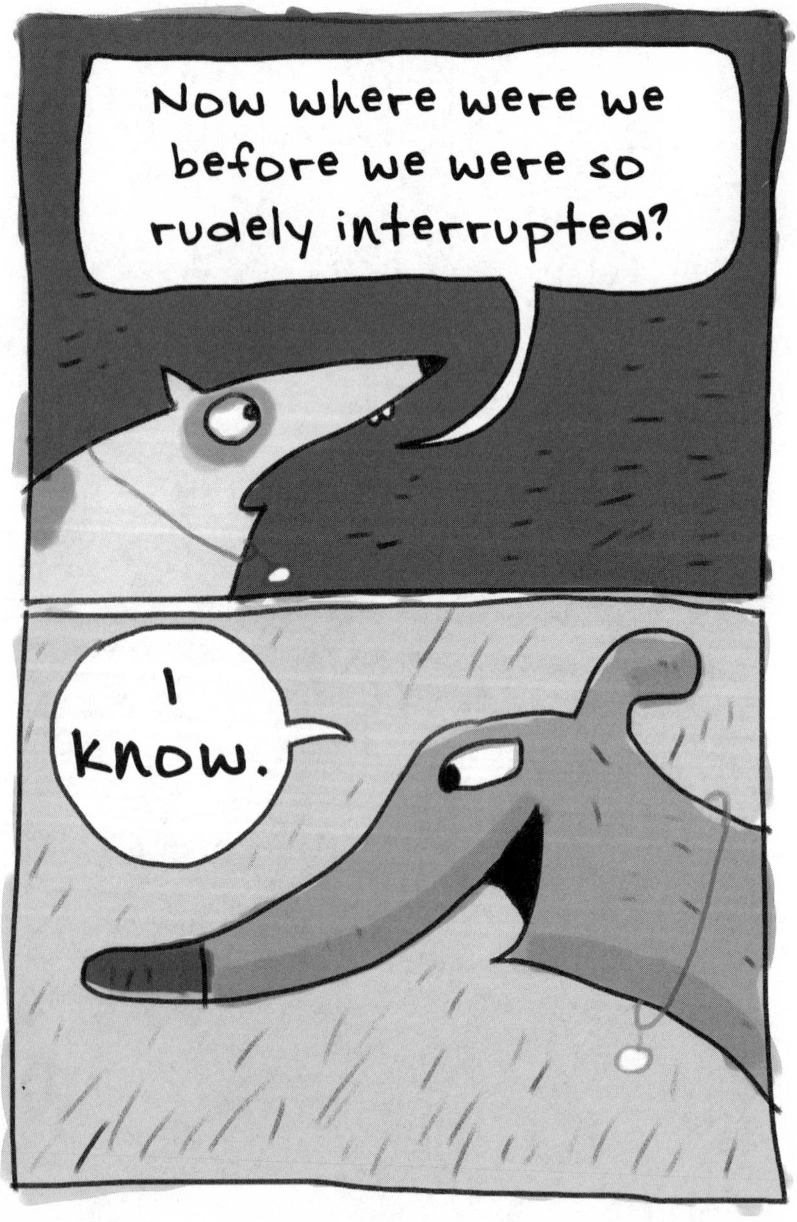
Now where were we before we were so rudely interrupted?
I know.

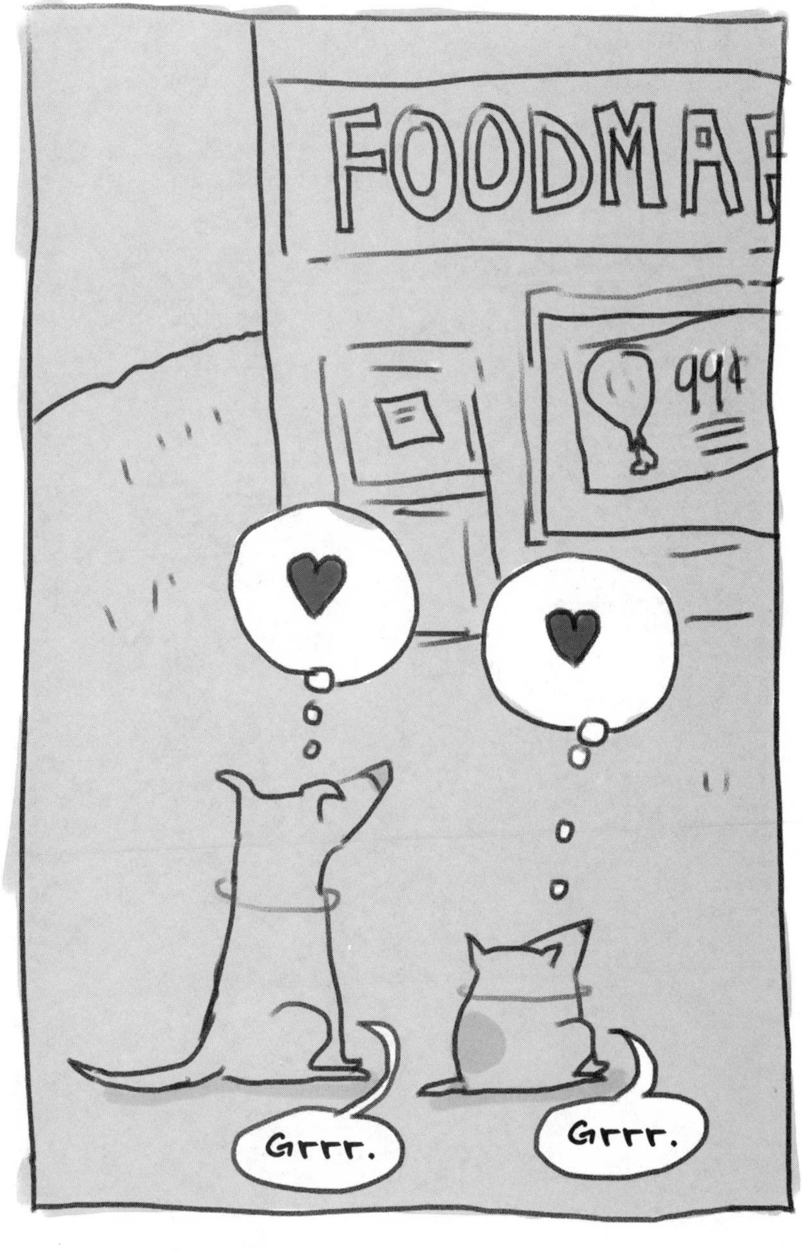
FOODMA
99¢
Grrr.
Grrr.

Scene
Ten

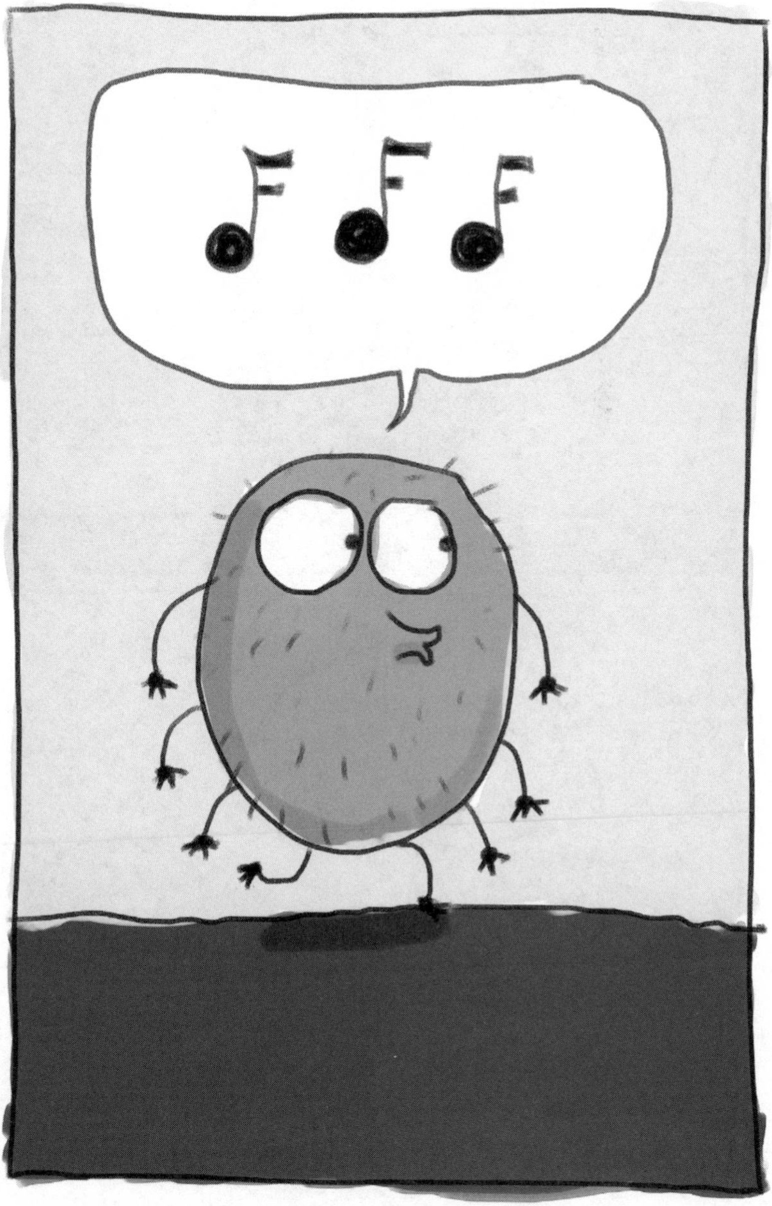

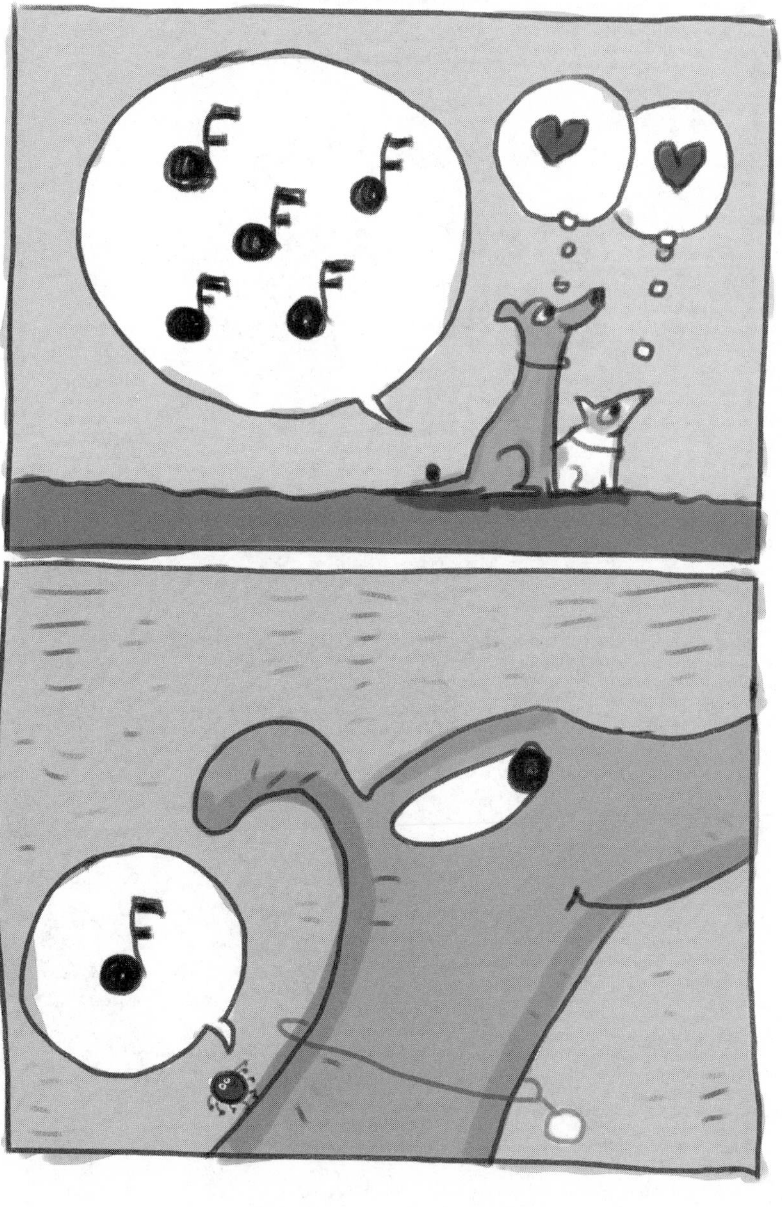

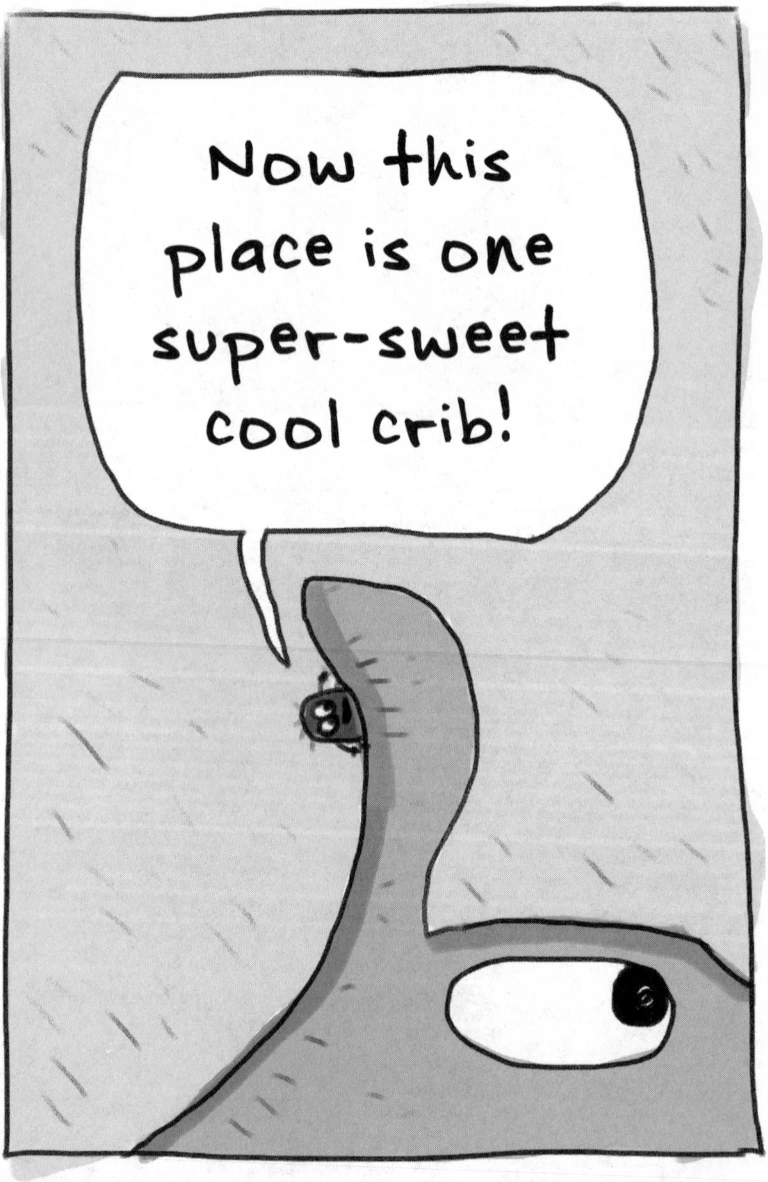
Now this place is one super-sweet cool crib!

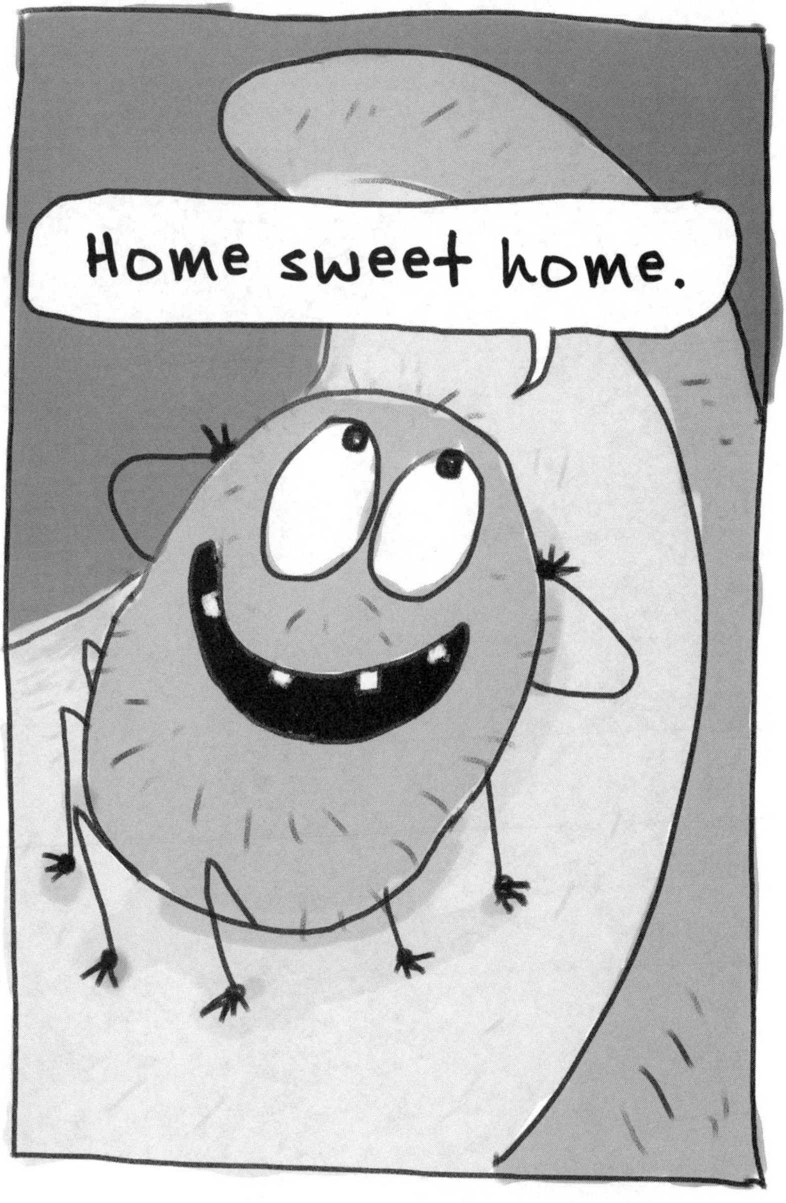
Home sweet home.

Scene
Eleven

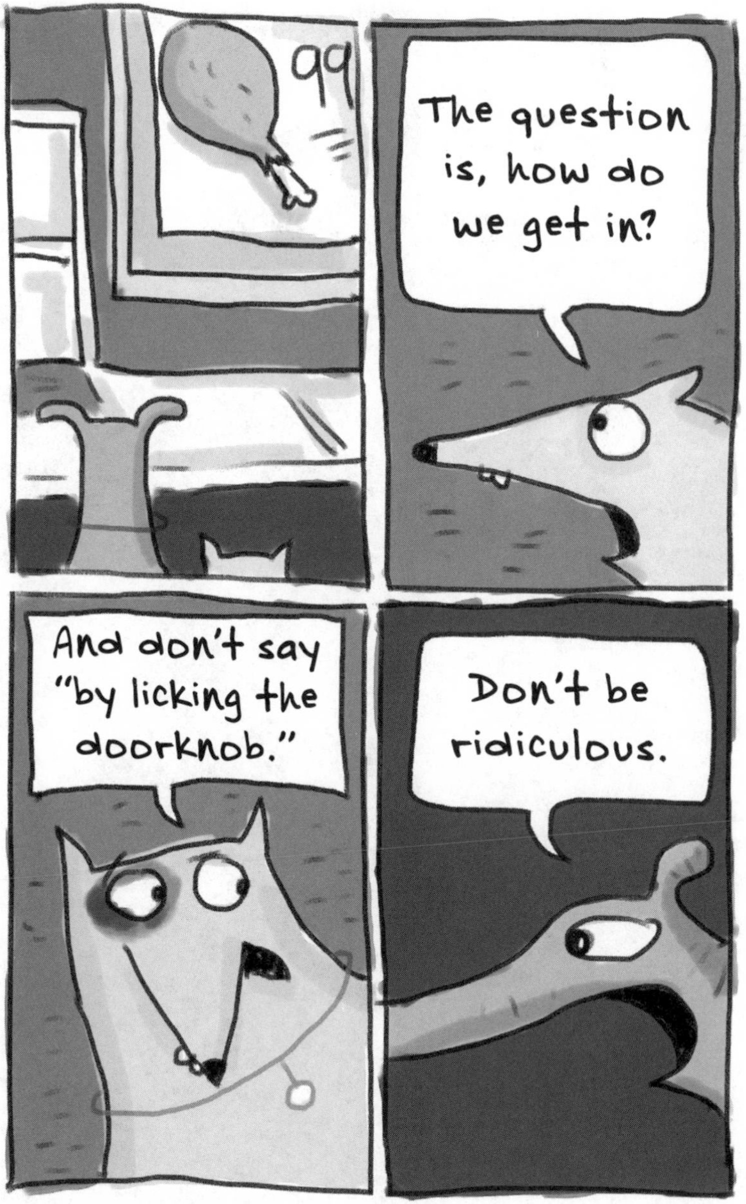
99
The question is, how do we get in?
And don't say "by licking the doorknob."
Don't be ridiculous.

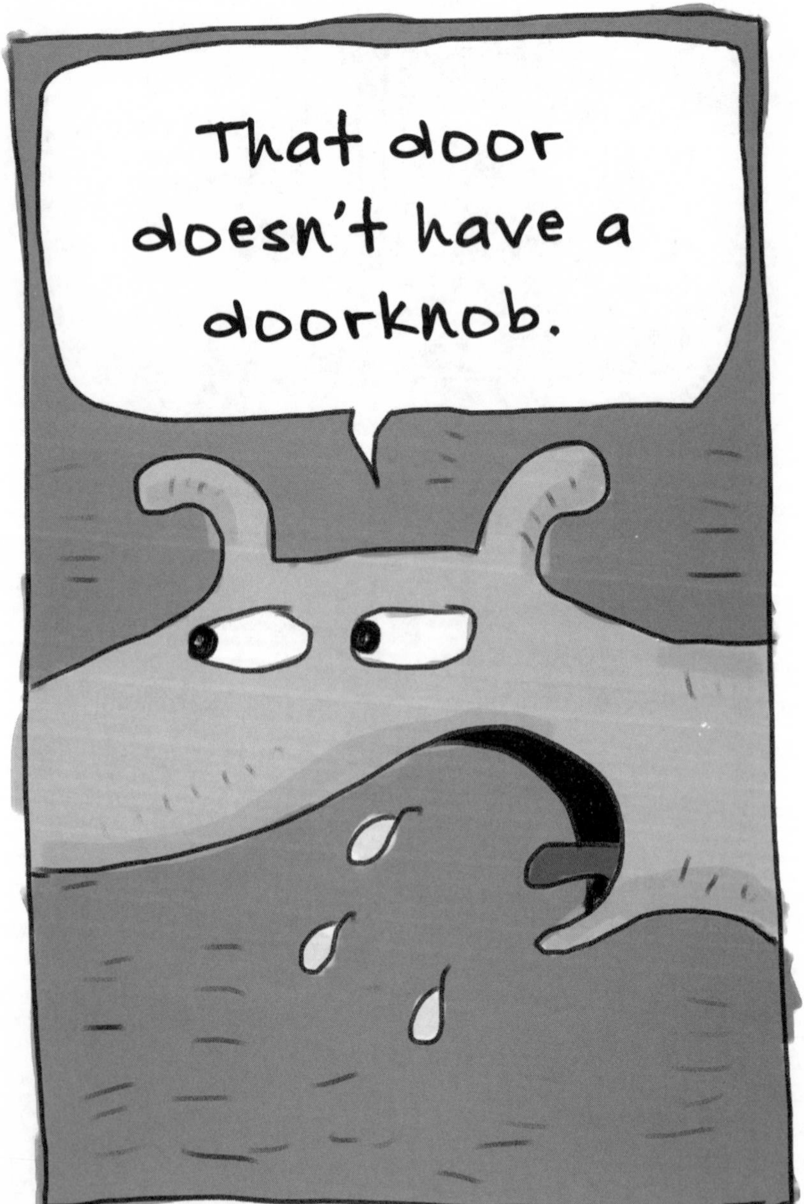
That door doesn't have a doorknob.

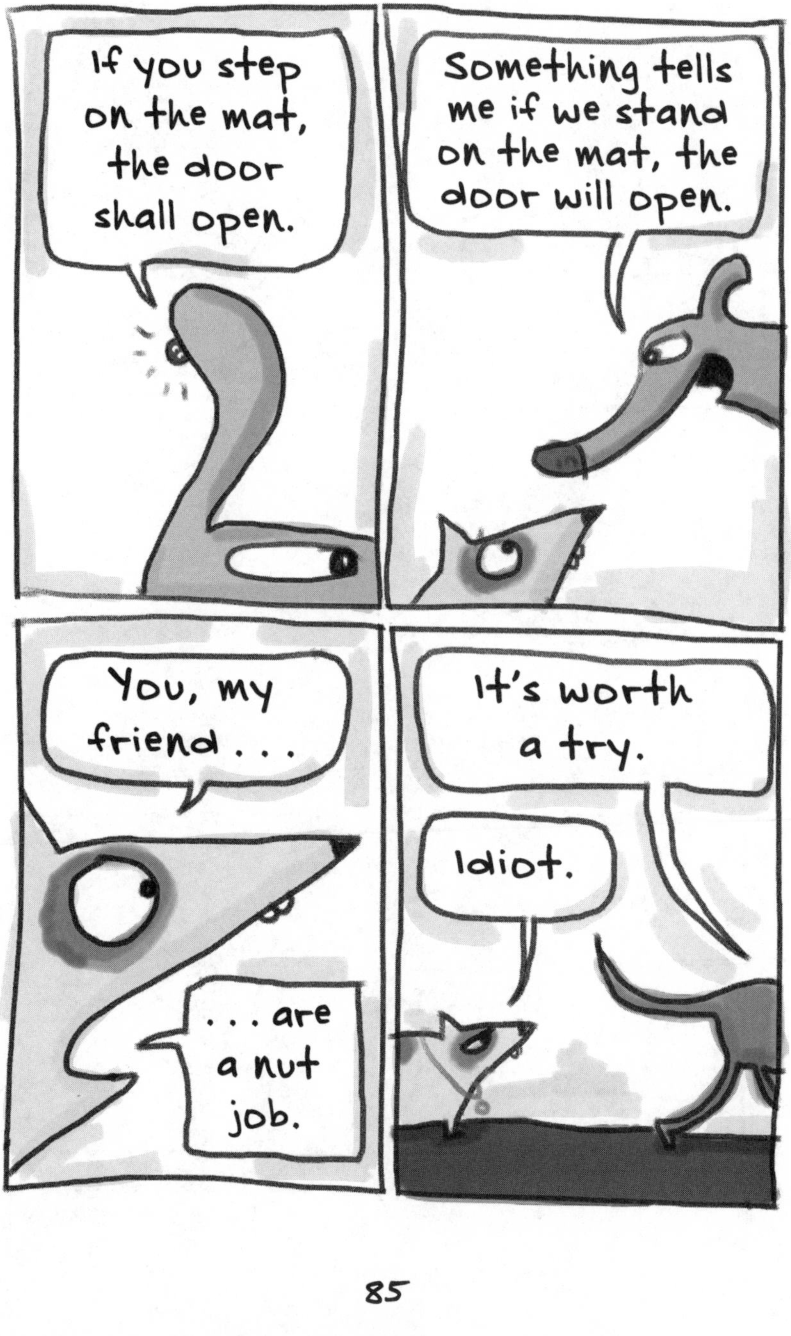
If you step on the mat, the door shall open.
Something tells me if we stand on the mat, the door will open.
You, my friend . . .
. . . are a nut job.
It's worth a try.
Idiot.

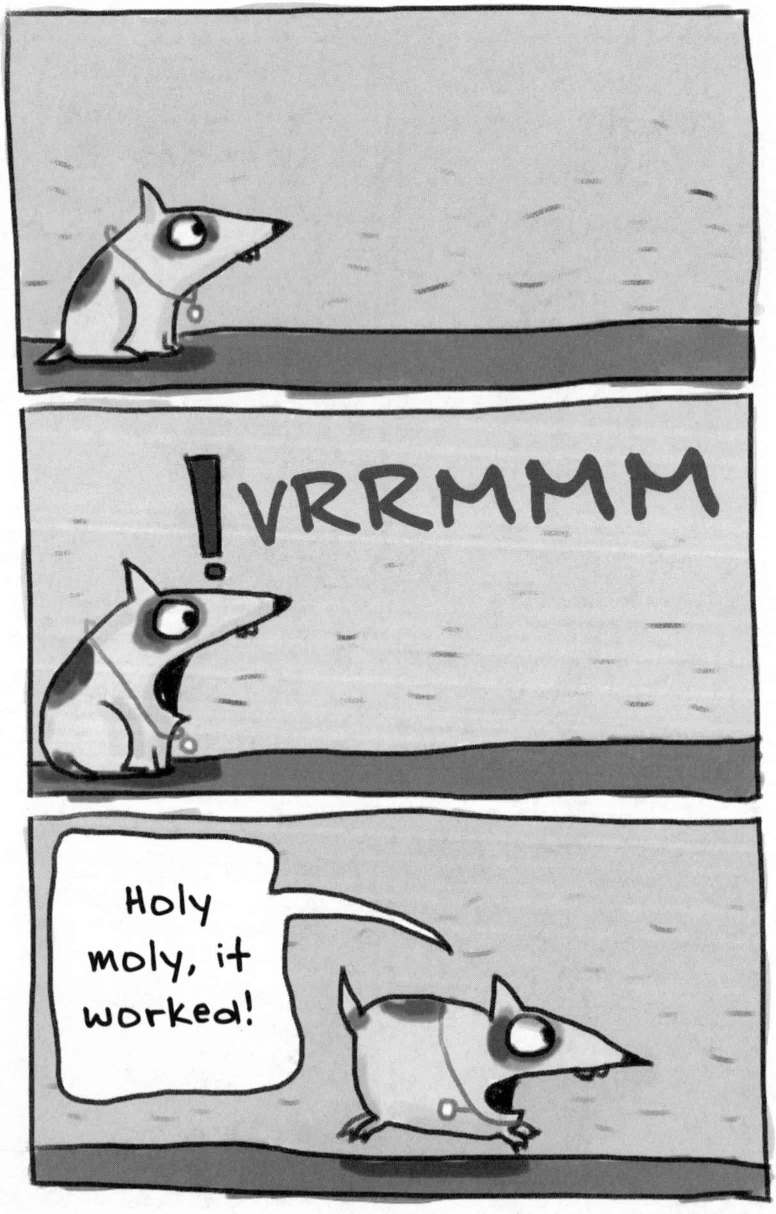
!
VRRMMM
Holy moly, it worked!

Scene
Twelve

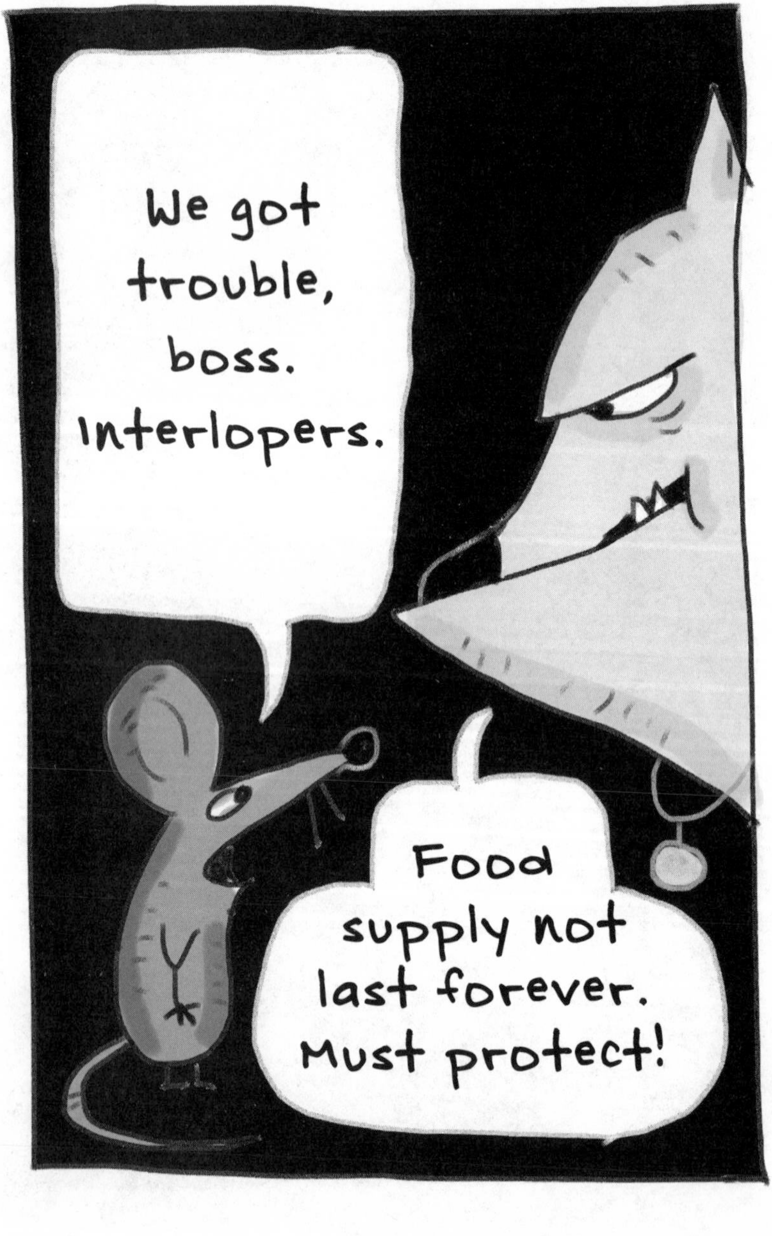
We got trouble, boss. Interlopers.
Food supply not last forever. Must protect!

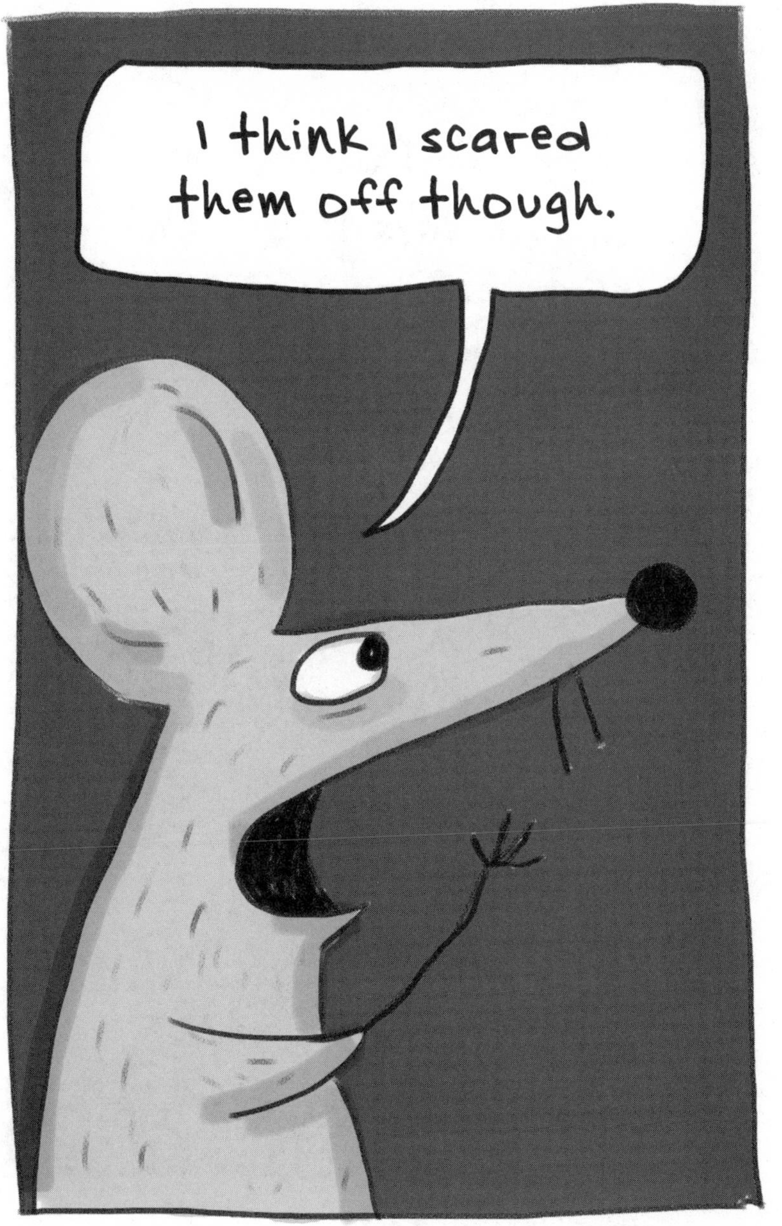
I think I scared them off though.

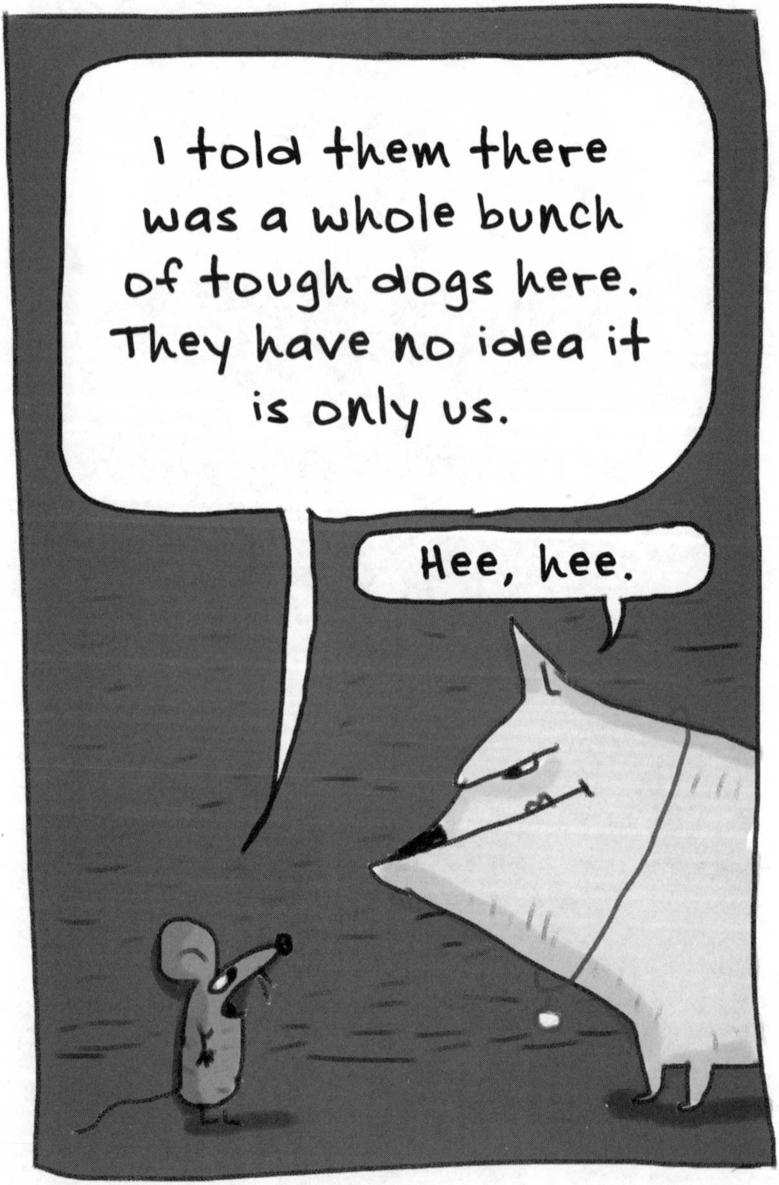
I told them there was a whole bunch of tough dogs here. They have no idea it is only us.
Hee, hee.

Scene
Thirteen

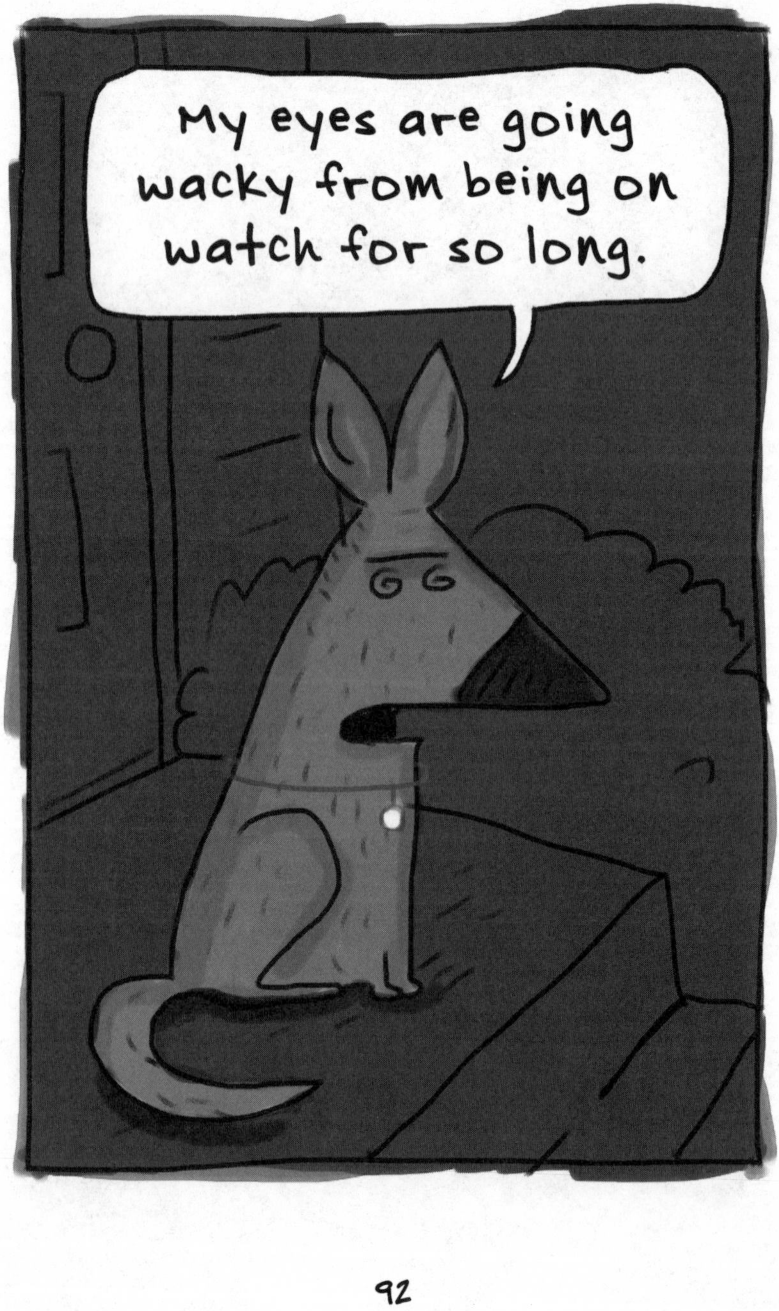
My eyes are going wacky from being on watch for so long.

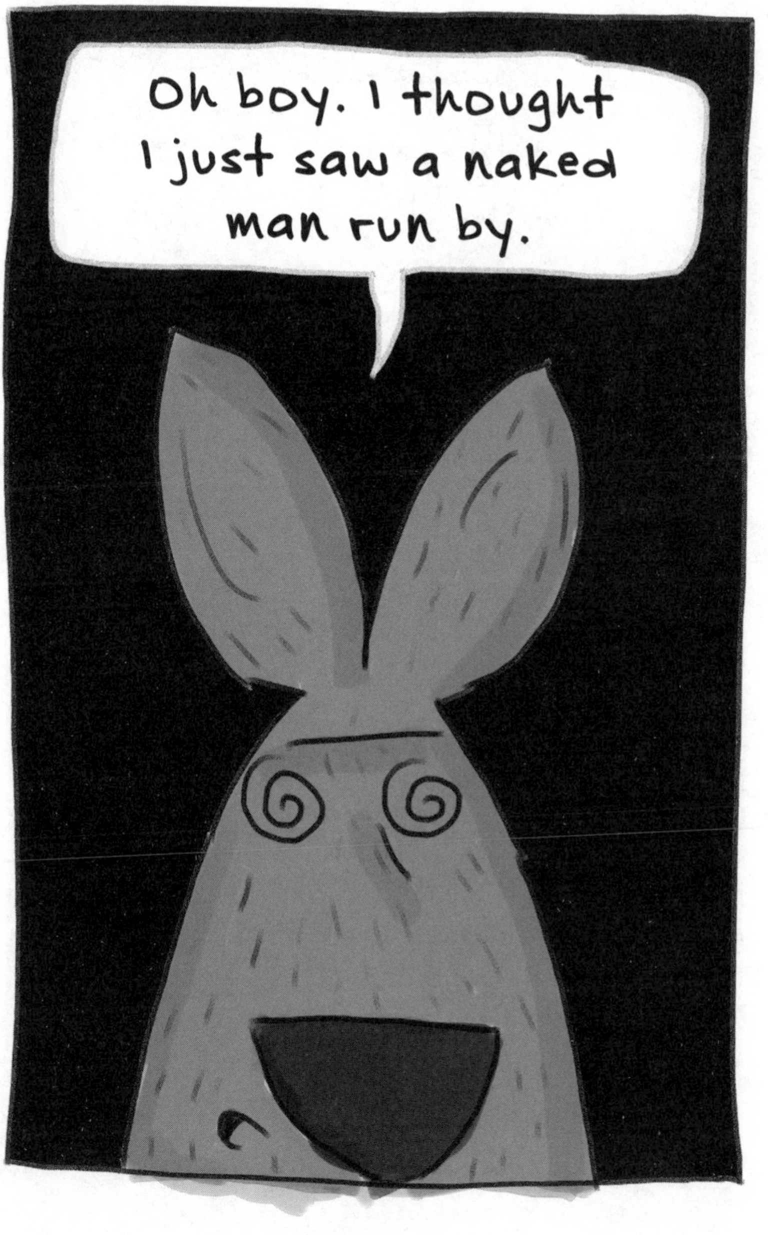
Oh boy. I thought I just saw a naked man run by.

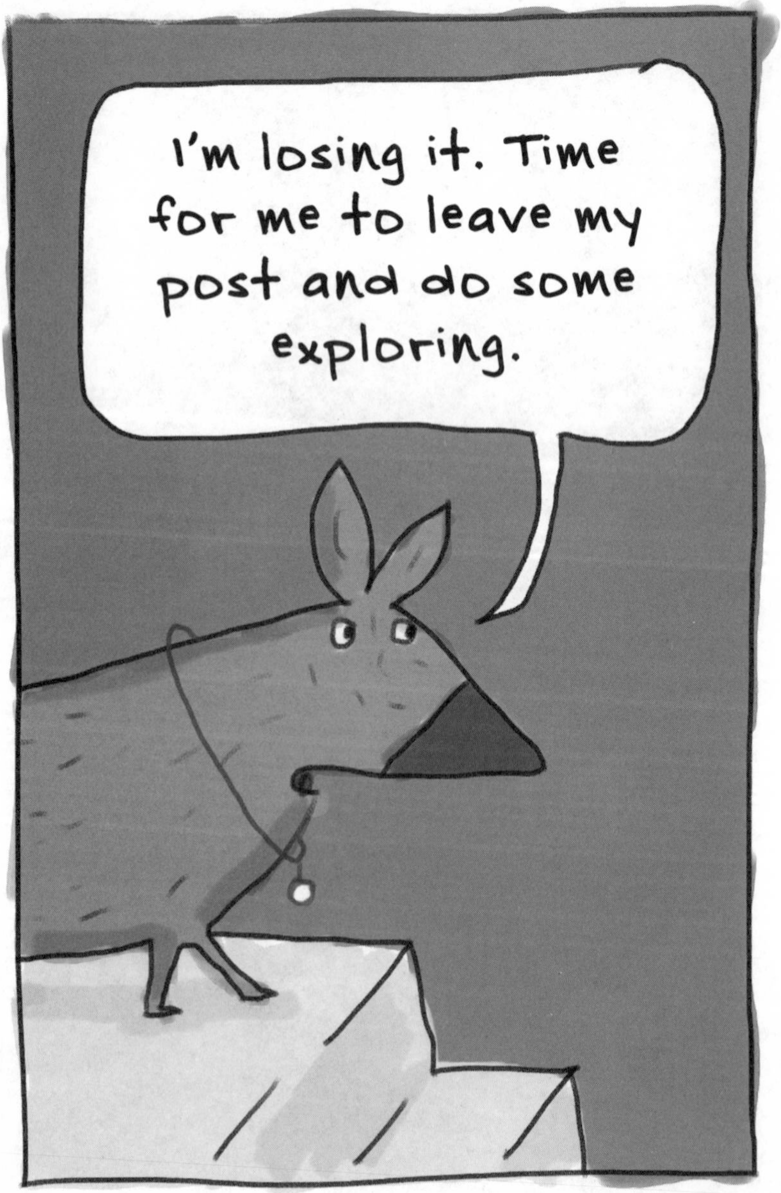
I'm losing it. Time for me to leave my post and do some exploring.

Scene
Fourteen

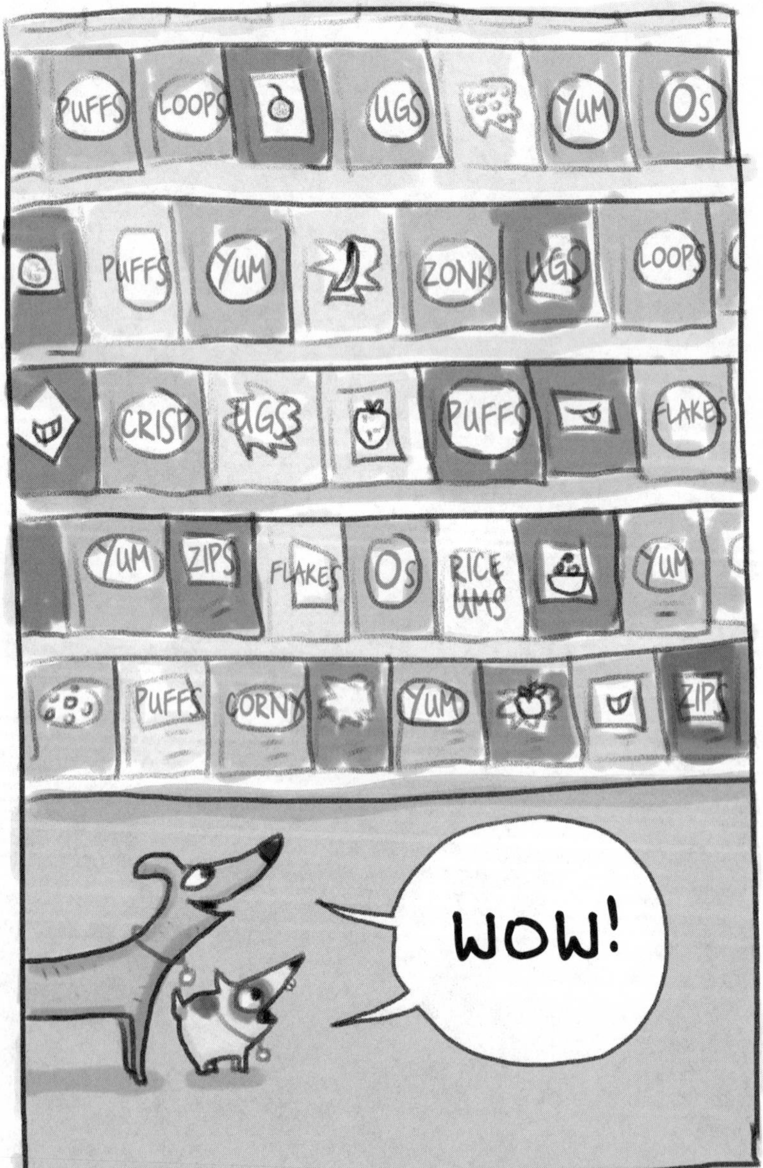
PUFFS
LOOPS
UGS
YUM
Os
PUFFS
YUM
ZONK
UGS
LOOPS
CRISP
UGS
PUFFS
FLAKES
YUM
ZIPS
FLAKES
Os
RICE UMS
YUM
PUFFS
CORNY
YUM
ZIPS
WOW!

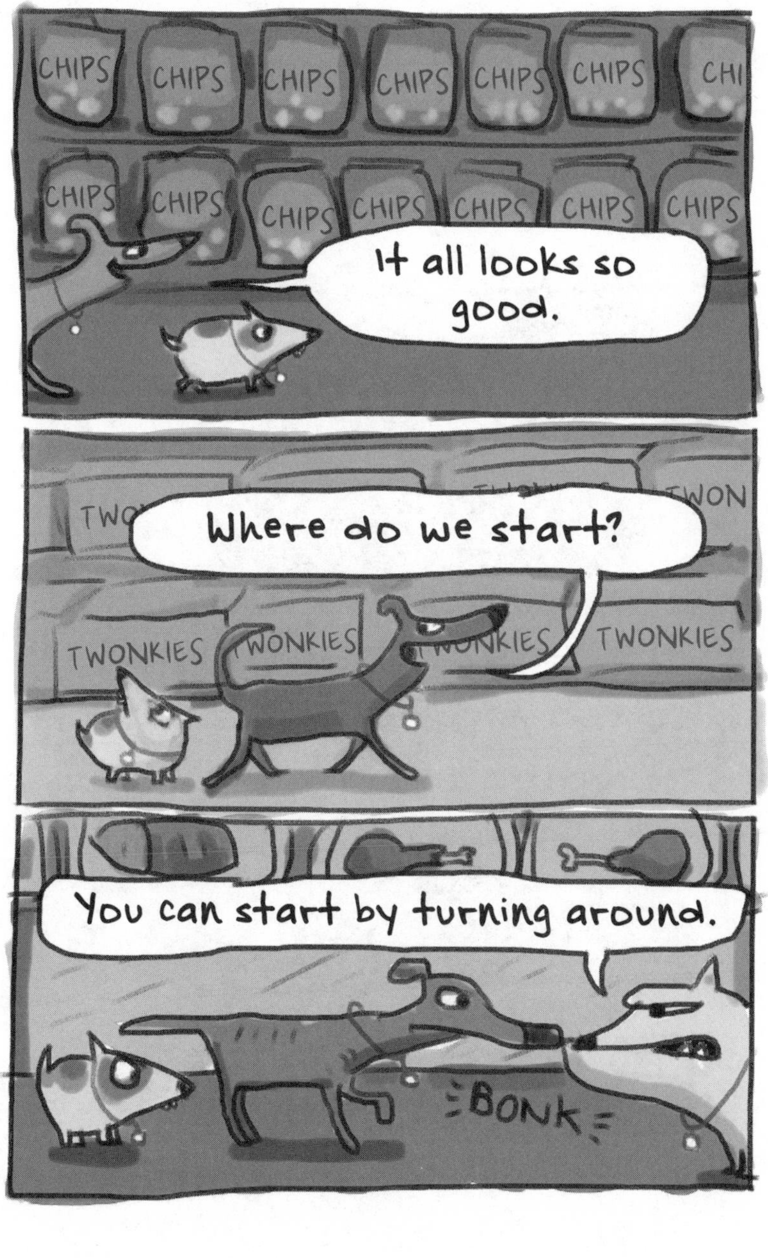
CHIPS
It all looks so good.
TWONKIES
Where do we start?
You can start by turning around.
BONK

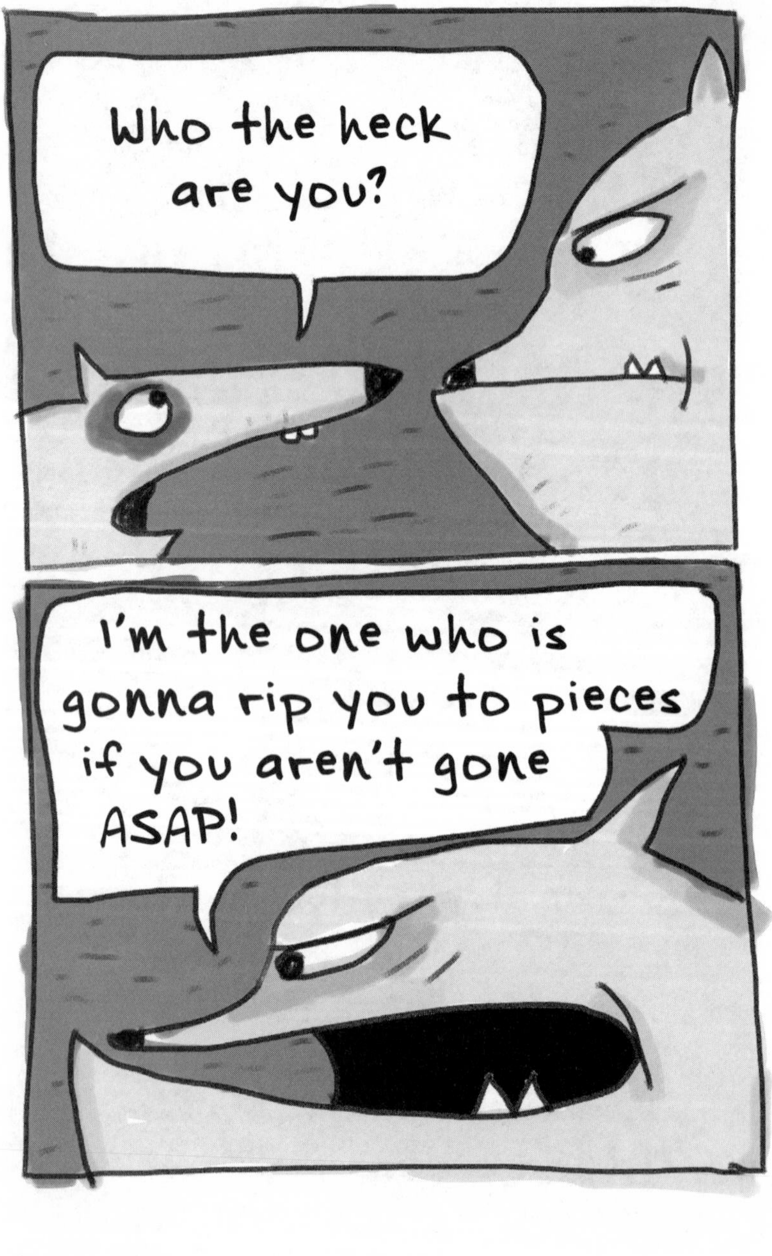
Who the heck are you?
I'm the one who is gonna rip you to pieces if you aren't gone ASAP!

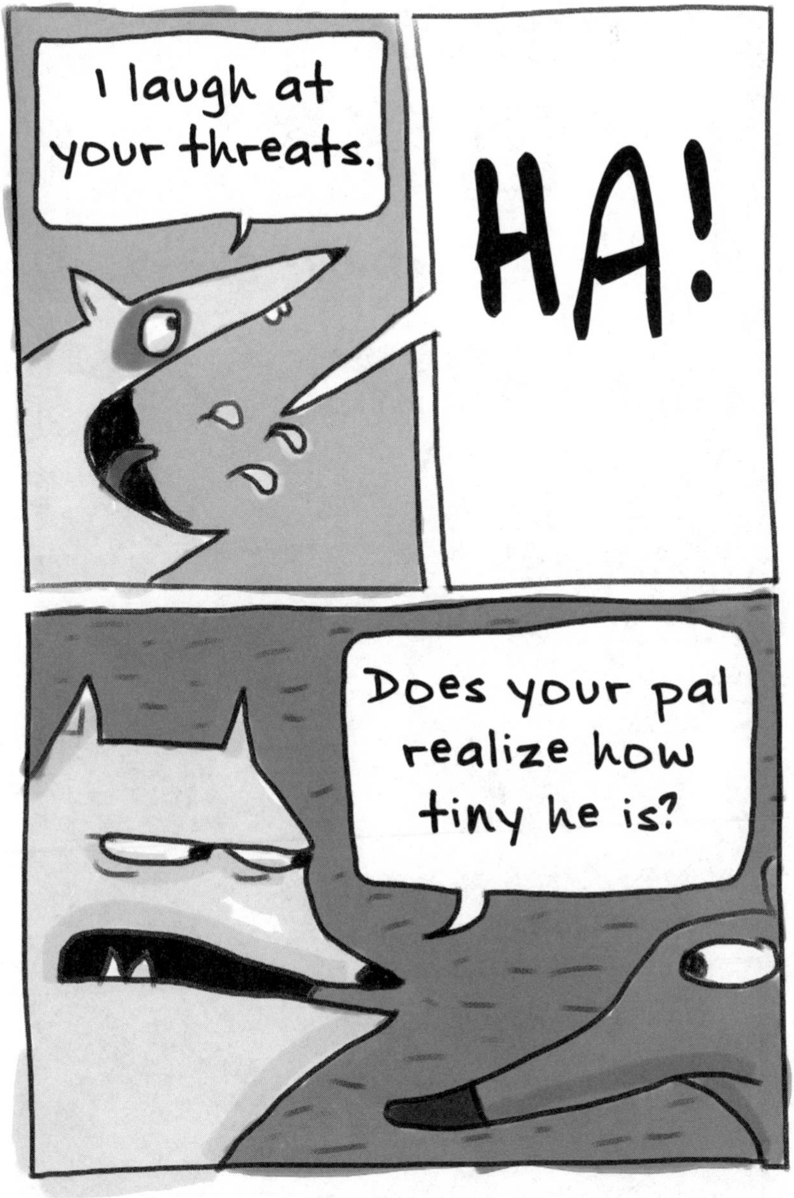
I laugh at your threats.
HA!
Does your pal realize how tiny he is?

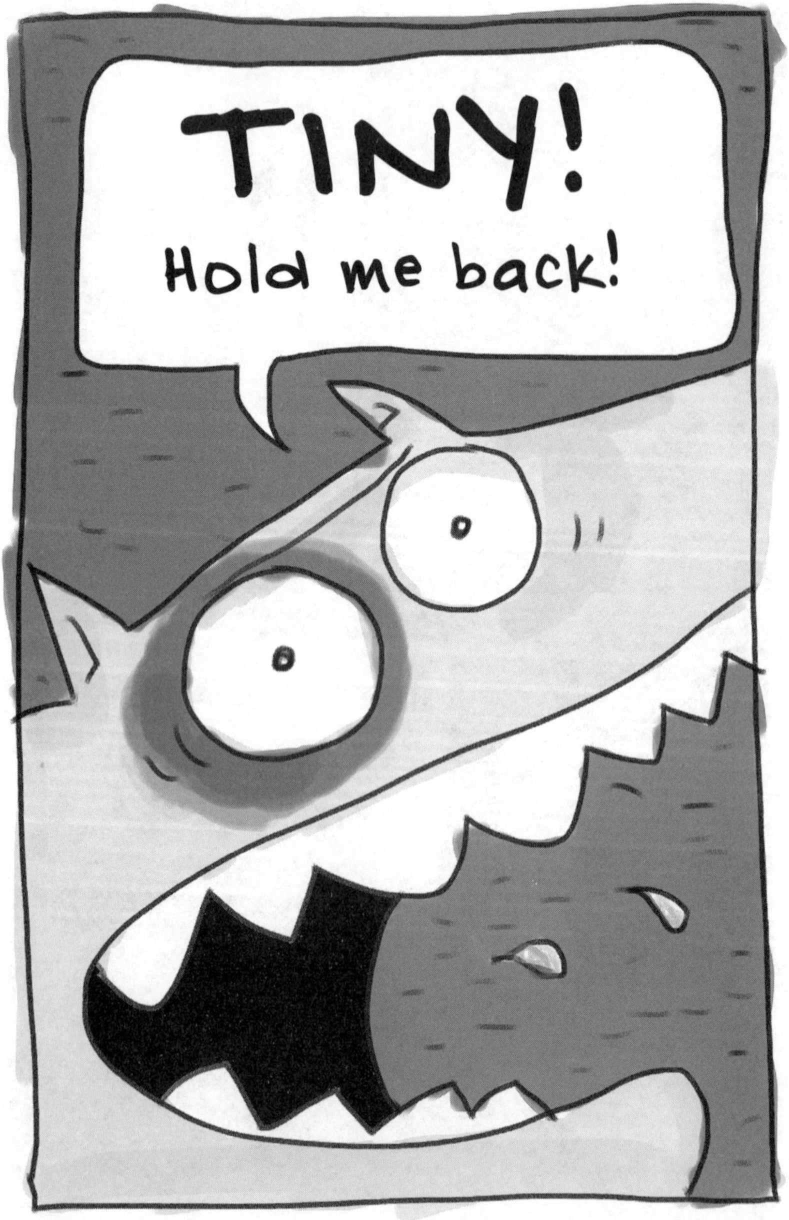
TINY!
Hold me back!

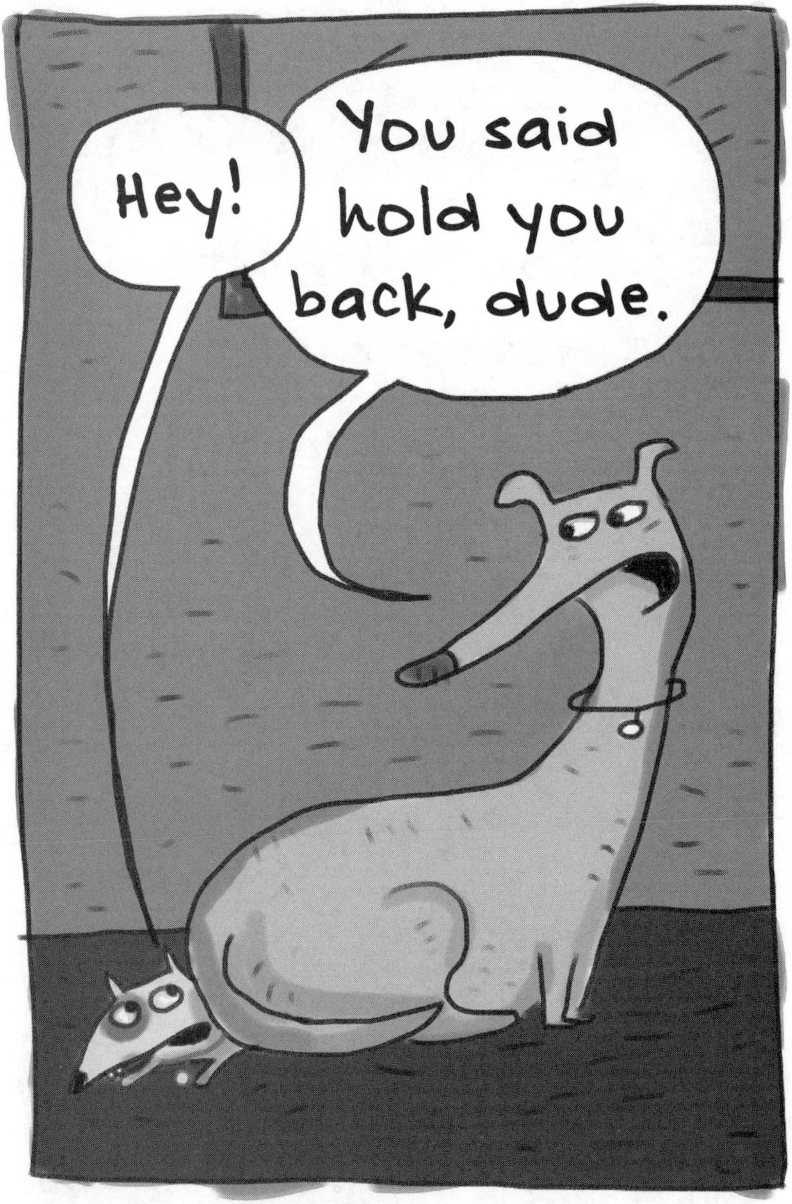
Hey!
You said hold you back, dude.

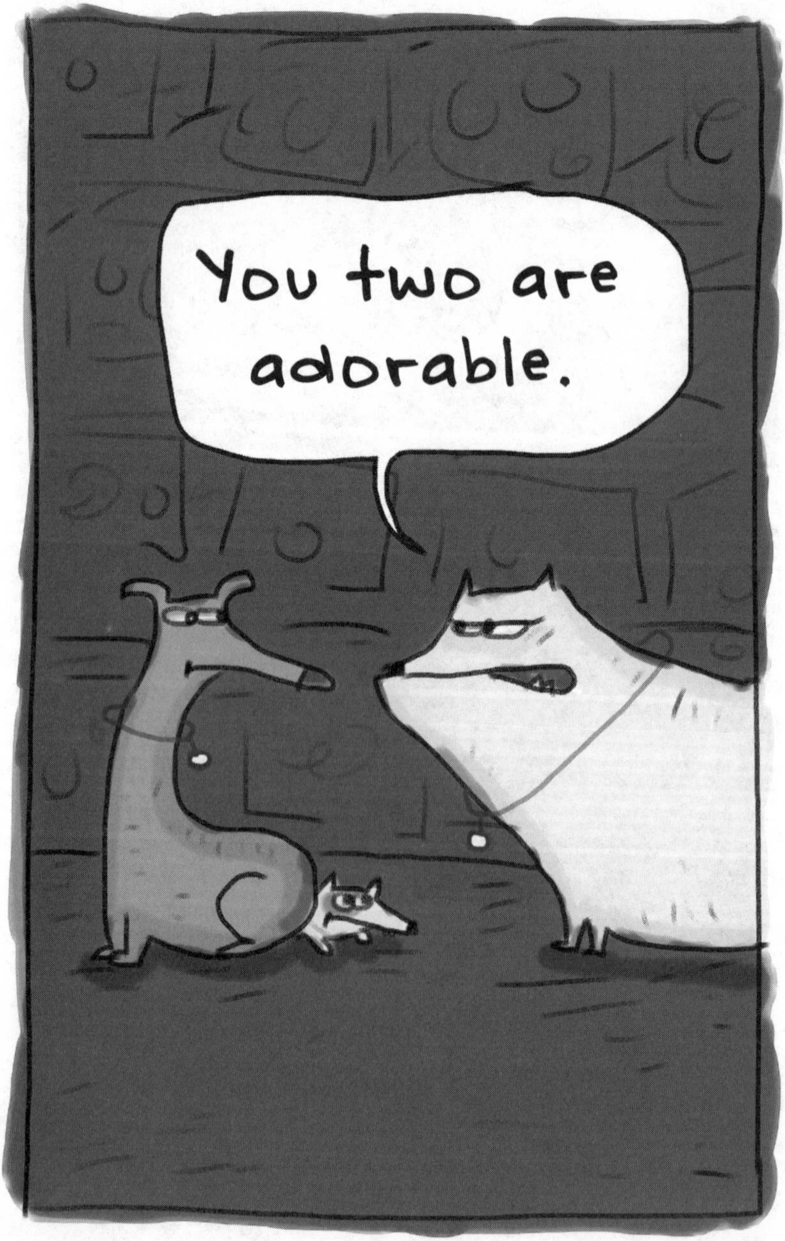
You two are adorable.

Let me tell you both something that might make you think twice about continuing this good dog/tiny dog routine. I am FERAL!

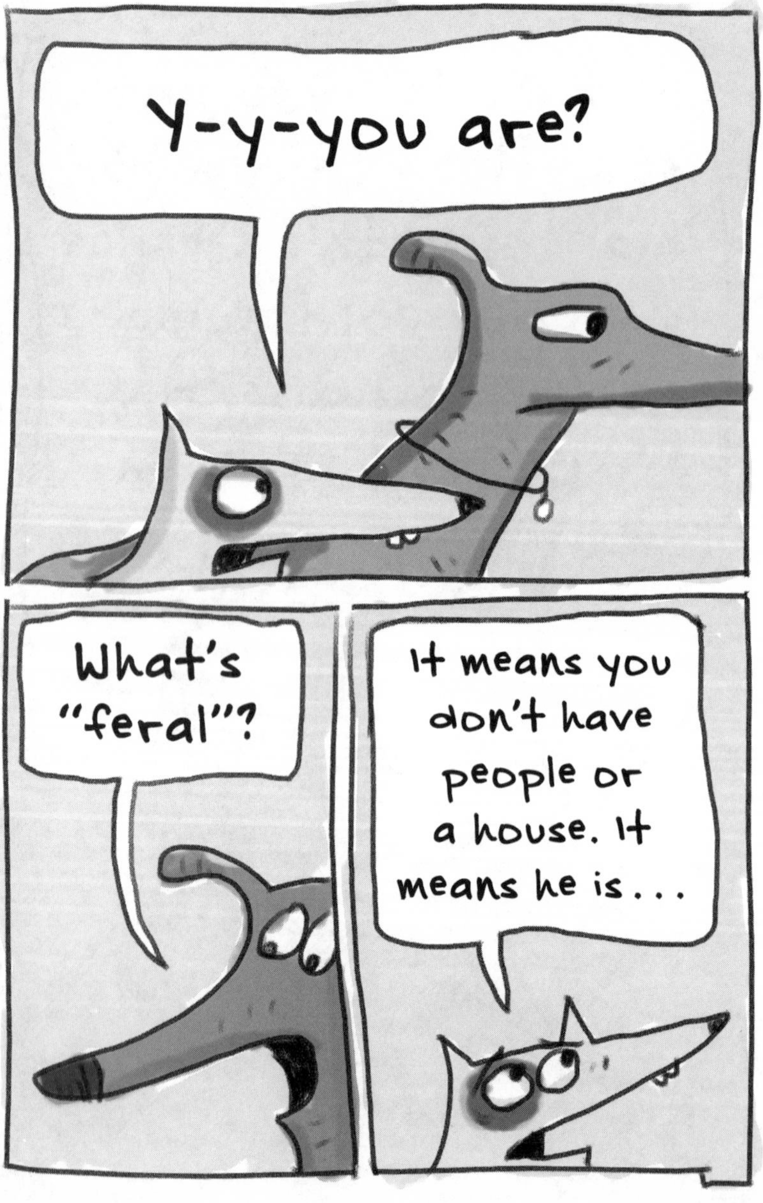
Y-y-you are?
What's "feral"?
It means you don't have people or a house. It means he is . . .

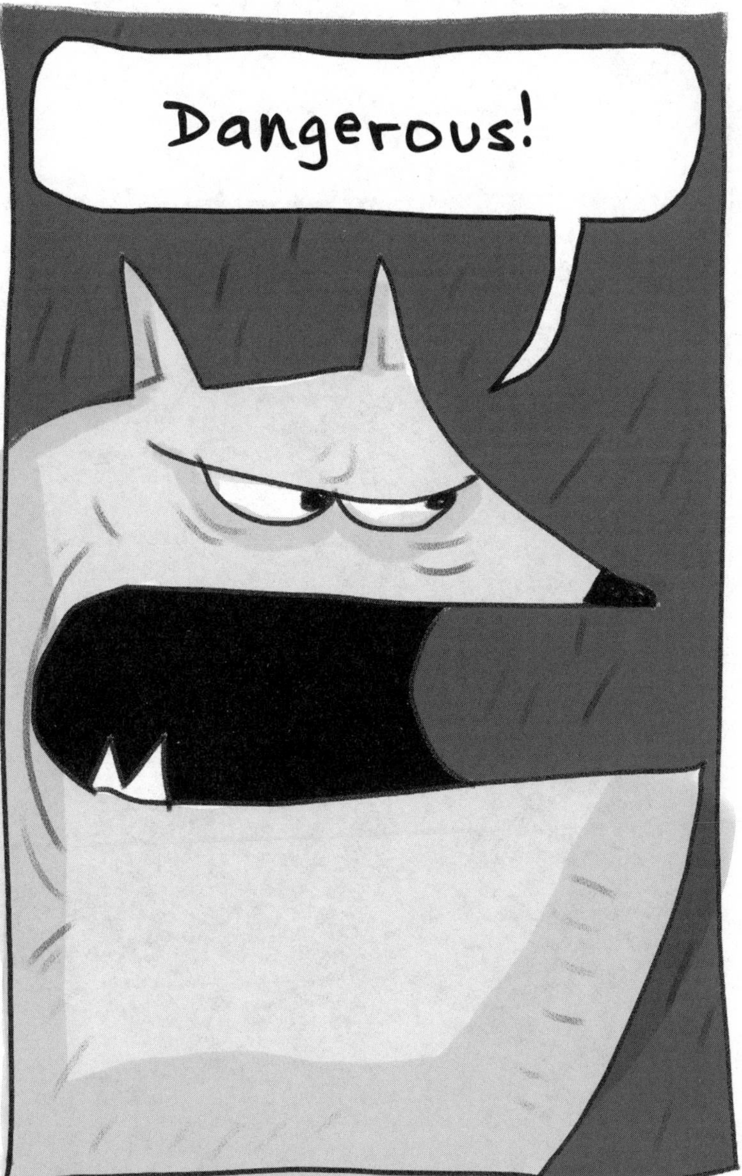
Dangerous!

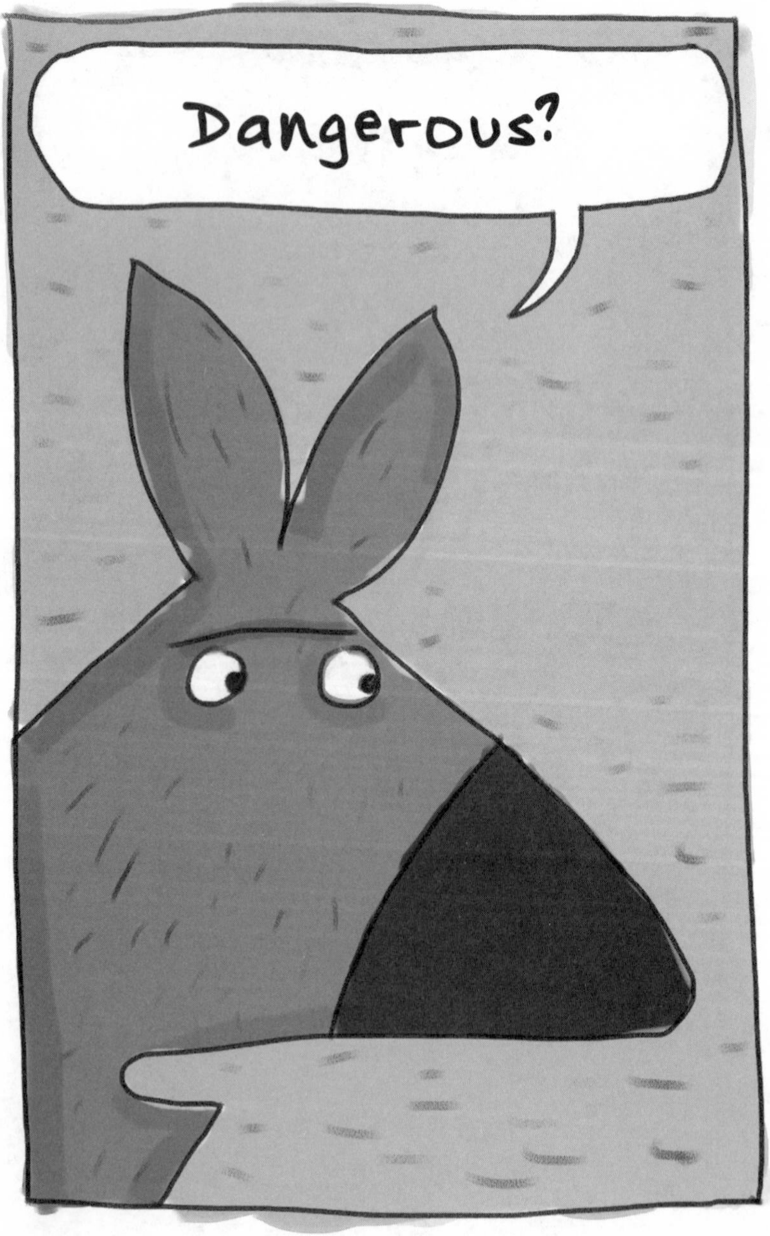
Dangerous?

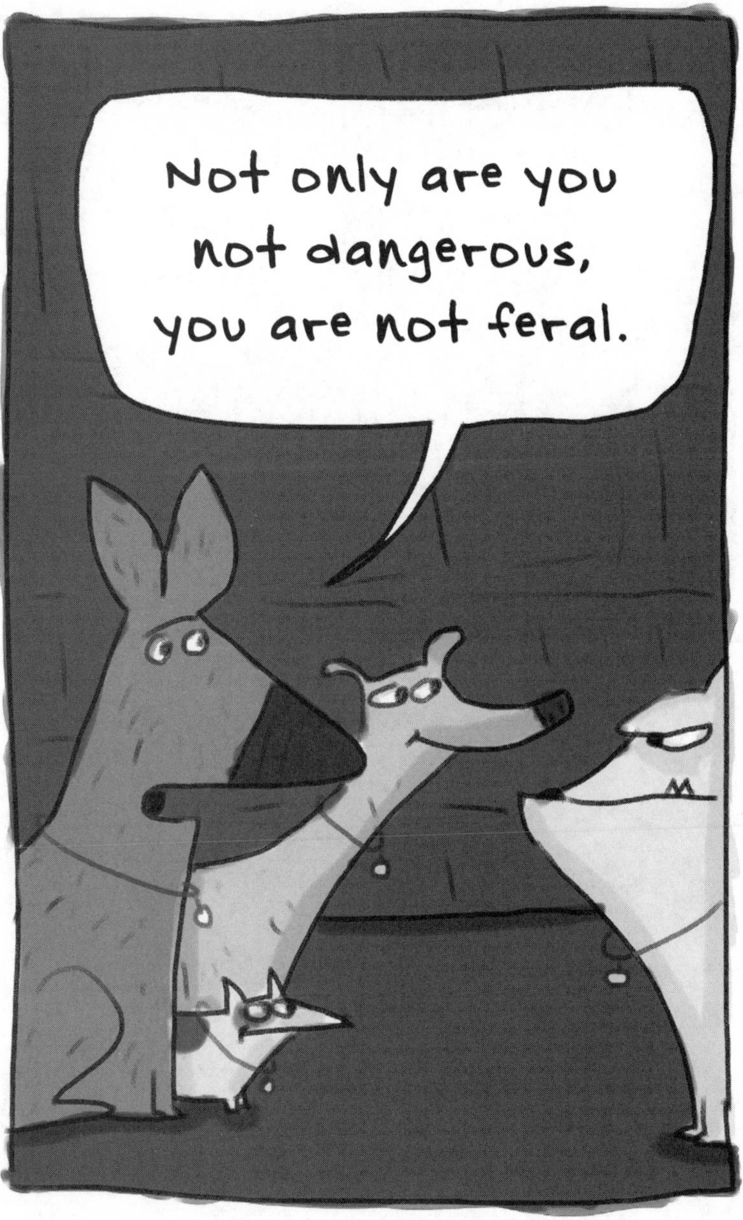
Not only are you not dangerous, you are not feral.

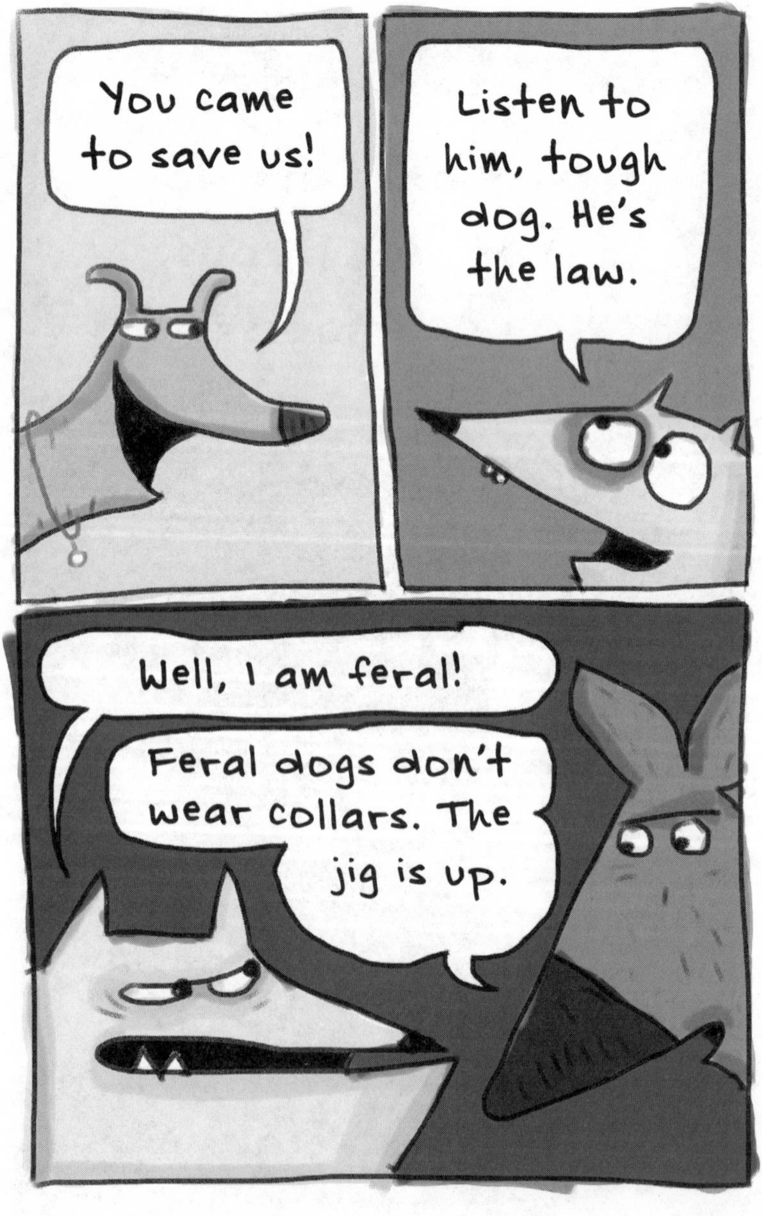

You came to save us!
Listen to him, tough dog. He's the law.
Well, I am feral!
Feral dogs don't wear collars. The jig is up.

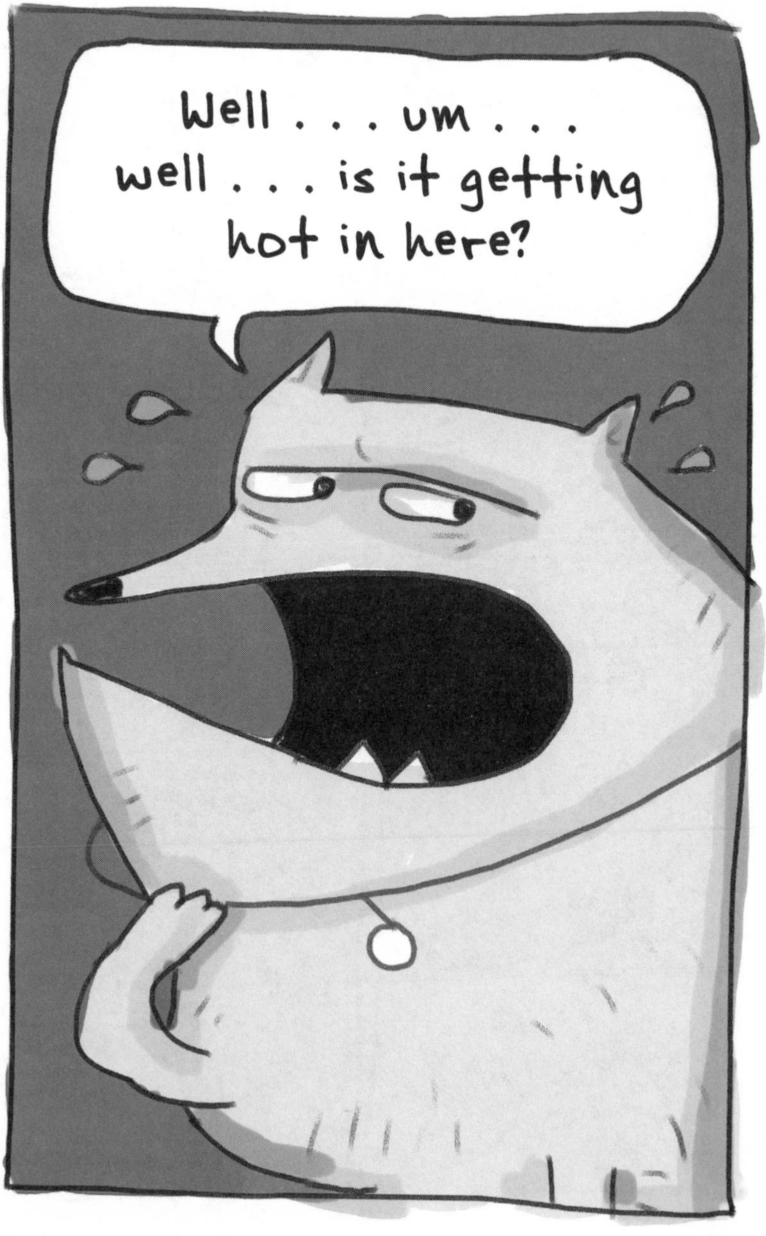
Well . . . um . . . well . . . is it getting hot in here?

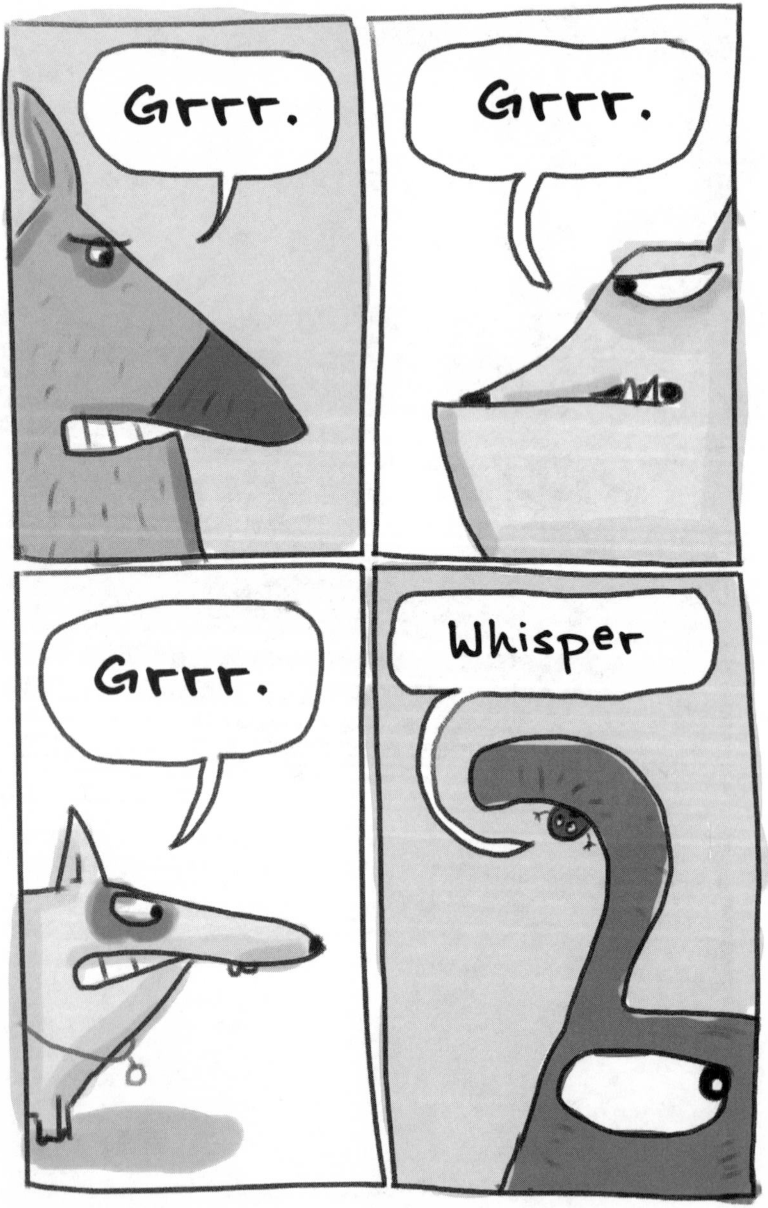
Grrr.
Grrr.
Grrr.
Whisper

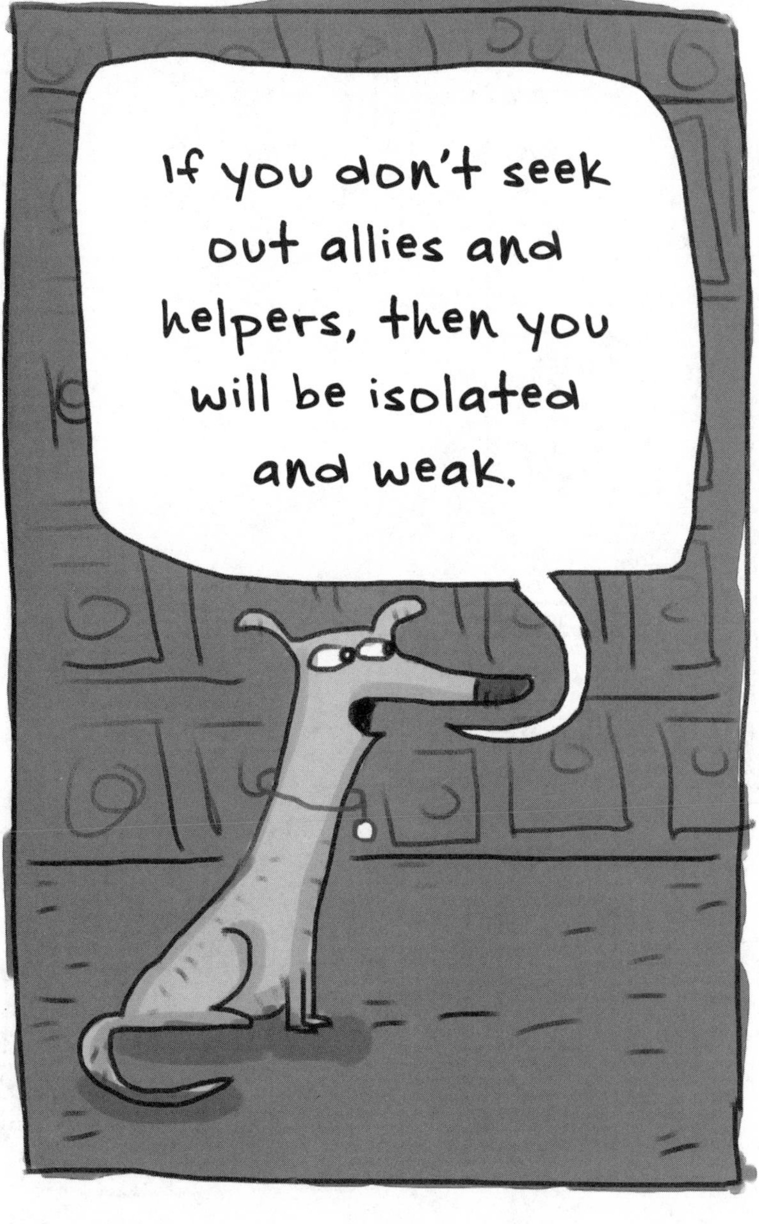
If you don't seek out allies and helpers, then you will be isolated and weak.

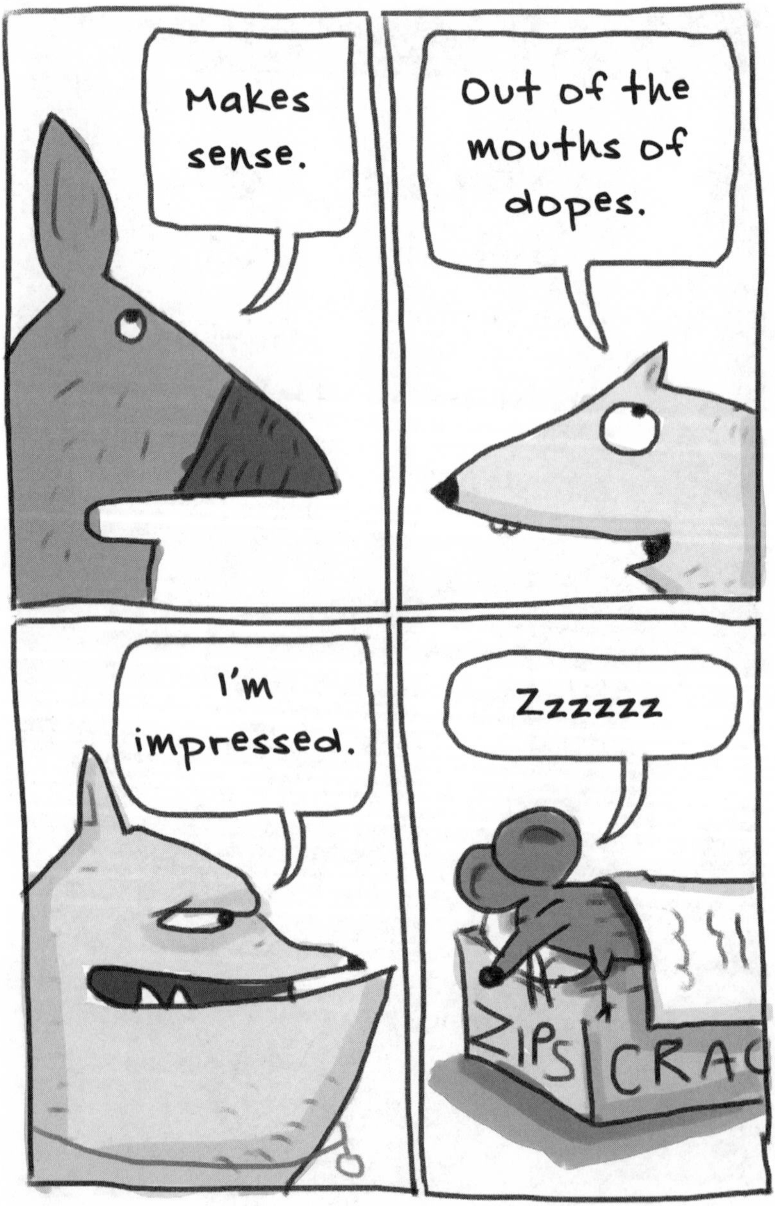
Makes sense.
Out of the mouths of dopes.
I'm impressed.
Zzzzzz
ZIPS
CRAC

Intermission

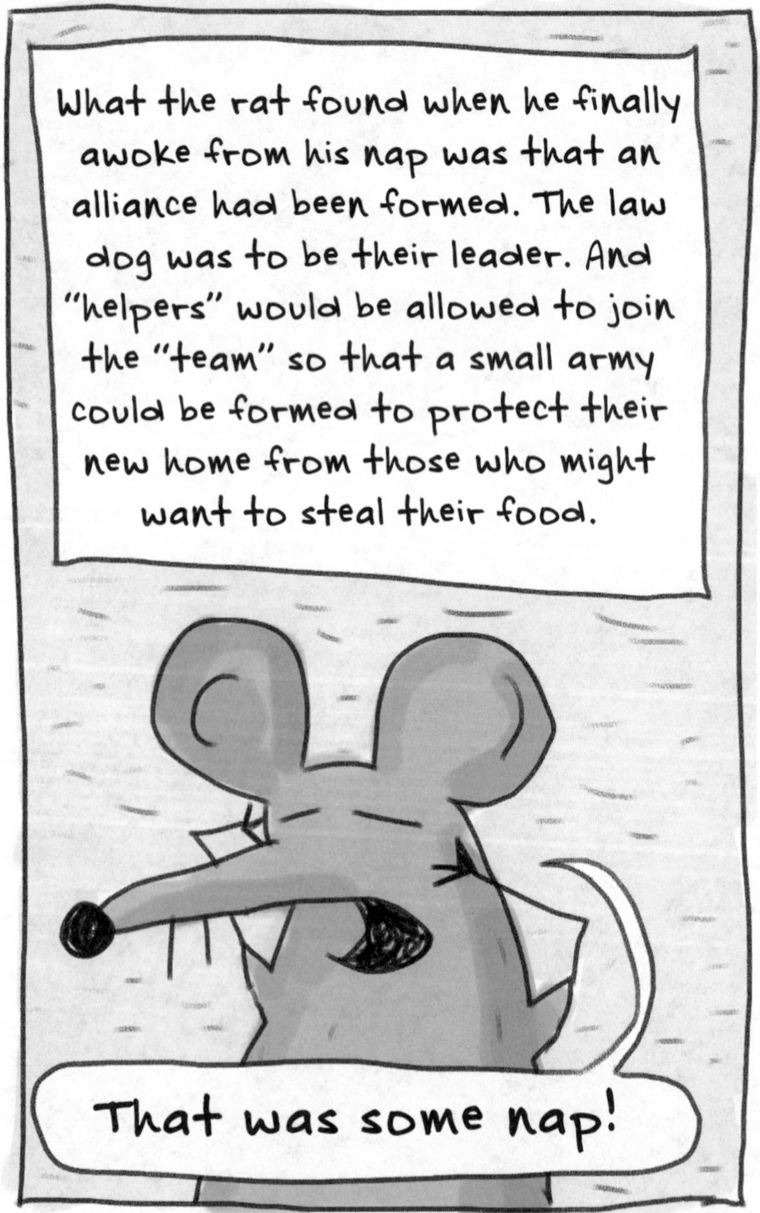
What the rat found when he finally awoke from his nap was that an alliance had been formed. The law dog was to be their leader. And "helpers" would be allowed to join the "team" so that a small army could be formed to protect their new home from those who might want to steal their food.
That was some nap!

Scene
Fifteen

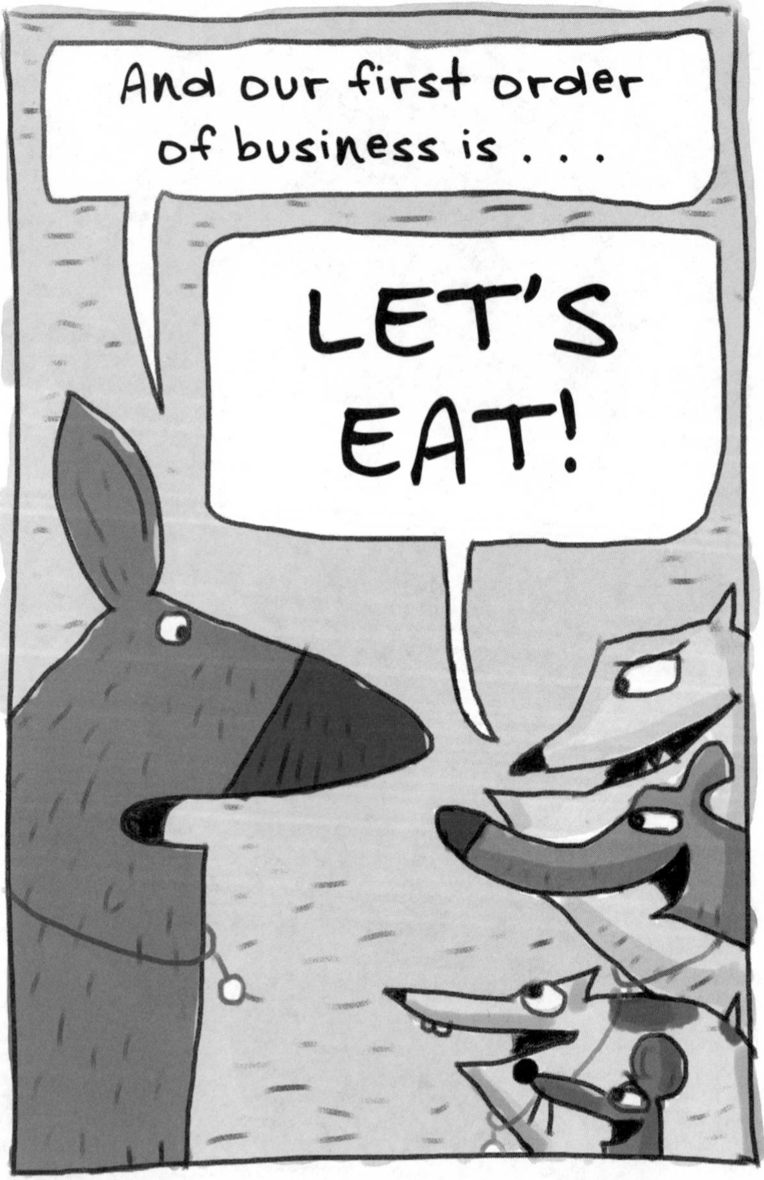
And our first order of business is . . .
LET'S EAT!

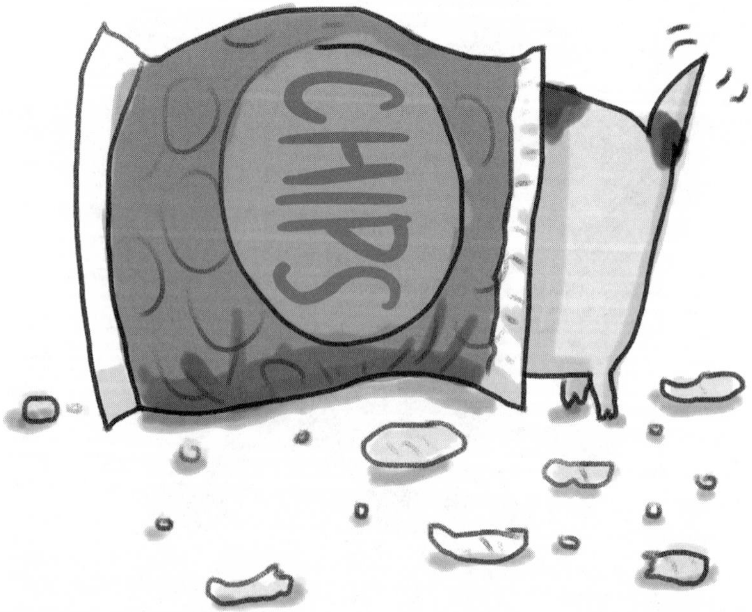
CHIPS

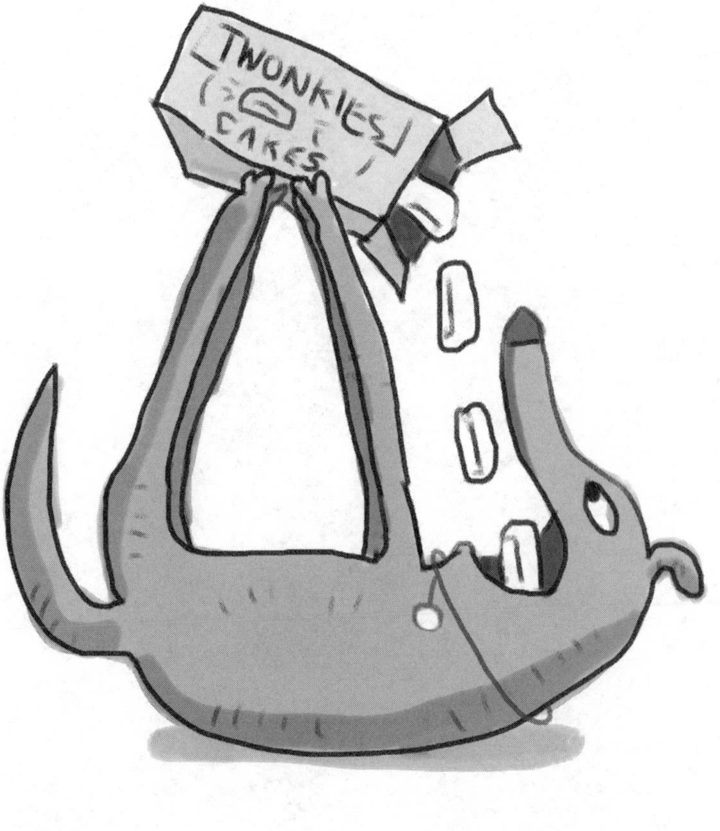
TWONKIES
CAKES

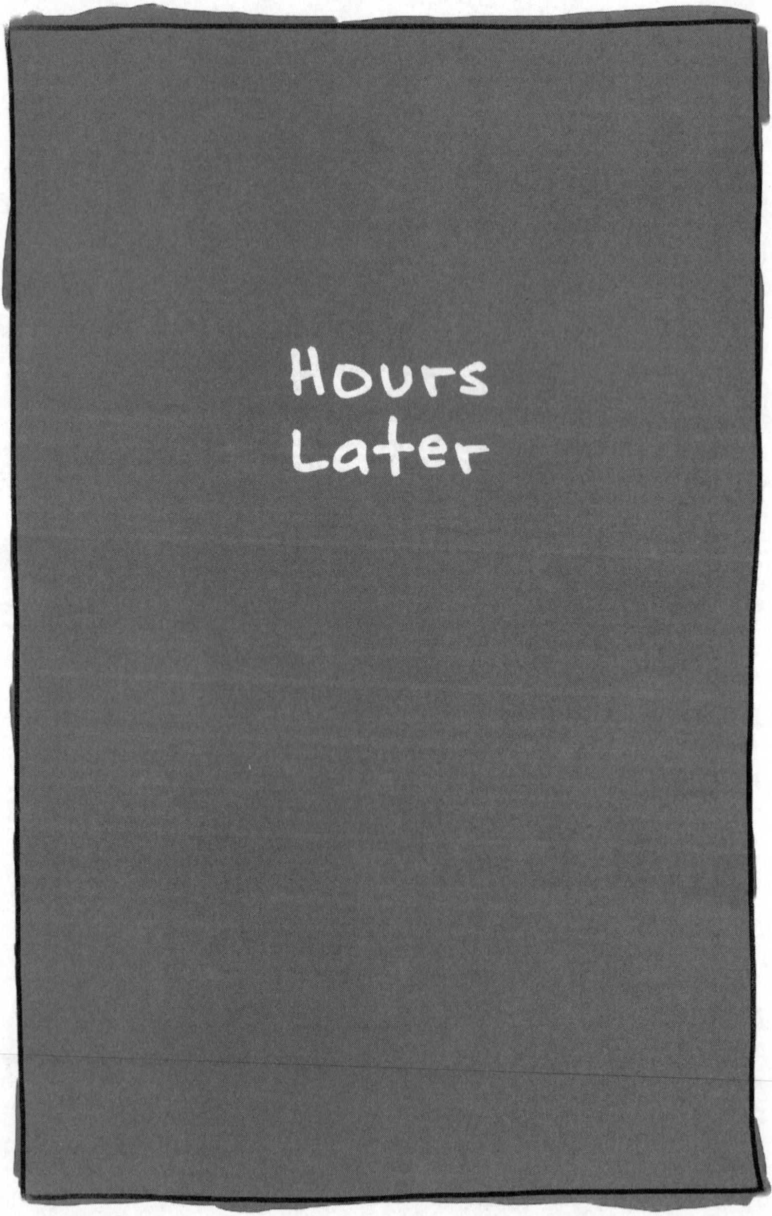
Hours Later

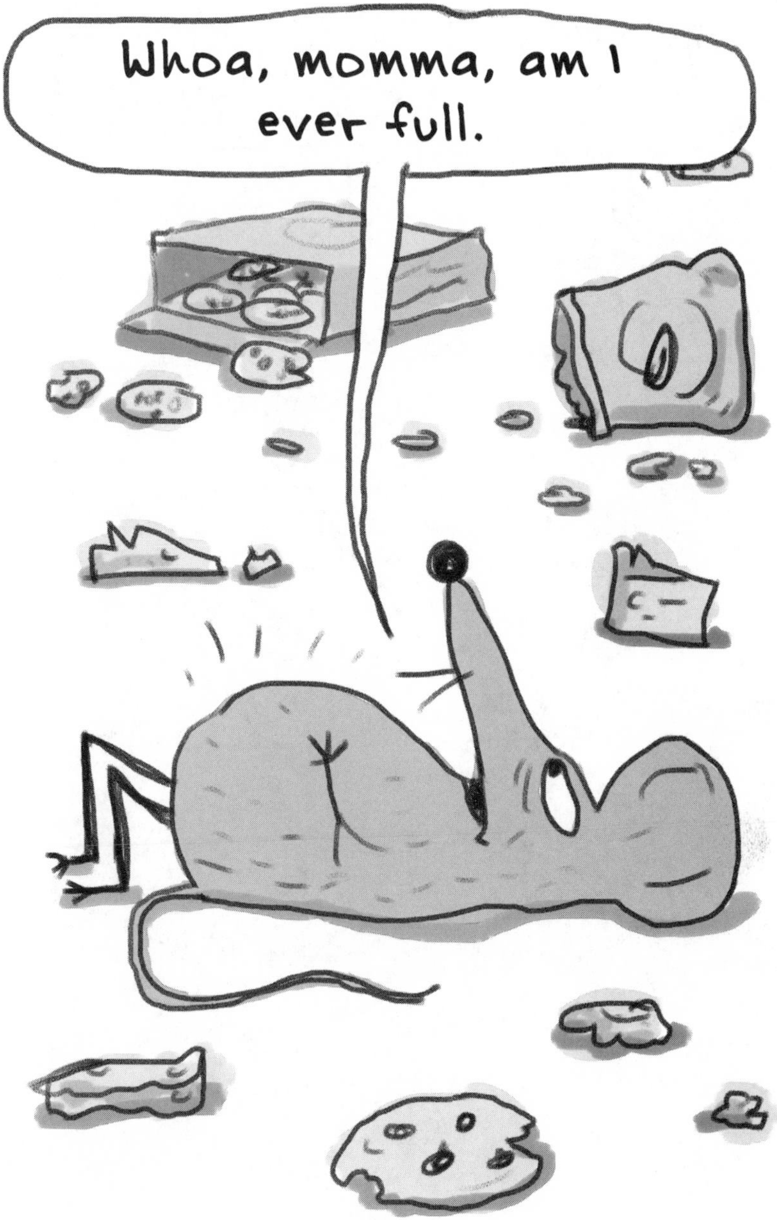
Whoa, momma, am I ever full.

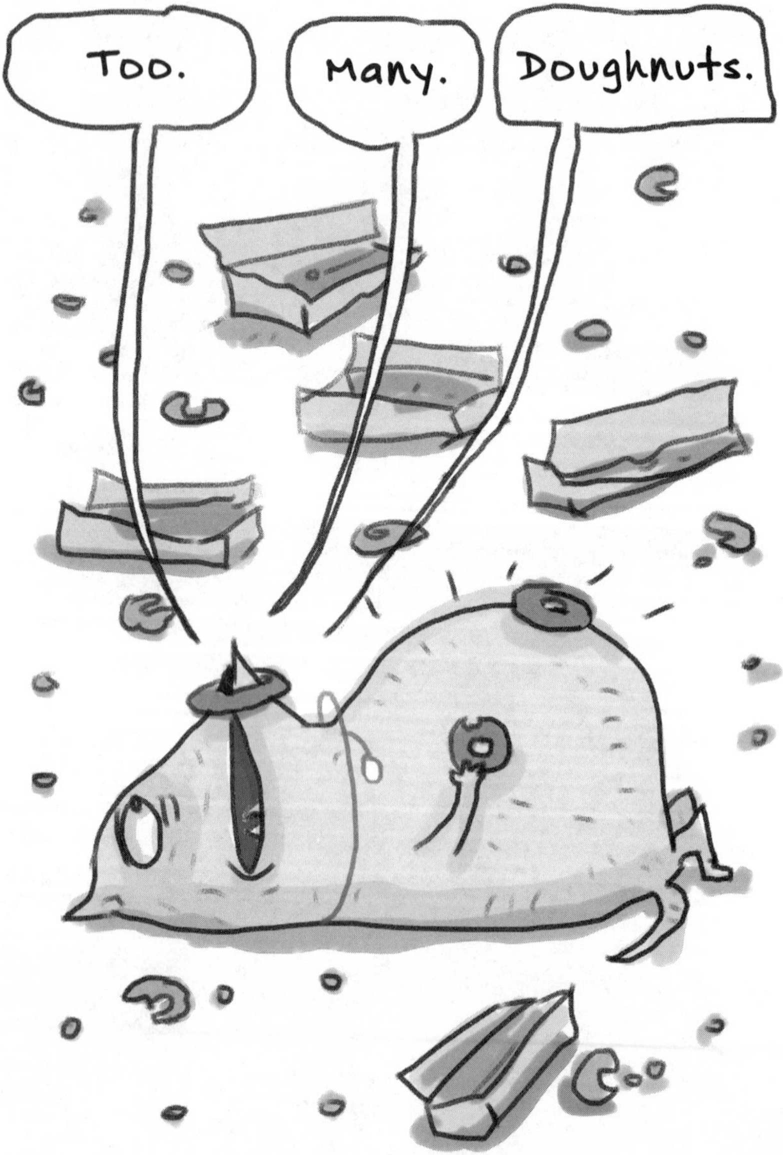
Too.
Many.
Doughnuts.

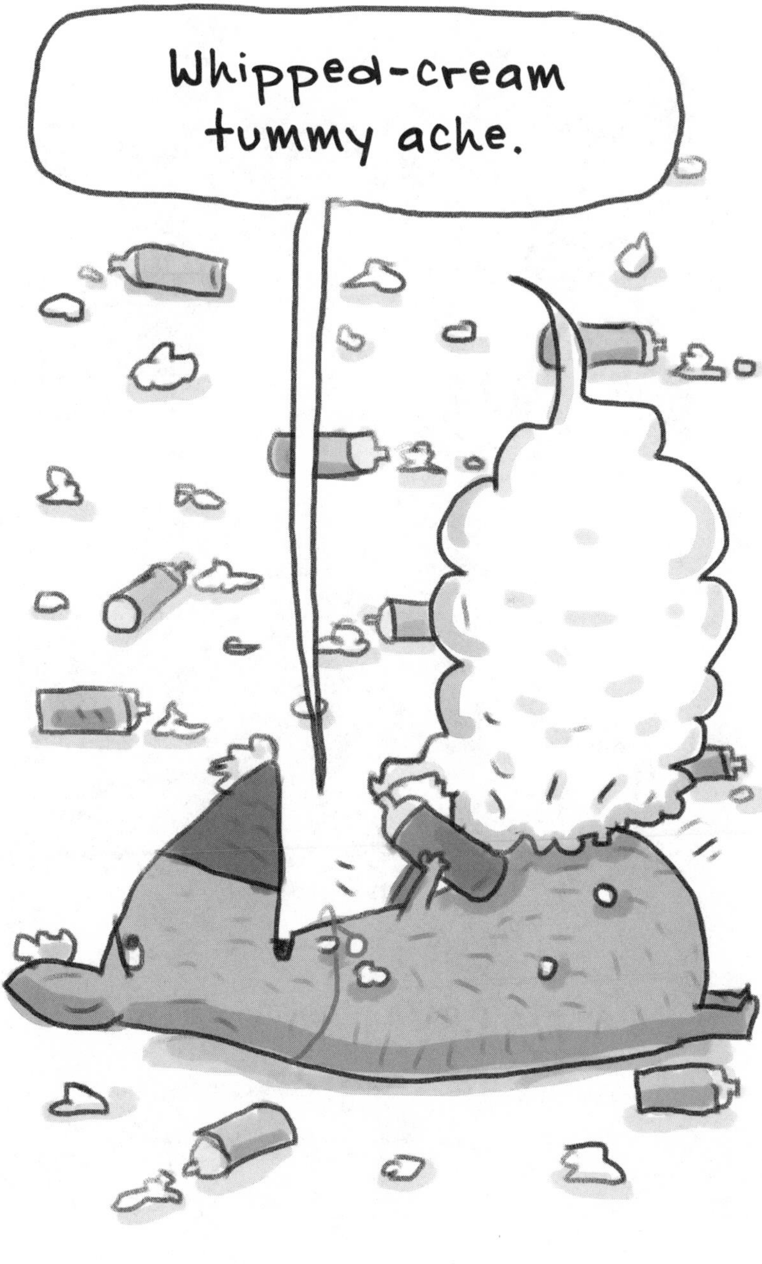
Whipped-cream tummy ache.

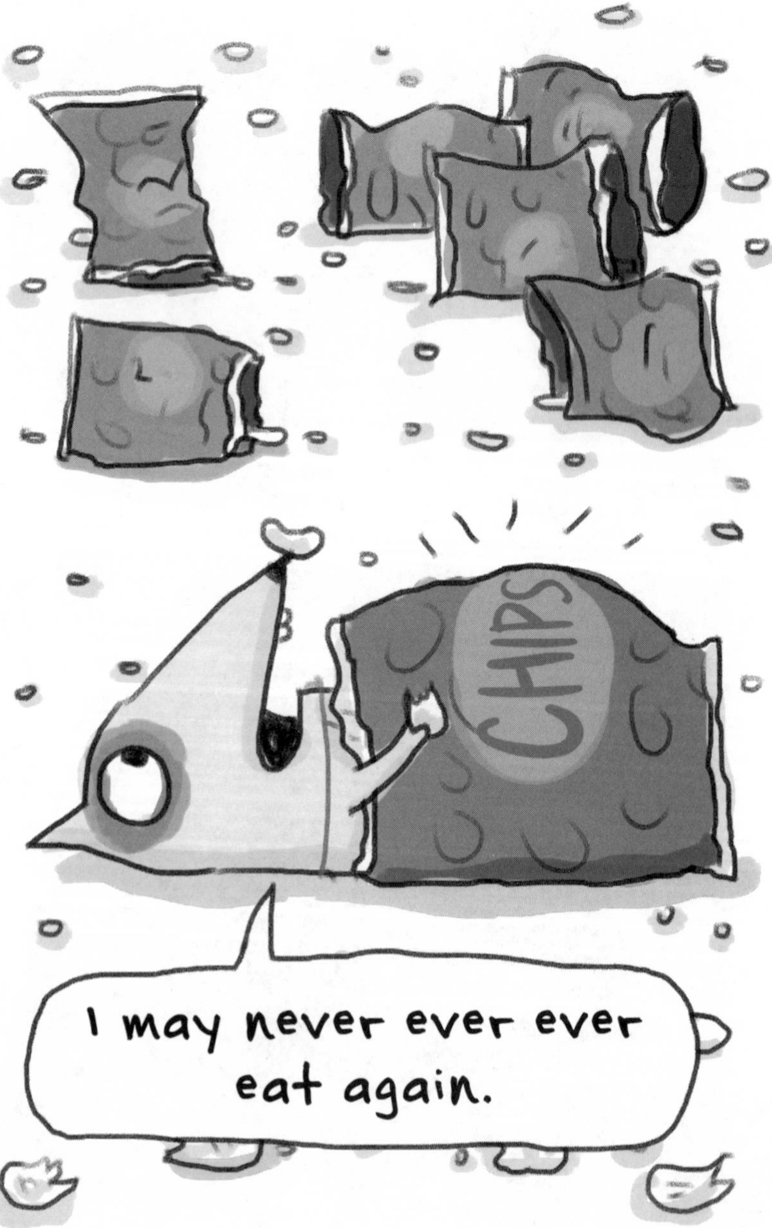
CHIPS
I may never ever ever eat again.

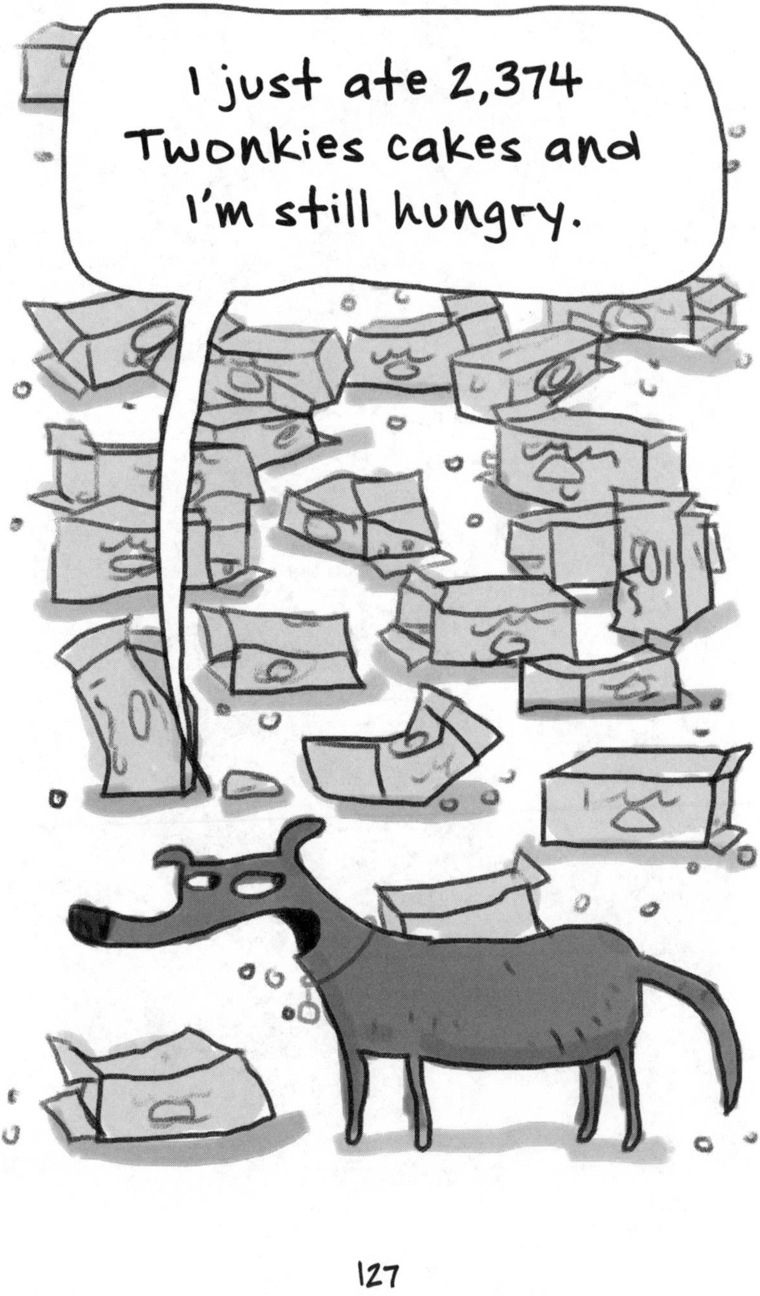
I just ate 2,374 Twonkies cakes and I'm still hungry.

Scene
Sixteen

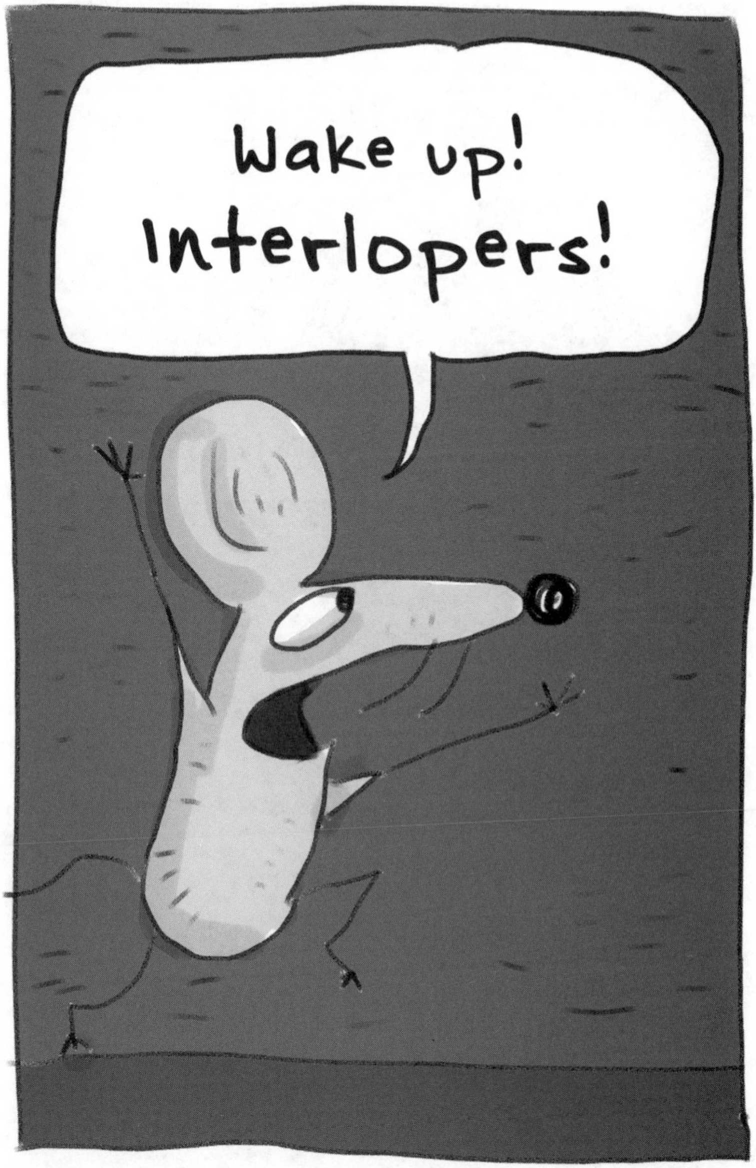
Wake up!
Interlopers!

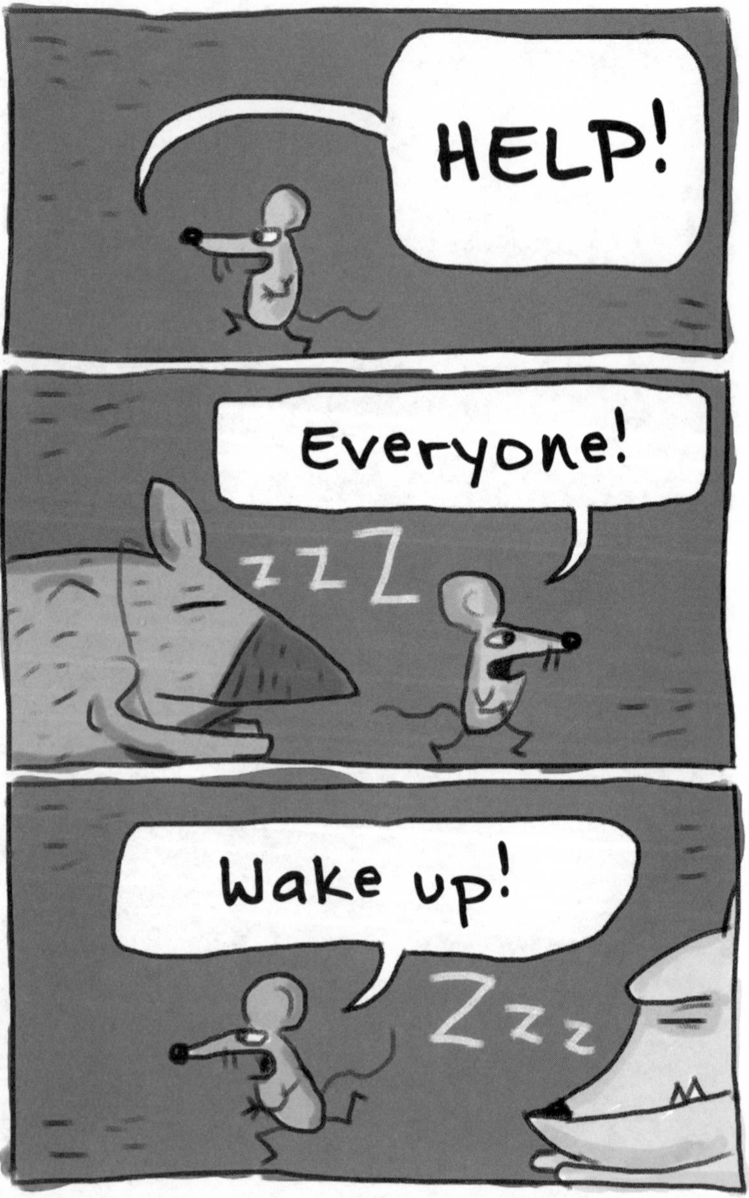
HELP!
Everyone!
zzZ
Wake up!
Zzz

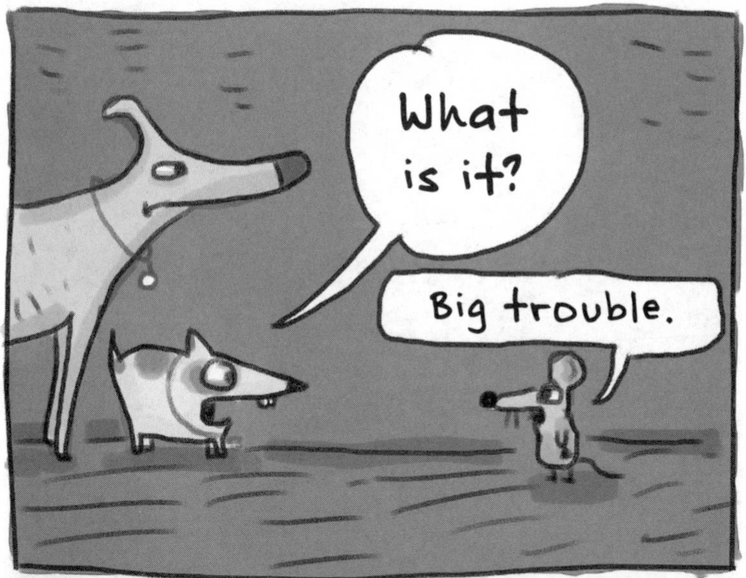
What is it?
Big trouble.

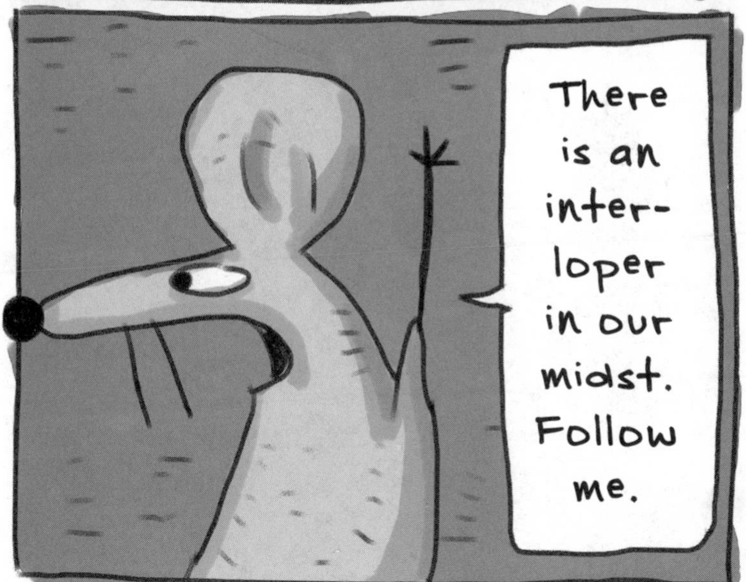
There is an inter-loper in our midst. Follow me.

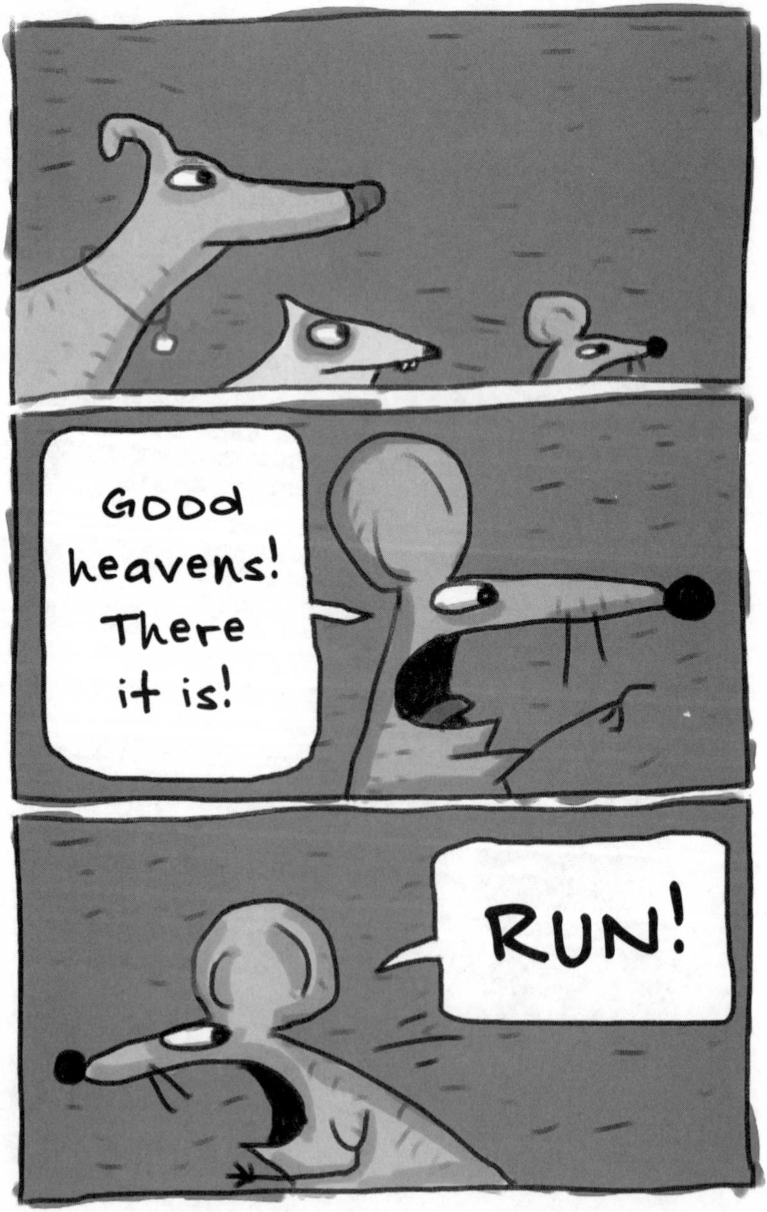
Good heavens! There it is!
RUN!

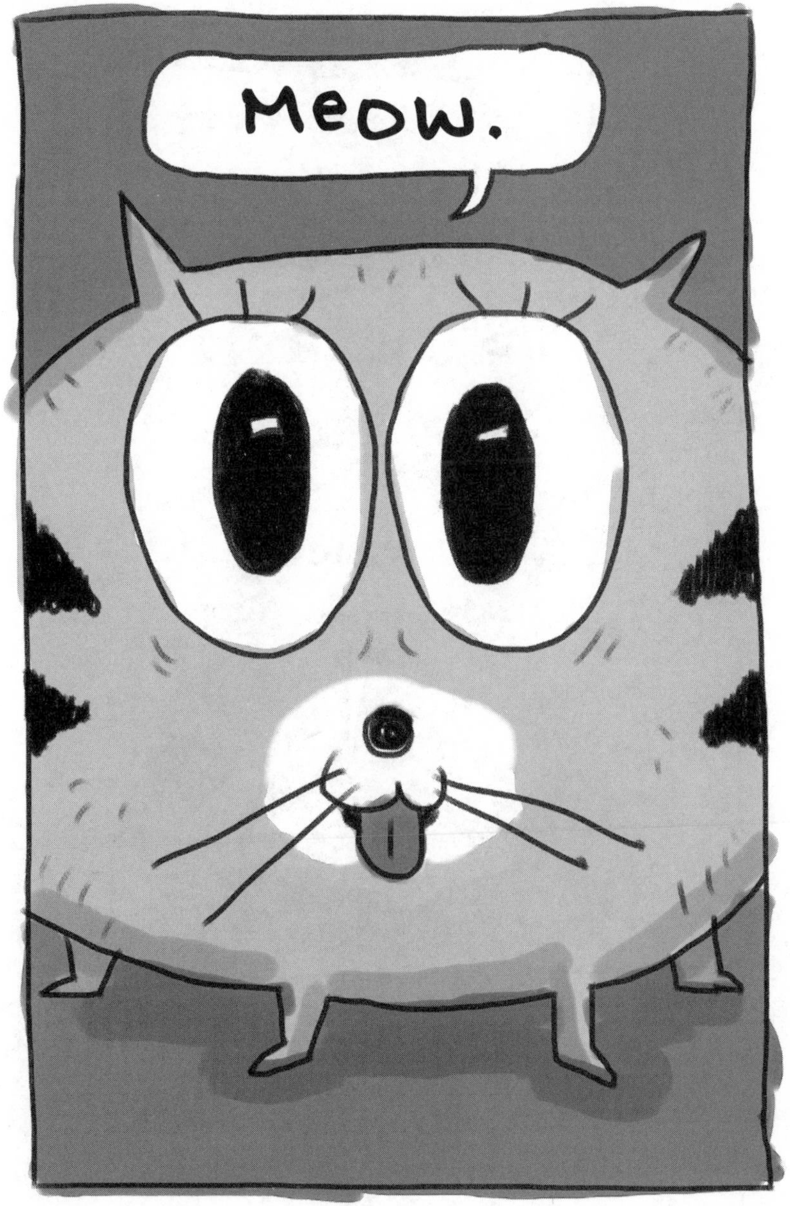
Meow.

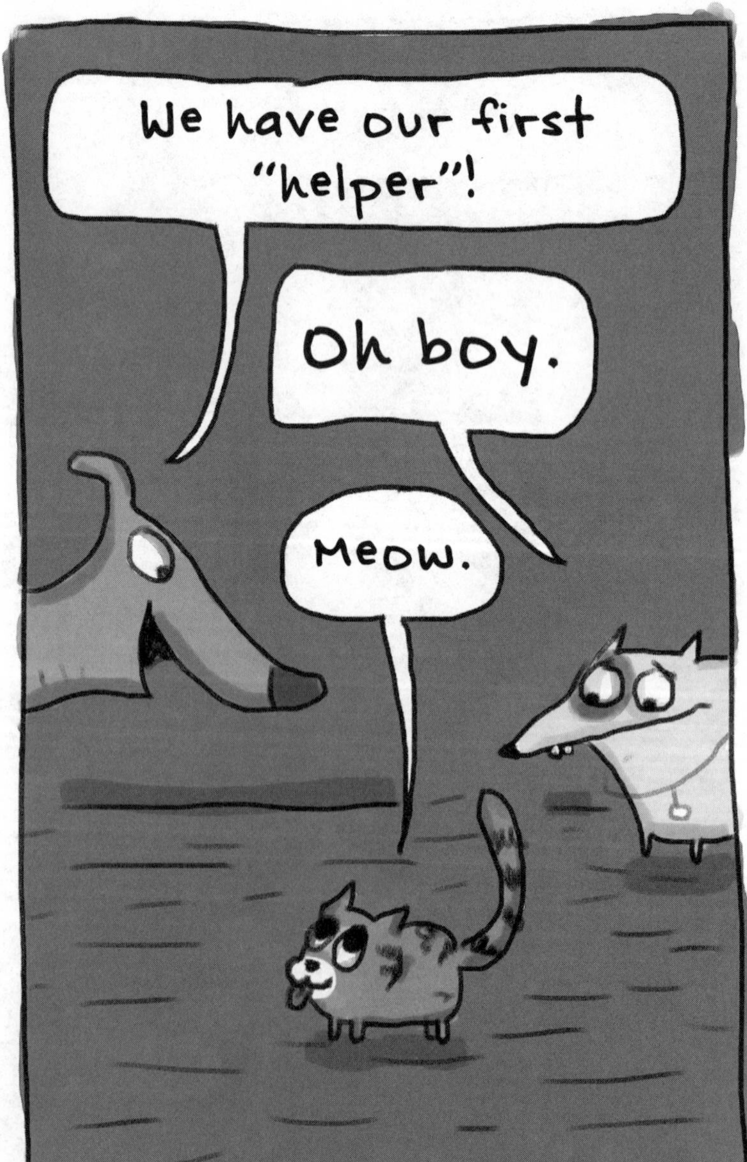
We have our first "helper"!
Oh boy.
Meow.

Scene
Seventeen

135

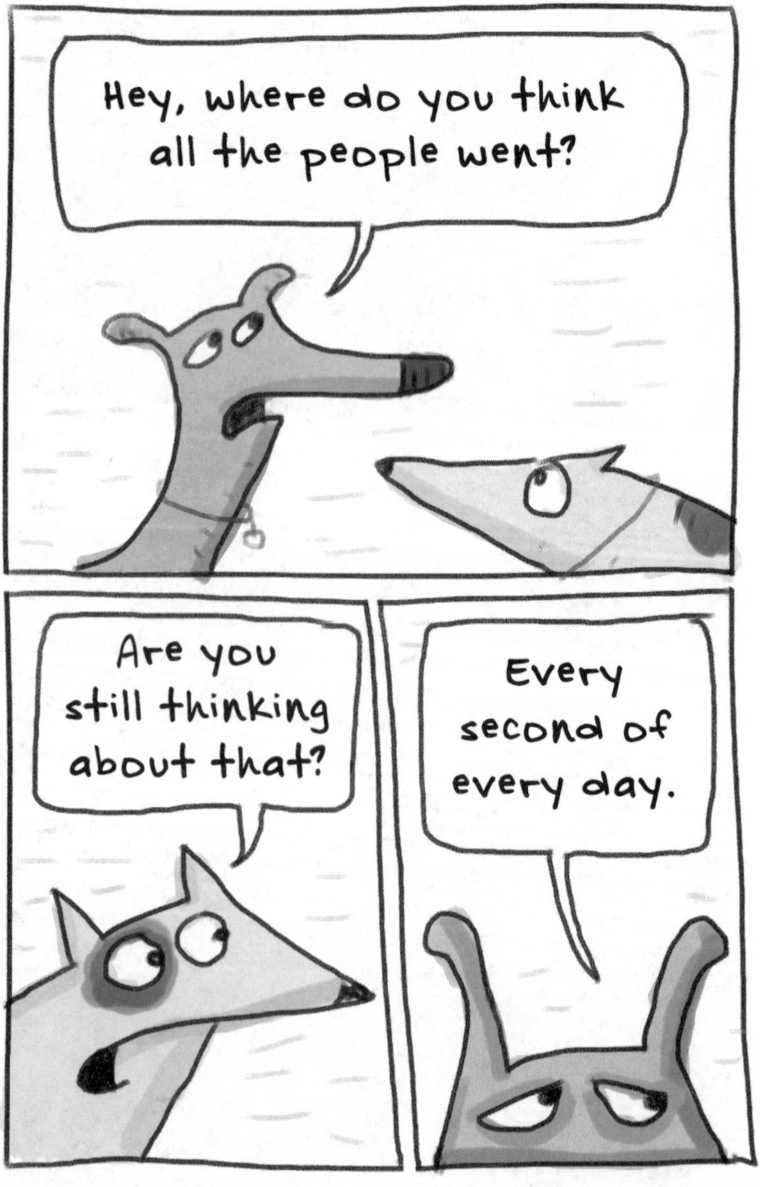
Hey, where do you think all the people went?
Are you still thinking about that?
Every second of every day.

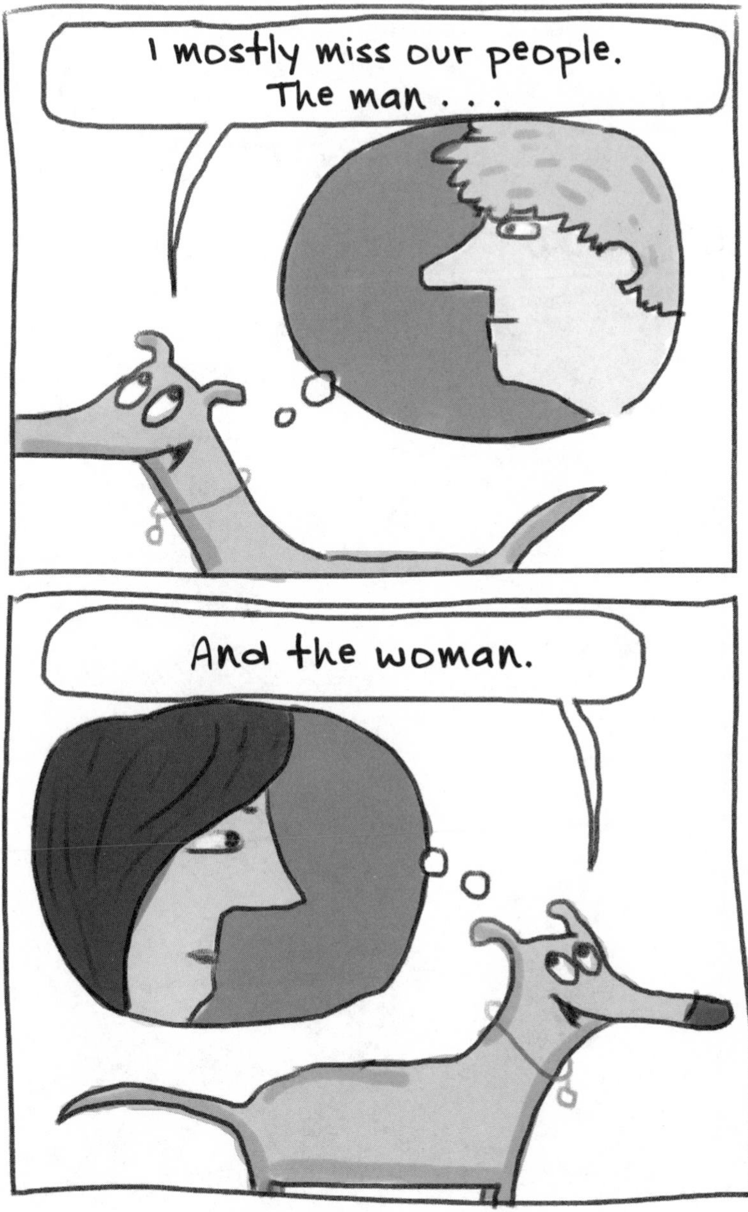
I mostly miss our people. The man . . .
And the woman.

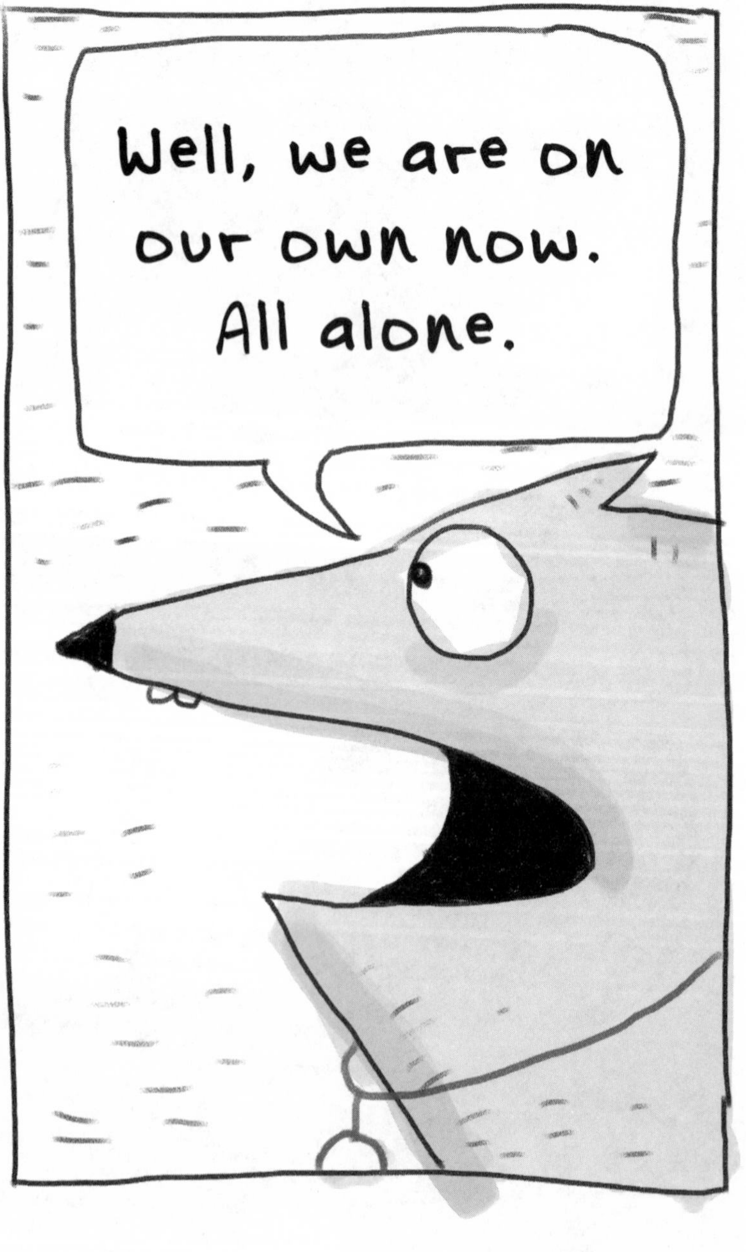
Well, we are on our own now. All alone.

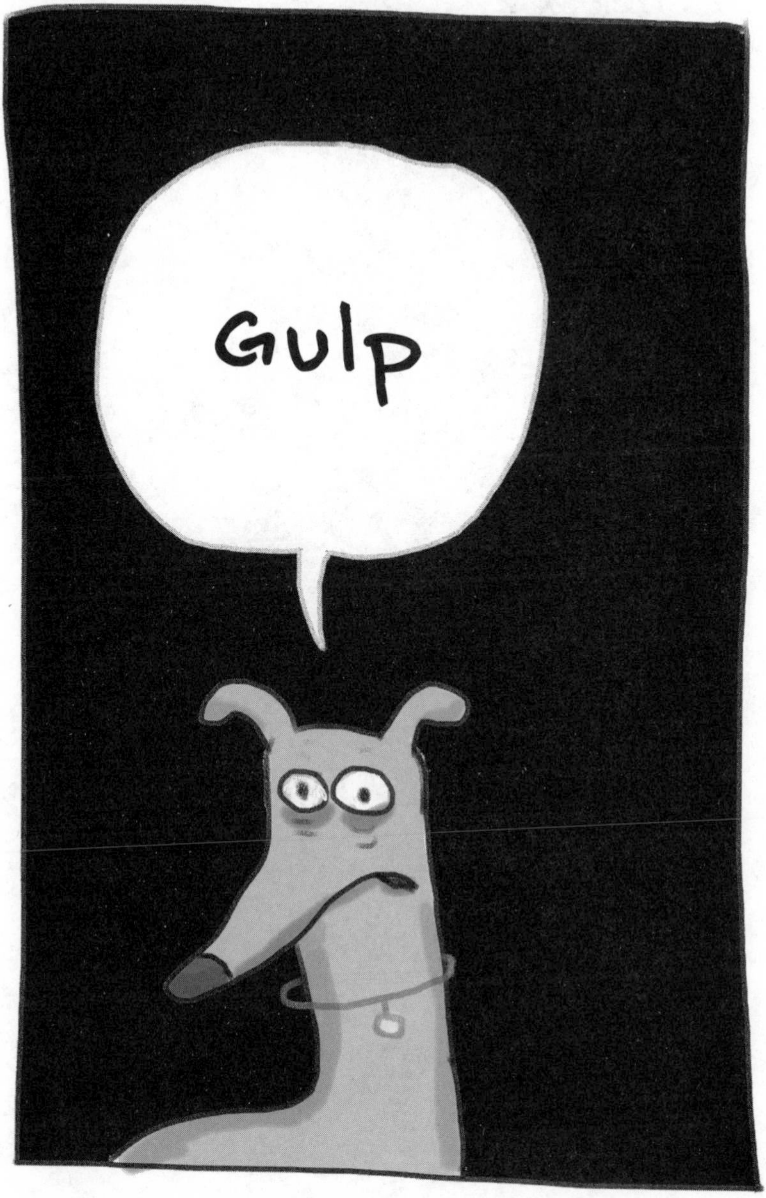
Gulp

Scene
Eighteen

140

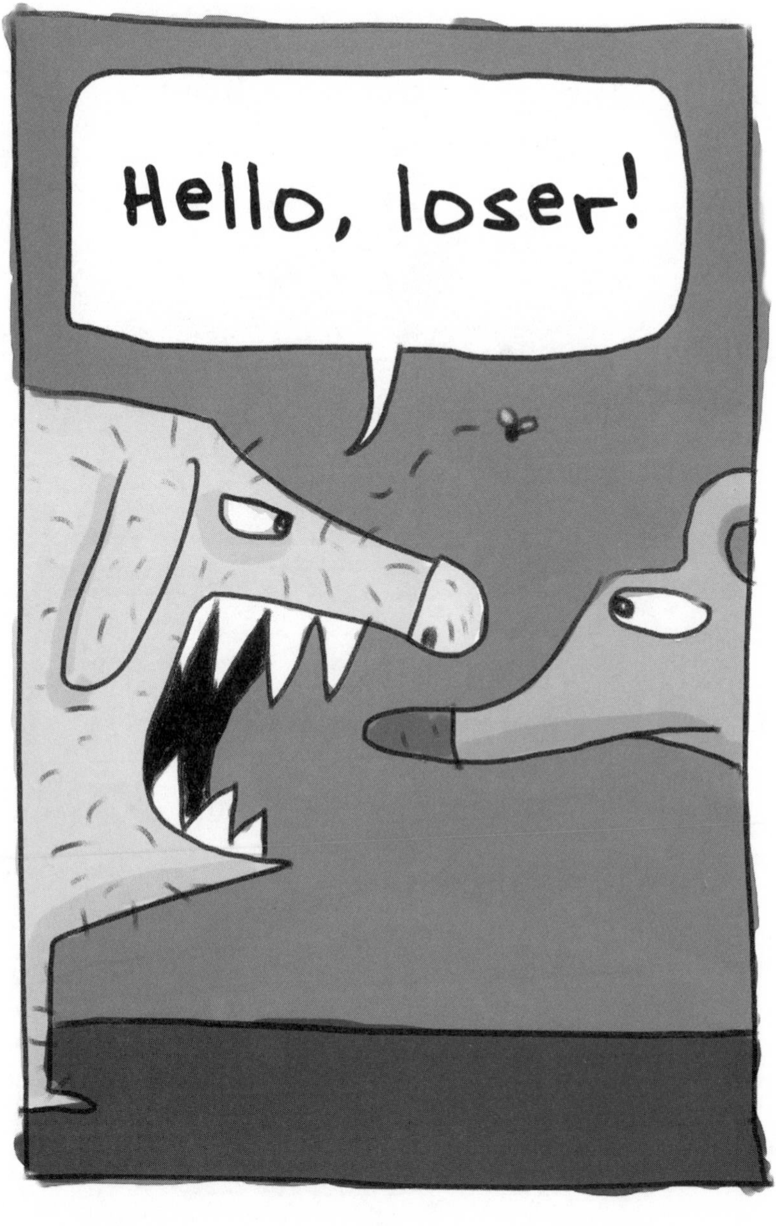
Hello, loser!

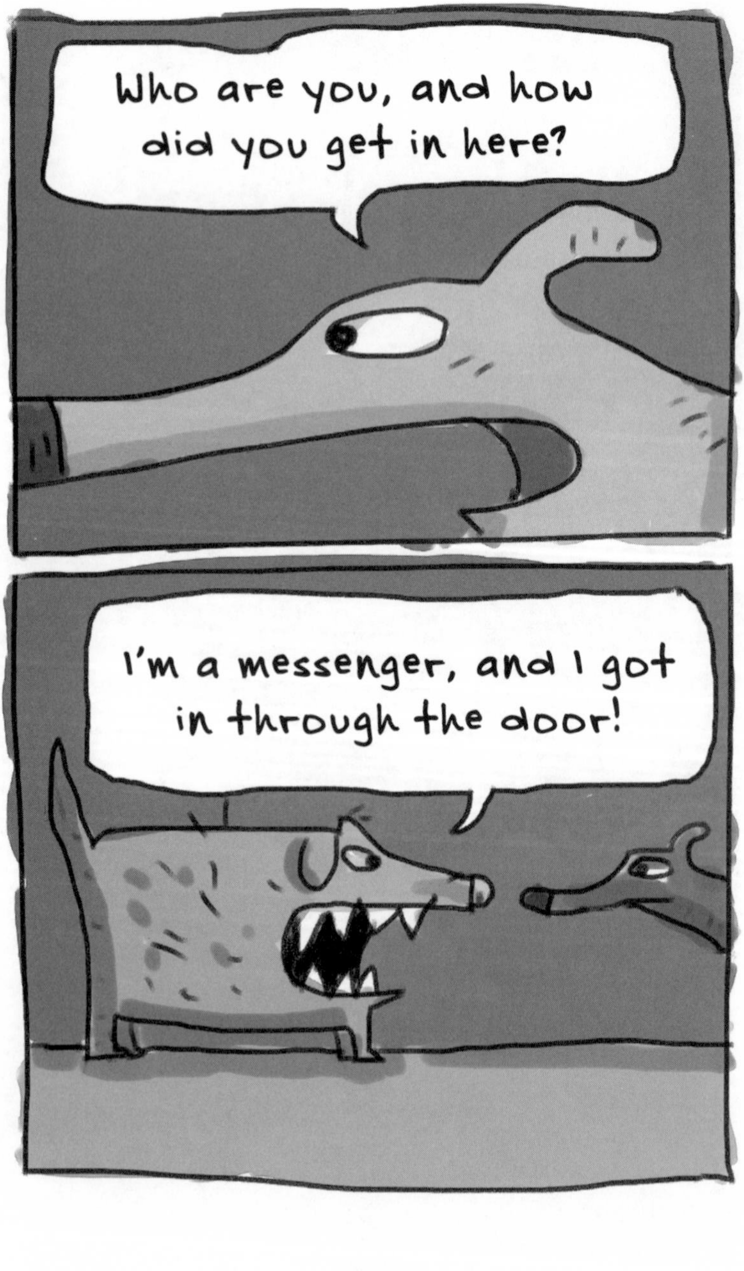
Who are you, and how did you get in here?
I'm a messenger, and I got in through the door!

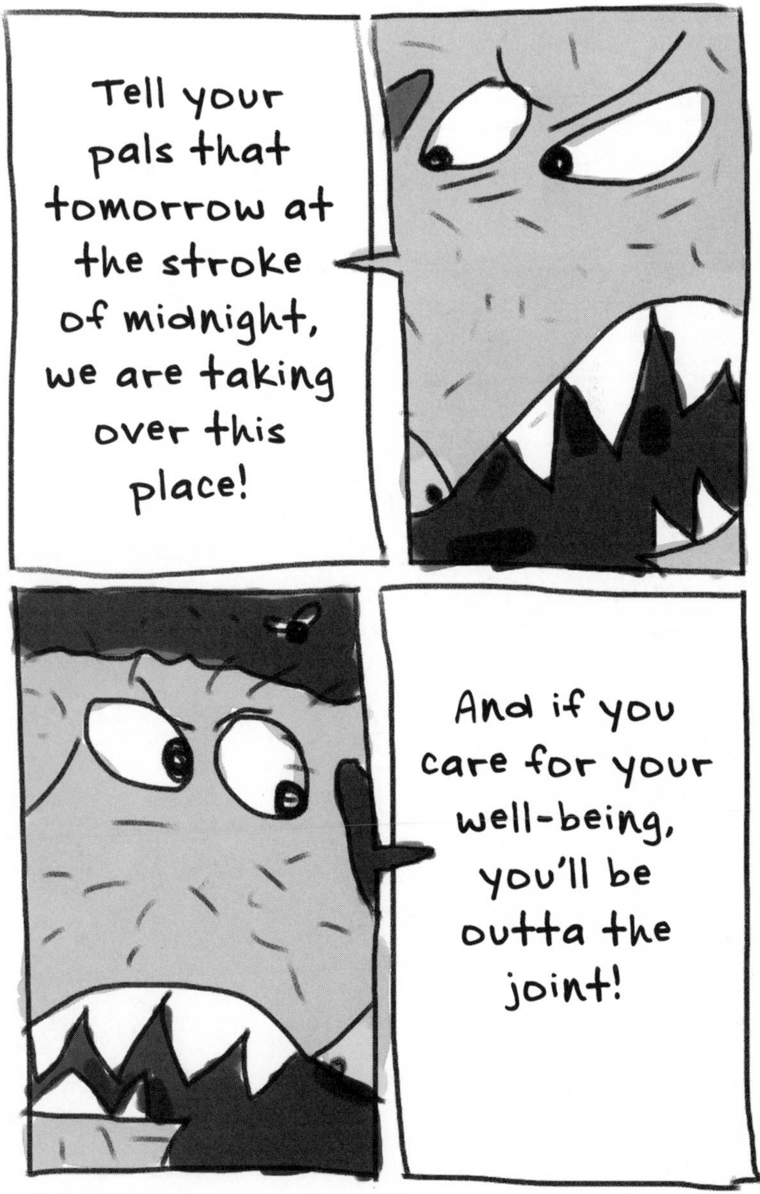
Tell your pals that tomorrow at the stroke of midnight, we are taking over this place!
And if you care for your well-being, you'll be outta the joint!

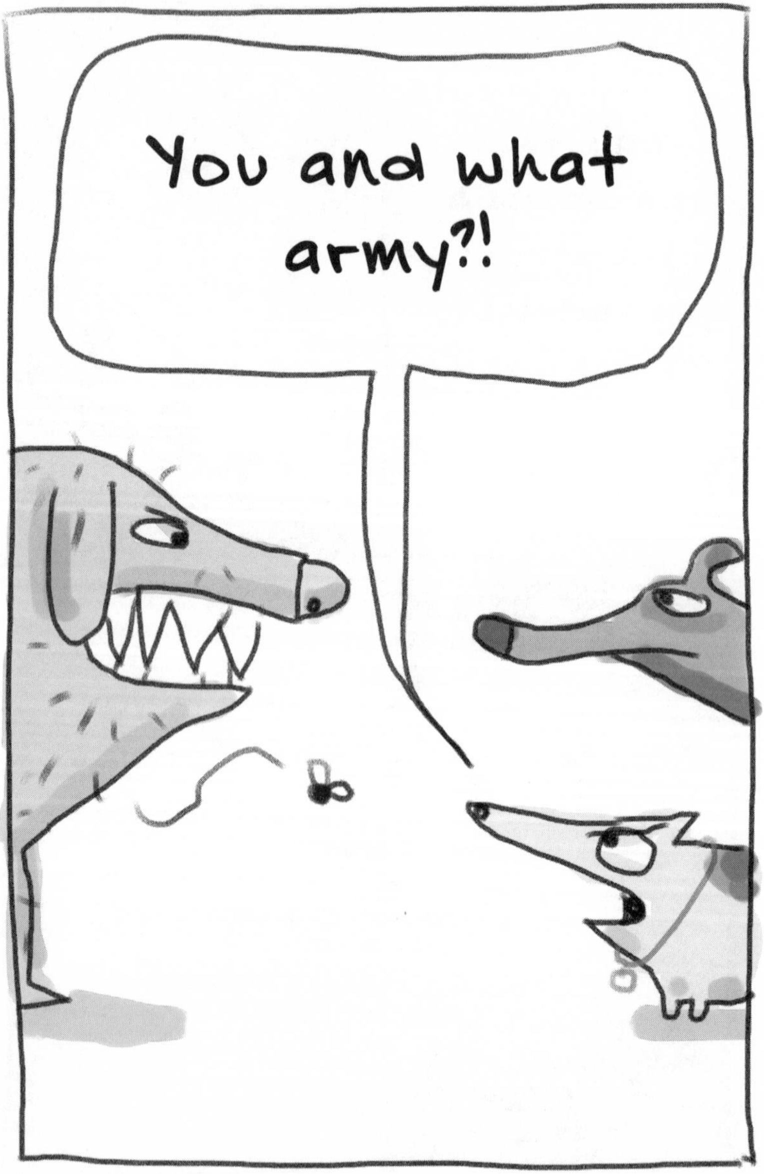
You and what army?!

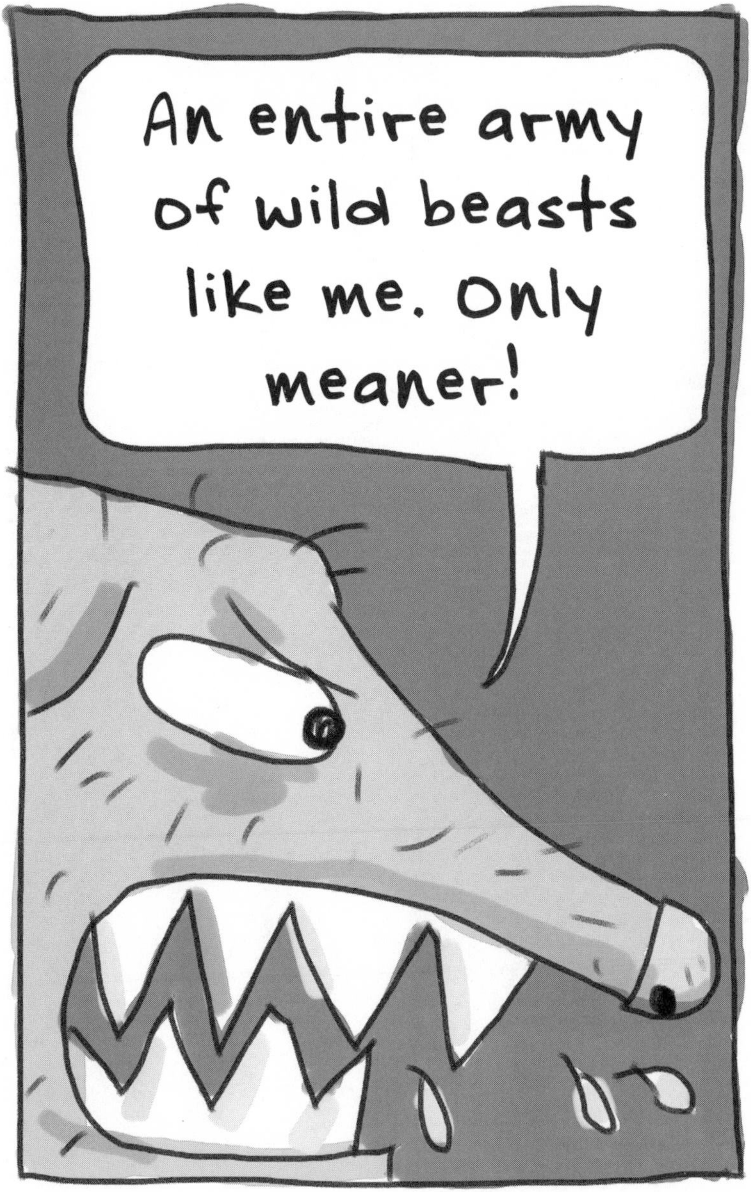
An entire army of wild beasts like me. Only meaner!

Scene
Nineteen

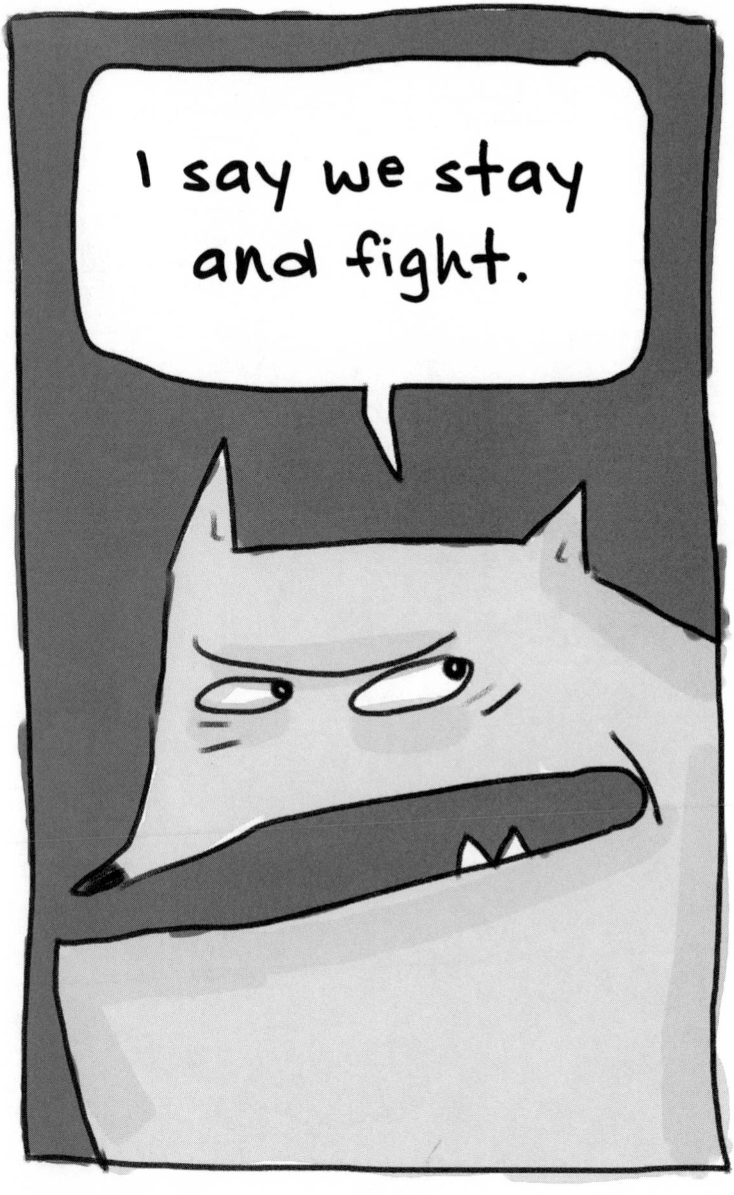
I say we stay and fight.

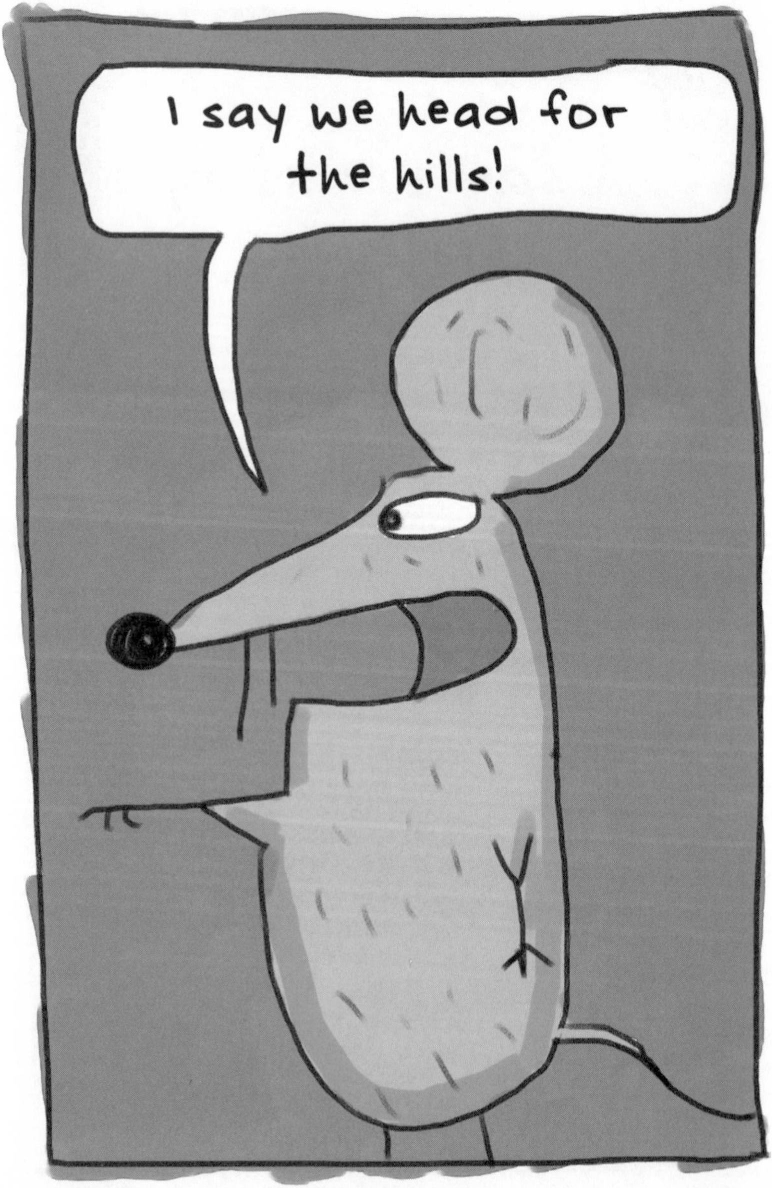
I say we head for the hills!

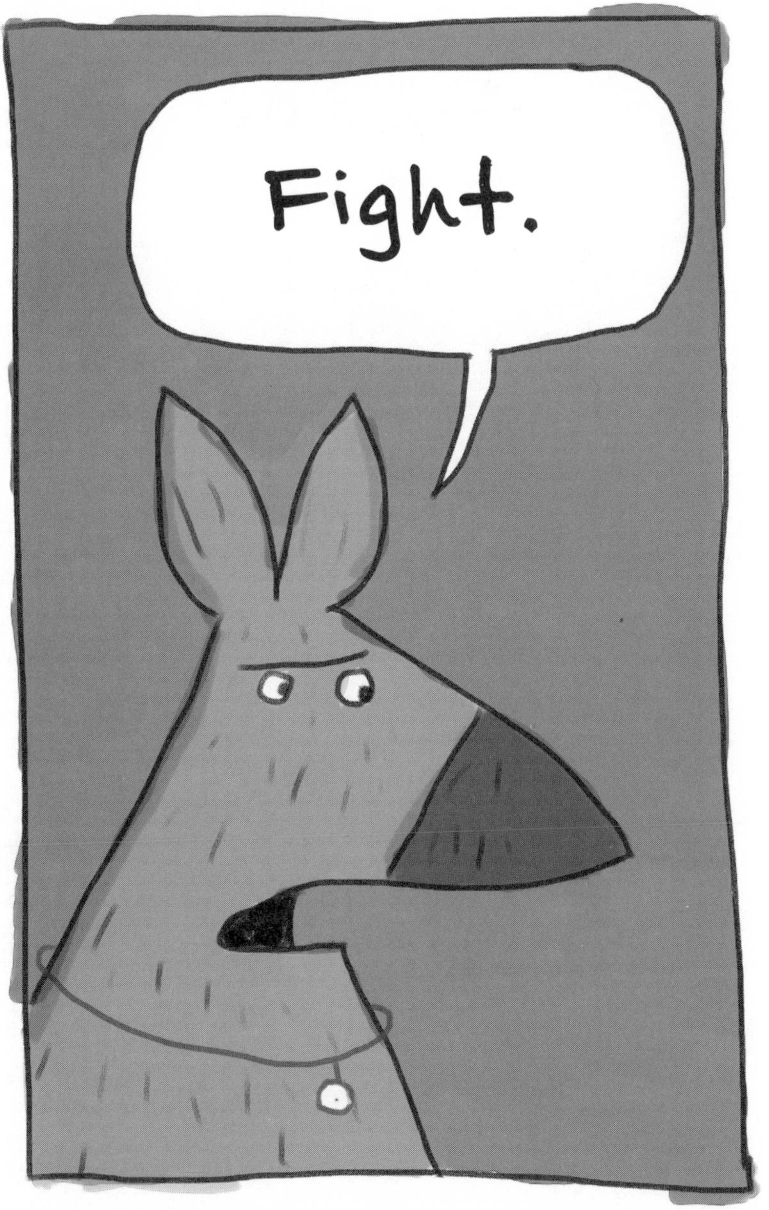
Fight.

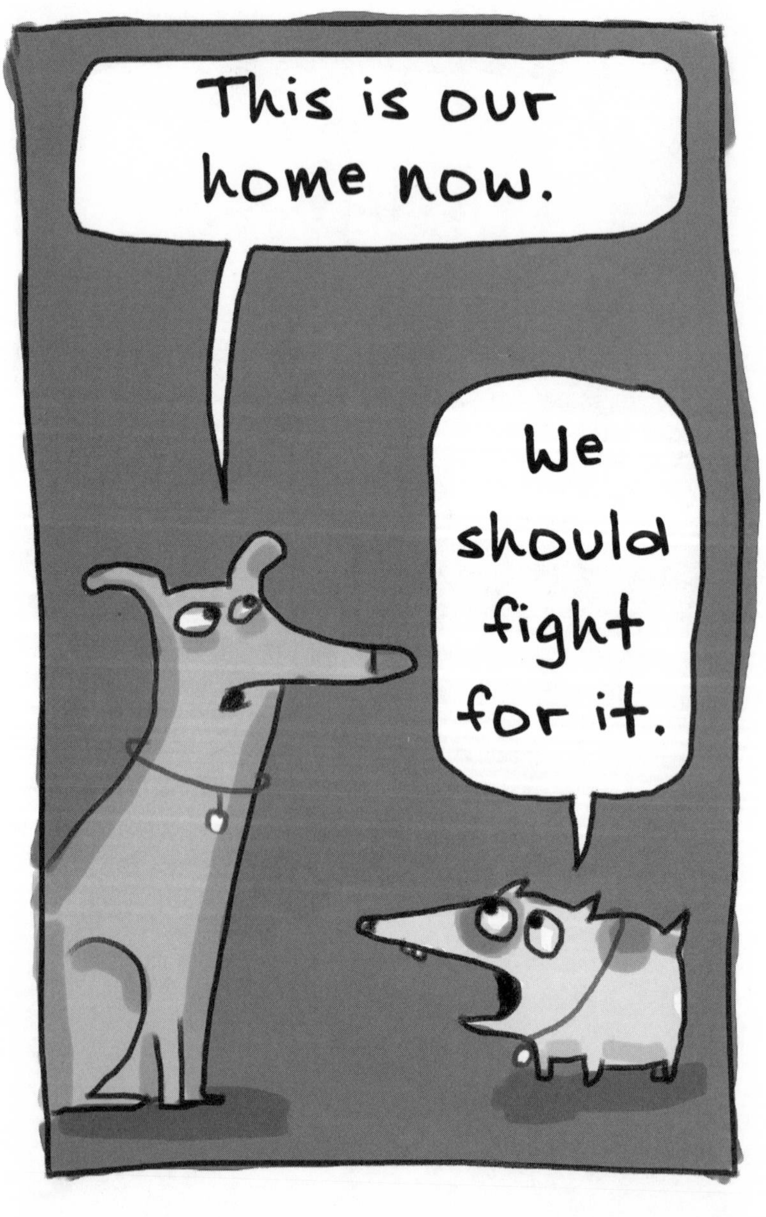
This is our home now.
We should fight for it.

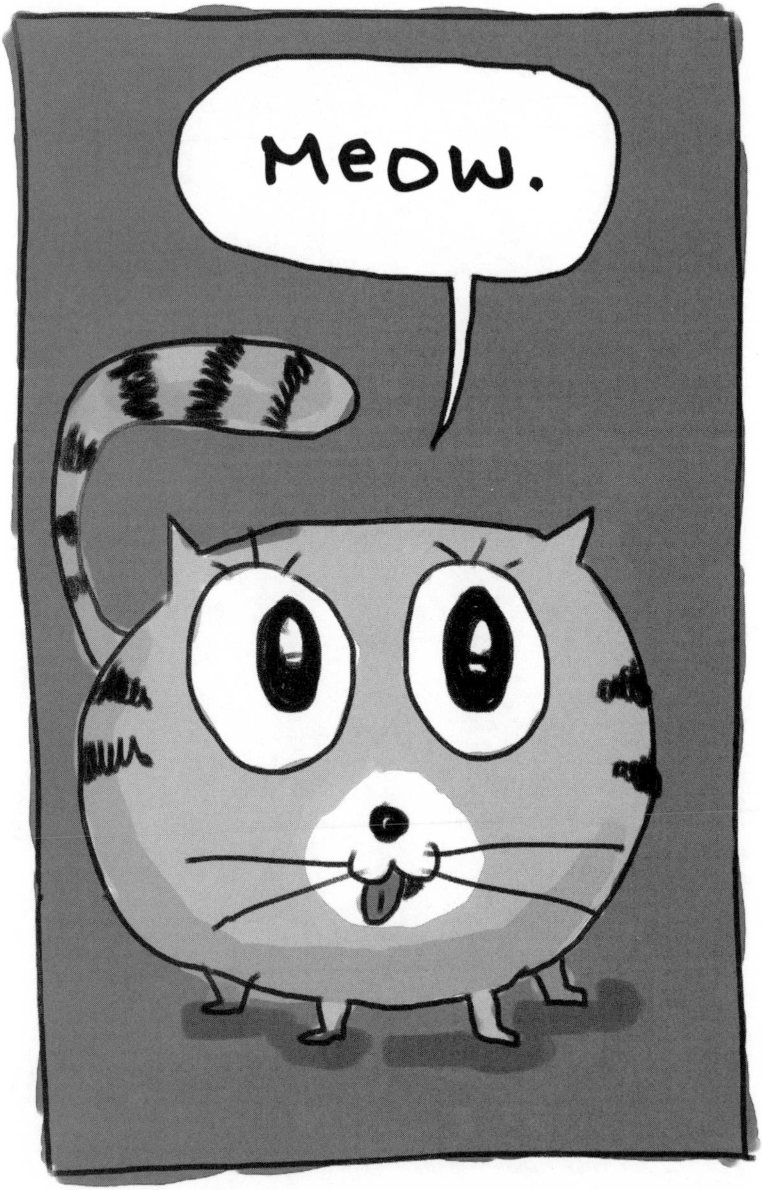
MEOW.

Scene
Twenty

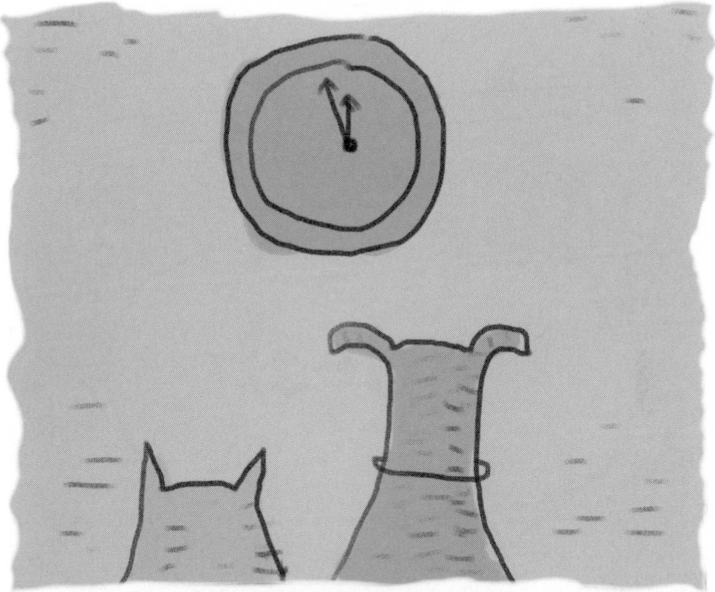

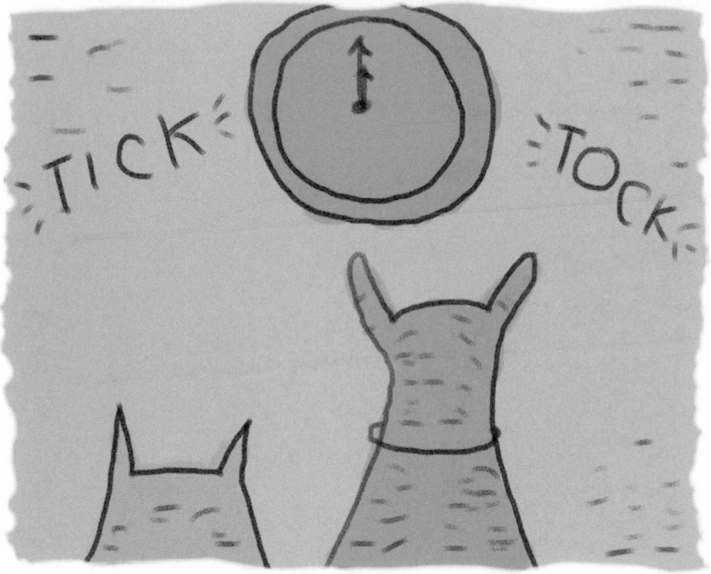
TICK
TOCK

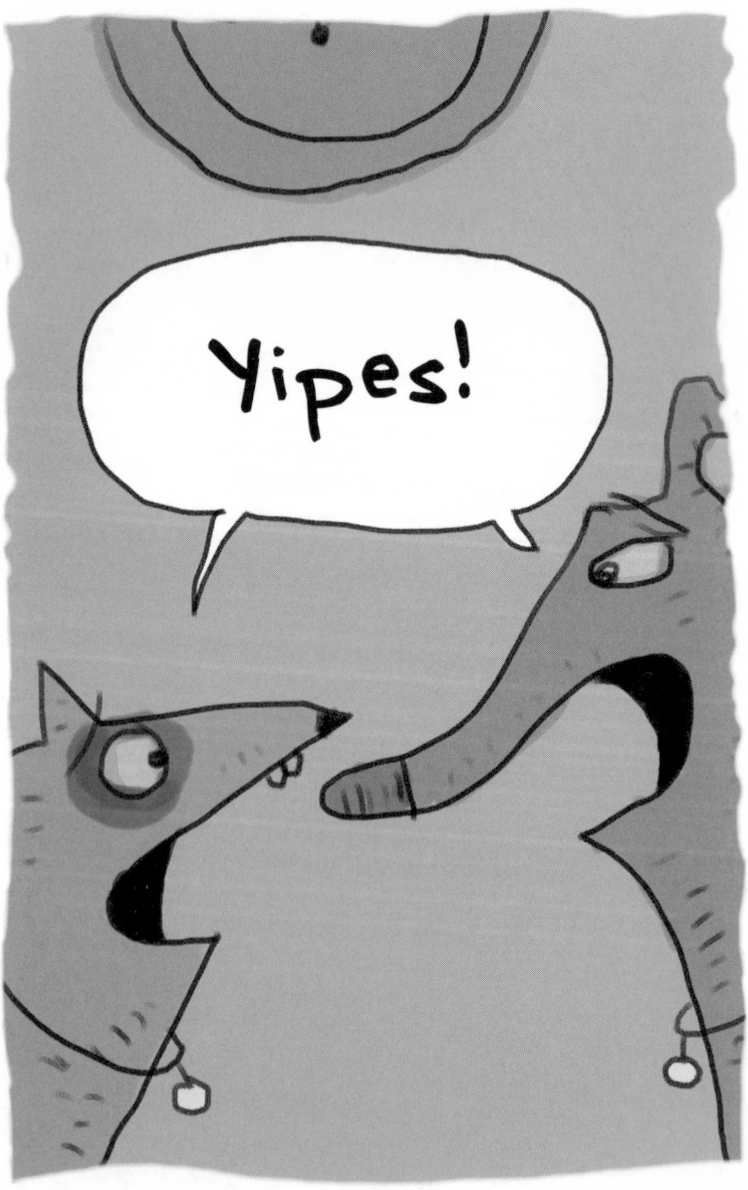
Yipes!

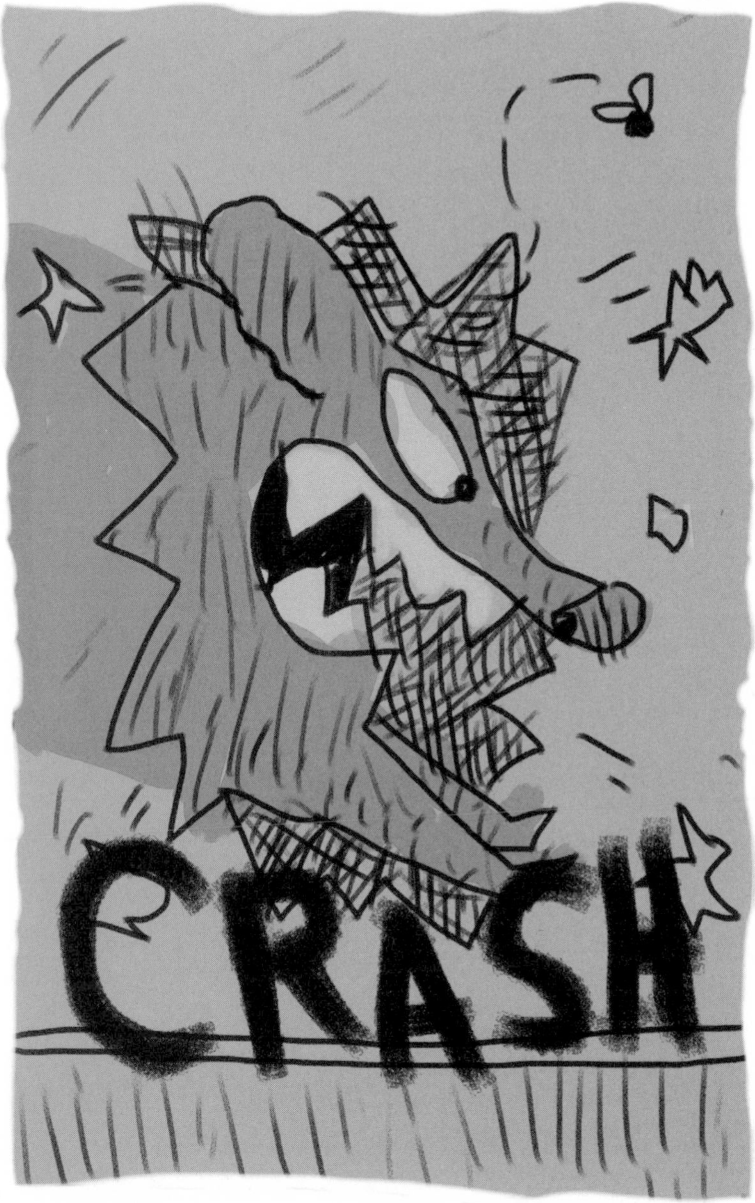
CRASH

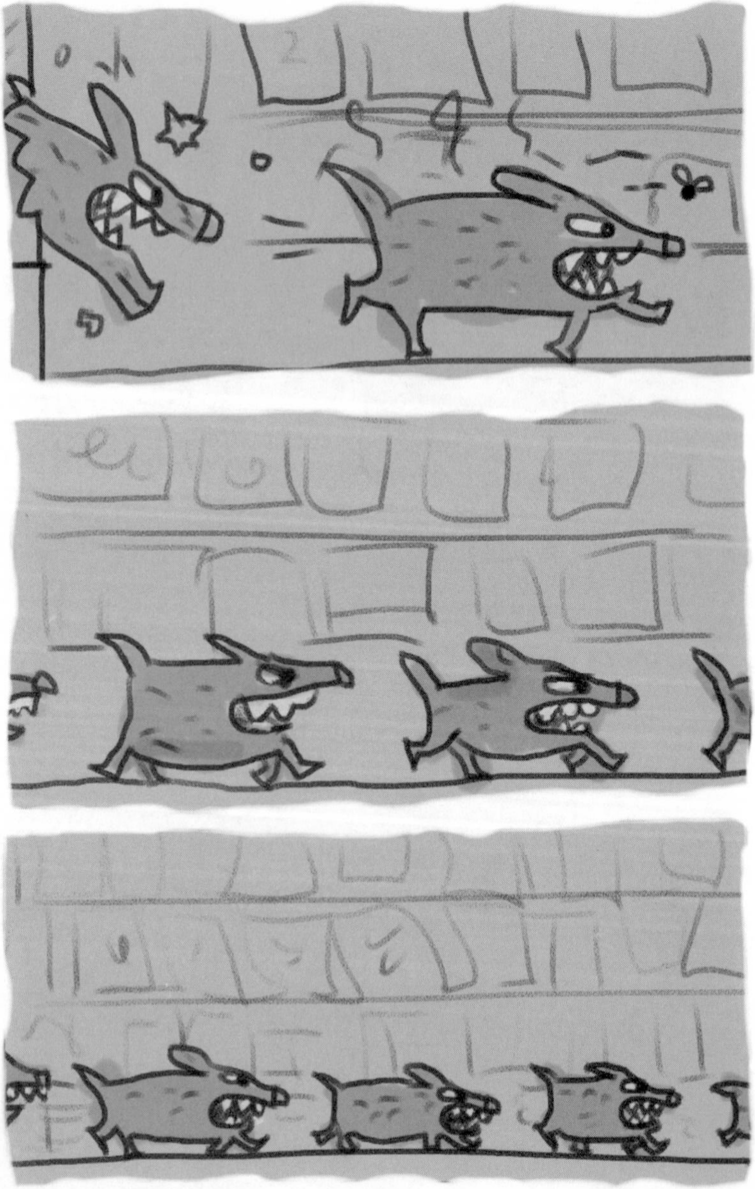

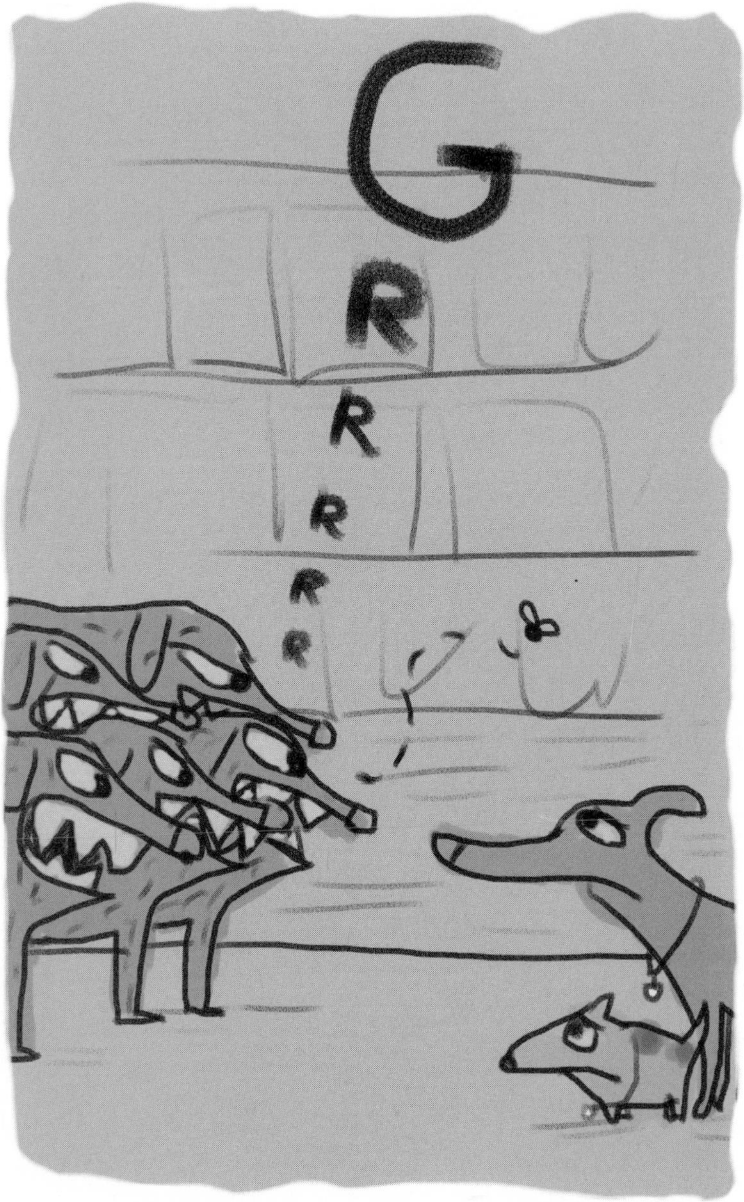
GRRRRR

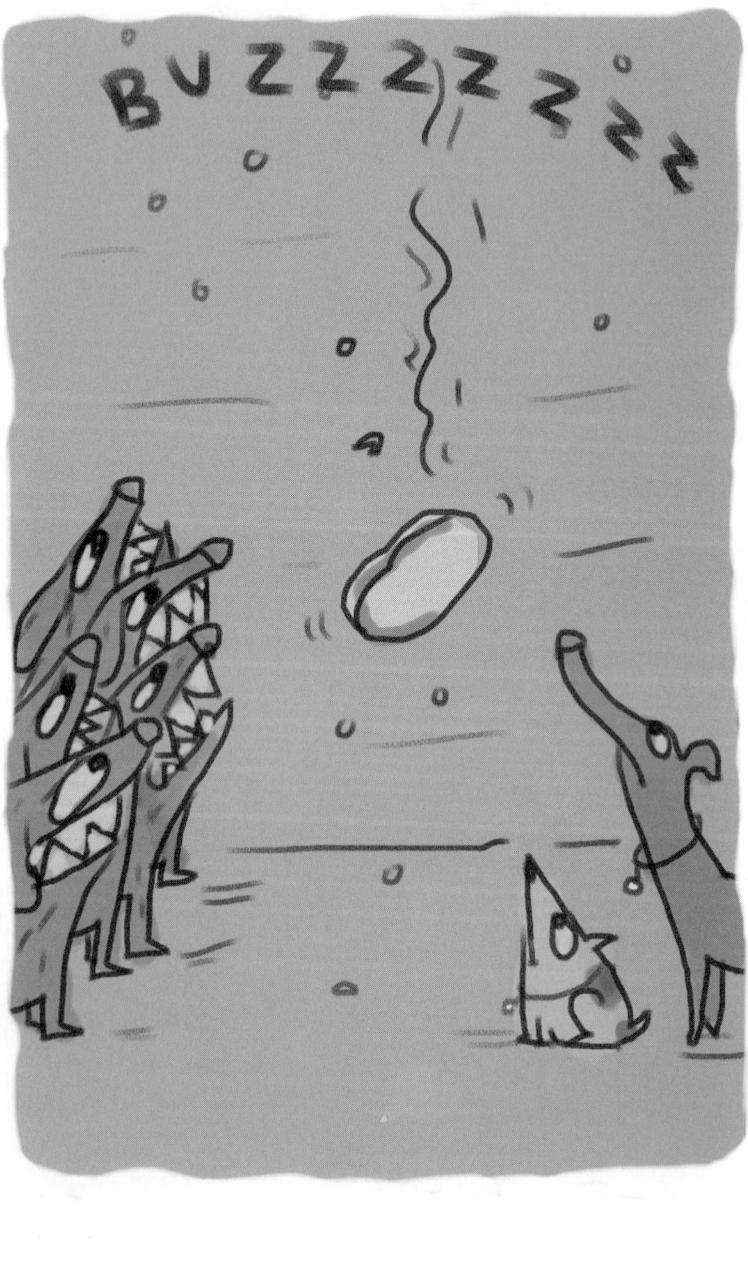
BUZZZZZZZ

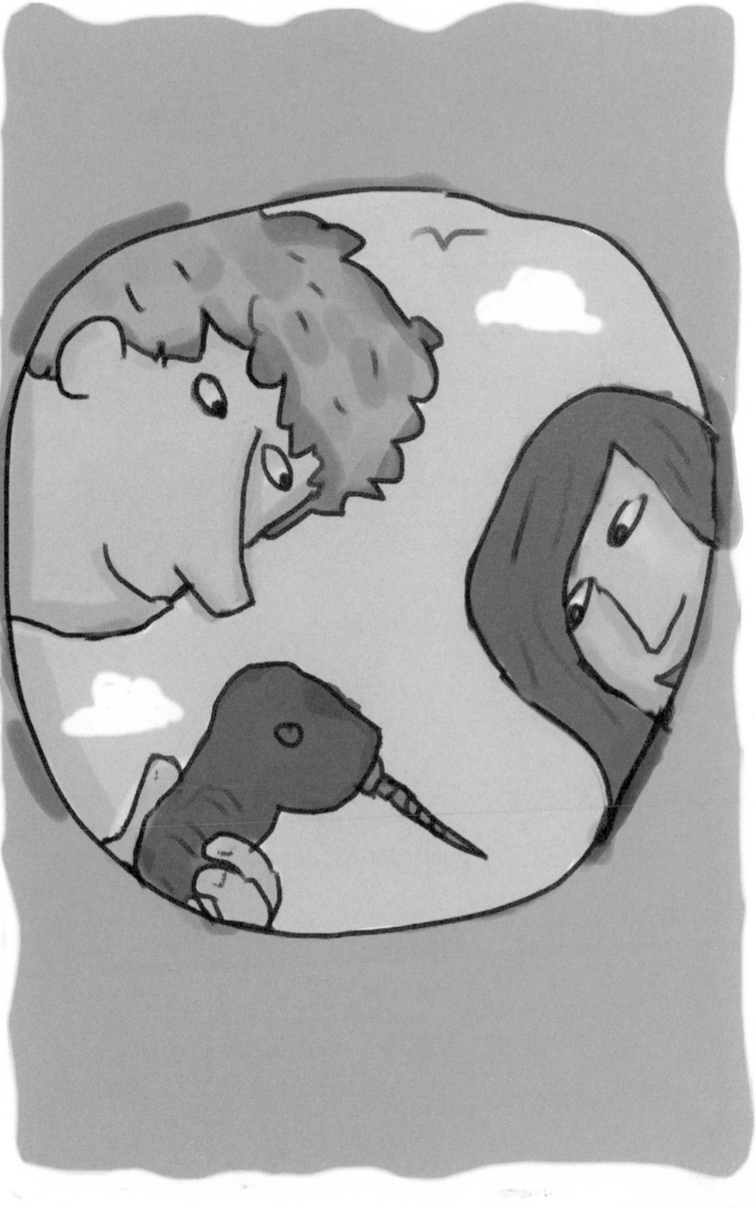

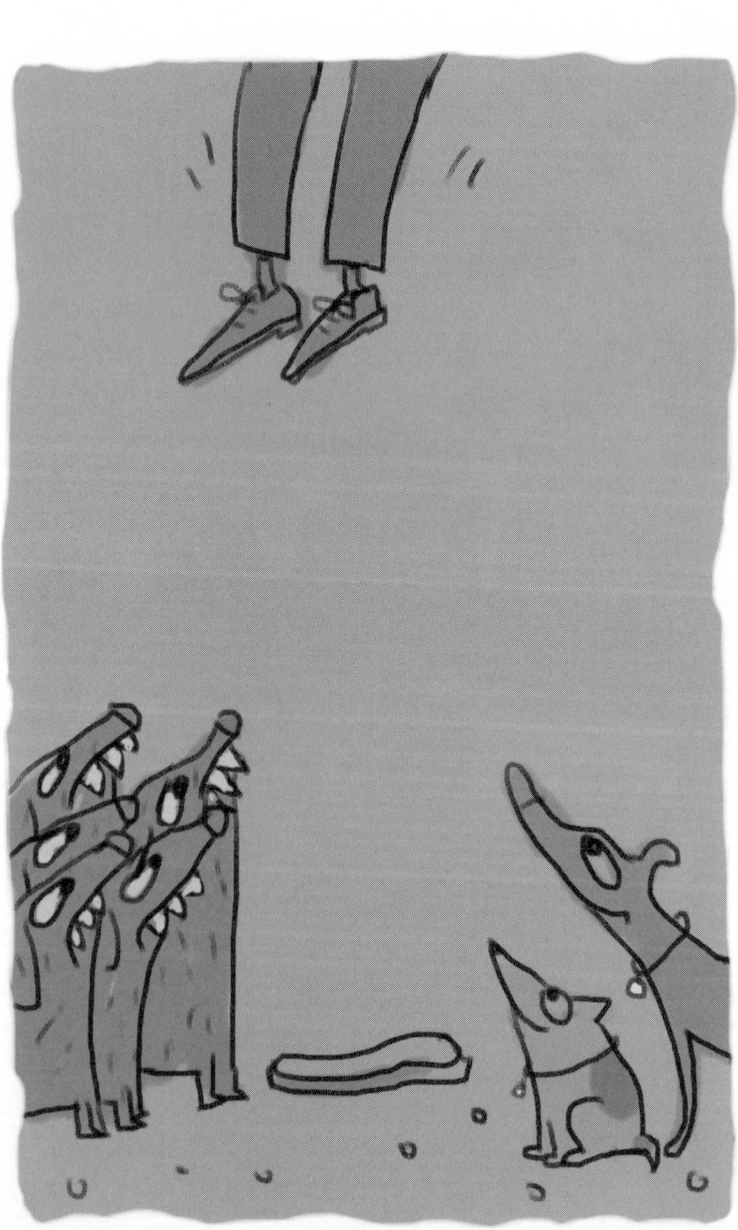

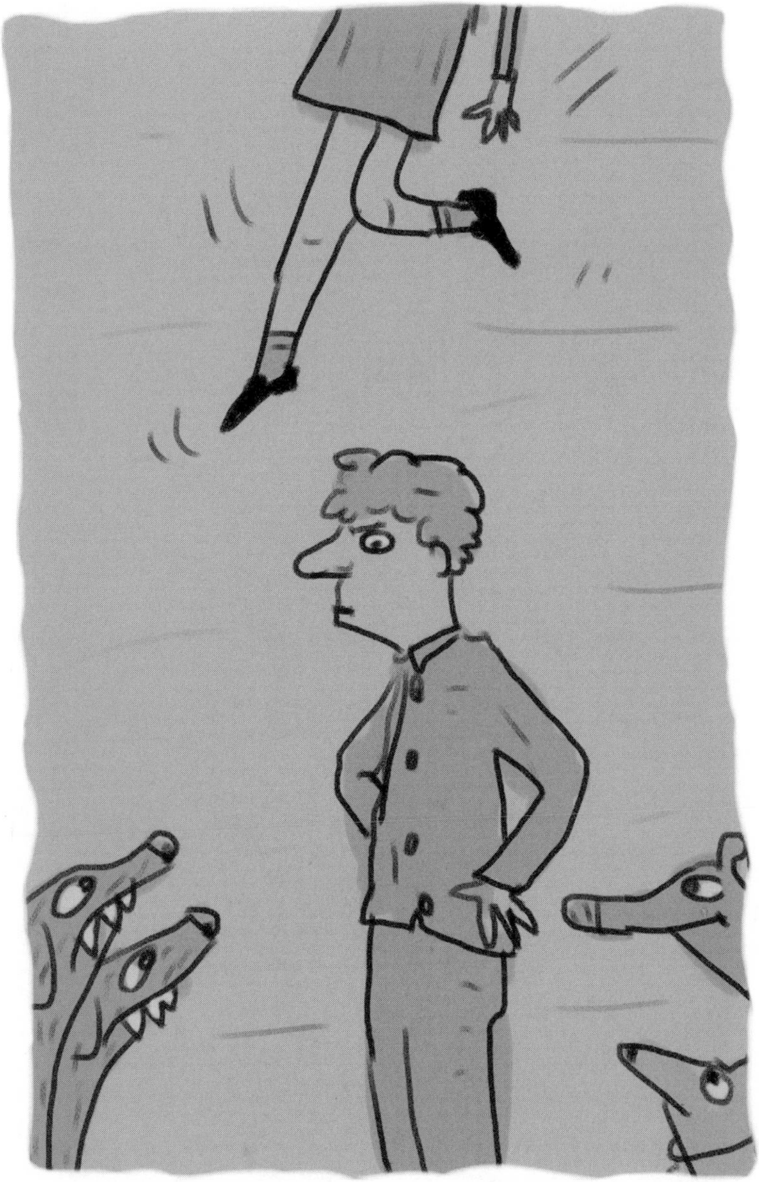

162

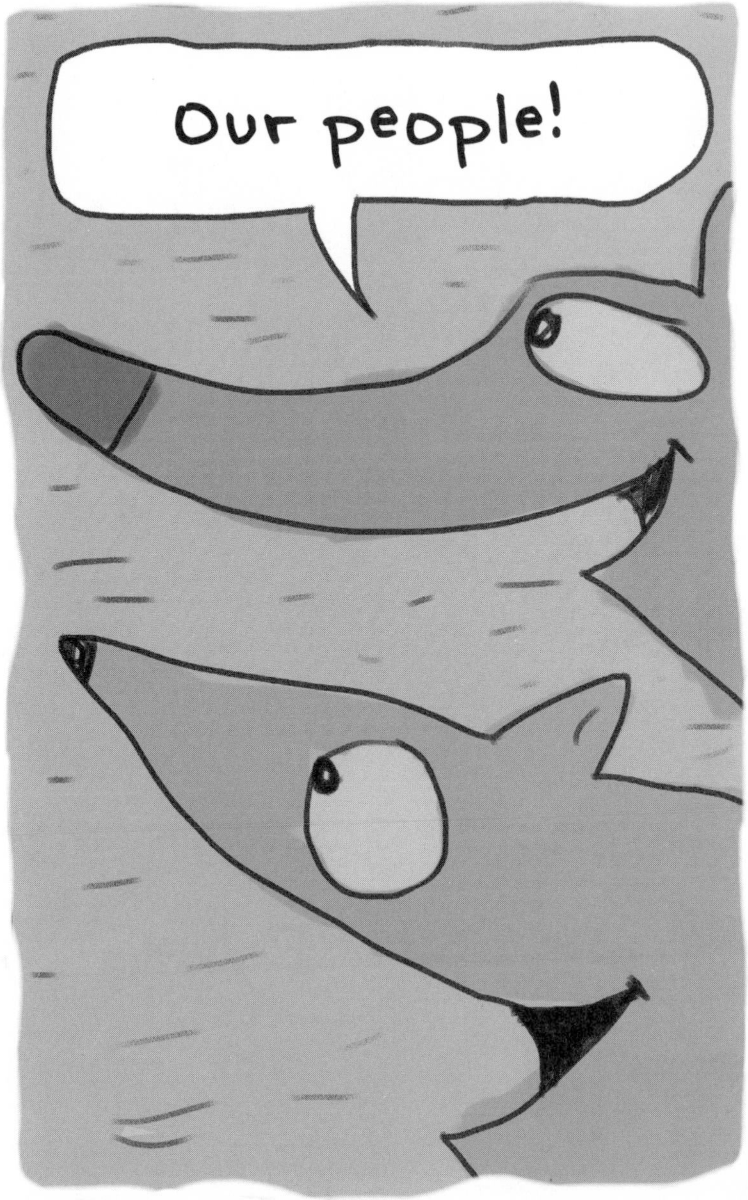
Our people!

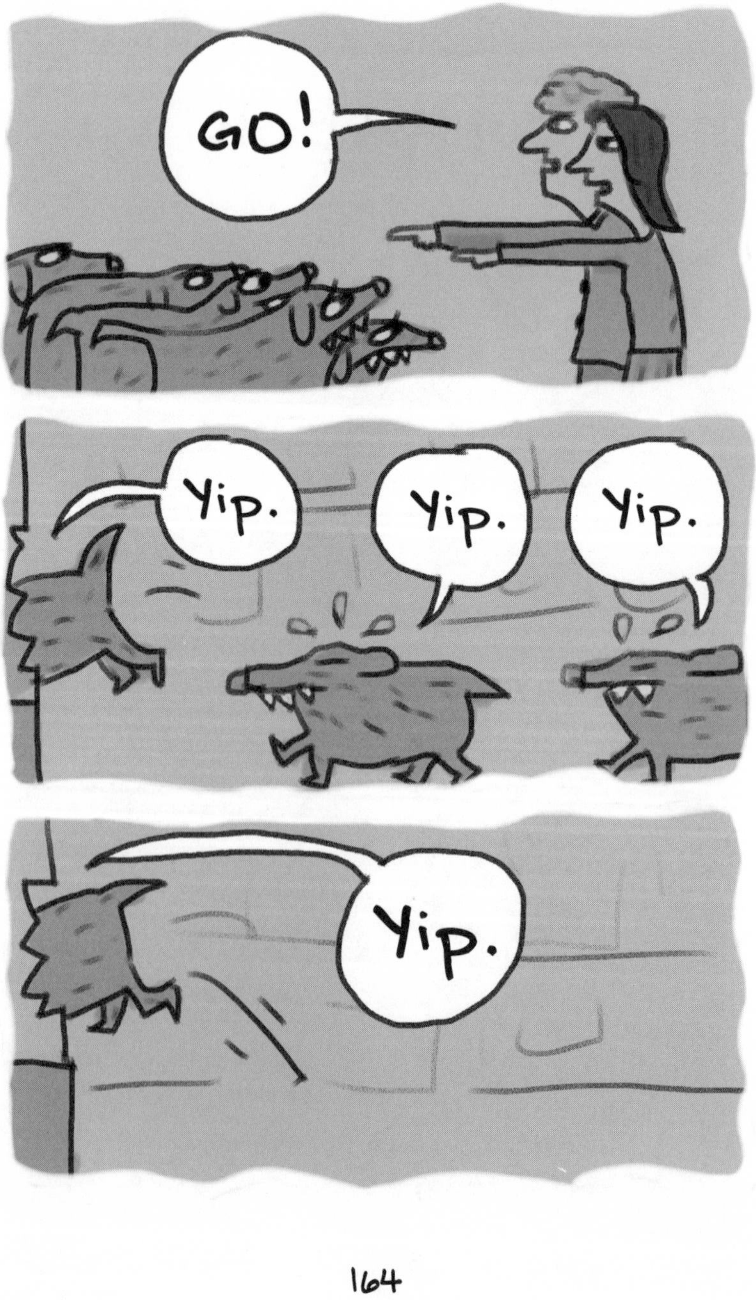
GO!
Yip.
Yip.
Yip.
Yip.

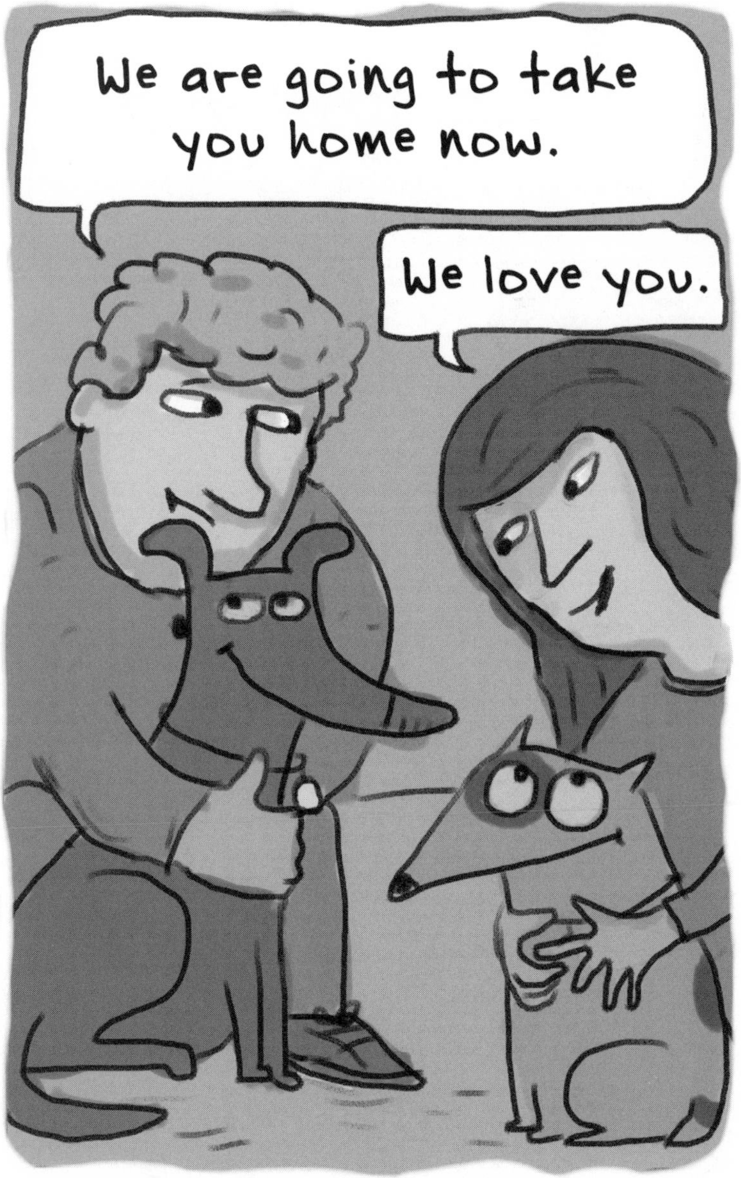
We are going to take you home now.
We love you.

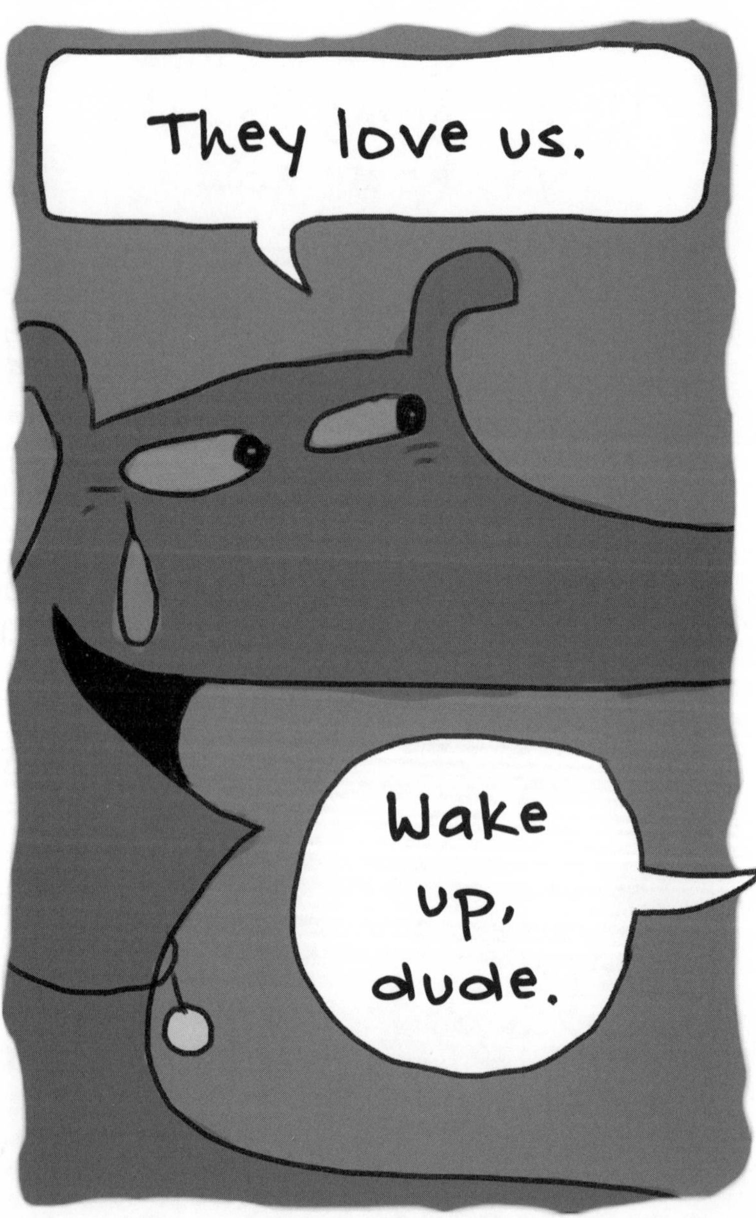
They love us.
Wake up, dude.

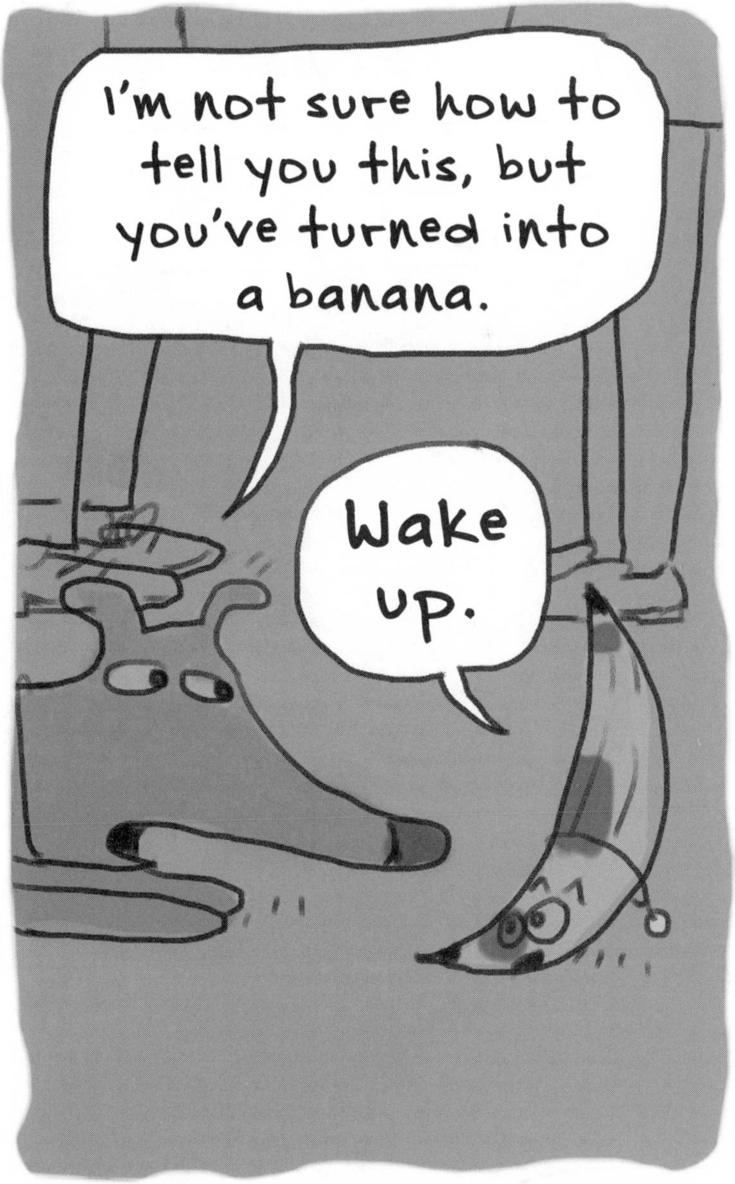
I'm not sure how to tell you this, but you've turned into a banana.
Wake up.

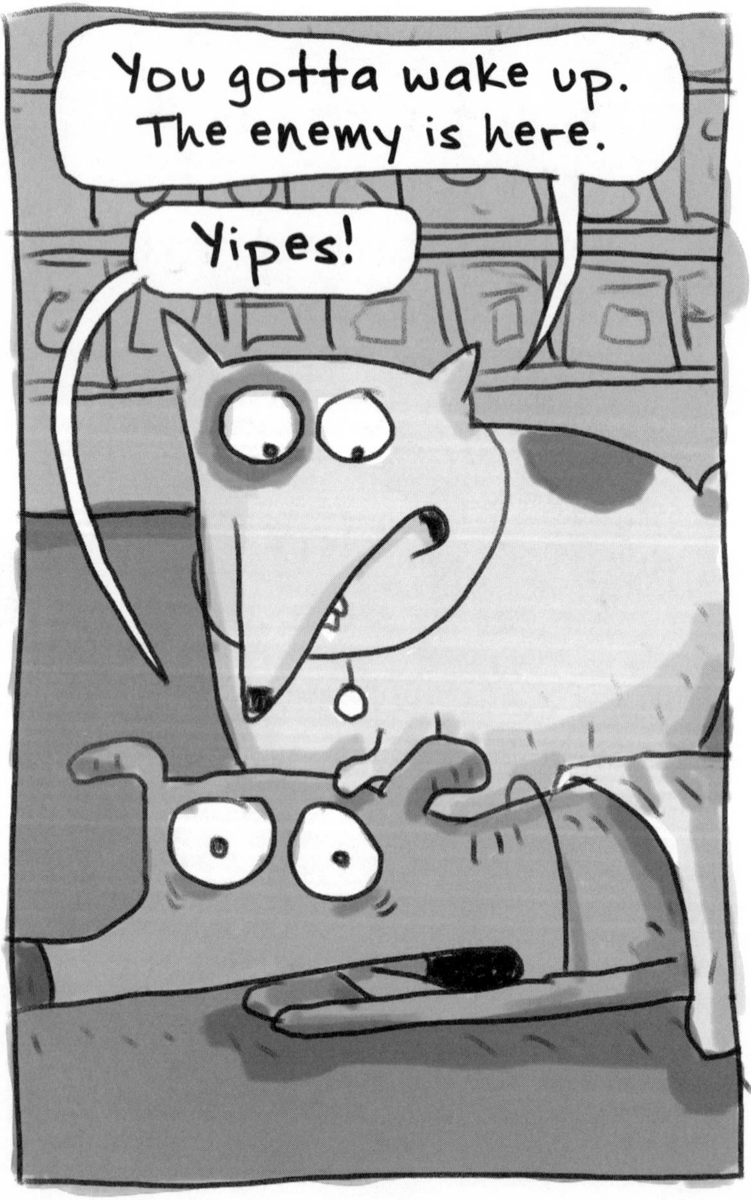
You gotta wake up. The enemy is here.
Yipes!

Scene
Twenty-One:
The Battle

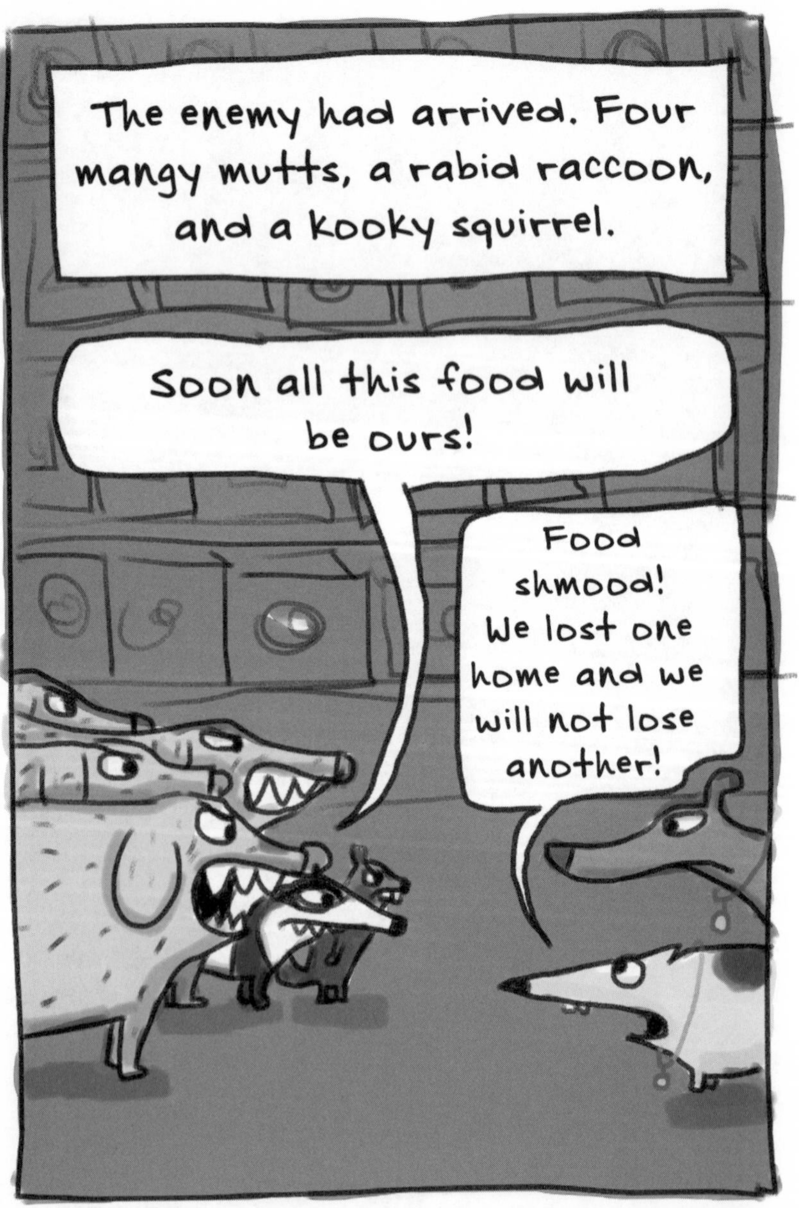
The enemy had arrived. Four mangy mutts, a rabid raccoon, and a kooky squirrel.
Soon all this food will be ours!
Food shmood! We lost one home and we will not lose another!

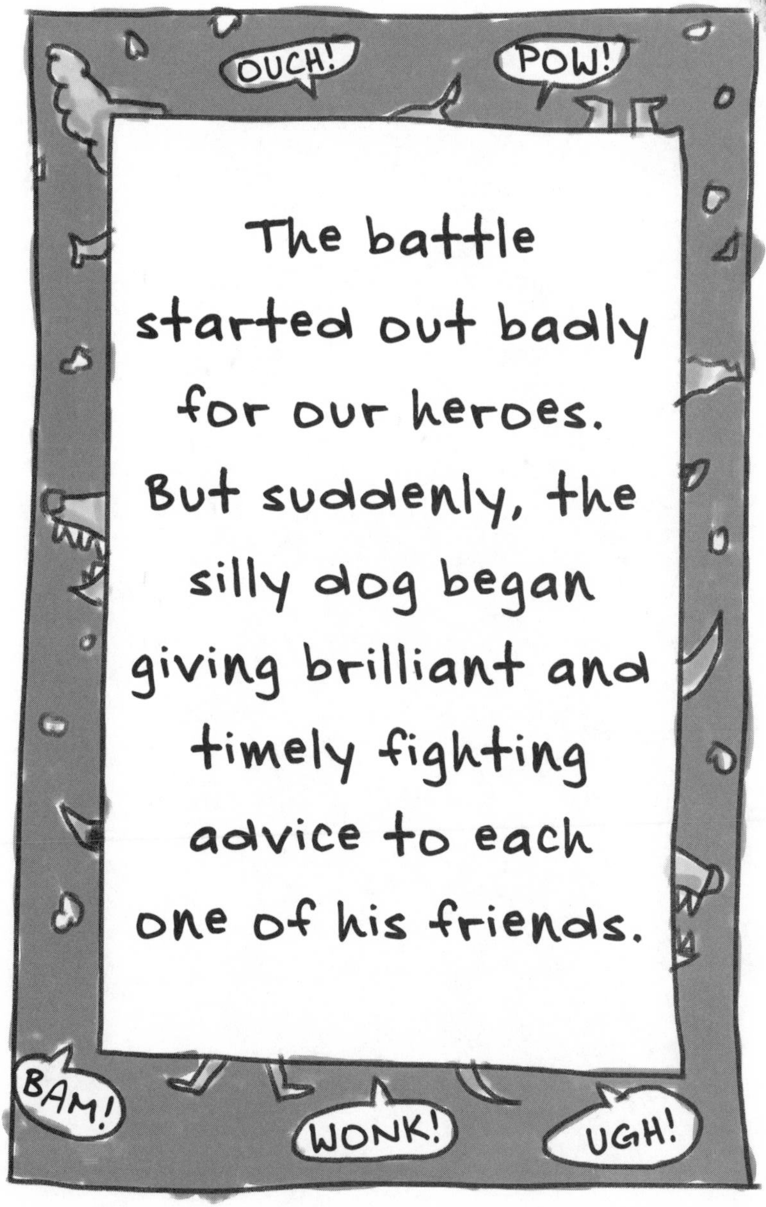
OUCH!
POW!
The battle started out badly for our heroes. But suddenly, the silly dog began giving brilliant and timely fighting advice to each one of his friends.
BAM!
WONK!
UGH!

Scene Twenty-Two: The Cop

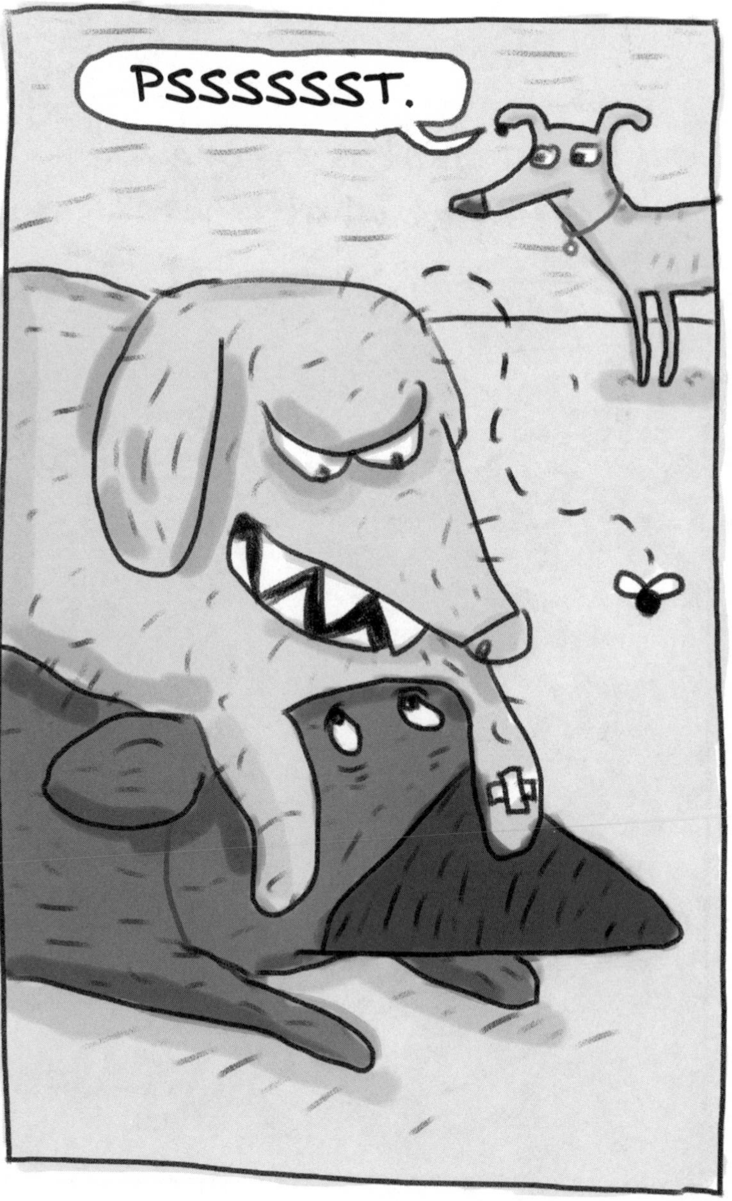
PSSSSSST.

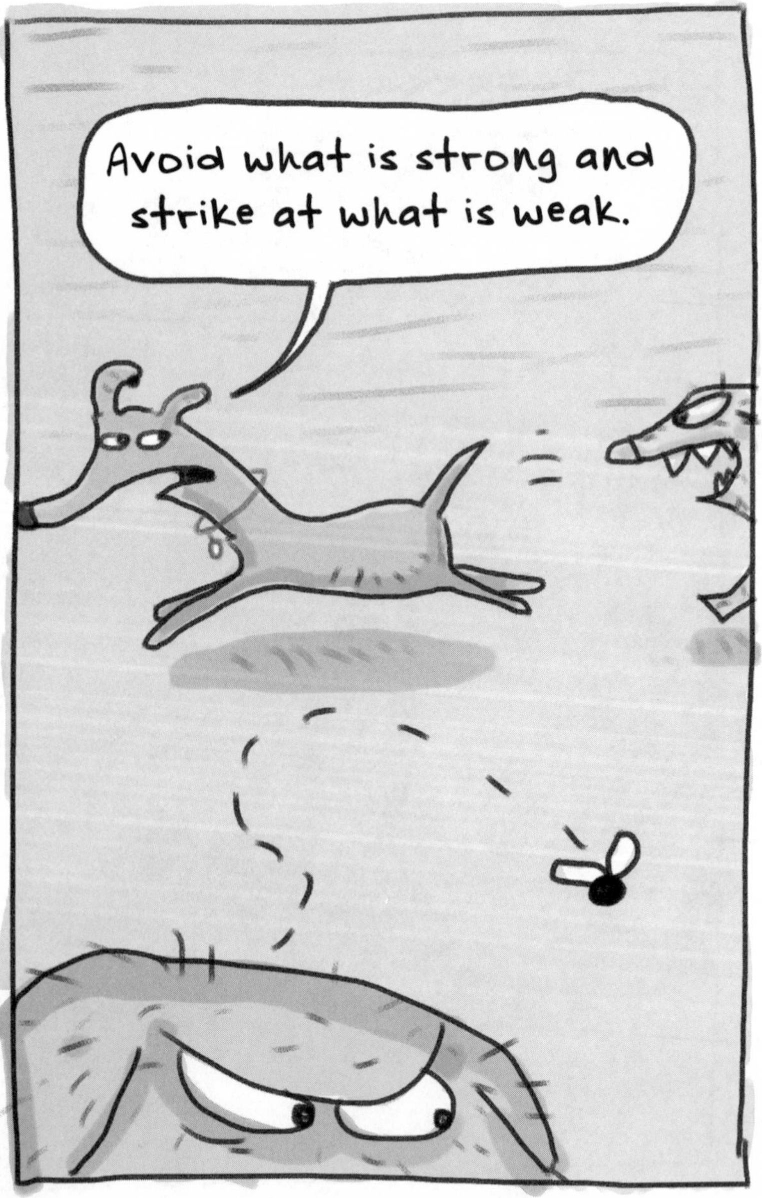
Avoid what is strong and strike at what is weak.

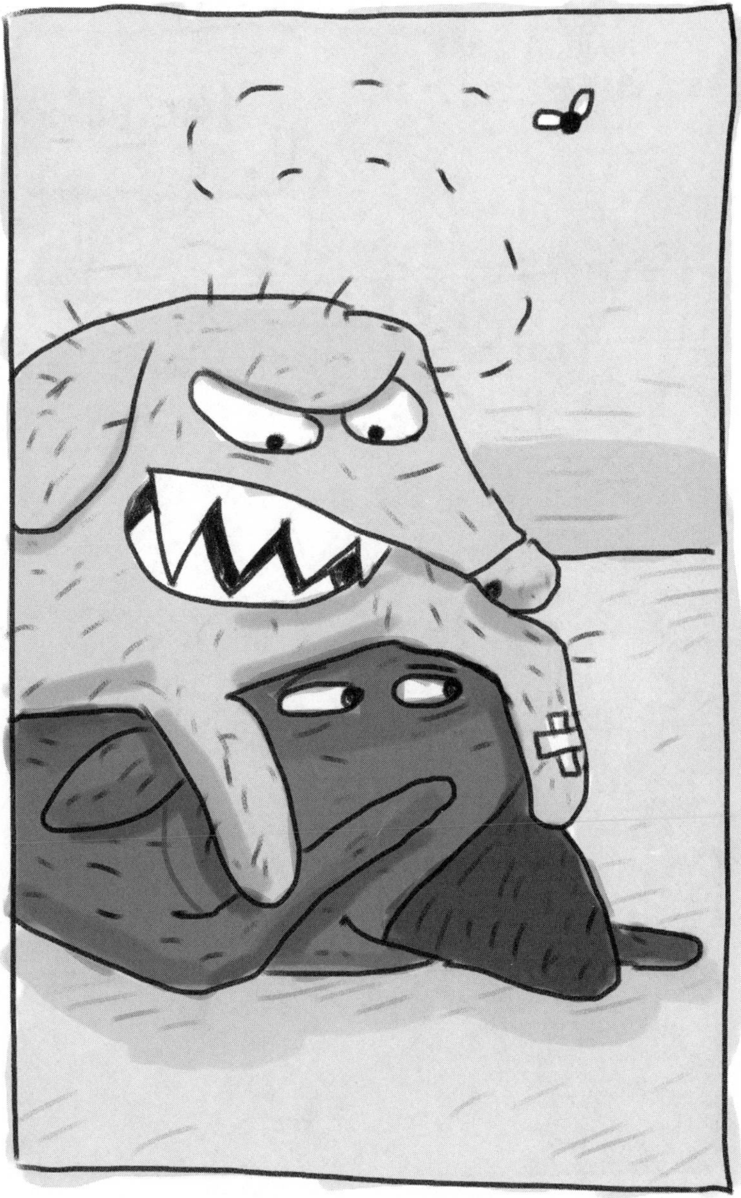

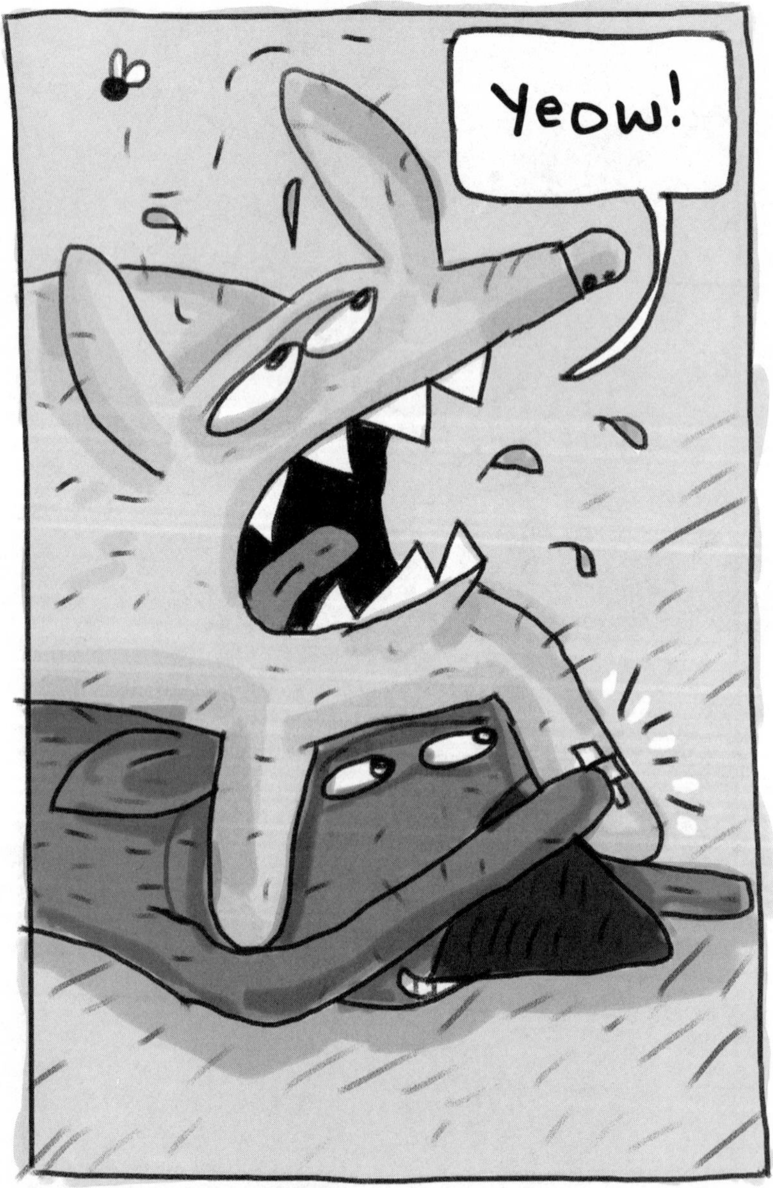
YEOW!

Scene Twenty-Three: The Boss

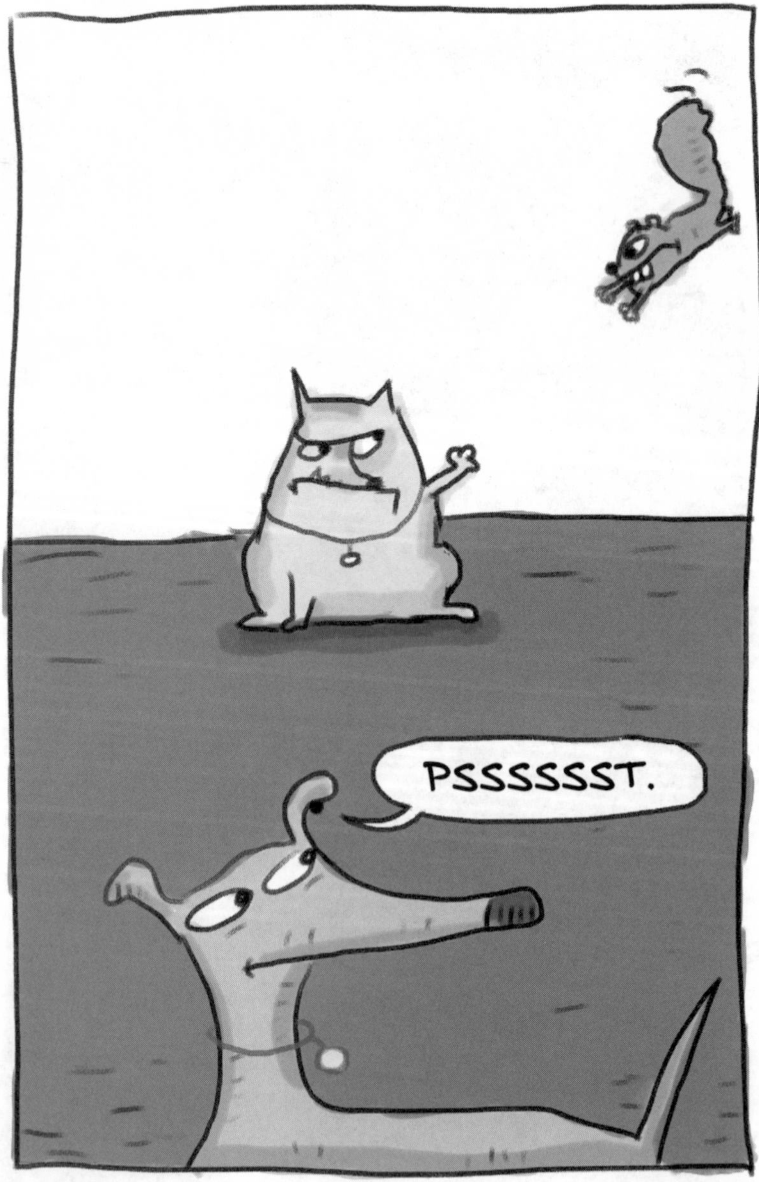
PSSSSSST.

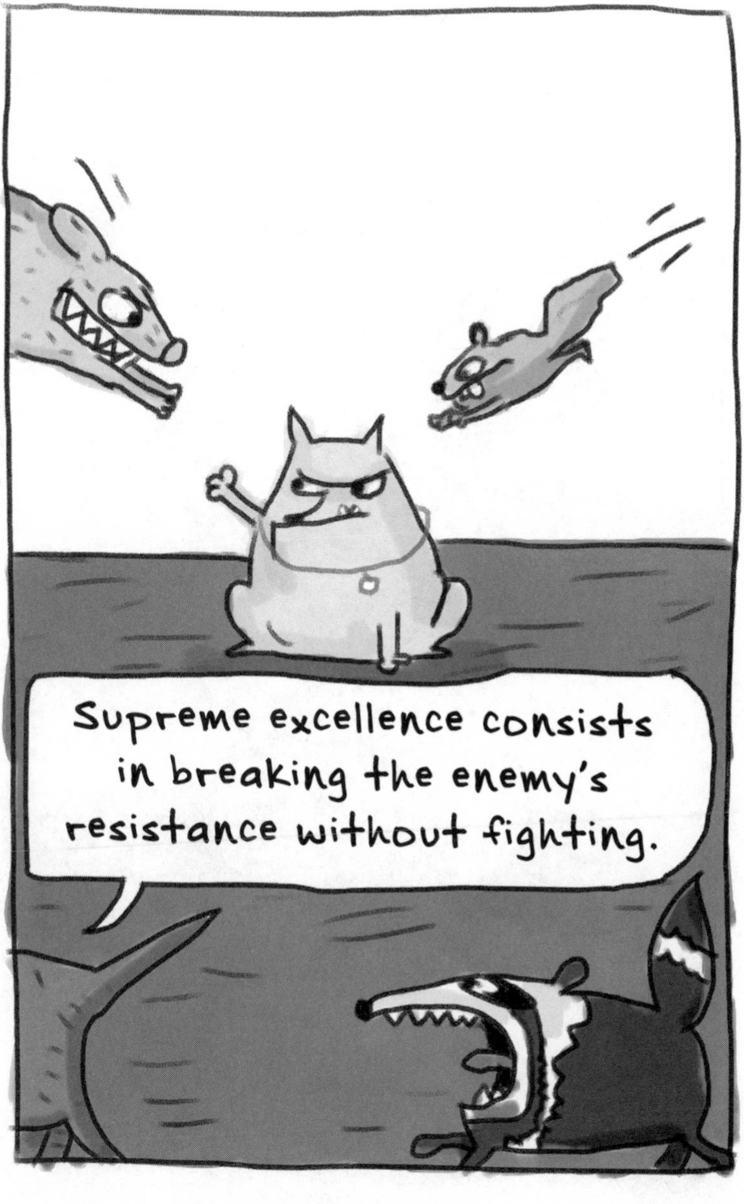
Supreme excellence consists in breaking the enemy's resistance without fighting.

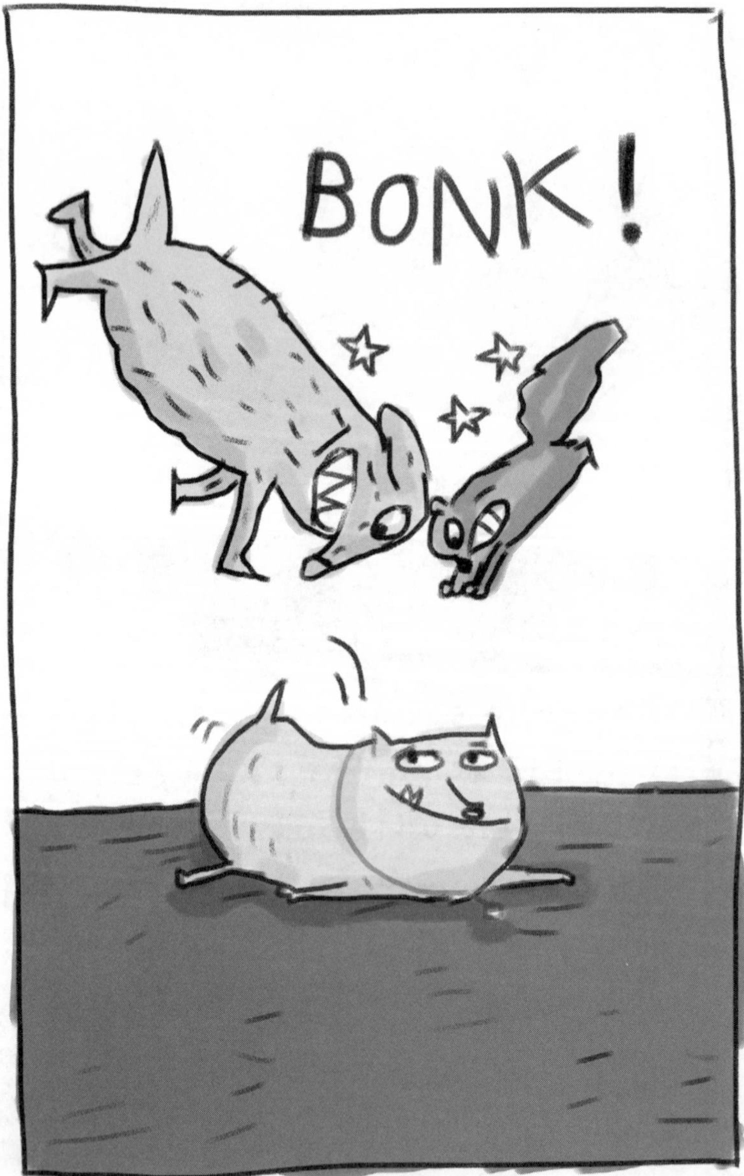
BONK!

Scene
Twenty-Four:
The Rat

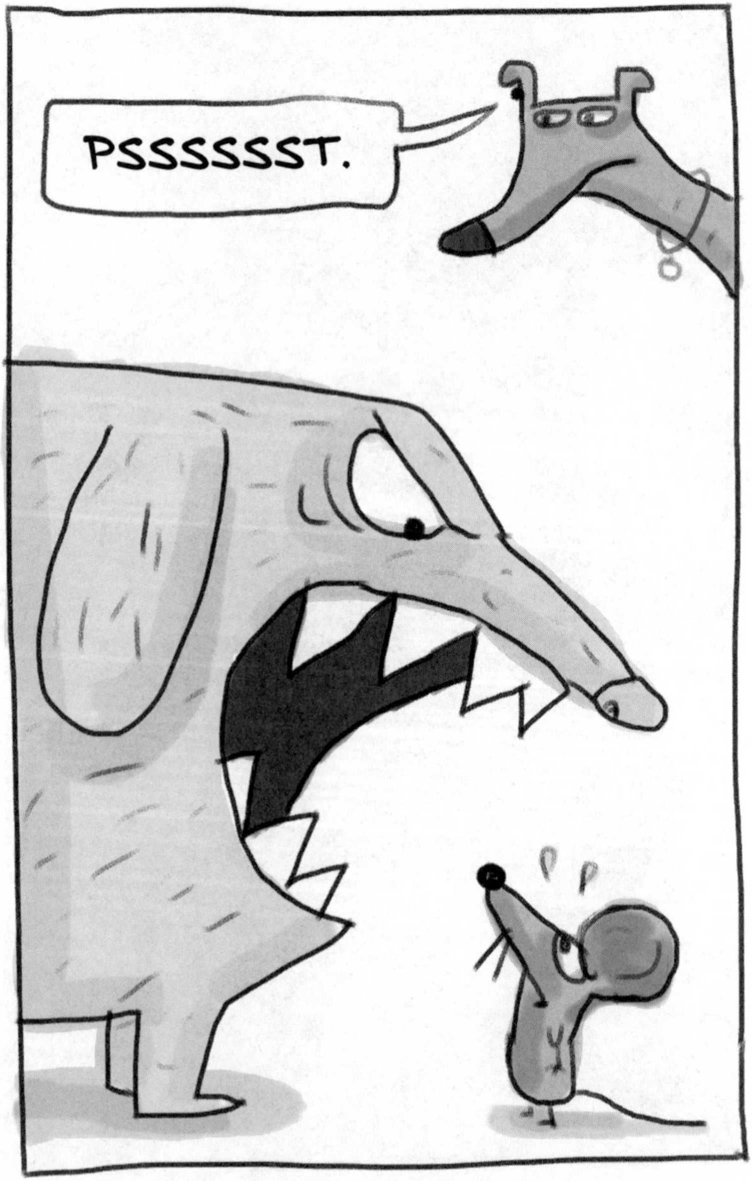
PSSSSSST.

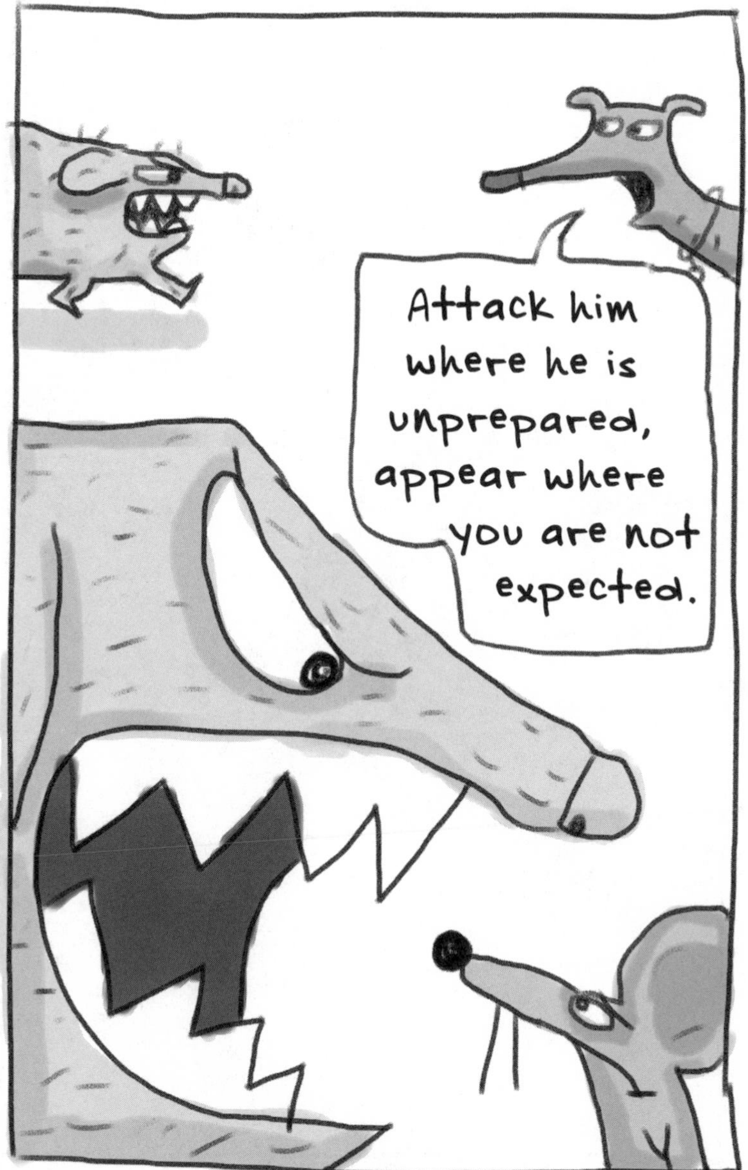
Attack him where he is unprepared, appear where you are not expected.

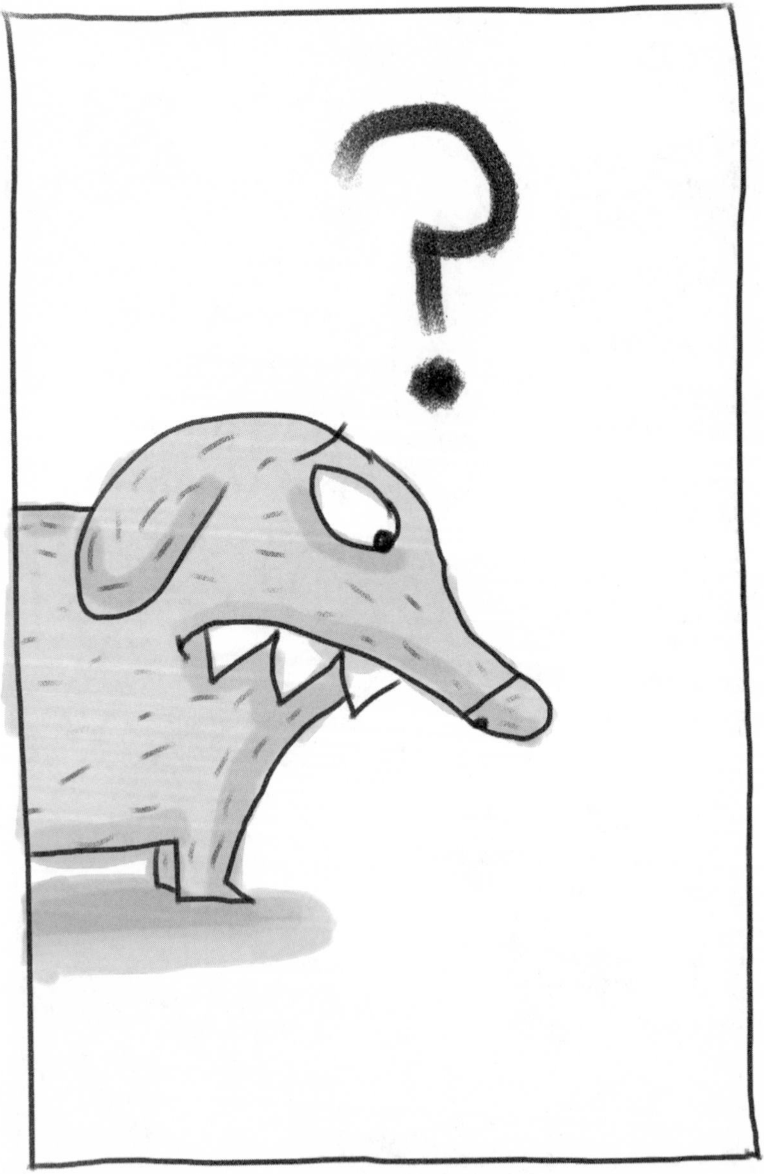

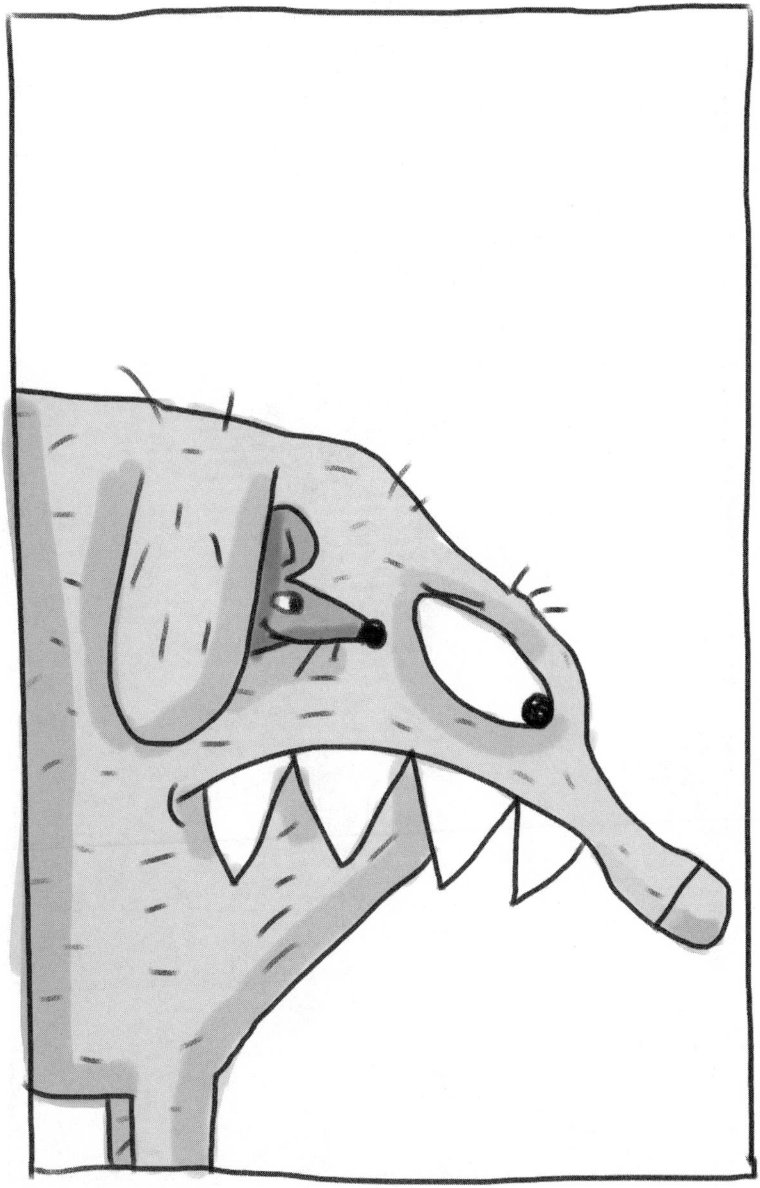

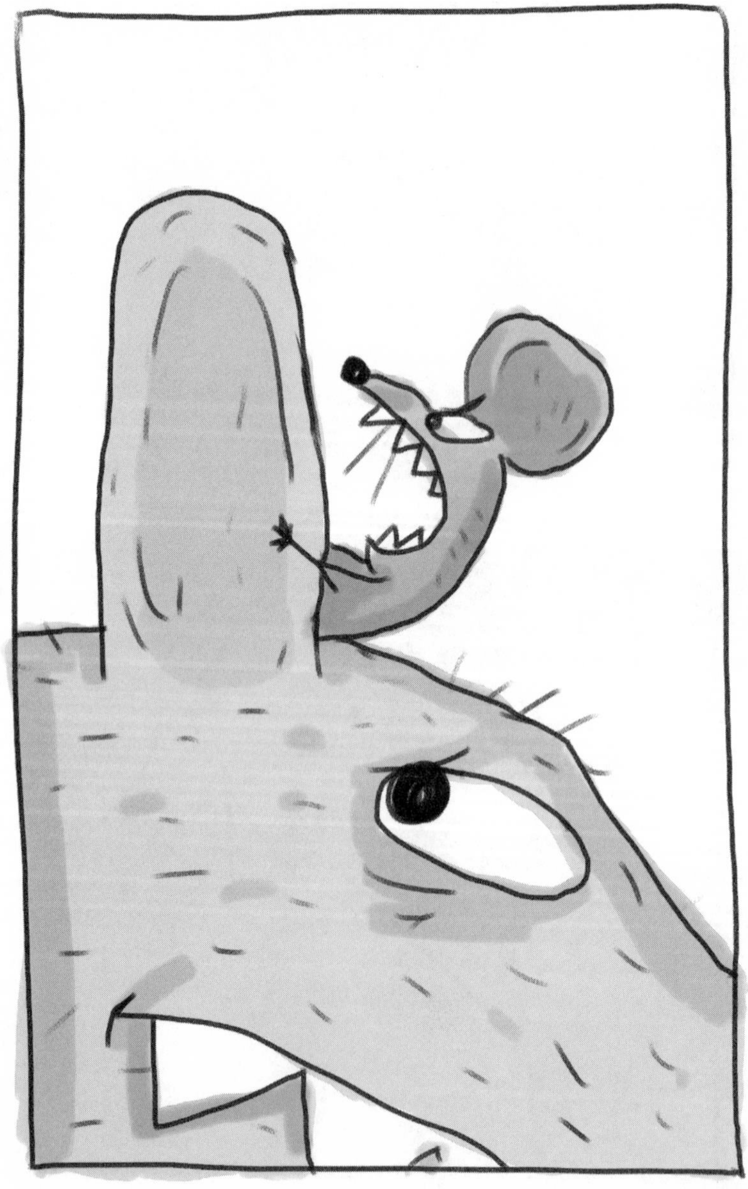

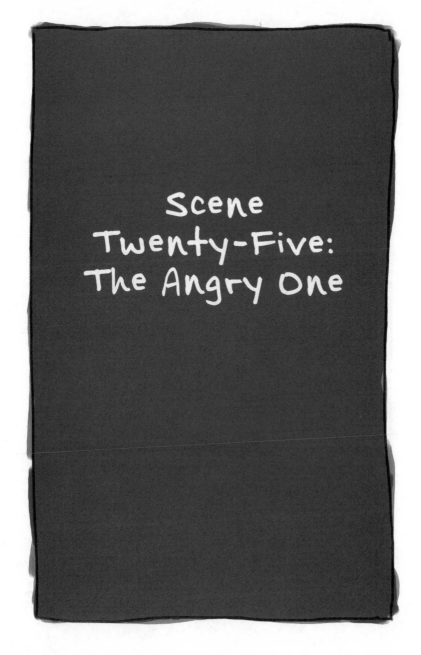

Scene
Twenty-Five:
The Angry One

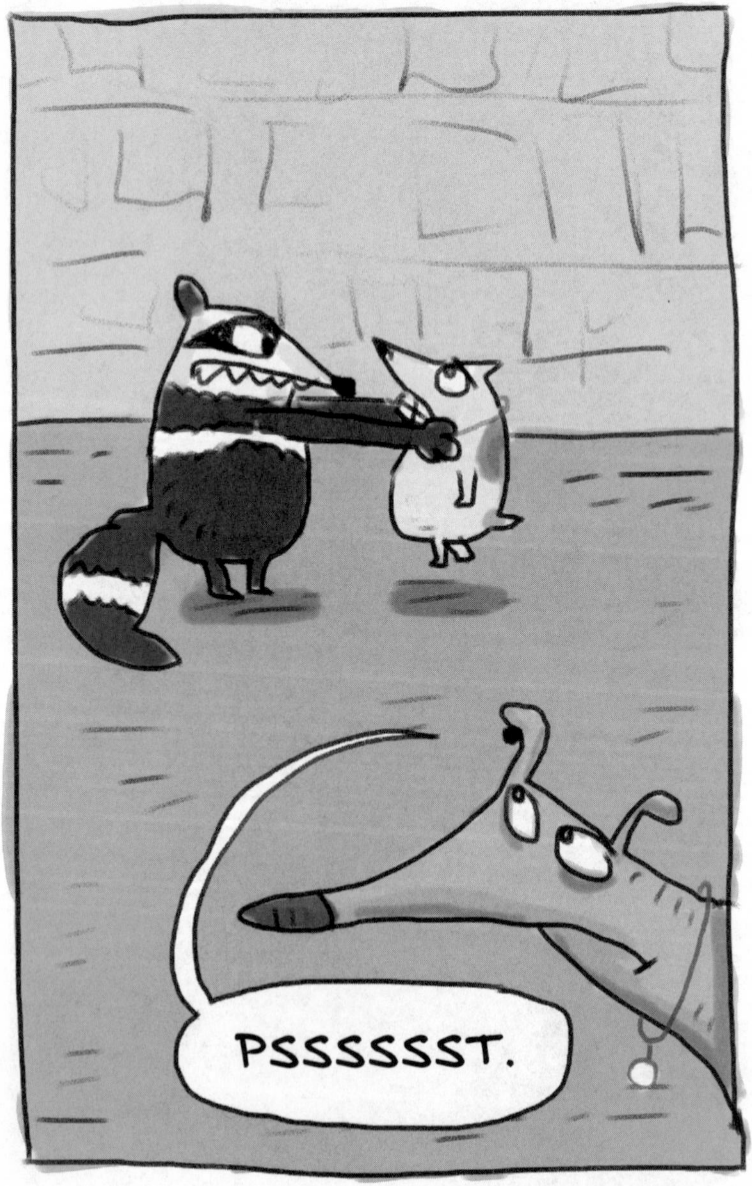
PSSSSSST.

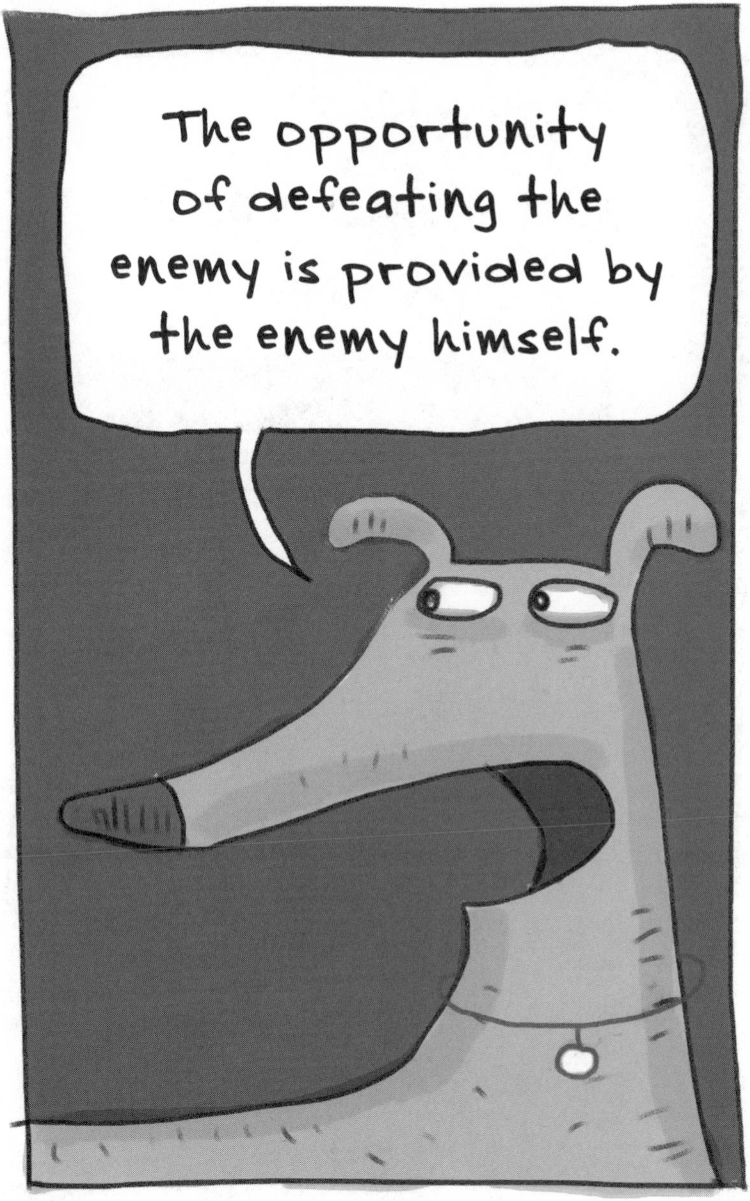
The opportunity of defeating the enemy is provided by the enemy himself.

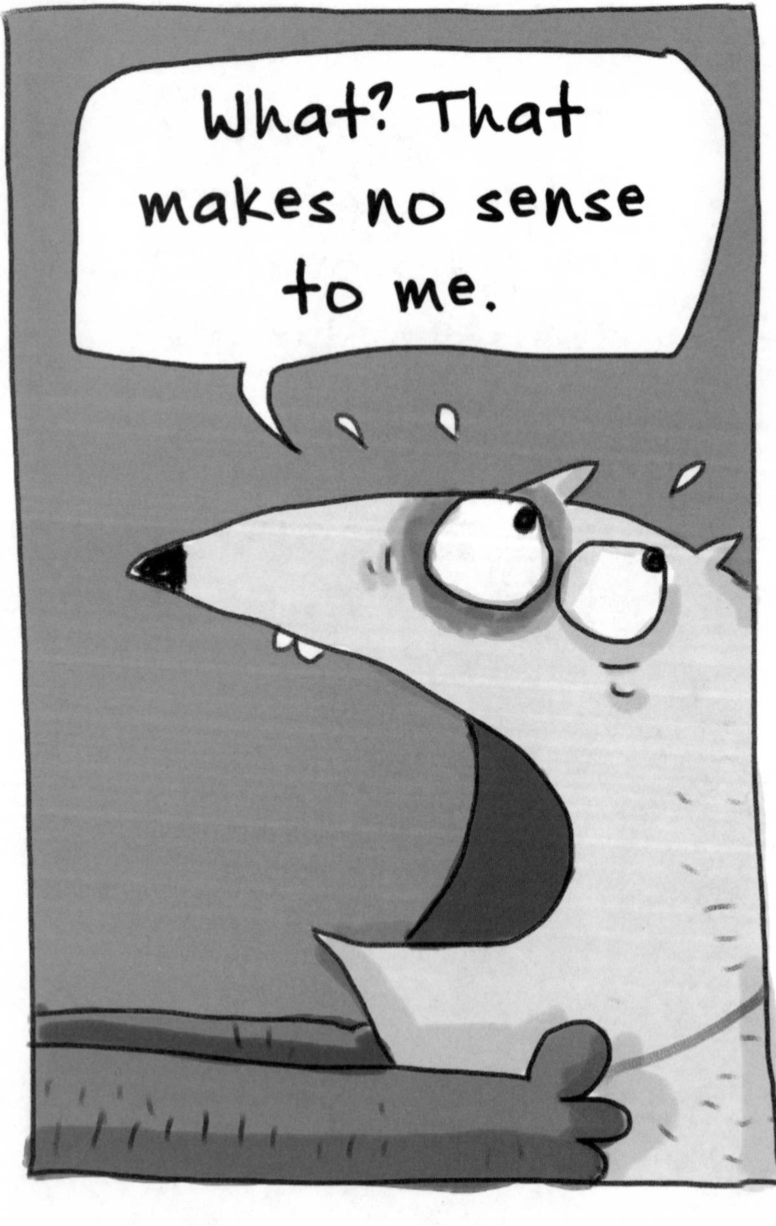
What? That makes no sense to me.

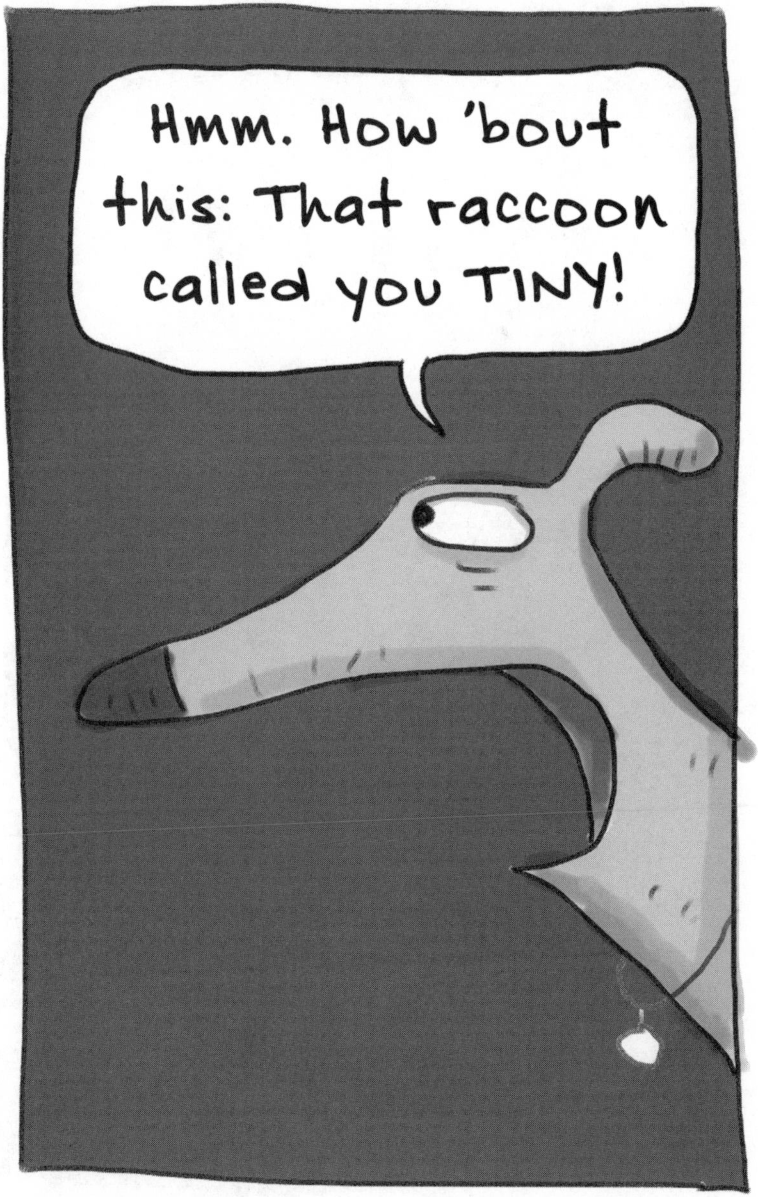
Hmm. How 'bout this: That raccoon called you TINY!

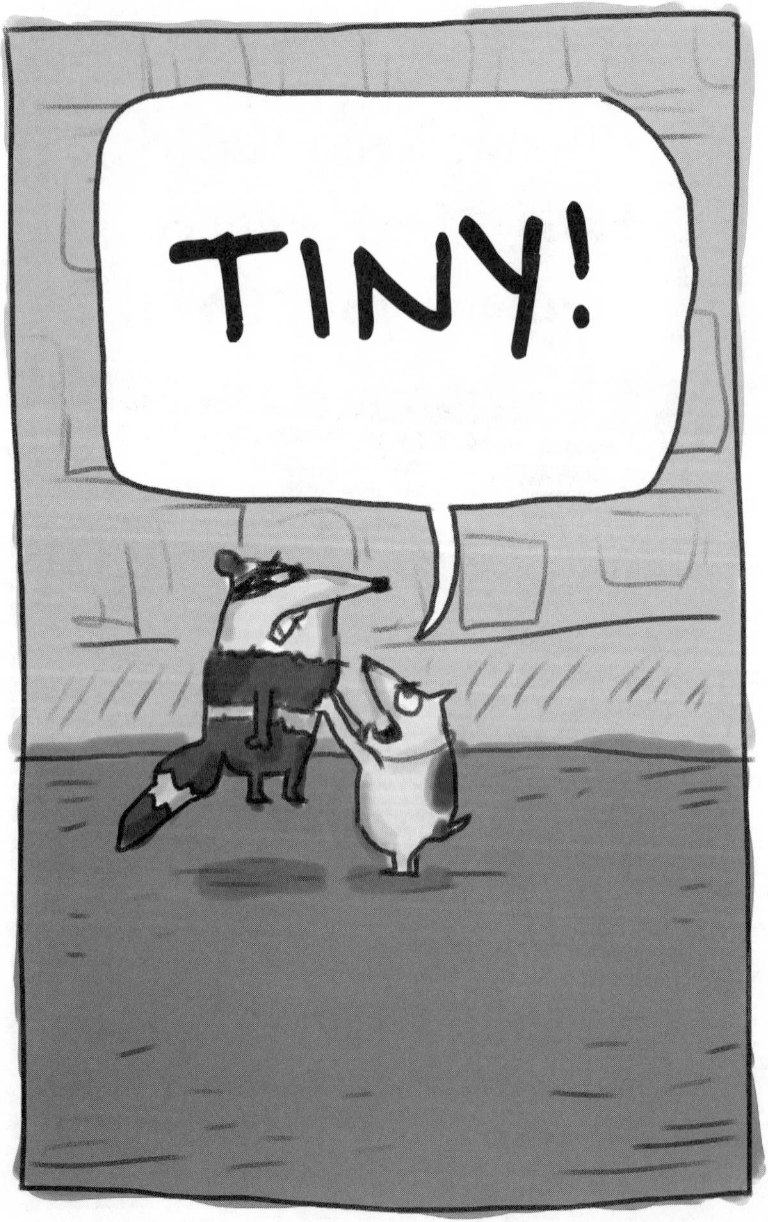
TINY!

Scene Twenty-Six: The Kitty

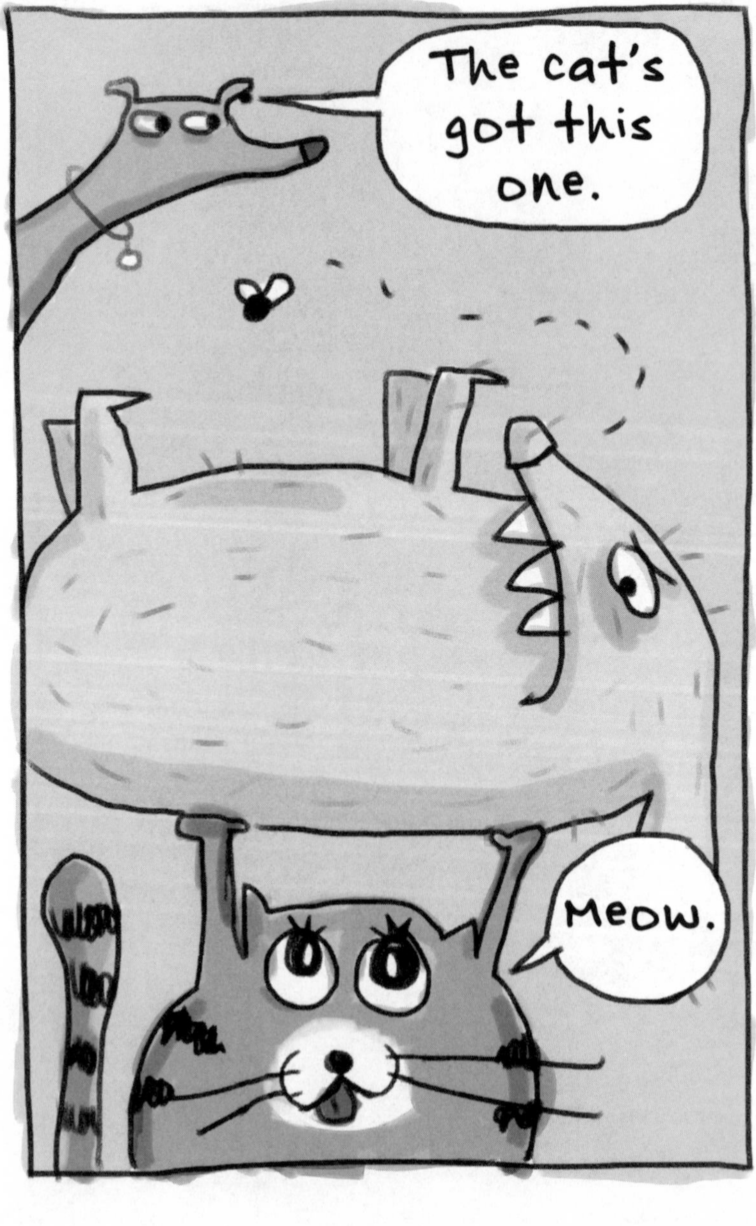
The cat's got this one.
Meow.

Scene Twenty-Seven: The Battle Turns

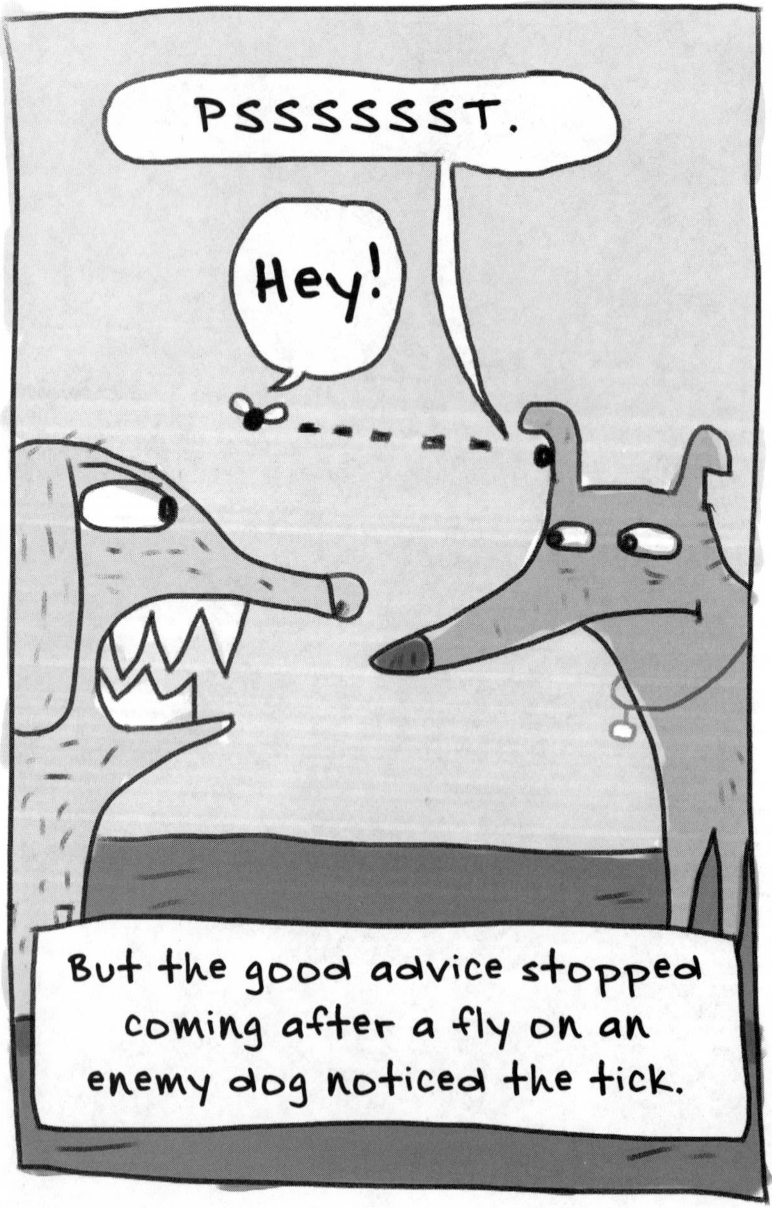
PSSSSSST.
Hey!
But the good advice stopped coming after a fly on an enemy dog noticed the tick.

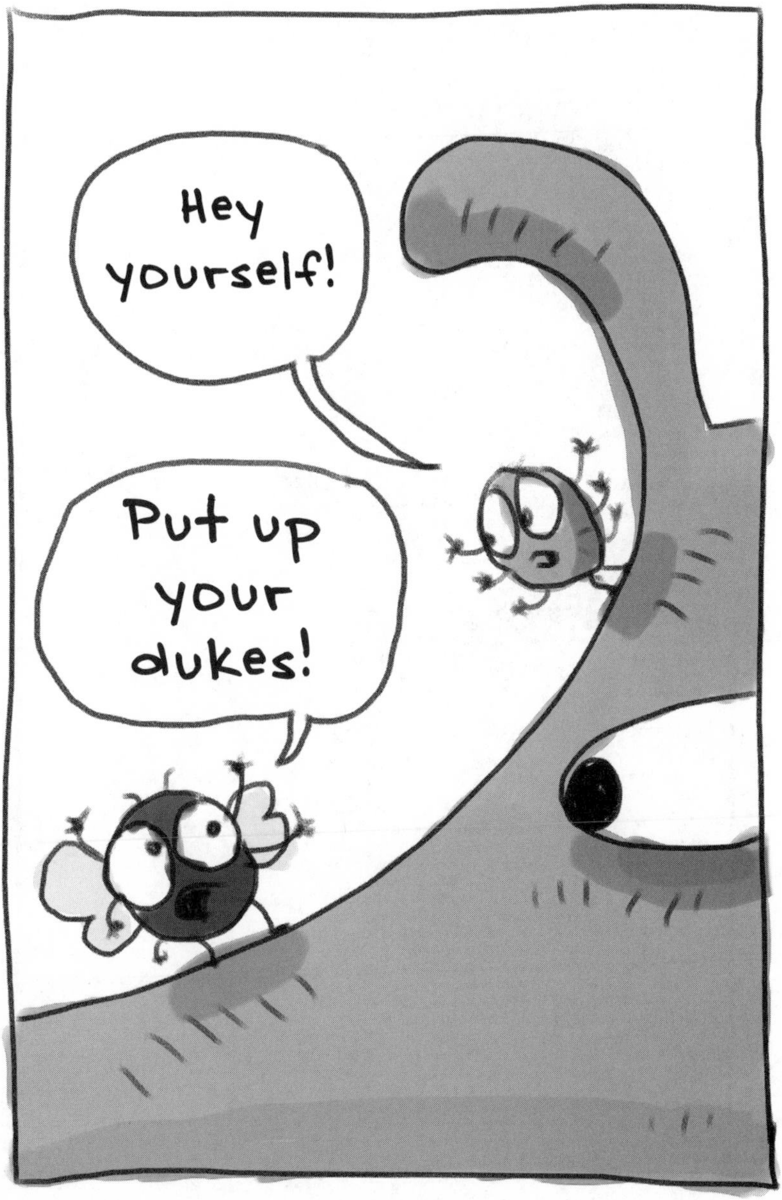
Hey yourself!
Put up your dukes!

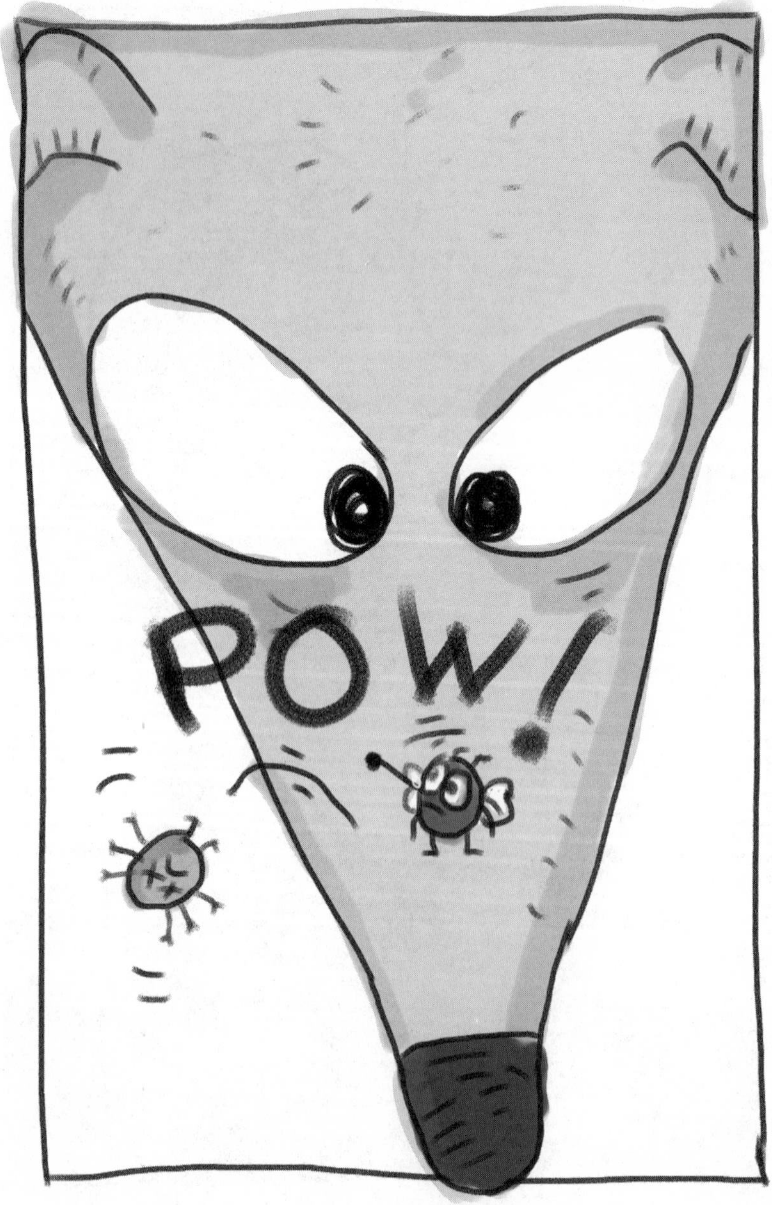
POW!

Scene
Twenty-Eight:
The Escape

Our heroes were just about goners. The enemy had them pinned in. Luckily, the angry dog found a secret way out. He stood guard and almost everyone got out. Almost.

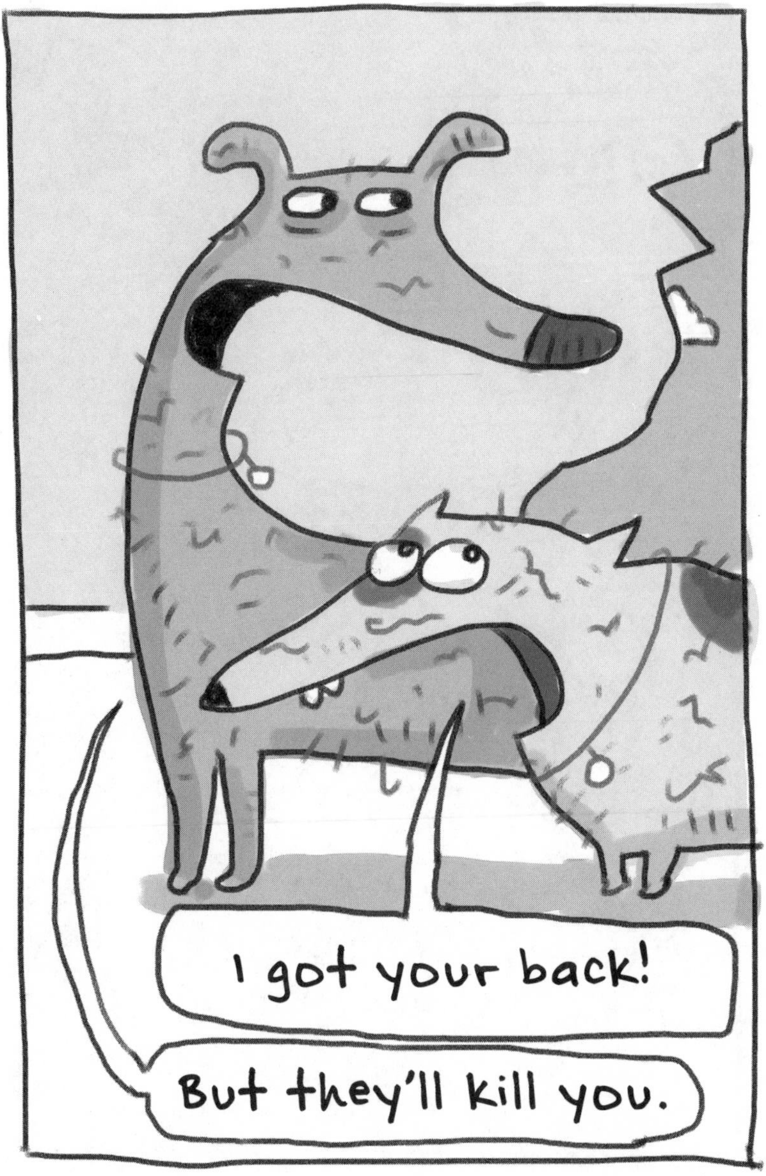
I got your back!
But they'll kill you.

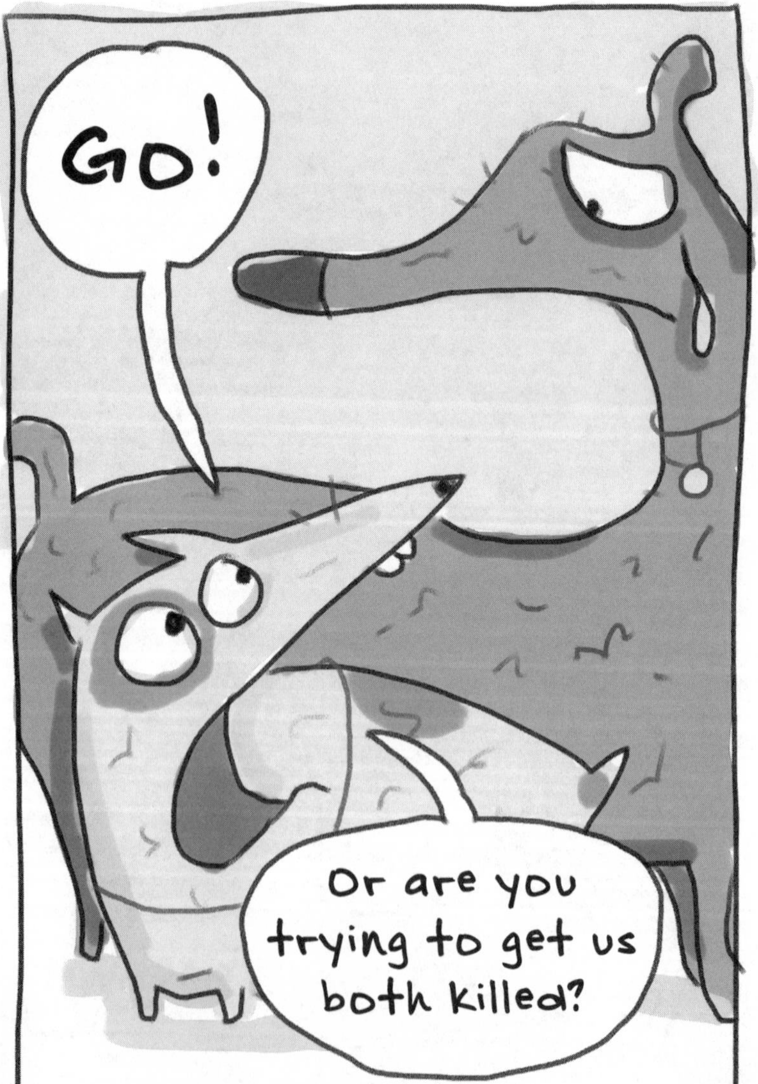
GO!
Or are you trying to get us both killed?

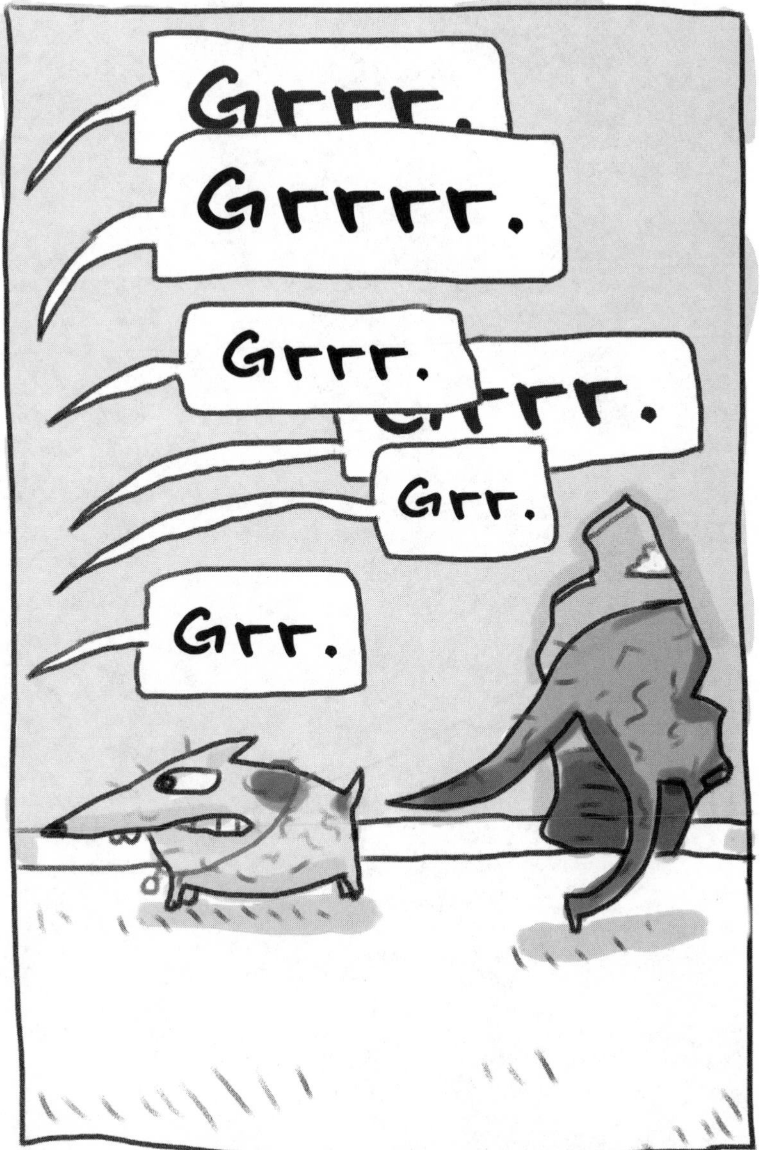
Grrr.
Grrrr.
Grrr.
Grr.
Grr.

Scene
Twenty-Nine

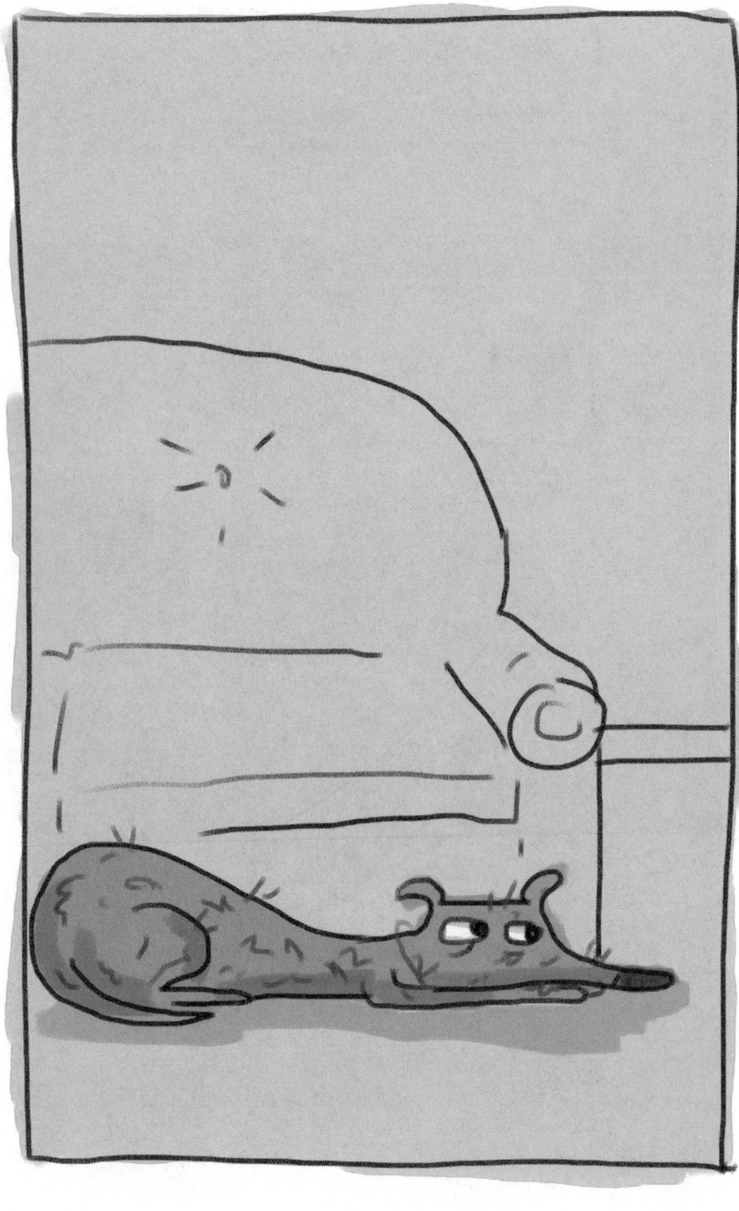

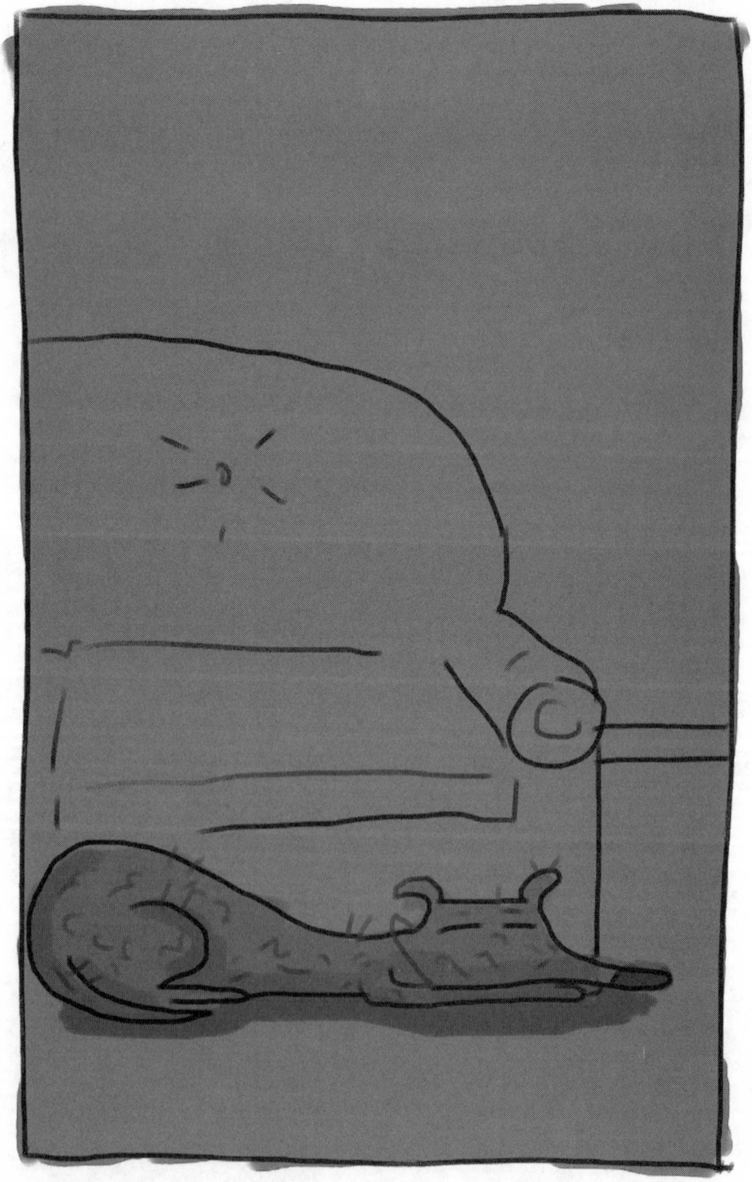

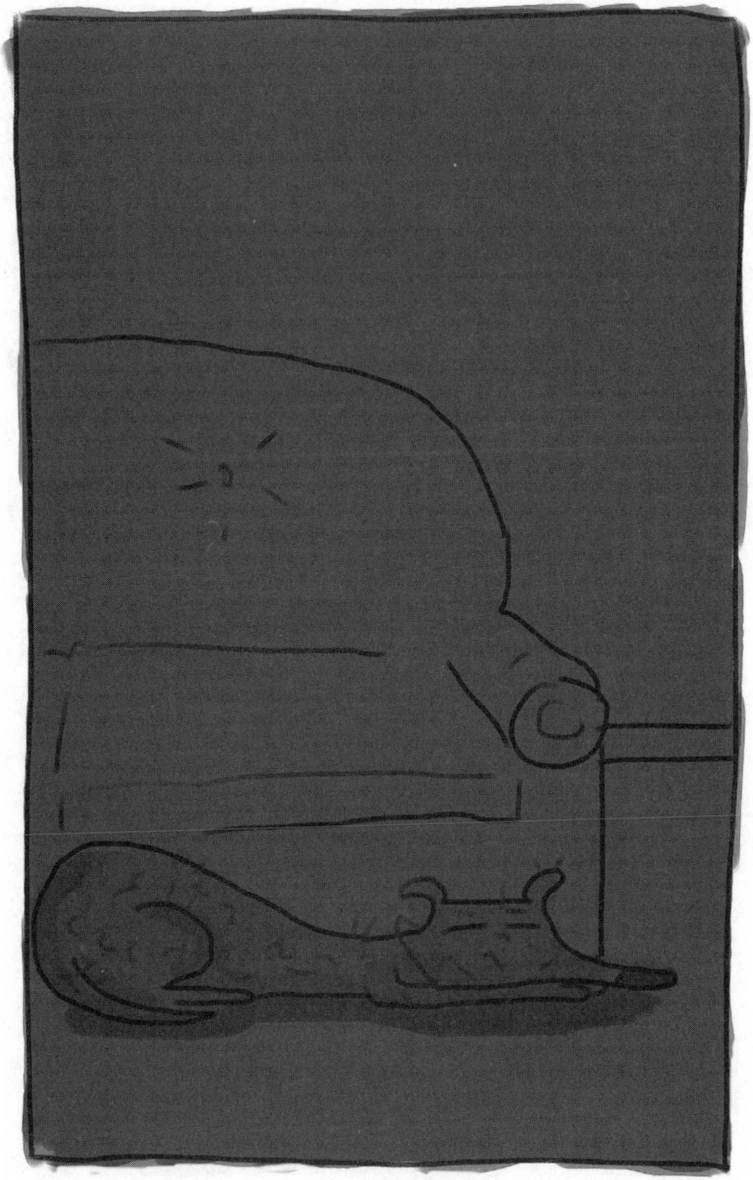

Scene
Thirty

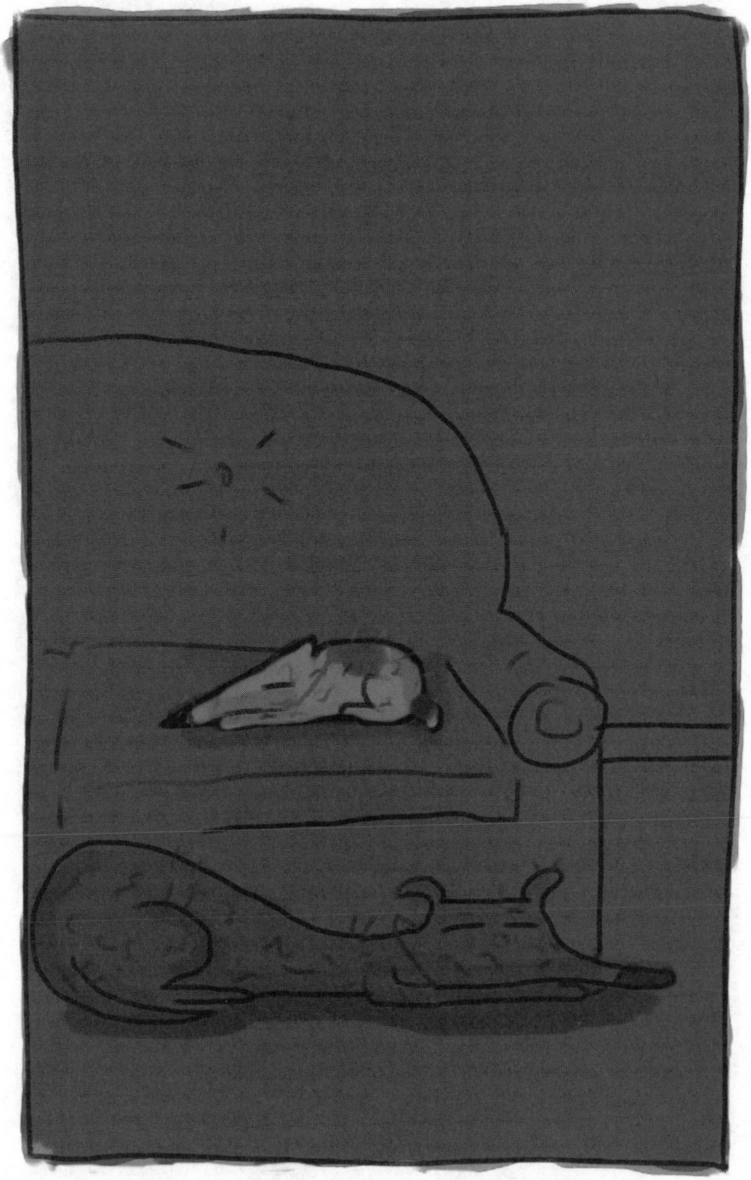

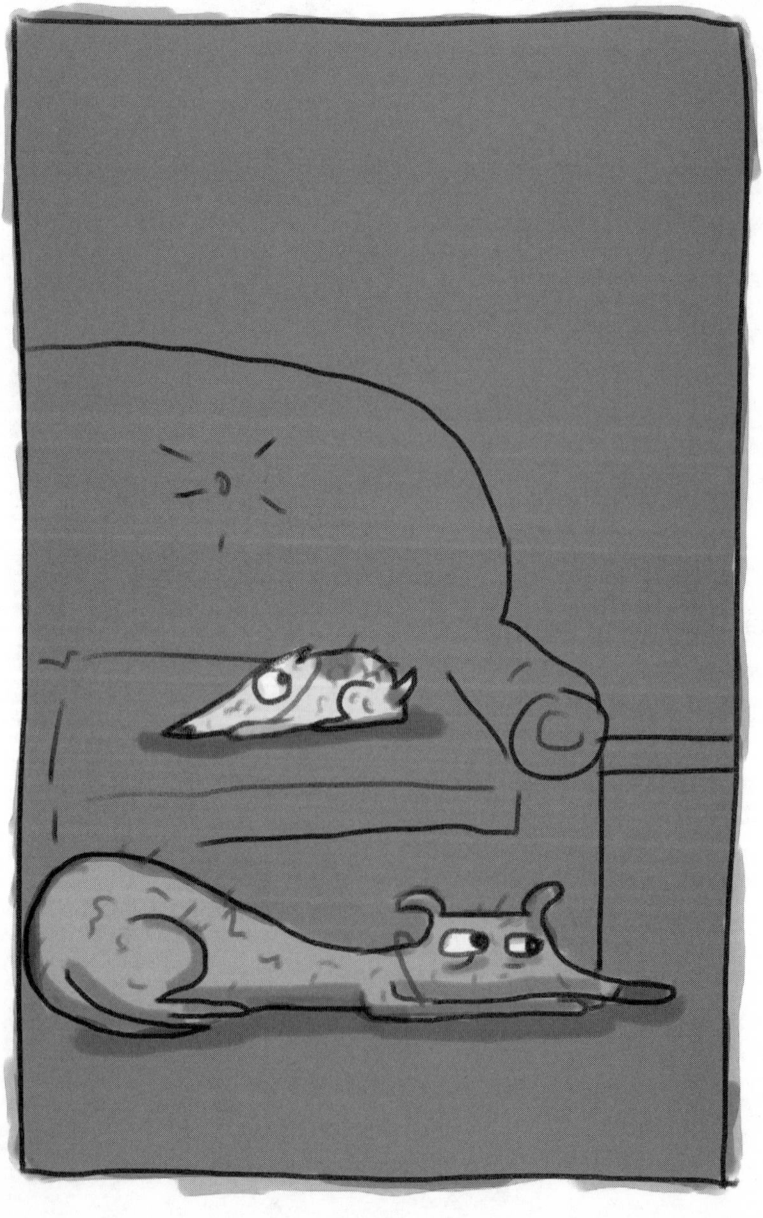

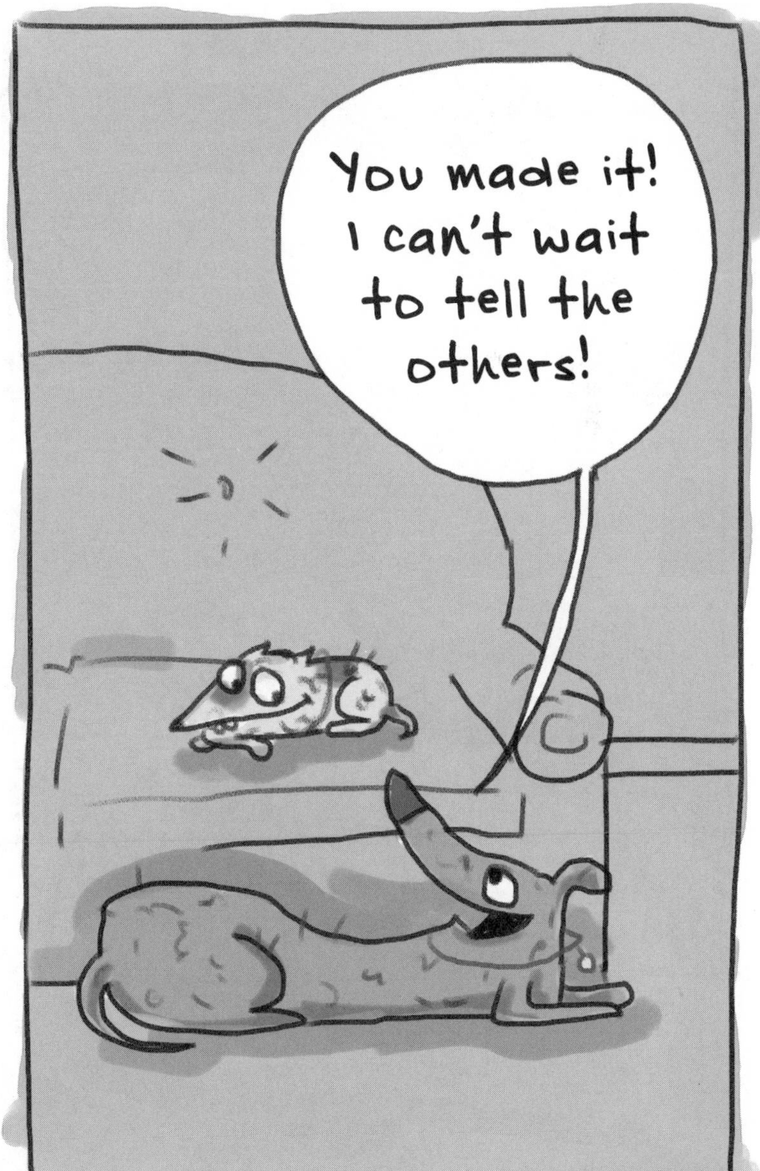
You made it! I can't wait to tell the others!

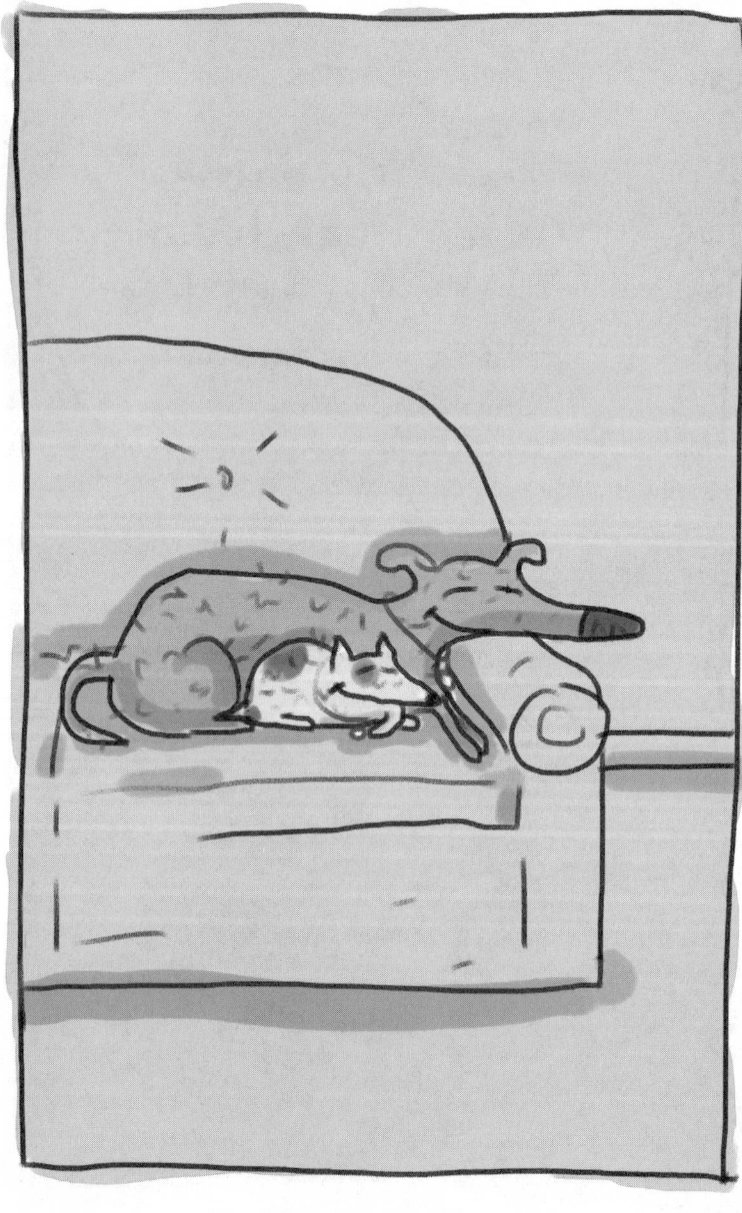

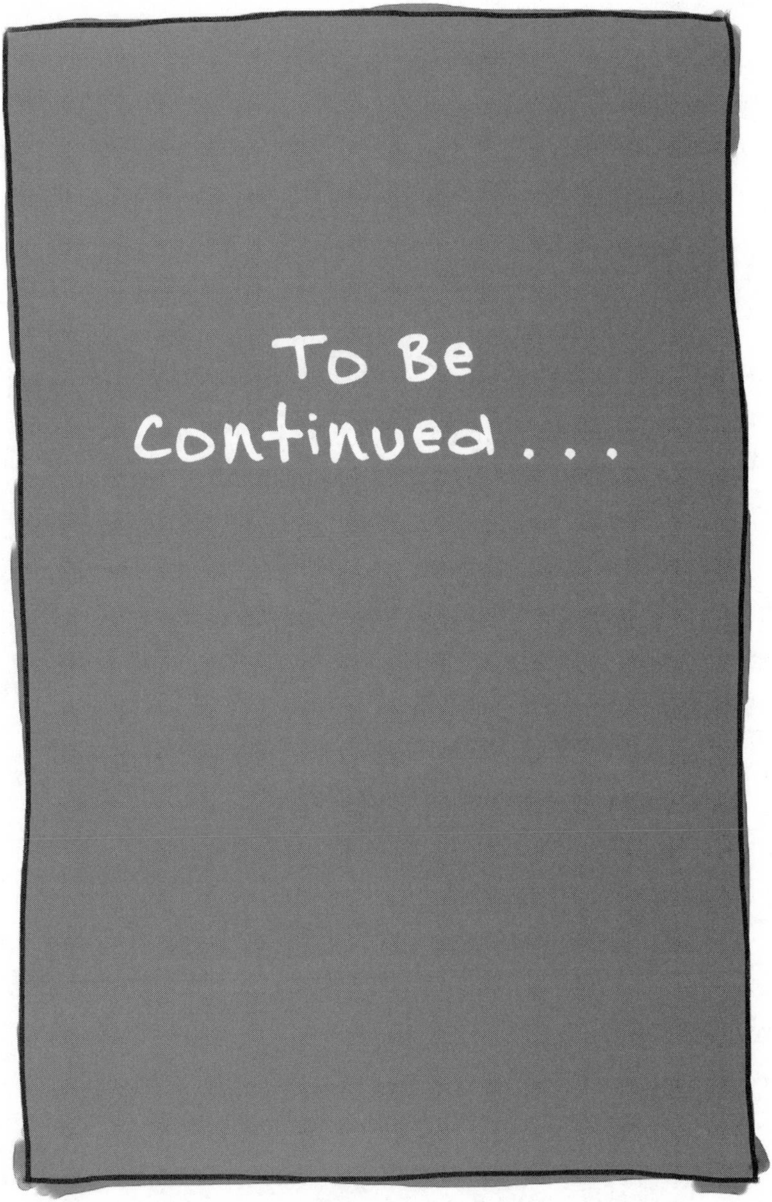
To Be
Continued . . .

Keep reading for a sneak
peek at Brownie, Apollo,
and the gang's next
adventure in

APOCALYPSE
MEOW MEOW!

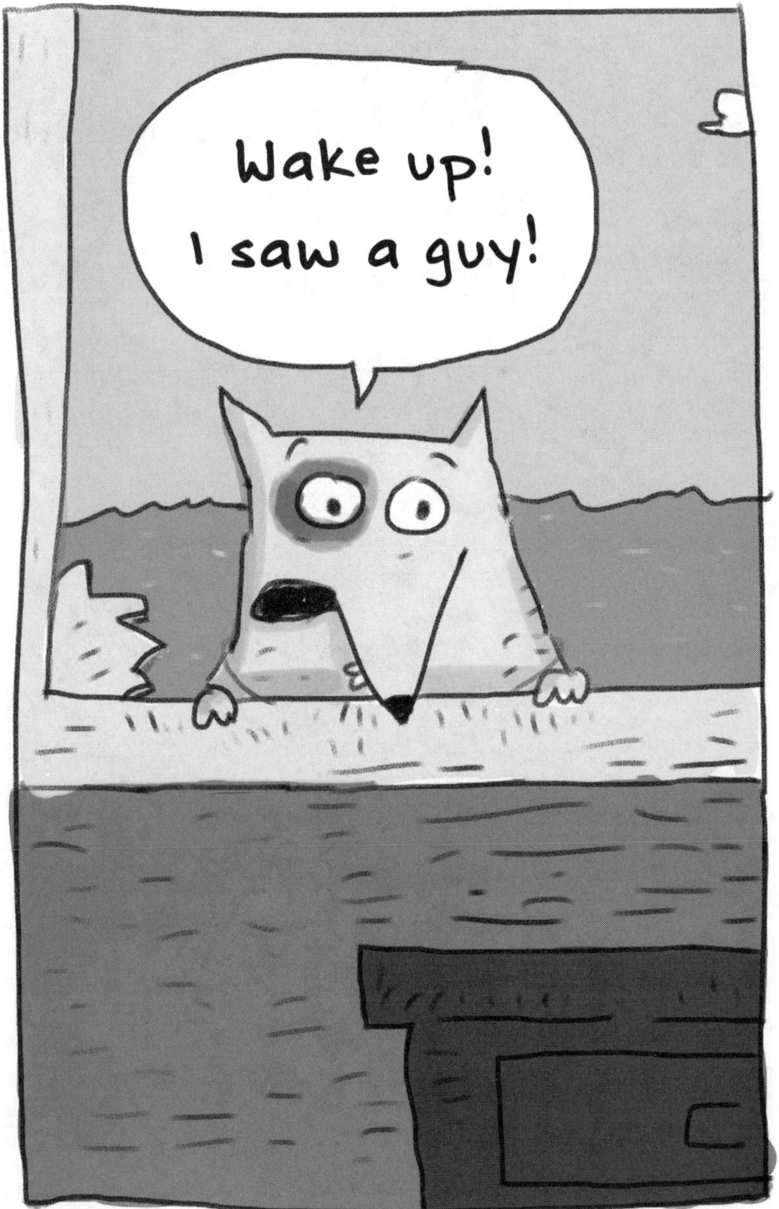
Wake up!
I saw a guy!

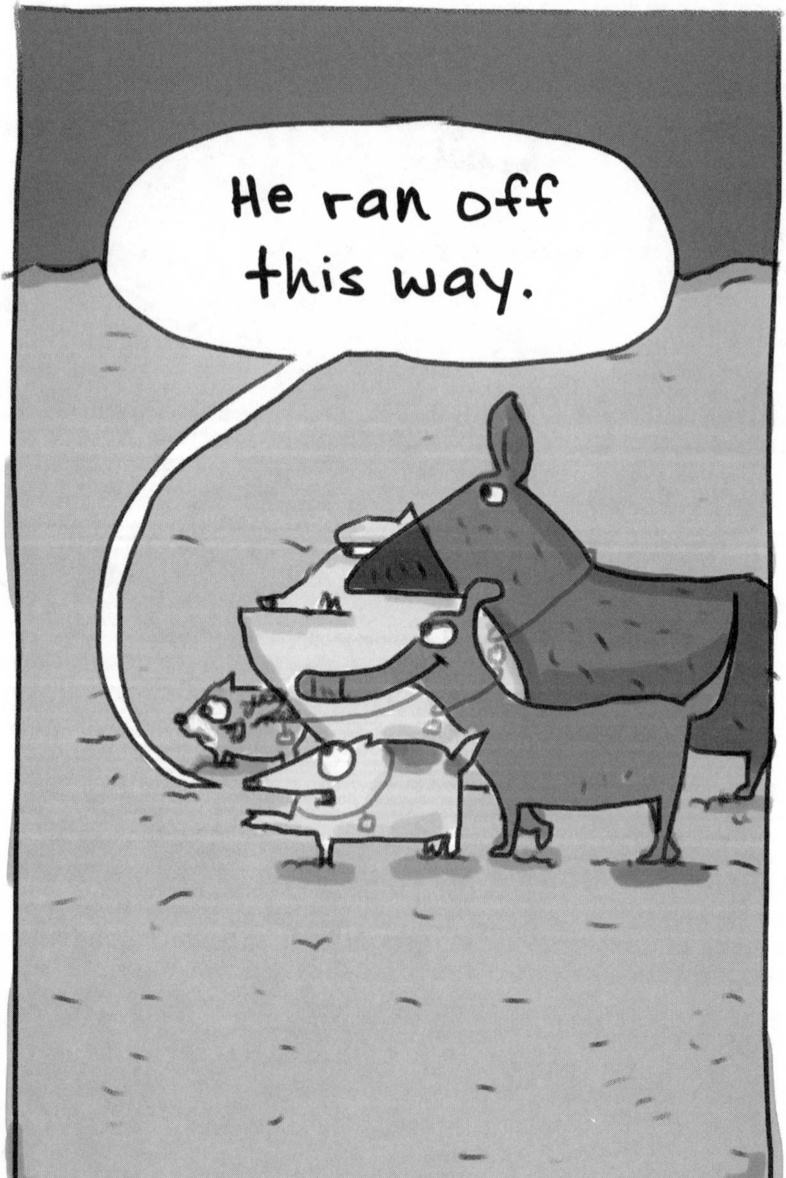
He ran off this way.

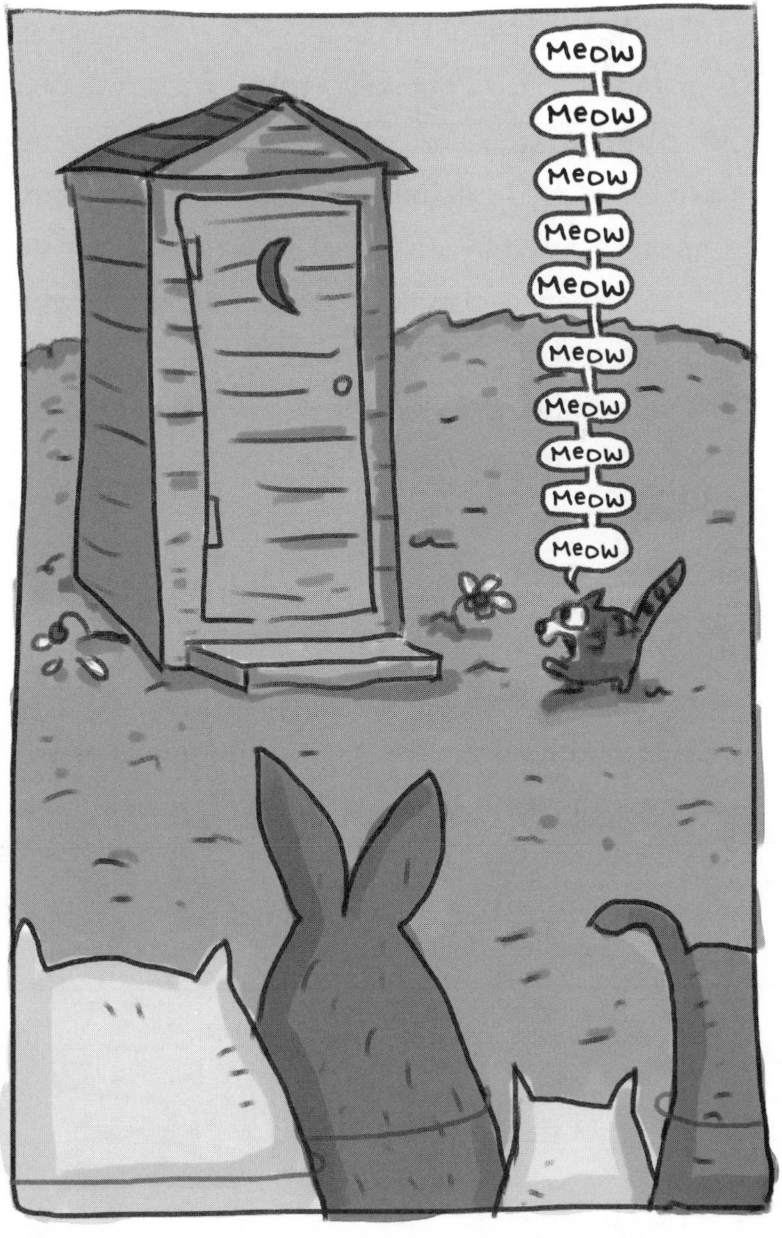
MEOW
MEOW
MEOW
MEOW
MEOW
MEOW
MEOW
MEOW
MEOW
MEOW

James Proimos III attended St. Mary's College of Maryland, where he obtained a BA in psychology. When not writing graphic novels, he takes on gigs as a quality control specialist in the video game industry. He currently lives in Maryland with his wife and goofy rescued mutt, as well as a housemate and that housemate's spunky Jack Russell mix.

James Proimos Jr. has written and illustrated numerous children's books, including the critically acclaimed picture book Year of the Jungle by Suzanne Collins. He's a former writer and creator for television, and a dad.